A VAST *and* GRACIOUS TIDE

A VAST *and* GRACIOUS TIDE

LISA CARTER

GILEAD PUBLISHING

A Vast and Gracious Tide
Copyright © 2018 by Lisa Carter

⌷⌷ GILEAD
⌷⌷ PUBLISHING

Published by Gilead Publishing, LLC
Wheaton, Illinois, USA.
www.gileadpublishing.com

Scripture quotations marked (NIV) are taken from the Holy Bible, *New International Version*®, *NIV*®. Copyright ©1973, 1978, 1984, 2011 by Biblica, Inc.™ Used by permission of Zondervan. All rights reserved worldwide. www.zondervan.com. The "NIV" and "New International Version" are trademarks registered in the United States Patent and Trademark Office by Biblica, Inc.™

This is a work of fiction. Names, characters, places, and incidents are products of the author's imagination or are used fictitiously. Any similarity to actual people, organizations, and/or events is purely coincidental.

ISBN: 978-1-68370-094-4 (printed softcover)
ISBN: 978-1-68370-095-1 (ebook)

Cover design by Jeff Gifford
Interior design by Beth Shagene
Ebook production by Book Genesis, Inc.

Printed in the United States of America.

18 19 20 21 22 23 24 / 5 4 3 2 1

Everything comes with a price, freedom most especially.

To the members of the United States military and for my Uncle Bill—who never quite managed to make it all the way home from Vietnam.

I am humbled by the incalculable price our armed forces have willingly paid so that the rest of us wouldn't have to. There is something of the sacred in your sacrifice. A love of country. A love for home.

I believe the longing for home is at the core of what it means to be human. And it is my prayer that you will all one day truly find the Home you've been made for.

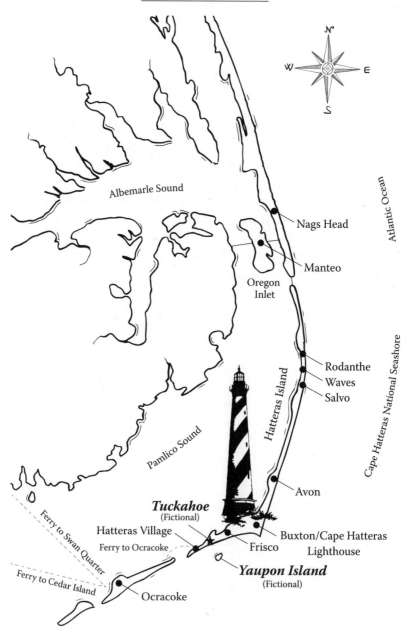

Outer Banks
of North Carolina

N
W • E
S

Atlantic Ocean

Albemarle Sound

Nags Head

Manteo

Oregon
Inlet

Rodanthe

Waves

Salvo

Hatteras Island

Cape Hatteras National Seashore

Pamlico Sound

Avon

Tuckahoe
(Fictional)

Hatteras Village
Ferry to Ocracoke

Frisco

Buxton/Cape Hatteras
Lighthouse

Yaupon Island
(Fictional)

Ferry to Swan Quarter

Ferry to Cedar Island

Ocracoke

Design by dc Graphics

*You see, at just the right time, when we were still powerless,
Christ died for the ungodly. Very rarely will anyone die for
a righteous person, though for a good person someone might
possibly dare to die. But God demonstrates his own love for us
in this: While we were still sinners, Christ died for us.*

ROMANS 5:6-8 NIV

Here Is Love

(Love Song of the Welsh Revival)
WILLIAM REES

Here is love, vast as the ocean,
Loving-kindness as the flood,
When the Prince of Life, our Ransom,
Shed for us His precious blood.
Who His love will not remember?
Who can cease to sing His praise?
He can never be forgotten,
Throughout heav'n's eternal days.

On the mount of crucifixion,
Fountains opened deep and wide;
Through the floodgates of God's mercy
Flowed a vast and gracious tide.
Grace and love, like mighty rivers,
Poured incessant from above,
And heav'n's peace and perfect justice
Kissed a guilty world in love.

Let me, all Thy love accepting,
Love Thee, ever all my days;
Let me seek Thy kingdom only,
And my life be to Thy praise;
Thou alone shalt be my glory,
Nothing in the world I see;
Thou hast cleansed and sanctified me,
Thou Thyself hast set me free.

In Thy truth Thou dost direct me
By Thy Spirit through Thy Word;
And Thy grace my need is meeting,
As I trust in Thee, my Lord.
Of Thy fullness Thou art pouring
Thy great love and pow'r on me,
Without measure, full and boundless,
Drawing out my heart to Thee.

Prologue

Sergeant First Class Caden Wallis grinned as his CO whistled—perhaps the fifteenth time today—that same tune again. On the floor of the Humvee, the six-year-old Belgian Malinois' ears perked. And Caden's canine friend, K9 Sergeant First Class Friday, barked.

Caden laughed. "Even Friday's sick of that song."

His team leader, Master Sergeant Joe Nelson, was the closest he'd ever come to a best friend, and to the younger guys Joe was a father figure. They'd all—Caden and Friday included—follow him without hesitation into a death trap if so ordered.

From the front passenger seat, Joe angled. His eyebrows arched, vanishing underneath his combat helmet. "Not just any tune. A hymn, but also a love song. 'Here is love,'" he warbled in his terrible off-key baritone. "'Vast—'"

The vehicle rattled over the bomb-pitted road, jostling them. Bracing, Caden grabbed hold of the side to keep from lurching forward.

Sanchez, team medic, cut his eyes at Caden and nudged Pulaski at the wheel. They took up where Joe left off, but in a shrill falsetto.

"'Vast as an ocean, loving kindness as the flood . . .'"

Joe rolled his eyes as they hammed it up.

"'Who his love will not remember? Who can cease to sing His praise?'"

Biting the inside of his cheek, Joe tolerated the impromptu concert. Anything to lessen pre-mission tension.

"'Through the floodgates of God's mercy flowed a vast and gracious tide . . .'"

Friday howled.

Sanchez and Pulaski broke into laughter, as did Joe.

Caden smiled. Joe was the best man he'd ever known. A godly man, the real deal. Caden wasn't into religion, but he'd come to believe that Joe's faith had somehow buffered them, protected them by proxy, throughout their long deployment thus far.

The only thing on Caden's radar was getting home to his girlfriend in one piece. Thinking of Nikki, his stomach cramped. She hadn't answered his calls in over a month. Sensing her handler's disquiet, Friday insinuated her head underneath her hand and licked his fingers.

Had Nikki, as threatened, grown tired of waiting for him?

The armored personnel vehicle jerked to a standstill. And the dust—always the dust—swirled through the open windows. In terms of mileage, the village wasn't far from base camp, but lately anywhere outside the wire had become a killing zone. Out of the other Humvees in the convoy, the rest of their team emptied onto the deserted street. Including the Afghan military officer.

Caden had taken a dislike to him during their extensive pre-mission planning. Maybe he was hyperparanoid, or maybe on his third tour he didn't trust any of the locals. The officer was a necessary evil in his opinion, considered essential in brokering the agreement between coalition forces and the tribal leader.

"Keep your head on a swivel for unfriendlies." Joe made eye contact with each member of their twelve-man Alpha team. "We're on foot from here."

Yazz—Navajo Hosteen Yazzie, their communications specialist—grunted. Caden seconded the feeling.

The dirt street disappeared into a maze of mud-brick dwellings three stories high. Row after row of potential sweet spots for a sniper. Or an entire terrorist faction. Silence reigned as the men assumed a defensive posture, clutching their M-4 rifles.

Joe adjusted the black-checkered shemagh around his neck. "I don't need to tell you how kinetic this area has been. The headman's support will pave the way to peace in this province."

Weapons Specialist Tavon Miller's dark face tightened. "So where is everyone?"

Scruggs—the newest and youngest team member—snickered. "Maybe the spooks didn't hand out enough chocolate when they set up this meet and greet."

Pulaski's mouth thinned. "Or we're walking into an ambush."

"What they pay us the big bucks for," Scruggs smirked.

Yazz sighed. "Not."

One look from Joe silenced the chatter. Their nerves were frayed. Too many back-to-back encounters of a deadly kind. But the quiet was unnerving. Caden grasped a tighter hold on Friday's leash.

"Glad you go first, Sergeant Friday," joked Pulaski, breaking the eerie hush.

The men had grown to love and depend on Friday. Her bomb-sniffing capabilities had saved their lives on more than one occasion.

Joe cut his eyes at the narrow street ahead. "And we've got your six."

Venturing deeper into the village, Caden and Friday did their job. The team and the Afghan officer followed Friday's lead. Only the sound of the men's boots on the hard-packed road broke the stillness. As Friday pulled forward on the leash, Caden's arms prickled. He felt the unseen force of a hundred eyes behind the mud-brick walls.

Suddenly, from somewhere behind Caden, the Afghan officer's shrill cry shattered the calm. "Allah Akbar!"

Caden's gaze swung over his shoulder just as the Afghan fired point blank at Joe. Tavon opened fire on the Afghan, pink mist spraying. Caden took a step intending to pivot, but Friday pulled down on the leash, sniffing his foot.

"What're you doing, girl? Hold—"

Something beneath his boot clicked. He half turned. Friday rammed her body against him. And at that moment he realized a second too late that he'd missed her signal.

The blast lifted him into the air amidst a searing pain. A percussive roar drowned out further sound. Darkness engulfed him.

When he regained consciousness, he found himself flat on his back. Blackened debris lay scattered in every direction. He blinked, waiting for the swirling dust and smoke to settle.

Gunfire erupted from the shadows, followed by the retort of the

M-4s. Savage yells reverberated off the walls. Responding with curses, the men hunkered behind whatever cover they could find.

Fear gripped his chest. "Friday? Where are you, girl?"

He struggled to rise, but his legs wouldn't cooperate. And despite the broiling noonday sun, a glacial coldness crept from his toes to his torso.

Where was his rifle? If he could find it . . . leverage himself upright . . .

But it had either been scattered out of reach or demolished beyond repair.

Someone slid to a stop beside Caden. Two others crouched as a defensive shield, protecting them and responding to small-arms fire from their unseen enemy.

"Helo inbound," Yazz shouted from a doorway.

Sanchez ripped open Caden's medical kit, the one-pounder every soldier carried in his gear.

"The sergeant first," Caden rasped.

Sanchez ignored him. Velcro ripped.

"A tourniquet?" His heart accelerated. "Where's—"

"I've got three or four minutes before you bleed out." Sanchez's lips flattened. "With all due respect, Wallis, shut up." He secured the tourniquet onto Caden's leg, positioned the Velcro strap, and tightened the attached rod.

Flinching, he bit back the scream of pain threatening to explode from his lungs.

Sanchez swallowed. "I'm sorry . . ."

It felt as if flames licked at his legs. "I'm on fire," he groaned.

The *rata-tat-tat* of gunfire continued. Amid the searing pain in his lower extremities, he heard the distant whir of the bird's rotors.

"Rick," he whispered.

Something in the New Mexican's face flickered before Sanchez clamped down his emotions again.

Caden fought against an onslaught of pain, so terrible it threatened to suck the oxygen out of his lungs. "I need you to put out the—"

Sanchez forced a fentanyl lollipop between Caden's clenched teeth.

Caden's hand inched toward his leg. Toward the wrenching,

LISA CARTER   15

mind-numbing pain. Instead of flesh, solid muscle or bone, a gushing warmth spurted between his fingers. A flowing fountain . . .

Echoes of Joe's favorite song filtered through his mind. He raised his hand and stared. A stream of crimson flowed between his fingers.

A vast and gracious tide . . .

His breath hitched as an unknown, helpless horror skyrocketed from the marrow of his bones. The white-faced figure of Sanchez blurred. The last sound he heard was Sanchez yanking open his own medical kit.

And Velcro ripping on another tourniquet.

Chapter One

PRESENT
THE OUTER BANKS OF NORTH CAROLINA

The explosive cawing of seagulls jolted her heart into overdrive. At the edge of the beach, she spun around on the deck of her boat. A gaggle of birds darted upward, their cries echoing on the wind, warning of danger.

Of predators.

McKenna Dockery clutched her camera, pressing it against her chest. She went still to identify the source of the misplaced noise that had almost sounded like gunfire. The island was narrow at this end, but on the other side of the dunes all was quiet, except for the relentless, pounding waves of the Atlantic rolling onto the shore.

Over the weekend, a tropical storm had battered the Outer Banks. Now the desolate yet wildly beautiful Yaupon was a treasure trove of sea glass. But no one except her ever ventured to Yaupon Island anymore, and it'd been a while since she visited.

She climbed out of the boat and reached for her plastic bucket. Ankle deep in the channel waters, she dug her toes into the sand, resisting the pull of the outgoing tide. Though late September, it was warmer than usual.

Curiosity overpowered her fear—and often her good sense, her father complained. Yet leaving her boat anchored in the sheltered cove, she traversed the beach and climbed the sandy trail winding over the dune. At the top, a stiff ocean breeze whipped tendrils of her hair into her eyes, obscuring her vision. She raked the strands out of her face and, lifting the camera hanging around her neck, peered through the telescopic lens. Her finger clicked the shutter button, the camera making faint whirring sounds as she scanned the deserted shoreline. Nothing she saw accounted for the *boom* she'd heard moments before.

Probably her imagination working overtime. Her dad had been ill last night. She'd awakened every time he struggled to make his way to the hall bathroom.

She tilted her head, listening, but heard only the soothing sound of churning waves and the skritching of the sand crabs on the beach below. Had she imagined the sound? Silence thrummed, underscoring the wind-swept abandonment of the isolated island off the coast of North Carolina.

Neither her dad nor Bryce liked her going off alone in the boat. She'd grown up on the Banks and knew how to handle herself on the water, but today . . .

Her skin prickled.

Gripping the camera, she gazed across the turbulent inlet that separated the small barrier island from the larger island of Hatteras. The air hung thick with trepidation. An early-morning fog snaked above the dark waters of the wetlands.

Suddenly the ever-present wind that buffeted year-round residents died. And quiet descended like a smothering blanket. No bird calls. As if they, too, waited. But for what?

An eerie stillness reigned, broken only by the tide lapping against the seashore. She fingered the cell phone tucked into the pocket of her denim shorts. No signal this far from Hatteras. A village had thrived here once beside a life-saving station, until repeated storms forced the villagers to relocate to Hatteras. Now only wild creatures remained.

She shook herself. This was ridiculous. Probably high school kids playing hooky. Though there had been a recent rash of more violent crime farther north on the Banks. Her dad, Tuckahoe's police chief, blamed it on a new player in the drug market. Connected to a Central American cartel, an unknown dealer was peddling an even more powerful and deadly drug. And where there was money to be made, so also came ruthless criminals to the otherwise peaceful Outer Banks.

As the police chief's daughter, she should've known better than to come here. Her hand shook as she replaced the cap over the lens. From Blackbeard to the gin runners of Prohibition, the barrier islands had proven a haven for unsavory elements.

Feeling eyes on the back of her head, a shiver of uneasiness traveled the length of her spine. She backpedaled the way she'd come. Underneath her windbreaker, tentacles of cold fear crawled up and down her arms. On the back side of Yaupon again, she sloshed through the knee-deep water of the cove. But she never took her eyes off the rotting stumps of the dock, the long-abandoned husks of boats. She groped behind her for the familiar fiberglass bow of her boat and heaved it off the sand, putting her back into it. Only then did she clamber onto the deck. Breathing heavily, she padded over to the controls. Turning the ignition, she brought the engine to life. And above the humming of the motor . . .

On a distant sandy rise behind the stark outline of stone foundations, a babble of voices. The words indistinguishable. Angry, loud voices.

Throwing open the throttle, she gunned the engine and headed for the safety of home.

❖ ❖ ❖

TUCKAHOE, HATTERAS ISLAND, NC

Caden startled awake, not quite sure where he was. But at the rolling crash of the waves, he remembered. And immediately wished to return to the oblivion from which he'd awoken.

As impossible as returning to his life before. He'd come to the end of the world. The end of the road. Soon the end of everything.

He rubbed the sandy grit from his eyes. Leaning heavily upon the piling underneath the pier, he strong-armed his way to his feet. Or rather, what remained of his feet.

Caden grimaced, stiff from his overnight sojourn on the sand. The last island ferry had dropped him off at Hatteras Village at midnight. The long journey to North Carolina had depleted his small cash reserve. First the train, then a bus. A fellow vet offered him a ride to the ferry landing in Swan Quarter. Once on Ocracoke, he'd caught another ferry—the free ferry—to Hatteras Village. Then he'd walked north on Highway 12 until he could go no further.

But this was as far as he needed to go. To fulfill one last desire. To complete one final mission.

Joe . . . Friday . . . Red-hot memories sizzled his brain. His chest tightened. He fought the panic. The urge to run. Not that running was an option anymore.

A pinkish glow bathed the shoreline in striations of golden light, shining through the breaks in the dunes. Caden ran a shaky hand over the stubble on his face.

He'd dreamed last night of running the long, grassy field at his old high school, a football tucked underneath his arm, his feet pounding the turf, darting and dodging the defensive line.

Nine months ago he'd awoken at Reed to the sensation of a blowtorch on his feet. And the pain hadn't lessened. How could anything no longer there still hurt so much? The bomb—a pressure-sensitive homemade device—had shattered his leg. Shredded his tissue into shards of flesh. Severed his left leg below the knee.

He owed his life to Sanchez. But Sanchez had done him no favors.

"Keep breathing. Stay awake. Don't you rack out on me." Sanchez had refused to abandon him until the C-17 deposited him at the combat support hospital in Kandahar, where they stabilized him.

There had then been a blessedly unconscious flight to Bagram Air Base outside Kabul. From there to Germany, where they'd removed the breathing tube in the Level One trauma center at Landstuhl. And ultimately to Walter Reed.

Seven days. Seven thousand miles. From Afghanistan to DC. From vibrant life to a living death. From wholeness to utter brokenness.

He'd endured multiple surgeries during his stay on Ward 57 to remove scraps of metal from his wounds. But as his calls and texts to Nikki went unanswered, the festering, gnawing fear inside him quadrupled.

"Take one day at a time," the doctor advised.

Many soldiers were wounded far worse than he had been, yet they'd overcome their disabilities. So he worked hard, harder than he'd ever worked in his life, to take back his life. To return to Nikki. To create a home with Nikki. To be the man Nikki deserved.

"You watch," he'd told the physical therapist in the amputee wing. "I'm going to climb those nine flights of stairs in record time. One month tops."

Caden glanced out from underneath the pier. Guys like him were trained to never quit. If one solution didn't work, they devised another plan. And if victory proved impossible, they died still trying. But this . . . He didn't know how to move forward from what had happened.

Nikki's last words had slashed his insides sharper than shrapnel, confirming everything he'd ever suspected about himself. And when she walked out of Reed . . . for the first time he heard oblivion call to him.

Stomach clenching, Caden scanned the blue-gray waters of the Atlantic. He'd always yearned to see the ocean—a desire fueled when the nurse deposited a brown parcel on his hospital bed. Inside the package he'd found ocean waves in the folds of fabric. A quilt. But it was the label on the reverse side he couldn't forget.

Always come home.

Foster homes didn't qualify as home—part of why he'd joined the army. And he'd found there for a time a family of sorts.

He pushed away thoughts of Joe and the brothers he'd left behind. There was no going back. Only forward.

"Your only limitations—" He could hear the prosthetist in his head. "—are the ones you make for yourself."

The quilt had gotten him through bad bouts of pain after intense PT. Wrapping around him like the arms of the mother he never had. The quilt kept him fighting.

Could he rebuild his life? Or was his life over? Eight months ago Nikki had answered that question for him.

He'd lost more than his leg in Afghanistan. He'd lost his pride, his chance for a life. And worst of all, hope.

That's when he made his decision. He had to end this—before the pain wore away at his resolve. No matter what, he'd not give into the temptation to numb the pain. He wouldn't—he'd rather die than become his parents.

A quick internet search revealed everything he needed to know to see the ocean for the first and last time. Everything he needed to find the quilter—*M. Dockery, Tuckahoe, NC*—named on the label.

Caden nudged the duffel in the sand beside him with his boot. Soon as he returned the blue-and-white quilt to its rightful owner, he'd return here. Stick to the plan. Go in deep until he could no longer see the beach. Waves would roll over him. He'd lose his footing. Saltwater would fill his lungs. Choking, gasping, he wouldn't be able to breathe. And then he—

He took a deep breath, the sea breeze bringing a briny aroma to his nostrils. Propping his hip against the wooden piling, he carefully— every movement minutely planned these days—hoisted the bag, ducked his head, and slung the strap over his shoulder. He fought to maintain his balance on the shifting sand. His knuckles whitened on the strap. He was hanging on by only a thread, and not just to his ruck.

Caden practiced the breathing techniques. Didn't help much, but the stabbing intensity of the pain abated somewhat.

He straightened. Refocused on his mission. He was tethered to this world by only the threads of a quilt. At least until eventide.

❖ ❖ ❖

McKenna's heart continued to thump long after the island disappeared behind the boat's wake. She steered across the channel toward the sheltered bay. Slowing the boat, she pulled back on the throttle and chugged into the Tuckahoe marina, maneuvering past a recreational boater headed out, a man with stringy gray-blond hair and brawny arms at the wheel. His short-sleeved tropical shirt with a riotous display of flora belied the beer gut above his cargo shorts. One of those aging hippies on a never-ending quest for the magic elixir of eternal youth. A stereotype of island escapism.

Before she got a close look at his face, however, the boater slipped Maui Jim sunglasses over his eyes. But she'd seen him before at Skipjacks. Odd he was still hanging around. Unless he was one of those weird writer types renting a house for the winter to pen his version of the Great American Novel.

Still, it was within a Banker's best interests to be friendly. Tourists were their bread and butter. She raised her hand to wave, but as the adrenaline escaped down her arm and through her fingertips, her hand shook.

His teeth flashed, a contrast against his peeling, sunburned skin, and then their boats were past each other.

Once inside the Tuckahoe harbor, she eased the boat into the rented berth and cut the engine. In one leap, she bridged the gap between the boat and the dock. The silver-weathered planks felt solid beneath her. She reached for her bucket—

"Top of the mornin' to you."

She whirled.

Beside his charter boat, a grizzled waterman lifted his hand in greeting. Laddie Ferguson, longtime family friend.

She willed her heartbeat to subside. It wasn't like her to get spooked. But after her unsettling experience on Yaupon, her nerves were frayed.

"Out early, aren't you now?" Beneath the brim of a stained ball cap, Laddie's bushy gray brows lowered. "Where you been?"

"Hunting sea glass." She secured a mooring line to a cleat on the pier. "You're heading out late, aren't you, Laddie?"

"Business to take care of this morning." Coming alongside, Laddie tied off another line for her. "I'll be out and about soon enough."

She glanced at her watch. "Thanks for your help." Still time before her shift, if she hurried. "Next time you're in the diner, I'll owe you a danish."

Behind the bristly beard, the waterman's lips curved, and creases from a lifetime of gauging sea horizons fanned out from his faded blue eyes. "Tell that grandmother of yours I said hello."

After leaving the bucket of sea glass in the bed of her truck, she crossed the marina parking lot to the public access path. At the bottom of the dune, she took the wooden steps two at a time. Topping the incline, she took a cautious, exploratory breath. Her pulse quieted. The sound of the waves always made her better, and she cast aside the strange foreboding she'd experienced on Yaupon.

She plodded through the sand until she stood at the water's edge. But despite the healing power of the wind and the waves, the old ache she'd come to consider a part of herself resurfaced. Grief had proven as slippery as an eel. Just when she believed she had a solid grip on it, a tsunami of breath-stealing anguish rolled in, taking her completely by surprise.

"Will it always be like this, God?" she whispered toward the leftover streaks of pink in the morning sky.

Silence, except for the sighing of the waves.

Three years since Shawn had died. She'd almost begun to believe there'd never be an answer. The tide frothed at her feet, flowing in and ebbing out. Kind of like her hope.

Every day, she lost more of Shawn. And one day—soon?—she feared she'd lose the memory of his laugh completely. Already, she no longer recalled the exact shade of his eyes. Blue-green? Or more green than blue?

Was this it for her? And if so, why did something within her yearn to find herself again—find her heart again—in someone else's arms? Why couldn't the life she had now be enough? A life with her dad and her grandmother, Lovey. Keeping the business afloat was a full-time job. So many had so much less. Was she ungrateful?

God, forgive me if I am.

Her eyes flicked upward toward the gulls wheeling in acrobatic figure eights in the sky. Something—Someone—whispered for her to wait. To be patient. To not lose faith.

To hold on to her hope.

But she'd become mired in a kind of emotional paralysis. Stuck between her life *Before* and an *After* she was afraid to embrace. Not if the future meant letting go of Shawn. She couldn't betray him like that.

Her heart ached at a sudden, quick memory of how Shawn used to smile when he watched her dance on stage.

Kicking off her flip-flops, she lifted her face to the morning sun. Soaking in the blessing. Claiming the promise. Lulled by the waves. The gentle sea breeze fluttered across her skin, imparting peace and strength. She staked her life and her heart on the fulfillment of that which she had yet to see. Choosing, despite the empty void, to trust while her dreams remained unfulfilled. When the pain and loneliness were at their height.

When, perhaps, faith meant the most.

❖ ❖ ❖

Rounding the curve of the shoreline, a flicker of movement at the water's edge caught Caden's attention. He noticed her legs first, homing in upon that which he no longer possessed. Encased in denim shorts, her legs went on forever.

She was a tall woman in a seen-better-days navy windbreaker. The unfurling of the sun highlighted the straight blonde hair skimming her shoulders. Eyes closed, arms outstretched, she arched one foot over the water and made a circling motion with her pointed toe, balancing on her other leg. She raised her arms above her head, her fingers artfully posed. Leaning sideways, she kicked upward. Her feet scissored above the surface of the water. He held his breath, transfixed. Yet she landed nimble, soft and sure footed as a butterfly lighting upon a leaf. Her knees flexed and straightened.

Poetry in motion.

Caden scowled at his useless leg and bit his lip until he tasted the coppery, metallic taste of blood. "Why do you hate me so much, God?"

As his sibilant whisper floated across the sand, the woman reeled midmotion. Her arms lowered from their duet with the sky. And she rotated, as graceful as the opening of a door, toward him.

For a long moment, they stared at each other. An eternity as they weighed the measure of the other. Until her eyes—blue like the Carolina morning—sharpened.

Something in those fathomless depths rocked him. Jarred him. A frightening intensity tugged at him. Read him down to his soul.

The soul he used to have.

His heart skipped a beat. He had to get away from here, from her, before she distracted him from his purpose. Before—

She stretched out her hand. Absurdly panicked, he pivoted without thinking.

And fell flat on his face.

Chapter Two

IN THREE STRIDES, MCKENNA REACHED THE MAN LYING ON THE sand. His pant leg had ridden up to his shin, revealing not actual flesh but a prosthesis.

Judging from his tactical pants, maybe a veteran. Dark hair feathered over the collar of an army-green T-shirt. Around his neck a metal chain glinted. Dog tags?

Something warned her not to help him. To save his pride and allow him to stand on his own.

"I got it," he grunted and rolled onto his side. "I don't need your help."

By sheer force of will—and locking her arms behind her back—she stopped herself from rushing to his rescue. "I wasn't offering."

At her tone, he stiffened. Using the duffel as a prop, he counterbalanced and crawled to a kneeling position.

She'd seen death in his face. His unvoiced intentions hit her like a blow. She'd seen a coming grave in those large, dark eyes of his. Sad, weary-of-life eyes. And a seething anger at an all-too-familiar enemy surged within her heart.

The man, perhaps a few years older, was gaunt. Late twenties. But he'd once been powerfully built with broad, muscled shoulders. His bent, emaciated frame was probably just under six foot. And behind the scraggly beard that framed his mouth, she imagined he'd also once been almost handsome. High cheekbones. A rugged jawline. Before pain wracked his features and flattened his lips into a thin, straight line.

Gasping, the man righted himself into a standing position. He tossed her a triumphant look. "I told you I could do it."

She shrugged. "Never doubted it."

The man glared at her. She glared back until his eyes darted over her shoulder to the waves. "What's that?"

Her breath hitched at the sight of the black-green object floating on the tide. She sped toward the water as the sea turtle flopped onto the shore. Sinking to her knees, she performed a cursory examination. A front flipper remained entangled in a fishing line. One of the back flippers had been severed, perhaps by the blades of a boat's propeller.

Belatedly, she remembered the other wounded creature by the dunes. But he was exactly where she'd left him. Still scowling.

She scrambled to her feet. "I could use some help here."

He jolted, nearly unsettling his carefully contrived balance. "You want me?"

She planted her hands on her hips. "I want you."

He blinked. And she blushed.

Averting her gaze, she brushed away the sand encrusting her knees. "I mean I need you. Really need—" She cleared her throat. "I need your help."

Pity demoralized. Responsibility inspired.

She studied him as indecision fought with something akin to dignity. Finally, he moved forward as self-respect gained the upper hand. His gait was jerky, uneven. She'd be willing to bet he'd ditched physical therapy too soon, before the benefits outweighed the pain.

He flushed when he caught her staring.

McKenna turned away, giving him the chance to approach without scrutiny. Reaching her side, he leaned closer. She prepared to be overwhelmed by the homeless stench of him, or alcohol. But he only smelled of the salty sea air, like everyone in Tuckahoe. Like her.

So maybe he wasn't homeless. Or homeless long. As a police chief's daughter, she knew enough to recognize a drug-induced haze in a person's eyes. This man's eyes were clear . . . except for the crushing weight of fear and a heart-wrenching childlike disbelief in the face of desperate pain.

McKenna pushed away a helpless feeling. This was why she hadn't gone into nursing. Her natural empathy unraveled her, rendering her useful to no one.

"I thought sea turtles lived in the ocean."

He had a strong, deep voice.

McKenna tilted her head. "When sea turtles get hurt, sometimes they get lost."

She resisted the temptation to point out the similarities between the turtle's injuries and his own. Despite the pain, intelligence also shone out of his dark eyes.

The man wasn't stupid. Suicidal, yes. Stupid, no.

His mouth twisted. "Where I come from, they'd shoot a horse in this condition."

A cowboy? Maybe the bow-legged gait wasn't solely a war wound.

She frowned. "We don't shoot turtles here."

His mouth hardened. "Maybe you should." A thread of anger flitted across the broad planes of his face.

She preferred anger to the other thing she'd seen in his eyes.

"Here's what we'll do." She outlined how she'd retrieve her truck, drive as close as she could get on the beach, and fill the baby swimming pool she kept in the truck bed for emergencies like this.

"We'll lift Cecil into the tub, then take him to the sea turtle rescue hospital."

"Cecil?" A laugh barked from between his lips. A rusty laugh, but a laugh all the same. "You know this turtle?"

Her lips curved. "Dr. Thompson lets me name the wounded ones I bring him."

The man raked a hand across the top of his dark hair. "A veterinarian?"

"Marine animal specialist. We share him with the aquarium over the bridge." She dusted off her hands. "We'd better hurry before Dr. Thompson heads to Manteo."

"You work at the animal hospital?"

She shook her head. "The turtle rehab is staffed by volunteers like me. We provide a temporary home for the wounded until we can equip them to survive on their own."

The man gave her the strangest look. "A labor of love."

Crinkling her eyes, she smiled. "Exactly."

Her smile dazzled him. Like a string of diamonds glinting across the water. A glittering trail of hope-encrusted bread crumbs. A commodity Caden had no use for. Not anymore.

She trudged toward the dunes. Sea oats waving in the wind, the woman disappeared from view. For a second he wondered if he'd imagined her.

But the creature—Cecil?—hunkered in the sand. So he wasn't going crazy. Or at least any crazier than he'd been when he arrived.

The injured turtle was real, so she must be real. The turtle-rescuing, beach-dancing woman. Tall, willowy, and blonde. Totally unlike Nikki. Her winsome smile had caught him by surprise. As did his unbidden response to the embodiment of hope she brought with her.

He stuffed the good feeling down. He'd help her with the turtle. Maybe she'd give him a ride to the diner.

Caden paced around the animal, his footprints sinking in the wet sand. He'd known the instant she noticed his leg. He could always tell by the slight hesitation, the hitch of breath. He'd steeled himself for the usual pity. But instead of pity—or disgust, in Nikki's case—there'd been something unexpected in the woman's face. A ferocity he recognized from fellow warriors in the height of battle. Though what Beach Girl believed she battled he hadn't a clue.

His gaze lifted as a blue Chevy truck rumbled onto the beach. Jumping out, she hurried around to open the tailgate. She handed him a plastic jug. "Fill 'er up."

Caden wasn't sure he could trust his footing in the foaming surf. What if he fell on his face and made a fool out of himself again? But she moved away, not giving him the chance to refuse.

Unscrewing the cap, he waded ankle deep into the water. So far so good. The water felt cool against his real foot, and sloshing, gurgling liquid filled the jug.

Heading up the incline with a confident stride he could only envy, she dumped the contents of her own container into the baby pool. "Just enough to make the ride to the clinic comfortable for him."

Sand was tricky, slippery. He moved cautiously up the slope and emptied his jug into the pool, pleased he hadn't disgraced himself. He retraced his steps to where she knelt beside Cecil.

"Loggerheads aren't as heavy as leatherbacks. And Cecil isn't full grown. Probably an adolescent, lucky for us."

Caden scowled. "Lucky for us."

Her eyes flicked at the bitterness in his voice. His knee protested as he lowered himself on the other side of Cecil.

"The hardest part," she warned, "will be lifting so you don't lose your balance."

He squared his jaw. Everything was hard. "Let's do it already."

"Okay. One . . . two . . . three." She hoisted her side free of the cloying sand.

Caden heaved and bit back a groan. But he toughed it out and took the brunt of the turtle's weight. Which was the way it should be. Soaking wet, Beach Girl probably wouldn't weigh much over a hundred pounds.

Together they lowered Cecil into the tub. The turtle fluttered what remained of his flippers. The woman clambered into the bed, gently splashing water over Cecil's pitted shell.

Breathing in short spurts, Caden was ashamed how such a small effort took so much out of him these days.

She gestured toward the crew cab. "Would you mind riding to the clinic to help me settle Cecil in case we don't catch the doc?"

"As long as you'll drop me off in town."

Jumping down, she slammed the tailgate shut. "Deal."

He yanked open the passenger door and tossed in his ruck. After inserting his torso into the cab like the therapist had shown him, he swung his legs inside.

Sliding behind the wheel, she inspected the dashboard clock and grimaced. "I'm supposed to be at work in fifteen minutes." She turned the key in the ignition. The engine sputtered before catching.

"Is the clinic far?"

Both hands on the wheel, she maneuvered off the treacherous sand. "Nothing in Tuckahoe is far."

He gripped the armrest, trying to cushion his joints against the jolt. "H-had the shocks checked r-recently?" He gritted his rattling teeth.

"Too expensive right now." She flung a sideways look at him. "You offering?"

"No . . . I'm not . . ." He made a motion toward his leg. "In case you forgot . . ." His lips clamped together.

"I didn't forget." She faced forward. "But maybe you should."

She had some nerve. Clenching his fists, he angled toward the passing scenery. Three minutes of blessed silence ticked by.

"Visiting someone on the Banks?"

This woman talked too much. He drummed his fingers on the armrest.

"Well?" She wasn't going to let this go.

"No." He cranked down the window, letting the wind buffet him.

They passed a post office and a grocery store. Two minutes passed. He knew because he fixed his gaze on the clock, waiting. And sure enough—

"Just passing through?" Her lips twitched. "Tuckahoe isn't exactly on the beaten path."

These never-met-a-stranger southerners didn't understand how to mind their own business.

He folded his arms across his chest. "I'm returning something to its rightful owner. I've got no use for it anymore."

"Nice of you. And then you're off to someplace else?"

"To nowhere else," he muttered under his breath.

"Only two ways on or off Hatteras Island—the ferry at Hatteras Village south or north on Highway 12 across the Bonner Bridge. How'd you get here?"

He glared. "Ferry."

She motioned toward the notch between the dunes lining the highway that revealed a tantalizing glimpse of blue ocean. "It's a nice place we call home. Tuckahoe has everything you'll ever need."

He snorted. "Like?"

"Like good people, ocean breezes, gorgeous sunrises or sunsets—take your pick." She smiled.

And something—it wasn't pain this time—banged against his rib cage.

She pointed to a clump of twisted, stunted trees where a white steeple pierced the azure sky.

"God and I aren't on a speaking basis."

She threw him a look. "Suit yourself."

He surveyed the terrain. "Not many people around."

"Summertime we get about forty thousand visitors. Bankers—that's what we year-rounders on the Outer Banks call ourselves—we work two or three jobs during tourist season to earn most of what we make the whole year." She quirked her eyebrow. "Like squirrels storing nuts for winter. But past Labor Day, we get the Banks to ourselves again."

"With no room for an outsider like me."

She turned off Highway 12 into the parking lot of a low-slung concrete building. *Tuckahoe Turtle Rescue Center*, the sign over the entrance read.

"There's always room." She glanced in the rearview mirror. "What's *he* doing here?"

A Town of Tuckahoe police cruiser pulled in behind them, and a thirty-something man in a short-sleeved, gray police uniform got out.

"Hey, Bryce." She left the door dinging as she hurried around the truck. "I'm glad you're here. I could use the muscle."

The athletic man with frat-boy good looks caught her around the waist. "I went to the marina. You took the boat out again, didn't you?" He shook his head. "You shouldn't take off with no one knowing where you are."

She lifted her chin. "As you can see, I'm fine."

Ice-blue eyes narrowing, the policeman tightened his arms around her in a proprietary way. "Aren't you supposed to be at work?"

Beach Girl and the man obviously had some sort of relationship. Caden's brow furrowed. None of his business.

Ever-fluid motion, she glided out of the man's hold. "I'm going to be late if you don't help me." She tugged him toward the pickup. "I ran into a situation this morning—"

Spotting Caden, the policeman's chiseled features underwent a transformation. "What have you done?" Lip curling, he jerked her to a standstill.

Caden's nostrils flared. He didn't like the guy manhandling her. Inside the cab, he unfolded his arms, his fingers flexing.

"Let go of me, Bryce." She pulled free. "He isn't the situation I'm talking about. I found an injured loggerhead on the beach."

Bryce's patrician nose wrinkled. "You don't even know his name, do you? A bum. A drug-crazed addict you picked up on the beach."

She slapped his hand away as he reached for her again. "Stop it, Bryce. He'll hear you. And he's not—"

"He's another stray," the policeman hissed.

"My ears aren't missing. Just my leg." He leaned out the window. "And the name's Caden Wallis."

She flashed him another one of those killer smiles. His gut quivered. The look Bryce threw his way was far from nice.

Her silver dolphin earrings jangled as she sidestepped the policeman. "But if you're on a call, I'm sure Caden—" She emphasized his name. "—can handle relocating Cecil to the tank inside the center."

The police officer's face darkened. "I came looking for you because Dispatch radioed me," he snapped. "Your dad was a no-show for roll call this morning."

She bit her lip. "He had a rough night. I realize he's been MIA a lot lately, but I'm sure he's on his way to the station."

An older man in surgical scrubs stepped out of the building, and she let out a breath.

"I thought I heard voices." The doctor peered into the truck bed. "A new patient?"

Caden fumbled for the door handle, but the officer leaned against the door, keeping it shut. "Wouldn't want a man in your condition to hurt yourself."

While Caden fumed in the truck, the three of them wrestled the kiddy pool with Cecil into the facility. Minutes later, she emerged with the policeman on her heels. He strolled toward Caden's open window.

"Somewhere I can drop you?" Not so much a question as a command.

Beach Girl yanked open the driver-side door. "I got this, Bryce. Stop being such a worrywart."

"You are so hardheaded," he growled, raking his hand over his close-cropped blond hair. "When will you learn not everyone is a good guy? Not everyone deserves to be rescued."

Anger flashed across her features. "I'm not the naive fool you think I am, Bryce."

His face fell. "I didn't mean . . . I just . . ."

She pulled the door shut. "Don't you have a drug dealer to catch, Officer Hinson?"

His eyes flitted to Caden. "How long are you staying in Tuckahoe?"

"Not long." Caden jutted his jaw. "No worries."

Bryce Hinson's brows lowered. "I'm not worried. But I consider the chief's family to be my family. And we take care of our own here on the Banks."

She revved the engine. "Goodbye, Bryce."

With a final death glare at Caden, he stepped away as she put the truck in motion.

On the highway again, her forehead scrunched as she glanced at the clock. "Where to now, Caden?" She favored him with another smile. His heart skipped a beat. Irritation shot through him at the pleasure he felt in its sunshine. There was this little dimple in her chin. An extremely friendly southern person, she probably smiled at everyone, turtles and dogs too.

"Drop me off at Skipjacks, please. If it's not out of your way." The ferry captain had told him the Dockerys owned Skipjacks. He'd go there, return the quilt, then leave. For good.

"I'm headed there too." Her cheeks lifted. "Although my grandmother is going to skin me alive for not being there when the doors opened."

"Good." He coughed. "I mean, not good that you're going to be skinned alive, but good that I'm not taking you out of your way. We're both headed in the same direction." He scrubbed the back of his neck. "Your dad's the police chief?"

Her face clouded. "With everything that's been happening, there's talk about him being forced to resign."

"What's been happening?"

Her fingers tensed on the wheel. "We serve a great breakfast at Skipjacks."

Okay, her dad's work was off limits. Not like he'd ever see her again once he got out of the truck.

She steered into the crushed oyster shell parking lot of a cedar-shingled restaurant on stilts. "Thanks for helping me rescue Cecil. How about the Fisherman's Breakfast Catch? On the house."

He bristled. "I don't need your charity."

She eased into the space nearest the ramp. "I park around back, but I'll let you off here." The engine idled in the handicapped spot—designed for a cripple like him.

Teeth on edge, he threw open the door and swung his legs over the side. He inched his way down and flinched when his leg made contact with the ground. The jarring motion set off a new round of aches in his stump. He bent to retrieve his ruck, hiding his pain.

He looked across the seat at her. "Thanks for the lift. For . . ." For one last chance to be useful.

She glanced at him through her lashes. "Maybe we'll run into each other again."

"Run?" He tightened his hold on the bag. "No chance of that."

Chapter Three

As the truck disappeared around the corner of the restaurant, he realized she'd never told him her name. And he'd not asked.

Caden reached for the glass-fronted door, and a bell jangled overhead. Inside, he hesitated, grateful for the cool current of air from the whirring ceiling fan. A placard read *Make Yourself at Home*.

He was here to make sure the quilt did just that.

The dining area boasted a smattering of blue-checkered tables with chairs. Booths lined the outer walls. Floor-to-ceiling windows provided a lofty view of the waterfront and the tidal marsh meandering to the Pamlico Sound. A larger-than-life menu was mounted on the back wall. A pass-through cutout revealed a commercial kitchen.

An auburn-haired seventyish woman perched on a stool behind an antique brass register. In a lavender shirt and charcoal-gray trousers, she chatted with a handful of men in ball caps and Wellingtons. Just the kind of woman he'd always imagined his own grandmother might resemble.

If either of his grandmothers had ever bothered to retrieve him from Child Protective Services.

Caden hobbled toward an empty booth. The lady at the register— his quilt lady?—looked busy. He'd order coffee and wait until she was free.

He thrust his ruck into the booth, then wedged himself on the opposite side. The enticing aroma of hash browns and scrambled eggs made his stomach growl. He hadn't felt like eating for a long time. But there was no need to fill his belly. He'd be nothing but shark food by sunset.

Balancing a tray of pancakes and orange juice, a fifty-something waitress in tight-fitting black jeans and red stiletto heels emerged from the swinging door of the kitchen. "Be right with you, hon. Soon as I deliver Pastor's order."

She rushed past, the aroma of breakfast meat and cloying perfume trailing in her wake. He barely had time to identify the scent—Shalimar—before she returned.

"What can I do you for, hon?" She plucked a pencil out of her upswept, golden blonde hair and tabbed through her notepad until she found a blank page. According to the name tag pinned to her fluttery red blouse, her name was Earlene.

Although his wounds weren't visible, out of habit he tucked his feet under the blue Formica table, keeping his leg hidden. "Coffee."

She made a note and paused, pencil poised.

"That's all."

Her red-tinted lips quirked. "Hon, if you don't mind me saying so, you need some meat on your handsome bones."

Caden shook his head. "Just coffee."

Her heavily mascara-rimmed eyes narrowed. "Cream and sugar?"

"Black."

"How did I know you'd say that?" She poked the pencil into her bun again. "Coffee coming right up, shoog." She ambled toward the pickup window.

Shoog. Southern for "sugar." An endearment Virginia-born Joe Nelson had used for his wife.

Earlene returned with his coffee just as a tall, lanky man in jeans and boots stormed inside the restaurant.

"Walt, honey, slow down," Earlene called out. Caden winced at the raw vulnerability in her eyes.

About Earlene's age, the man combed his fingers through the short ends of his gray-blond hair. "Didn't hear Baby Girl leave. I got a call about her."

The man appeared frazzled, his movements jerky, an all too familiar expression on his weary, once handsome face. There was a hint of pain in his blue eyes, and barely masked exhaustion. Which over time had apparently carved deep lines upon his face.

Caden swallowed past the boulder in his throat. Not going to happen to him. Not once the sun descended below the horizon.

"Where have you been, Walt?"

"S-somewhere I had to be." Walt tugged at the cuffs of his green plaid shirt. "But my girl—"

"Walt, it's fine. She's in the kitchen."

If Earlene could have curled herself into the man's angular frame, Caden reckoned she would have. As it was, she still held his coffee. Should he reach for it?

"Pour yourself a cup and go talk to her." Earlene flitted a hand toward the far wall.

Caden's gaze followed her gesture, and for the first time he noticed the trophy case on the other side of the counter. Not filled with the usual trophies, the case contained lots of ribbons—mostly blue—and a photo of the old lady cashier standing beside a large quilt.

So she *was* his quilt lady.

"Relax, Walt." Earlene patted his arm. "Take a breath."

Walt's thin mouth creased into a vague smile as he shoved off toward the kitchen.

She peered after him for the duration of a heartbeat, her eyes consumed with an unrequited longing. Caden fiddled with a sugar packet. After Nikki's betrayal, he knew that feeling.

Earlene's breath caught in a small half sob as she swung around and plunked the mug in front of him. Hot black liquid sloshed over the rim of the cup. She grabbed a handful of napkins. "I'm—I'm so sorry, shoog." Her hand shook, dabbing at the tabletop.

He should've ordered the cream—anything to take the pinched, hopeless look out of her eyes.

"I might take some cream after all, Miss Earlene." Using a napkin, he caught a rivulet of caffeine flowing toward the edge. "If it wouldn't be too much trouble, ma'am."

A pool of moisture welled in her ocean-blue eyes. Maybe all the islanders—Bankers, Beach Girl had called them—sported blue eyes.

Earlene gave him a tremulous smile. "Wouldn't be any trouble at all, shoog. What else can I get you?"

He almost smiled back. Almost.

"I'm looking for M. Dockery." His gaze drifted toward the old woman. "I'd like to speak with her when she gets a chance."

Earlene pushed the soggy napkins to the far side of the table. "Will do. And I'll be back with a cloth to clean up this mess."

Wending around the throng of tables, she nudged one old codger with her hip before heading behind the counter. "McKenna," Earlene yelled. "A man wants to talk to you."

Caden jerked, the cup halfway to his lips. The old woman at the register stilled. Like someone had flicked a switch, the chatter instantly died. Every head turned in his direction.

He reminded himself yet again that his wounds didn't show.

"Soon as I flip this omelet," someone hollered from the kitchen.

His eyes darted to the cash register. The old lady hadn't budged.

Remembering the need to map out his moves, he carefully got to his feet and unzipped the bag. Extracting the quilt, he angled as Beach Girl ambled out of the kitchen, a white apron wrapped around her lithe form.

She swiveled to Earlene. "Who'd you say was looking for me?"

Earlene gaped at him, a dishcloth limp in one hand. "Sweet tea and hush my mouth . . ."

When Beach Girl caught sight of him, genuine warmth lit her face. "Caden, I'm so glad you decided—"

Her gaze latched onto the quilt. She froze. Color drained from her face as her knees buckled.

And with reflexes he hadn't used since Kandahar, he caught *M. Dockery* in his arms as she fell.

Her first coherent thought? Somebody ought to shut up the squawking hen.

Actually, not true. Tucked beneath someone's chin, encircled in strong, masculine arms, McKenna's initial sensation had been one of extreme comfort.

A hand, callused but gentle, brushed a lock of hair out of her eyes. "McKenna?"

His beard scraped against her earlobe. She nestled deeper.

"McKenna?"

Her name sounded different coming from him. She liked the low scrape of his voice.

"Somebody call 9-1-1!" Earlene screamed. Ah, the squawking hen.

McKenna's eyes popped open.

Caden Wallis let out a breath, the warmth fanning her cheek. Mortification mounted. She—who'd never fainted in her life—had collapsed into a stranger's arms.

Her weight had unbalanced him. Both of them were sprawled across the booth. She'd knocked over a wounded vet. A man who struggled to stand upright.

"I'm so sorry. Did I hurt you? Let me . . ." She struggled, trying to get off him. Would the embarrassment never end? "For the love of sweet tea," she whispered.

Caden's chest rumbled beneath her.

Her eyes darted to his face in time to see him crack a smile. *Crack* being the operative word. He quickly clamped down as if his face might break from the unaccustomed strain.

She scrambled free. "This isn't funny."

His eyes held amusement as he righted himself. "This is the most fun I've had in a year."

"McKenna!" screeched Earlene.

Other voices shouted for her dad, and the cacophony rose. "Who is he, hon?" "What's going on here?" "What's he doing with Shawn's—"

Placing two fingers in her mouth, McKenna unleashed the ear-splitting whistle Dad had taught her at the tender age of eight. Earlene winced. Lovey, a funny smile plastered on her wrinkled face, didn't budge from her stool behind the register.

"Everybody calm down. I'm okay."

"I'm not." Caden fell against the upholstery, hands to his ears. "Warn a guy next time."

Her father stepped forward with one hand on his gun belt.

She stood and gestured to the booth. "Everyone, I'd like you to meet Caden Wallis."

Her father scowled. "Bryce said there was a man . . ."

Fresh irritation with Bryce flared inside McKenna.

The quilt in his arms again, Caden pushed to his feet. "I'm looking for the quilter who made this."

And once again McKenna felt herself going cold. How did he— Where did he—

Dad wheeled toward the cash register. "Do you know this man, Mother?"

McKenna held up her palm. "I've got this, Daddy."

"Leave the boy alone." Lovey fluttered her hand. "She said she's got him."

Chuckles rang out as diners returned to their tables.

"That's not what I said, Lovey."

"Mother? Earlene?" Dad barked. "What's going on here?"

Earlene retreated to the drink dispenser. Lovey didn't look up from counting change. "Go on about your business, son. No harm will come to McKenna."

McKenna stared pointedly at her father. "Yes, *Chief.* Don't you have places to be?"

"I'll be at the station." Dad scowled at Caden. "Across the street." He stalked out, the bell jangling.

She sank back into the booth, Caden on the other side. She fingered the quilt lying on the table between them. "This is what you were returning to its rightful owner?"

Caden's dark eyes softened. "Did you make this quilt?"

"Where did you get this?"

"At Walter Reed. After . . ." He swallowed.

"I sent it to a group who takes quilts to wounded veterans." Her voice went husky. "I couldn't bear for it to never be used."

"The quilt blocks capture the movement of water . . . like the way you danced—" He bit his lip.

Her cheeks reddened. She hadn't danced in front of anyone since she left the troupe. Since Shawn.

"The quilt spoke to me. Made me feel better. Comforted." His eyes, as dark fringed as a raven's wings, dropped away. "I'd never seen the ocean. It gave me a good excuse to come."

She straightened. "Never?"

"I'm from Oklahoma."

"A cowboy."

His lips twitched. "Sort of."

She smiled. "Thought so."

His eyes fastened on the region of her mouth. A curious, melted-butter feeling warmed her.

"I spent my high school years on a ranch for foster kids who didn't adopt out. We were expected to work."

Unexpected pain jabbed her heart. She reached across the table for his hand. "I'm sor—"

A frisson of electricity sizzled between them. Stung, she drew back. He stared at the place where her fingers had touched his skin.

"Quilt static. Sorry."

A pulse jumped in his cheek. "Those people were good to me." He sighed. "Long as I helped the football team win championships." He scrubbed his forehead. "I aged out. We haven't kept in touch."

Something inside her ached at what he'd said. And hadn't said. He'd worked for approval, and something told her Caden Wallis had continued to perform.

Until he couldn't anymore.

But there was something else going on beyond his injury. Something worse?

Soldiers with strong support networks recovered faster from the wounds of war. Those without that kind of support . . . didn't.

Turning back a corner of the quilt, she traced the words on the label with her finger.

He leaned forward. "*Always come home.*"

She found herself unable to look away from his eyes. "So you did."

His mouth opened. He closed it with a snap. "I brought the quilt home." He laced his hands together on top of the table. "To you."

Strong, capable hands. Capable of expertly palming a football, she imagined. And yet also capable of a gentleness she'd experienced first-hand. Her heart thudded. "You said the quilt was something you had no use for anymore."

He gripped the tabletop and pushed to his feet. "Correct."

Inexplicable panic streaked through her. "Wait." She placed a restraining hand on his arm. Another crackle of electricity. He froze. The skin on her arm goose pimpled.

"Before you take off somewhere—" She allowed the unspoken "nowhere" to hang between them for the space of a breath.

He sank into the booth again.

"I wondered if maybe you'd help us out at Skipjacks today." The words tumbled out of her mouth. "Our cook, Alonso, didn't show again. Since Lovey's hip surgery, she doesn't do well standing for long. Earlene's alone on the floor and Dad . . ." She blew out a breath. "Dad doesn't seem to be having a good day."

His face remained a stoic, maddening mask.

She started to squeeze his hand, but thinking better of it, she placed her palm flat on the table. "I've stepped in to cook, but the dishwasher's not working. If you could wash the dishes so we don't get behind on the orders . . ." She couldn't seem to stop jabbering. "I'd pay you a fair wage. You'd be doing me—us—a tremendous favor if you'd stick around." She inhaled. "For a while."

"I don't have a while to spare." The coldness of his words hit her like a punch to the face.

"Till sundown, then." What could she say to make him stay? Why did she care if he did or not? "Sunsets on the island are not to be missed."

A flame of interest—in the sunset?—flickered in his dark brown eyes. She resisted the urge to drown in those pools of liquid chocolate.

"Just today. Till you kick me out." His lips twisted. "You won't be the first."

Chapter Four

HE'D OVERDONE THE PHYSICAL EXERTION TODAY, BUT SOMETHING deep within Caden rejoiced at the chance to do something worthwhile again.

After he finished the dishes, he nudged McKenna away from the stove. "Help Earlene. I got this."

She floated past him to heap coleslaw on a hot dog. "My hero."

Caden lifted the fries and racked them above the boiling grease vat. Hero? Guilt surged as he thought of Joe and Friday. He wasn't anybody's hero. But he couldn't resist the urge to watch as Beach Girl moved around the stainless-steel kitchen and shoved orders through the cutout toward Earlene. McKenna Dockery didn't so much move from one place to the other as glide. As if every step were choreographed for his enjoyment.

He scowled at the bubbling onion rings. So not true.

McKenna had tucked the quilt back into his ruck. "For the time being," she'd said.

Skipjacks closed at two. Spotting a toolbox under the sink, he decided to see if he could fix the dishwasher. He pulled the machine out from the wall and unhooked the water line. He fiddled. He probed. He experimented.

"I'll probably need help getting to my feet after being on my knees this long," he muttered.

Someone squatted beside him. "Sure—" It sounded like *shore.* "—thing."

Earlene.

"Can I hand you something, shoog?"

His eyes flitted toward the woman. "The wrench." He chewed the inside of his cheek.

She handed him the wrench. "Anything else?"

"Who's Shawn?"

Limber as a teenager, Earlene sat down beside him. "McKenna's fiancé. Died three years ago. One week before the wedding. The quilt was to be her wedding gift to him."

A pang needled him, but he shifted away from it. His own pain—emotional and physical—was more than he could deal with most days. Besides, McKenna, Earlene, and the Dockerys were none of his business. How had he gotten sidetracked?

Earlene rose. "Everything you wanted to know?"

He returned to the job. "More than I needed to know." More than he'd wanted to hear.

"Then my work here is done."

"Wait." He frowned as she slipped from the kitchen. "You said you'd—"

"Did you need something?" McKenna flitted into the kitchen. She gasped. "Caden Wallis, did you go and fix this dishwasher?"

He lumbered to his feet. "Don't get excited yet. First, let me—"

"Lovey!" she shouted through the cutout. "Come see what Caden has done."

He dropped the wrench with a clang into the toolbox. "I told you, McKenna, to wait for me."

The oddest look flitted across her features as Lovey and Walt ambled into the kitchen. Police Chief Walter Dockery, now in uniform. Gun belt, Caden didn't fail to notice, at the ready.

Great. An audience for his latest inadequacy.

Lovey rested her hip against the sink. "Let's see."

The chief glowered. If the dishwasher flooded the kitchen, would he arrest him? Or shoot him?

Making sure the door was good and closed, Caden jabbed the On button. Water whooshed inside. Something mechanical whirred. And he released the breath he'd been holding.

"Woo-hoo!" McKenna proceeded to—as southerners called it—hug his neck. His arms went round her of their own volition. But remembering her dad's gun belt, he dropped his hands.

Lovey smiled. Chief Dockery appeared a tad less forbidding. But only a smidgeon. When the radio mic on his shoulder crackled, he stepped away. Seconds later, he poked his head back around the door.

"Got a lead on a local connection to the dealer we're after. I'm headed to Kitty Hawk to execute a search warrant." His gray-blue eyes gouged Caden. "I appreciate you helping Skipjacks today."

Wait for it. There was always a "but," in Caden's experience. Would Chief Dockery escort him to the ferry or merely "encourage" him not to miss it?

He lifted his chin.

"I reckon since you've done what you came here to do—"

Not really.

"—you won't be hanging around."

"Daddy!"

Lovey pursed her lips. "Walter, there's no call for rudeness."

Walt never so much as blinked. "I'm sure you have places to go. People to see, Sergeant First Class Wallis."

McKenna's eyes widened. "You ran a background check on him?"

The last few months he'd lived in a hazy blur of pain and emptiness. With the team on a six-month deployment to Africa—without him, of course—there'd been no reason to return to Fayetteville. Especially with Nikki and her new boyfriend living there too.

He didn't blame Dockery for checking him out. "I'd have done the same."

It was the kind of thing a good father and son did to protect those he loved. Not that he'd ever had a good father. Nor the chance to be anyone's son.

Walt's eyes narrowed. "I reckon we understand one another."

"Yes, sir, we do."

The police chief straightened. "I'll be on my way, then."

With an apologetic look, Lovey shuffled after her son.

McKenna grimaced. "I don't know what has gotten into Daddy. He's been under a lot of pressure with the drug task force."

Caden scanned the kitchen for his ruck.

"Let me guess." She tapped her forefinger on her chin. "The ranch."

His gaze traveled back to her. "What?" Her upper lip made a perfect bow to the pleasing fullness of her bottom lip.

"Where you learned to repair things."

By sheer force of will, he dragged his attention away from her mouth. "I should go."

The smile in her eyes died. "I promised you a sunset." She feathered a blonde strand of hair behind her ear.

"But your father—"

"I owe you a day's wages."

Where he was going, he wouldn't need money.

"After the sunset, I can give you a ride to the ferry."

This was a one-way trip, not that she needed to know that.

She motioned to his leg. "Unless you're too much of a coward to see how pretty sunsets can be around here."

And just like that, sweet McKenna was replaced by the bossy McKenna who'd already forced him to tackle more today than he ever dreamed possible after Afghanistan.

McKenna steered the truck into the Cape Hatteras Lighthouse parking lot. In the seat beside her, Caden craned his neck at the majestic black-and-white spiral-striped lighthouse.

She'd already learned one truth about the mysterious Caden Wallis—focus too much attention on him and he shied away like a nervous stallion. Uncomfortable with words, he held his feelings tight inside himself as if he expected to have to pay for each one.

Perhaps he already had.

Lovey had made it her personal mission to force-feed him a hamburger and milkshake before leaving Skipjacks. Her grandmother would have him filled out and healthy again in no time.

Time. Just what she—he—was running out of.

He gestured at the swath of broom sedge between the parking lot and the ridge of dunes. "I always wanted to see a lighthouse."

She drummed her fingers on the steering wheel. "The view is better from up there."

"Yeah, well . . ." He tensed. "No way."

She locked eyes with him.

"You've got to be kidding me."

Caden Wallis was quick on the draw, she'd give him that.

He crossed his arms over his chest. "Absolutely not."

"Only a small group booked the last tour. The ranger was able to fit us in."

His eyes dropped. "I can't, McKenna."

She cocked her head. "I didn't figure you for a quitter."

His eyes flashed. She'd hit a nerve.

"Stop feeling sorry for yourself. You lost your leg, not your brain. Take back your life, Caden."

He clenched his jaw. "I . . . can't."

"You mean you won't."

A mulish expression darkened his features. "Like you said, I mean I won't."

Something flew right into her. At the waste. The unnecessary squandering of his life. When so many, like Shawn, didn't get a second chance.

"Then get out." She leaned across him and thrust open his door. "When the going gets tough, cowards fall away."

"Fine." He gripped the seatbelt strap so hard his knuckles whitened. "I'll climb your stupid lighthouse." He scowled. "But I won't make it to the top."

Relief washed through her. "You *will* make it. You don't have to do this alone."

Unclipping the seat belt, he slung his legs out of the cab. "For someone as pretty as you, you're a bully, McKenna Dockery."

"I'm not a—" Wait. Had he just called her pretty?

But he'd already slammed the truck door, rattling everything inside. Including her. He jerked his thumb at the visitor center. "Are you coming or what?"

❖ ❖ ❖

Why did she care what happened to him?

Caden gripped the railing, took a breath, and willed himself over the next step. True to her word, she waited on the step below. No pressure. No hurry. Yet prodding him not to quit.

He used to relish this kind of thing. Pushing himself to his limits and beyond. He would've done something like this before breakfast without breaking a sweat and then rucked twenty miles carrying fifty pounds without a second thought.

Step after trudging step, he kept going. Onward. Higher.

Why did she bother with him? She'd been the only one lately who bothered—maybe the only one left who truly cared.

"Hatteras Island is like this skinny arm jutting out from the North Carolina mainland." She made a sweeping motion. "Cape Point and the lighthouse are the elbow."

On a landing, he placed his hands on his thighs, desperate to breathe. He'd lost his stamina. Yet she didn't appear the least bit winded.

"Did I tell you the Cape Hatteras Lighthouse is the tallest lighthouse in the United States?"

"You did not." He peered over the railing. "But you might've mentioned that before forcing me to climb it."

The rest of the group had already made it to the top. Even for the physically fit—which he was not—it was a strenuous climb.

"I didn't want to run the risk of demoralizing you."

The stairs curved in an upward spiral. "Just how many steps are there, McKenna?"

She arched her eyebrow. "Do you really want to know?"

Caden shoved off from the wall. "Tell me once we reach the top."

Her answering smile stole his breath again. Breath he didn't fully regain until he clambered out onto the viewing platform at the top of the lighthouse.

Leaning over the iron railing encircling the structure, she gazed over the churning waves. "Two hundred and forty-eight."

He collapsed against the wall.

"I'll lock up once you're done." The lady ranger shepherded the others toward the stairs. "Take your time."

"Thanks, Julie." McKenna pointed. "Hatteras Village and the ferry terminal are over there."

He followed the direction of her finger. The two-lane artery of Highway 12 curled far below them.

"There's our little town, Tuckahoe. Between the bridge and the ferry are a handful of villages." She circled over to the north-facing railing. "Salvo, Waves, and Rodanthe. The tri-villages."

And in between, long empty stretches of shoreline.

"Most of the island belongs to the Cape Hatteras National Seashore and is unavailable for development. Just how we like it."

"Thanks for the bird's-eye tour."

"And the most important direction?" At the rim of the earth's horizon, the sun bathed them in a molten-gold light. "Heaven." She smiled, crinkling her eyes. "But no rush to go there."

The reddish-orange glow reflected off the waves. Maybe up here was closer to heaven. Worth the struggle.

McKenna took his hand and laced her fingers in his. His heart pounded from more than lack of oxygen. Like that peculiar sizzle when she'd touched him before. Other than the impersonal care of medical professionals, it had been a long time since anybody had touched him. He could grow too attached to someone as generous as McKenna. Misread it as something more.

Something impossible for someone as broken as he was.

Caden had learned early—the hard way—about needing other people. A life lesson temporarily forgotten with Nikki. And look how well that had worked out for him.

"Have you given any thought to what you're going to do next?"

Yeah, he had. But for now he put that out of his mind and just drank in the scent of her. Sunshine. Sea salt. Cocoa butter.

"It's kind of hard to map out your life when you're on a twelve-story marathon."

"You chose life, Caden. No taking it back."

And a desire he'd not realized made its way to the surface. "There is one thing."

"What?"

He shrugged to show he didn't care one way or the other. "I wish I could be there when my team returns to Fort Bragg from their latest deployment." His voice caught. "To honor the ones who didn't make it home."

She studied his face. "I think you can do anything if you decide you want it badly enough. When does your team return?"

He scrubbed his hand over his face. "Early November."

"If you worked hard, you could be ready. Might be better to stay where you've got people who care about your recovery."

"Care?" Something stronger than bitterness chipped away at his resolve.

"You'd be doing us a favor too. Alonso's done this before. Left us without explanation for days. Skipjacks is still minus one short-order cook. Plus Lovey's dying for a chance to feed you."

She spoke in a rush of words, which he noticed she did when she wanted something badly. And she badly wanted him to stay. Which, over the course of his lifetime, put her in a minority of one.

"We could have you healthy before you know what's hit you."

He cut his eyes at her.

"Not the best choice of words." She planted one hand on her hip. "And I have a few ideas of my own."

He gestured toward the stairs. "That's what I'm afraid of."

But the picture she painted was a future he hadn't foreseen. A future he was afraid to believe in. Only delaying the inevitable.

"Give yourself a chance. Please, Caden."

What could it hurt to stay awhile? To be with the guys one last time? He ought to get better just to prove Nikki wrong about him.

Yet something insidious—wearing Nikki's face—screamed inside him that he needed to get out while he could. To find the nearest riptide and finish what he'd planned. To allow oblivion to forever enfold him in its numbing, watery embrace.

"It's time for me to go."

Descending, they stepped out of the lighthouse into the fading light of day. McKenna tugged at his arm. "One more look at the ocean."

They followed the path out of the parking lot, stopping at the top of the rise. She watched the waves crash onto shore. And he watched her.

"It's both beautiful and frightening." She smiled at him. "If you know what I mean."

Fear and yearning knifed his chest. "I know exactly what you mean." Putting some distance between them, he took one last look at the foaming waves. "I need to go."

The warmth dimmed from her eyes. Better for her to believe him a quitter than for her to believe she could save him. There was no saving him.

In the truck on the highway again, she didn't say anything. He darted a look at her set, determined features. He'd hurt her by refusing her generous offer. More generous than someone like him deserved. But he couldn't afford hope. He wouldn't survive its loss. Because that's what always happened. In the end, hope left.

All of a sudden, she veered off the road into a pullout and killed the engine.

"Why are we stopping?"

"My house is through the trees." She flitted her hand. "I didn't check our beach this morning for stranded turtles. I'll just be a minute."

Over the dunes, the faint roar of the ocean called him. He was done with her stalling tactics. He reached for the door.

"Did you know that turtles always return to the beach where they were hatched? No matter how far they've wandered, they always come home."

Grabbing his ruck, he got out of the truck. "I'll walk from here." He shut the door with a click.

She stepped out of the truck too. "The ferry is miles away."

"I'll get there eventually." His mouth flattened. "Same place I've been headed since I was born."

"You want to die?" She made a sweeping motion toward the beach. "I won't stop you this time."

Nostrils flaring, he glared at her.

She glared back. "There are easier ways to die."

His breath came in ragged spurts. "You can't imagine—"

"If you truly wanted to die, you could've jumped off the ferry before you even arrived on Hatteras."

He gritted his teeth. "The quilt. I told you—"

"Somebody would've found the quilt and made sure it got to us. I don't for a minute believe you really want to die." She jabbed her finger into his shirt.

He crossed his arms. "You'd be wrong." But the uncertainty in his voice belied his words.

"I think you desperately want to live. You just don't know how yet."

Silence roared like storm waves between them.

McKenna raised her chin. "Here's what I've learned about sea turtles like Cecil. Sometimes, when they're injured, they get lost somewhere along the way. They need our help to make it home."

Home. A pipe dream. His Achilles heel.

"Goodbye, McKenna. Thank you for today." Their gazes locked. "For the sunset."

She pressed her lips together. "You're welcome," she whispered.

Before he lost his nerve, he walked away, heading south.

She slammed the truck door and stalked past him. Her flip-flops slapped against the pavement as she headed toward the public access path to the ocean. Shoulders stiff, she took the wooden stairs two at a time and soon disappeared from view.

He stopped, hesitating. This time, instead of Nikki, for reasons he didn't fathom he visualized McKenna as she'd been that morning on the beach. Arms lifted, her graceful dance as the tide frolicked at her feet. Poetry in motion. Sunshine.

Over the sandy ridge, the waves crashed. Vast. Powerful. Final.

And then, somewhere beyond the dune, McKenna screamed.

Chapter Five

Adrenaline pumping, Caden lurched toward the access path. McKenna met him halfway, still screaming. He grabbed hold of her.

"I thought it was a turtle. Tangled in a net." She put her hand to her throat. "But it wasn't."

Caden held out his hand. "Show me."

She led him to the water. The surf rolled over a man lying face down in the sand. The waves tugged at his body, giving the dead man an illusion of movement.

"The tide's going to take him out to sea, Caden."

Without stopping to think, he plunged into the water. He flinched as the cold sliced through his clothing. Grasping the white-corded net, he heaved the man beyond the tide line to where she directed.

She fished her phone out of her pocket. "Shouldn't we call 9-1-1?"

Caden assessed the victim. "This one's beyond help. Has been for a while."

"How do you know?"

Caden grimaced. "In Afghanistan you learn these things the hard way. Not to mention . . ."

"Not to mention what?" She bit her lip.

"The bullet holes that caved in the back of his skull."

He turned the man's body over. The dark, lifeless eyes of a man in his thirties stared sightless at the sky. A Skipjacks logo adorned his shirt.

She gasped. "Alonso."

"The missing cook?"

She lifted frightened eyes to his. "Why would anyone . . . ?" She swallowed, hard. "This kind of thing rarely happens here. As in never."

The barrier islands were like a strand of gleaming pearls. But despite the ocean breezes, white sand, and gorgeous sunsets, death had come ashore.

❖ ❖ ❖

McKenna sat on the bottom step of the access stairs. Someone—maybe Bryce—had thrown a lightweight fleece around her shoulders. Lovey's quilt group had made the blankets for first responders to give to victims of crime.

She must be in shock. Everything around her had shrunk to a narrow, darkened tunnel. Sounds were muted. Yet colors appeared more vibrant, like the flashing red-and-blue lights on the police cruisers parked on the sand. Crime-scene tape cordoned off the body. The beach was awash with Tuckahoe police officers. Everyone but her father.

McKenna shivered. She couldn't believe Alonso was dead. He hadn't worked at Skipjacks long—about six months—but his cooking had been great . . . when he bothered to come to work. She'd wanted to fire him when he failed to show Labor Day weekend—the last hoorah of the tourist season—but her father had talked her out of it.

Where was her dad? Still in Kitty Hawk? As second in command, Bryce had taken charge of the investigation.

The Criminal Investigations Team—not as grand as it sounded, since this was Tuckahoe—had erected floodlights on the beach. The team gathered evidence from the crime scene while the medical examiner made a preliminary assessment of the body.

It had been Caden who took the phone out of her trembling hands to dial Dispatch. Unlike her, he'd been perfectly calm. Standing over a dead man, too detached. What sort of person looked at the wrecked skull of another human being and apparently felt nothing? Perhaps her instincts about a man she barely knew were off course.

They'd been separated as soon as the first responder arrived. Standard procedure until statements were taken. But as an outsider, his statement had taken three times as long as hers. Finally, the officer moved away to question motorists who'd gathered, attracted by the lights.

Now, at the edge of a dense clump of red cedars—shaped by the forces of the wind, salt and tide—Caden held himself rigid and strangely vigilant.

She'd seen the bullet entry wounds. But there'd be an autopsy anyway. Alonso had been murdered execution style. Two bullets fired at close range. She wasn't a police chief's daughter for nothing.

Instead of the young, always-laughing Latino cook, she feared she'd forever see his shattered face in the rictus of death. A ghastly, greenish white. And the smell of his water-bloated body—

Her stomach heaved, and she retched into the cord grass. Almost immediately, a cool hand rested on her forehead, sweeping the hair out of her face. Caden.

She flushed, wiping her mouth. "I'm sorry."

His eyes shadowed. "No one should grow used to it."

But he had. What memories of death did he hold? What had Caden become accustomed to?

Caden placed his palm against her cheek, and she was stunned by the comfort his touch evoked. Their gazes caught, a visceral connection. She found herself wanting to offer him comfort in return. For the hurt he'd suffered as a child. For the scars of war, both physical and emotional. And for the unknown something that had broken him, driven him to desperation.

His eyes widened, becoming opaque. She wasn't good at hiding her emotions. He leaned closer. Her lips parted.

"McKenna, I—"

Out of nowhere, Bryce tackled Caden. They hit the ground with a thud, Caden taking most of the hit.

"Stop, Bryce." Throwing off the blanket, McKenna jumped to her feet. "What are you doing?"

Bryce shoved Caden's face into the sand and planted a knee in his back. Caden wrestled against Bryce's weight, but Bryce was heavier and had the advantage.

"I'm arresting him." He grabbed Caden's arms, pulling them back at an unnatural angle.

Pain flashed across Caden's features, but he didn't make a sound.

McKenna pulled at Bryce. "Stop. You're hurting him."

Caden tried bringing his arms to a comfortable angle.

"You're my witness." Bryce cuffed him. "He's resisting arrest."

"He is not resisting arrest." She came at Bryce, shoving him off Caden. "This is unnecessary force. Why are you doing this?"

"I'm arresting him on suspicion of murder. The murder of Alonso Garcia."

She shook her head. "You can't."

He hauled Caden upright. Caden stumbled, trying to find his footing. She took hold of him to steady him. But taut with anger, Caden shook her off too.

"Caden didn't kill Alonso." She jutted her jaw. "He was with me all day."

Bryce kept a tight grip on Caden's forearm. "We'll see what the autopsy reveals about time of death."

Caden rubbed the sand from his mouth against the fabric on his shoulder. "You've got no evidence to justify an arrest."

Bryce jerked Caden. "I've got enough to hold you for questioning."

McKenna clenched her fists. "This isn't right, Bryce Hinson, and you know it."

"Stay out of this, McKenna. You don't know anything about this loser. This isn't any of your business," Bryce growled.

"Isn't it?" A chilling glint in his dark eyes, Caden's voice dropped to a dangerous purr.

She blinked at the sudden change. This wasn't the man who'd held her in his arms when she fainted. This wasn't the man who'd kept the hair out of her face when she was sick to her stomach.

This was the man who'd casually stood—bored?—over Alonso's body. She shouldn't forget he'd been trained to kill. Bryce was right. She didn't know much about Caden.

She swiveled to Bryce. "What's he talking about?"

The men glared at each other. If looks killed, both of them would've been dead in the sand at her feet.

Caden's eyes went half-mast. "I think Hinson understands what I mean."

"That's Officer Hinson to scum like you." He yanked Caden forward, towing him toward the squad car. "Let's see how you like cooling your heels—" He laughed. "I mean your one heel in jail."

She took a quick intake of breath. "Bryce . . ." That had been cruel, unlike the man who'd become her friend since Shawn's death.

Bryce rammed Caden inside the cruiser. Spinning sand beneath its wheels, the cruiser roared down the highway to Tuckahoe. She followed in her truck.

Trust your gut, her dad always said. Trust your instincts about people. Yet for some reason Bryce had taken an instant dislike to Caden. Was Bryce trusting his instincts, or was the outsider just a convenient scapegoat?

She wasn't going to stand by and watch Caden get railroaded. That wasn't justice. That wasn't the Tuckahoe her father had worked for over twenty years to create.

Pulling into a visitor space at the station, she spotted the chief's car. Bryce must've called him from the crime scene. She hurried inside.

Neither Bryce nor Caden were in sight. But her dad blocked her path to the officer-only area.

"You know the drill, McKenna. No one without a badge goes any further."

"I go to your office all the time."

Her father folded his arms over his chest, an imposing figure. "Not tonight, you don't."

"Dad, you didn't see Bryce on the beach. The way he treated Caden. The way he worked him over. Who knows what he's doing to Caden while we're standing here wasting time."

Her father's eyes went steely blue. A look reserved for those who broke the law. "Are you accusing one of my men of improper conduct?"

She swayed on the balls of her feet, clenching and unclenching her hands.

"Do you wish to make a formal complaint against Officer Hinson?"

Her breath came in rapid, short bursts. "No."

"Then I trust you will go home and not impede our investigation."

So he was going to be that way about it.

McKenna moistened her lips. "Caden was with me all day."

"I saw him at Skipjacks about 7:30 a.m." Her father's thick, graying brows bunched together. "When exactly did you first run across him this morning?"

Calculating that initial awkward meeting plus the discovery of Cecil coupled with the time it took to transfer the injured sea turtle to her truck . . . She backtracked the minutes. "It was at least 6:15 when I pulled into the marina."

Her dad's eyes narrowed. "You were up early this morning. Where did you go, McKenna?"

Despite everything he'd taught her about body language reflecting guilt, her eyelids flickered. "Hunting sea glass. Turtle patrol." Technically true.

Her father raised his eyebrow. She wasn't good at deception. Never had been.

She bit her lip—another sign of lying—and forced a smile. "So I met Caden around 6:30?"

"Was it 6:30 a.m. or not?"

She lifted her chin. "It was."

"This is important, McKenna. You're sure?"

She met his gaze head on. "I'm positive."

He stared at her a minute. She held her breath, unmoving. Shiftiness in body or gaze—another telltale sign of lying. Though more omission in this case. But she'd made a habit of always telling the truth, so after another second he relaxed his stance.

"You're looking better than you did this morning, Dad."

"I feel better than I did this morning." He rested his hands on the gun belt. "Though I didn't even have time for my usual cup at the station until now. Gina—" The only female officer on the Tuckahoe force. "—clocked me in this morning. You need to head home. Check on your grandmother."

At seventy-nine, Lovey was tougher than either McKenna or her police chief son would ever be.

"Not unless you make sure Caden gets fair treatment until he's released."

Her father snorted. "If we release him."

"You already ran background on him, Dad."

"Sergeant First Class Caden Wallis came back clean. But once we get this man's prints in the system, we'll see if he is who he says he is."

"What possible reason would he have for killing Alonso?"

Bryce came through to the reception area. "So he could take his place at Skipjacks."

"Why would he do that, Bryce? That makes no sense."

"He admitted that he came looking for you, McKenna." Bryce curled his lip. "A stalker."

"That's ridiculous." She threw out her hands. "He came looking for a quiltmaker."

"Bryce has a point, McKenna."

"Dad!"

"Not hard to find pictures of anyone on the internet." Bryce's mouth flattened. "Like those photos of you dancing with the tour company."

Her father's mouth hardened. "Caden Wallis—or whoever he is—is staying right where we've put him until the ME issues his report."

She stamped her foot. "I told you how he dragged Alonso's body to the tide line so the current wouldn't take him out again."

"Quick thinking," Bryce sneered, "to account for any of his DNA on the body. A body practically left on your doorstep, McKenna."

"Why are you so determined to pin the murder on Caden, Bryce?"

Her dad rested his hands on his duty belt. "No one is pinning anything on anyone."

Bryce broadened his shoulders. "When's the last time Tuckahoe had a murder? You think someone we know killed Alonso? Would you prefer we round up old Laddie Ferguson?"

"I know Caden didn't kill anyone."

Bryce wrinkled his nose. "How can you know that about a man you met less than twelve hours ago?"

She bit her lip.

"Just go home, McKenna," Bryce grunted. "Let us handle this."

Her nostrils flared. "You don't get to tell me what to do, Bryce Hinson."

A hurt look flitted across his handsome features.

Her father drew himself up. "But as long as you're living in my house, I do. And I'm telling you to go home."

Resentment rose in her chest, burning like acid. If Shawn hadn't died and Lovey hadn't needed her to run Skipjacks, she'd be free. But instead she was chained by her apron strings to the family business.

Lest she say things that couldn't be unsaid, she marched out. Under the streetlight she dialed Lovey's attorney friend, Talbot Rivenbark. This wasn't over. Not by a long shot.

Though after what happened to Alonso, not something to joke about.

❖   ❖   ❖

"Either charge my client, Chief, or release him."

The elderly southern gentleman in the seersucker suit and bowtie bore a strong resemblance to a lawyer one of Caden's foster moms used to watch on television.

"Since the judge refused your petition to hold him longer—"

"Judge Evans, your golf buddy, right?" snarled Bryce.

A look of pure pleasure crossed Talbot Rivenbark's wrinkled features. "Better keep your officer on a leash, Walt. I'm this close—" He held his gnarled forefinger and thumb inches apart. "—from charging your department with unlawful arrest, police brutality, and the kitchen sink."

"You don't have anything, you old—"

Chief Dockery laid a restraining hand on Hinson's arm.

Rivenbark's eyes sparkled, the years shedding off him like water off a dog. Caden would bet in his day Rivenbark had been a topnotch criminal defense attorney. With a sinking feeling he wondered just how much this topnotch, if retired, criminal defense attorney was going to cost him.

"That short fuse of yours, Hinson," Rivenbark tsked, "It's going to be your undoing one day. Mark my words, young man."

"I'll mark your—" Hinson surged across the interview table.

Only Dockery's hand against his chest stopped him. "Calm down, Bryce."

Rivenbark rose. "My client and I will be on our way now." He gave

Hinson a supercilious smile. "If you'd be so good as to remove the cuffs."

Hinson gritted his teeth.

"Uncuff him, Bryce."

The chief wasn't pleased. Caden had no doubt that, soon as he and the lawyer left the station, somebody was going to get heck. Like how Joe used to ream them out if they screwed up.

Muscle ticking in his cheek, Hinson released the metal links around Caden's wrists. "You'll get yours, Wallis," he growled for Caden's ears only.

Rivenbark waited for him at the door. "Y'all have yourselves a fabulous day." Spreading the good-old-boy routine a little thick, in Caden's opinion.

Taking possession of his ruck, he slipped outside before the chief changed his mind or Hinson dreamed up new, unsubstantiated reasons to hold him. On the sidewalk, he shaded his eyes. He'd spent a miserable pain-ridden night in a jail cell. Just when he'd believed his life couldn't get any worse, it had. Like being suspected of murder.

All because he'd tried to do the right thing in returning the quilt to *M. Dockery, Tuckahoe, North Carolina. Always come home.* Should've known better. No good deed went unpunished.

He cleared his throat. "Mr. Rivenbark, sir, I appreciate everything you've done for me. And I promise I'll compensate you soon as I—" The sight of McKenna's truck pulling into the station parking lot brought him up short.

Rivenbark winked. "Your bill has been remitted in full."

"By who?"

"Speak of the angel and up she jumps."

Caden frowned. "What?"

"McKenna, my darling girl." Rivenbark swept her into an embrace. "Every time I see you, you look more like that gorgeous grandmother of yours."

Clad in jeans and a T-shirt, McKenna hugged the old guy. "Thank you so much, Mr. Rivenbark." She cut a glance at Caden. "I don't know what we would've done without you."

"Alas, if only Lovey Styron one long-ago day—before she became Dockery—had felt the same."

McKenna touched Caden's sleeve. "Did they hurt you?"

When she looked at him like that, with those big, blue eyes of hers . . .

"It's Tuckahoe, not Mogadishu." He trained his attention on the crack in the sidewalk. "I've been in far worse places."

A neon-green sports coupe with the diminutive Lovey at the wheel veered in beside McKenna's truck.

Rivenbark adjusted his tie. "I'm off to a museum-committee meeting with Dr. Stanhope."

Caden stepped in front of him. "About your bill."

Rivenbark waved at Lovey and headed for her vehicle. "Like I said, taken care of in full by the Dockerys."

An awkward silence fell as Lovey and the attorney rode away.

Caden scowled. "I don't like being beholden."

"I'm getting that." McKenna's mouth thinned. "But if somebody hadn't paid Talbot to come, you'd still be rotting in a jail cell on your way to a murder charge."

He gnashed his teeth. "I didn't kill your cook."

"I believe you, or I wouldn't have called Talbot. And it wasn't me who paid the bill. Lovey doesn't believe you killed Alonso either."

He wasn't used to people believing in him. Now he owed an old lady a large sum of money. Money he knew the Dockerys didn't have to throw away on him.

"I'll pay her back." He clenched his jaw. "Every cent."

She gave him a cool look. "Kind of hard to do that from the bottom of the ocean."

This had gotten out of hand. It had seemed so simple when he left Reed. Return the quilt, then take a long walk off a short pier. But things had gotten complicated the moment he met McKenna Dockery on the beach.

He scrubbed his face. "Did you hire another cook?"

"Why?" She arched her eyebrow.

She was going to make him ask for the job. He gritted his teeth. Fine.

A warm, sea breeze lifted a tendril of her hair. His fingers twitched, remembering the feel of those strands, like corn silk. Before he gave in to the urge to touch her hair, he stuck his hands in his pockets. "I'd like to work the grill until I repay your grandmother."

She tilted her head. "We could work out an arrangement, if that's what you want."

"That's what I want." The least of what he wanted, actually, but he'd learned a long time ago he'd never get what he longed for most.

She fingered the cleft in her chin. "I'm thinking it'll take you till early November."

He tried not to look at her lips. "Oh, yeah?"

"In time for you to meet your team at Fort Bragg."

Despite common sense, a sliver of hope wormed its way past the pressure building in his chest. "Is that right?"

"We'll take food out of your wages. There's a spare room off the kitchen at our house. In return for lodging, you could make repairs around the diner, the boat, the house, my truck . . ." She sighed.

"McKenna . . ." He shook his head to clear it. "Your father is going to have a fit. And then he'll shoot me."

"Let me handle my dad." She flashed him a smile. "He's never refused me anything I really wanted."

Despite her perennial optimism, he had a bad feeling. This wasn't going to end well. Not well at all.

But it was either the job or the ocean. And sometime over the last twenty-four hours, without realizing it, he'd chosen life.

Chapter Six

THE ENGINE TICKED, COOLING IN THE DRIVEWAY. SITTING IN THE cab, McKenna assessed Caden's reaction to the two-story, cedar-shingled Banker house.

"It looks like home." He dropped his eyes. "I mean, it looks like a great place to grow up."

She thrust open the truck door. "This area is known as Indian Woods. Highest point in Tuckahoe. The ocean lies through the patch of wax myrtle over there." She fluttered her hand.

He cocked his head. "I hear waves."

"You can see the beach from upstairs. Waves are the last thing I hear every night before I go to sleep."

"That sounds nice. Will you give me a tour?"

She made a face. "That'll take about five minutes."

Oyster shells crunched beneath their feet. She stopped at the bottom of the porch. By now she knew better than to offer to help him do anything.

Duffel bag on his shoulder, he gripped the railing. "One step at a time, right?"

She got out of his way as he negotiated the stairs. Like most homes on the Banks, theirs was raised to avoid flooding during a storm surge. She turned the doorknob.

"You don't keep the house locked?"

"The tourists and the trouble they bring are long gone."

"After what happened to your cook, you might want to rethink that, McKenna."

Barking erupted from inside the house. He froze. "You have a dog."

"You don't like dogs?"

An emotion she couldn't decipher glinted in his eyes. "I-I'm not comfortable with dogs."

"Ginger is very gentle. Children love her. She's not aggressive, I promise."

As soon as she opened the door, toenails clicked across the foyer. Caden stiffened. Spotting a familiar face, Ginger picked up speed. McKenna inserted herself in front of Caden to ensure that in her exuberance Ginger didn't flatten him.

"Hey, Ginger." She crouched. "Hey, girl." Tail wagging, Ginger licked her face.

"*What* is *that*?"

Holding on to Ginger's collar, she glanced at Caden. "Our dog."

"That's not a dog. It's a red pom pom."

"She's a labradoodle." McKenna brushed her cheek against the silky fleece of Ginger's deep red coat. "This girl loves to snuggle, don't you? She's super intelligent. Never met a stranger. I found her half-starved a few years ago, abandoned."

"Another stray? Cecil. The dog. I'm sensing a pattern."

McKenna ignored the jab. "Labradoodles are as close to nonallergic dogs as you can get. They also make great service dogs."

Caden drew up, scowling. "A dog is the last thing on earth I need."

He gave new meaning to the word *churlish*. She'd never met anyone who made it so difficult for people to like him.

McKenna clenched her teeth. "Anybody ever tell you that one day your face is liable to freeze like that? It wouldn't hurt you to smile."

"Since this is the only face I've got, I'm sorry you find me so repulsive."

Problem was she didn't find Caden Wallis, surly as he could be, repulsive at all.

"Maybe I should apply for a prosthetic face to match my prosthetic leg." He sneered. "Go for the whole freak-show package."

"That wasn't what I—" She tapped her flip-flop on the pine floor, counting to ten in her head. She took a breath, a long one. "Over the last few days, Ginger has become very attached to Dad."

"What's wrong with your father?" He shook his head. "Never mind. None of my business." He eased across the threshold, eyeing Ginger. "He didn't look sick when he put me in jail."

"Probably a virus, but he's not one to let illness keep him from his duty." She sighed. "I wish you and Dad had gotten off to a better start. You two have a lot in common."

His eyebrows rose. "Oh, really?"

Ginger's eyes were alive with curiosity about their guest.

"Yes, really. Dad was in the National Guard during Desert Storm." She chewed her bottom lip. "Are you going to be okay about Ginger? She'd love to meet you."

For a brief second, she was sure he was going to refuse. And she was suddenly uncertain about how this arrangement would work if he had a thing against dogs.

A muscle beat in his cheek. "I-I guess." He swallowed.

Not a ringing endorsement, but she'd take what she could get.

She brought Ginger closer. "Sit . . . Sit . . . Good girl." On her haunches, Ginger was the picture of adorable. "How could anyone not love that face?"

He stroked his chin. "I'm assuming you mean Ginger's face since we've established you find me less than attractive."

"I never said I didn't—" She pressed her lips together. "Of course I meant Ginger."

Hadn't she?

"Ginger, this is Caden." She looked at him. "Let her sniff your hand."

He tensed, something like panic flitting across his features. Almost when she'd begun to believe he never would, Caden reached out, but his hand shook. Perhaps he'd had a bad encounter with a dog in the past.

Ginger's black nose did a thorough job sniffing him. He visibly flinched, however, when her tongue licked his hand.

"Would you like to pet Ginger?"

His brow furrowed. "No . . . I don't think I will."

McKenna pursed her lips. "If you're afraid—"

"I'm not afraid." His gaze snapped to hers. Reaching out, he hesitated a second before finally placing his hand on Ginger's fluffy head. Ginger, as was her nature, nuzzled his palm.

Some of the lines across his forehead eased. He combed his fingers deeper into Ginger's wavy curls. "It's—she's—her coat is like silk. Soft."

"Ginger likes you."

Despite his almost pathological need to keep people at arm's length, so did McKenna. But as Lovey always said, not everything that came into her head needed to come out of her mouth.

"We're in the family room." She motioned to the staircase. "There are three bedrooms upstairs. For Dad, Lovey, and me."

Tongue panting, Ginger pressed against his side. He gently but firmly pushed her away. "Where's your mom?"

What was it with him and Ginger? Everybody loved Ginger. Frowning at him, she called Ginger over to her side. "My mother died in a car accident on the mainland when I was five."

"That must've been hard."

She studied him. "Not as hard as losing both your parents."

His mouth flattened. "The foster care system was a step up from living with either of my parents."

"How old were you when you were placed?"

The impenetrable mask fell over his face again. "Seven."

"Are either of your parents alive?"

"Probably not. My mother was a drug addict." He shrugged. "The man she said was my father—or at least the only man I remember— was a drunk. And the alcohol brought out the mean in him."

She'd seen enough from her father's line of work to have a pretty good idea of what his childhood must've been like before foster care. "I'm sorry."

A flicker of annoyance crossed his otherwise impassive features. "I survived. It made me stronger." His eyes narrowed. "And I'm aware the same could be said about losing my leg."

Her eyebrows rose. "I wasn't going to say that."

"Sure you were."

Lifting her chin, she headed toward the rear of the house. "Dining room . . . The kitchen." Ginger's toenails *click-clack*ed as she followed them. "Here's the guest suite where you'll be staying."

He had to be exhausted. He was moving slower than yesterday.

"What's the deal between Earlene and your dad? Are they dating?"

"Don't I wish." McKenna leaned against the kitchen table. "Lovey says they had a thing when they were teenagers. But when Dad returned from Kuwait, he brought my mom with him. Earlene was crushed."

"Being replaced isn't easy."

Interesting choice of words.

He didn't elaborate. "Yet Earlene works at Skipjacks."

"That was later. After she married a truck driver with a nasty right hook."

Caden's eyes became black pools devoid of light. "I don't like men who hit women."

With his background, she didn't suppose he would.

"Not long after my mother died, my dad took the domestic disturbance call. He got Earlene out of that situation. Suggesting it'd be in the trucker's best interests to hit the road."

Caden gave her a wry look. "Or take the ferry instead?"

"Something like that."

He gave her a lopsided grin that buckled her knees. Stole her breath. Made her heart zing a hundred miles an hour.

Maybe it was a good thing Caden Wallis didn't smile more often. A smile like that could break a girl's heart. Probably already had.

Flushing, she motioned to the screened porch overlooking the marsh. "Lucky for you, this time of year the mosquitoes aren't as hungry."

"So you keep saying. Lucky for me," he growled.

And just like that, the bitterness was back. Perhaps Bryce was right. What did she really know about this broken man?

For the first time, she realized how isolated the house was, the highway obscured by the dense thicket of yaupon holly and gnarled live oaks. Ginger was a wonderful dog, but a guard dog she was not.

Time to put some distance between them. Her tender heart had gotten her into trouble before. This had been a mistake. "Dad will be home soon." No harm in throwing that out there.

Caden's jaw jutted. Like he knew what she was thinking.

"The bed's made. There's fresh towels in the bathroom." She was talking too much and too fast again. "I'll leave you to get settled. Ginger needs to let off steam."

She practically bolted through the screened door. Ginger bounded across the lawn to do her business. McKenna rushed down the steps, willing her heartbeat to settle, yet shuddered when the door slammed behind her.

Were her instincts wrong about him? After Shawn, she'd promised herself she'd never get involved with another servicemember. Much less one as fragmented as Caden Wallis.

No matter how altruistic her motives, this probably wasn't a good idea. There was something inherently wild, slightly unpredictable, and marginally dangerous about him. Probably even before being wounded, he'd been a complicated man.

She, on the other hand, wasn't too complex. She loved Tuckahoe. She loved the wind and the waves. She loved her family. She used to love to dance. But after Shawn . . .

McKenna blew out a breath. She'd closed the door on that dream. Lovey and Skipjacks needed her.

Caden Wallis was an unforeseen ripple in her otherwise uneventful world. As for the unexpected ripple of chemistry between them? Her heart hammered. Not just a ripple. More like a shock wave. And with it a vague sense of nagging guilt. This connection she felt for Caden—

Tires crunched on gravel out front. Time to head off her dad. She hurried around the house.

Unfolding from his cruiser, Dad looked furious. "I got a text from your grandmother. What were you thinking?"

"Caden needs our help, Dad."

"You don't know anything about him, McKenna. Offering him a temporary job because you're shorthanded is one thing. Inviting him to stay in our home is another."

The longer this drug investigation dragged on, the deeper the furrows on his forehead. The pale, greenish cast around his mouth had returned. Was he sick again today? Consumed with the case, he wasn't taking care of himself.

She flicked her hair over her shoulder. "You of all people should understand how hard it is for a soldier to make the adjustment to civilian life."

He rested his arms on top of the car door. "This man has been through a horrific experience. But there are more than physical consequences from war. It's the emotional and mental wounds I'm worried about."

She opened her hands. "Where's your compassion, Dad?"

"Where's your common sense, McKenna?" He gritted his teeth. "This isn't some stray cat you're bringing home."

"I realize that, Dad."

"Do you? A man has been murdered, McKenna."

"The ferry captain corroborated that Caden was on the ferry at the time Alonso died. The real question is whether Alonso was murdered elsewhere and dumped here or if he was killed in Tuckahoe. What's your working theory?"

"We're still working the crime scene." Her dad shook his head. "The coroner can only provide a window for time of death. A window during which Caden arrived on the island."

"And murdered a man he doesn't know? You've found no connection between Alonso and Caden."

"I've got no proof they didn't know each other either. We don't know much about Wallis. Certainly not enough to let him sleep here." He rubbed his forehead. "This man's got issues."

She stood her ground. "We've all got issues."

"Why are you so determined . . . ?" His mouth thinned. "This is about Shawn and that blasted quilt, isn't it?"

She sucked in a breath.

"You couldn't save Shawn, so you're on a mission to save this one?"

Tears pricked her eyes. "That's not true."

But deep in her heart, she wasn't so sure. Was this about Shawn? She couldn't forget the strange pull she'd felt since meeting Caden. Was she using Caden as a means to move beyond her own emotional paralysis? Either way . . .

"Please, Dad," she whispered. "I need to do this. For a lot of reasons."

"Supper only." He let go of the car. "Then he's going to have to find other arrangements if he wants to stay in Tuckahoe. And that's my final word, McKenna."

McKenna clamped her teeth together.

"It's my job to protect you, Baby Girl." His gaze traveled toward the house. "I'll leave it to you to break the news."

This was so unfair. Caden hadn't deserved to lose a leg, and he didn't deserve the accusations thrown against him. She had no proof, but somehow she believed he was innocent. Problem now? Proving it to her father.

❖ ❖ ❖

Caden wasn't used to being idle. Grabbing the notepad off the desk in his room, he walked around the ground floor, taking inventory of what needed fixing.

Oil the hinges on the screen door. Fix the steps leading off the screened porch. Mend the broken spindles on the porch railing. Elevate the sagging roof on one end of the front porch. McKenna's truck needed a thorough overhaul. And then there were the repairs at Skipjacks.

He had his work cut out for him. But for the first time in months, he felt a stirring of hope. That there might exist an After for him.

It was then he overheard McKenna's impassioned argument with her father outside. He squeezed his eyes shut as reality crashed over him. He was a murder suspect. If the police chief and Hinson had their way, he'd spend what was left of his miserable life rotting behind bars.

Backtracking, he lurched to the kitchen window, staring sightlessly at the silver ribbon of marsh water glinting through the tangle of bushes.

Hatteras, with its handful of small coastal villages, was a close-knit community. At best, outsiders were tolerated. At worst, they became an easy target on which to pin a crime. Caden should disappear before Dockery threw him in jail. Yet there was the money he owed Lovey. He'd never been one to break his word. And he'd promised to help at Skipjacks. McKenna needed him.

Caden slammed his fist on the countertop. She didn't need him. Nobody needed him. He'd done nothing but disrupt her life since they ran into each other on the beach yesterday. Though in truth she'd done as much to unsettle his life as he had hers.

And it wasn't like getting off the island was easy. He had no means of transportation. But for whatever it was worth, he could still walk. So if he was going, he had to go now.

Leaving everything behind, he slipped out the screened porch, wincing at the squeak of the door. He'd not be fixing that or anything else on the list. He edged down the steps.

His back plastered to the siding, he poked his head around the corner of the house. The Dockerys and Ginger had drifted to the front porch. He assessed the terrain between him and the highway. If he kept to the maritime forest, he could skirt the driveway and reach the road with no one the wiser. From there, he could hitch a ride north and disappear on the mainland. He didn't want to live the rest of his life as a fugitive, but what choice did he have?

Caden gained the cover of the trees. What choice had he ever had except to do whatever it took to survive? Somehow, despite the odds, he'd always managed to land on his feet.

He grimaced. Landing on his feet wasn't a guarantee anymore.

Breathing hard, he burst onto the highway. He glanced over his shoulder to the second story of the house, visible above the tree canopy. If someone were to look out a window, he'd be spotted immediately.

A couple of vehicles blew past, heading south. In the distance, a truck shimmered in the heat, radiating off the asphalt like a mirage. The Dodge Ram 1500 Big Horn barreled toward him. His heart pounded. It was now or never.

Stepping into the road, he raised his arm. The black truck slowed. This was going to work. In less than sixty seconds he'd be speeding away from a place that had brought him nothing but trouble. Free and clear.

Free, perhaps. But his name—the only thing he'd somehow managed to preserve—not in the clear. Nothing screamed guilty as much as running. As for the hurt his leaving would cause McKenna . . .

Something squeezed inside his chest. No one had believed in him for a long time. Including himself.

Dropping his hand, he fell back onto the shoulder of the road. He couldn't do this to her. He couldn't do this to himself. This might be his last chance to reverse the downward spiral.

As the truck drew even with him, the window rolled down. He got a quick glimpse of a shaggy-haired, graying older guy. Jimmy Buffet blared from the radio. Then the engine revved, and the aging surfer dude accelerated past him.

Drawn by the crash of waves beyond the trees, Caden skirted the house again and followed a well-worn path through the mudflats to the towering dunes.

At the edge of the ocean, the unfathomable vastness mesmerized him. The rise and fall of the undulating tide kept him spellbound. Unending and inexorable. Like the song Joe used to sing—

"Hey."

Caden jerked.

"I thought you heard me coming."

He'd lost not just his leg but his skills, too, if Beach Girl could creep up on him undetected.

"You've found my favorite spot in the world." McKenna gestured to a couple of Adirondack chairs half buried in the sand in front of a blackened fire pit. She lifted her face to the late afternoon sun like a sunflower soaking in its beams.

Sunshine is what he envisioned whenever he thought of McKenna. And he was beginning to think of her a lot. She alternately beguiled and petrified him.

McKenna opened her eyes and he lowered his, afraid she'd read his thoughts. She already read him better than anyone ever had. He'd prided himself on keeping carefully constructed barricades, but he seemed to have no defenses when it came to her.

"What made you decide not to go?"

There she went again.

"You'd have to be dumb not to consider it. I would have in your situation. But why didn't you?"

Caden wasn't about to admit his greatest fear had become the fear of disappointing her. No need to give her unnecessary ammunition. He felt exposed and vulnerable enough as it was with her.

"How old are you, McKenna?"

"Twenty-six." She narrowed her eyes. "Why?"

Same age as Nikki. Though he'd bet his life not in terms of mileage.

McKenna frowned. "How old did you think I was?"

"I thought you were younger."

Her family had the tendency to overprotect her. Or maybe just since her fiancé died.

She pursed her lips. "How old are you?"

He gave her a half smile. "Twenty-eight. But I feel older." He tore his gaze away. "A lot older."

"Young enough to complete the punch list you left in the kitchen?"

Sticking his tongue in his cheek, he broadened his chest. "If there's still time before dinner, how about I start by washing your truck?"

McKenna smiled. A smile that did curious things to his self-imposed walls. "You'll have time. Lovey texted—"

"Your grandmother texts?"

McKenna laughed. "She and Mr. Rivenbark are going to dinner with the director. She won't be home till later."

"Tuckahoe has its own museum?" He cut his eyes at her. "Next thing you know, there'll be a chain restaurant on every corner."

She rolled her eyes. "God save us from that."

It wasn't that he didn't believe in God. He just didn't believe God believed in him. Some—including Joe—might say God had saved him from death. But from where he was standing—on only one leg—Caden wasn't sure God had saved him. Not from a fate he considered worse than death. In the end, Joe's God hadn't even saved Joe from death. If a good guy like Joe could die, what hope did somebody like Caden have?

Sometimes he thought the guilt alone might eat him alive.

"I've been thinking, Caden . . ."

He glanced at her. "About what?"

McKenna made a small circle in the sand with her toe. Barefoot again. What did she do in the winter? Or maybe it didn't get cold here. He wouldn't be here to find out.

She'd gone quiet. Was she thinking about Shawn?

"I was thinking we could both use a friend."

"A friend." He cocked his head. "You and me?"

Her head came up, eyes flashing. "Why do you make that sound so ridiculous?"

Somebody ought to tell her that in moments of extreme happiness or anger, her eyes went as navy blue as the sea. What would her eyes look like if he kissed—

He reeled.

"What's wrong?"

He scrubbed his face and the image from his mind. "Friends? A man and a woman?"

"You don't think that's possible for people with mutual interests?"

Is that what they had? Mutual interests? Maybe so. If nothing else, keeping him out of jail and getting him on a ferry headed to Bragg come November.

"Never had a woman friend before."

Her eyes widened. "Seriously? Never?"

Caden's relationship with Nikki had been many things. Friends wasn't one of them. The only friends he'd ever had were on the team. Including Friday, lost to him now forever.

His mouth twisted. "Why not?"

She muttered something under her breath. He caught ". . . most contrary, ornery . . ." and decided it might not do his self-esteem any good to listen too hard.

He stuck out his hand. "Friends."

She looked at his fingers long enough he started to get nervous. This had been her idea, hadn't it?

"Okay . . ." She slid her hand into his, and a bolt of fire and ice surged like a current from his shoulder, down his forearm to his hand, and passed through his fingertips into hers. He jerked. She let go.

His arm—and his heart—felt fried. No static electricity this time. It had been a mistake touching her. A no-touching policy would have to be imposed. His nerve endings tingled.

Wrapping her arms around herself, she gave him an uncertain smile. "You coming?"

Caden sighed into the wind. "I'm coming."

He should've run when he had the chance. This . . . this *thing* with McKenna—he refused to give it a name—would not turn out well for him.

Nothing good ever did.

Chapter Seven

FROM THE HEAD OF THE TABLE, MCKENNA'S FATHER GLOWERED AT Caden. Ginger lay between their chairs, a canine Switzerland.

She tried to mitigate her father's lack of hospitality by talking. Her fallback when nervous. But her attempts at conversation were met with grunts from her dad while Caden said nothing. No surprise there. Eventually, she lapsed into silence.

"Thanks for dinner." Caden pushed back from the table. "I'll help you with the dishes."

Her father stood just as quickly. "*I'll* help McKenna with the dishes."

Caden's nostrils flared. Dad had made him angry. Not necessarily a bad thing. He'd lost that hunched, defeated look. "I won't stay where I'm not welcome. I'll sleep on the beach."

McKenna rose, her chair scraping against the pinewood floor. Ginger whimpered.

Her father crossed his arms. "You can sleep here tonight."

Caden's brow wrinkled. "But—"

"Oh, Dad." McKenna touched her father's sleeve. "Thank you."

"Where I can keep an eye on you."

Caden's mouth flattened. "You still think I'm involved in Garcia's murder?"

"Let's just say you're a person of interest in an ongoing investigation." Her father gave him a thin smile, not really a smile at all.

But it was more than she'd expected from her dad. Not as much as she'd hoped, but with that, she'd have to be satisfied. For now.

Caden retreated to the guest room. Not long after, Lovey arrived home. They each headed upstairs. Ginger trotted into her dad's bedroom.

Much later, McKenna startled awake, her heart pounding, to find Ginger whining beside her bed. She glanced toward the greenish glow of the digital clock on the nightstand. Three a.m.

Her father had once told her this was the time many people allowed death to take them.

"Ginger?" she whispered. "Is something wrong with Dad?"

The dog pawed the floor.

"Hush, Ginger."

The tropical storm that had passed over the island had done nothing to break the summerlike heat. Through the open window, a breeze ruffled the curtain. Night noises filtered inside. Frogs in the marsh. The strident rasp of cicadas.

Propping on her elbow, she listened for other sounds. Was her father ill again? He'd gone to bed with a blinding headache.

She swung her legs over the side of the bed. Leaving her bedroom, she padded across the landing. Her dad's door was ajar. She poked her head around the frame.

The bedside lamp cast a muted light. Sitting at his desk, her father had fallen asleep in his uniform, his head pillowed on his arms. In the stillness of the night air, she heard his steady breaths. Only then did she allow herself to breathe more freely.

Ginger let out a soft woof, her tail banging against the floor. "Ssh," She held her finger against her lips. "Let Dad sleep."

She checked on Lovey. Her grandmother's gentle snores were as regular as the tide. McKenna backed away. But Ginger prodded her legs, nudging her toward the stairs.

McKenna placed her hand on the dog's head. "What's wrong, girl?"

Ginger knocked her hand away. McKenna gulped. The memory of Alonso's water-bloated body floated through her mind.

But whatever the problem, it was downstairs. A job for the police chief.

Yet it could also be nothing. A trick of the wind. The old house settling. And she wasn't willing to rouse her father when he needed sleep so badly.

Ginger refused to be ignored, herding McKenna to the stairs. Hugging the wall, she crept down the steps. Too late she forgot that the third tread creaked.

The sound seemed deafening. She froze. But nothing leaped out at her.

Ginger rammed McKenna in the back of her knees, nearly sending her tumbling. "I'm going," she grunted. Where was a flashlight when she needed one?

Hand over heart, she descended, finally reaching the ground floor. She stopped at the end of the couch. Nothing appeared out of the ordinary in the family room. She tiptoed into the kitchen. A shard of light shone from beneath the guest room door.

Could Ginger be trying to tell her something about Caden?

Adrenaline pumping through her veins, she eased a knife from the butcher block. If this was a false alarm, he'd think she was crazy. Which maybe she was, since she'd invited "a person of interest" to be their houseguest.

She inched toward the bedroom. Gripping the knife, she turned the knob. Swung open the door—

Perched on the edge of the bed, Caden looked up, startled. But his eyes . . . His eyes stole her breath. She rushed into the room, dropping the knife on the dresser with a clatter.

"Get out!" he growled, white-lipped with pain.

"What's wrong? Let me help you."

Ginger sidled around McKenna and loped over to him. Her tongue rolled out, licking his leg. His remaining leg.

She gasped, unable to withhold her shock. Dragging her eyes from the raw, festered skin on the stump, she met Caden's tortured gaze.

His clenched features reddened. "I told you to get out."

She stepped farther into the room.

Defiance and agony shone from his eyes. "Pretty, isn't it? Grotesque, hideous, and gruesome. Or so I've been told." His fingers squeezed the mattress in a death grip.

Anguish of body and soul. And of the two, the wound to his soul by far the worst. Whoever had told him that must've been someone close or he wouldn't have believed it and it wouldn't hurt so bad.

"I repulse you. I'm a freak."

"You are not a freak." She took another step forward, as cautious as one might approach a wounded forest creature. "And you do not repulse me. What you saw in my face was just surprise."

She'd never hated anyone in her life. But in that moment, if she could've somehow gotten her hands on the person whose words had wrought such damage to his spirit . . . she wasn't sure what she would've done. But it would've been something terrible.

He glowered at Ginger. "Et tu, Lassie? You just had to rat me out to her."

Making sympathetic noises, Ginger rubbed her face against his gym shorts.

Beads of sweat dotted Caden's brow. A spasm of unbearable, unspeakable pain distorted his features. He bit his lip so hard dots of blood appeared.

How long had he been suffering, trying not to wake anyone?

Reaching out, she closed the distance between them.

"Stop. Please," he whispered. "McKenna . . ."

He hadn't wanted her to see his stump. Nor him like this. He was embarrassed. More than embarrassed. He was ashamed. And the realization broke something inside her.

Dropping her hand, she glanced at the prosthesis, leaning against the nightstand.

"You overdid it," she gestured. "You wore it too long."

He clamped his teeth together. "Phantom pain." The sensation must've passed because he slumped, his T-shirt wet with perspiration. Utter defeat carved his posture.

She couldn't leave him like this. Something within her wouldn't let her, even if she'd wanted to. Which she didn't. She ventured closer, her shadow falling over him.

"Will it hurt if I sit beside you?"

He didn't lift his head. "No."

She took that as the only invitation she was likely to get. The bedsprings squeaked as she sank onto the bed. "Is it always this bad?"

"Not always." He wouldn't look at her. "Worse in the last few months."

"But once is too often." She touched his thigh.

He looked at her then, his brow knotted. A muscle drummed in his cheek.

"The nights are worse for me. Stress probably triggers my most severe episodes."

"Same for my dad. The last couple of nights . . ." She laced her fingers together. "He's not in the office much. I'm not sure what he's doing or where he goes. These days, law enforcement seems to have taken a back seat with him. I'm not sure how much longer the town council will allow Dad to be police chief."

Caden's eyes mirrored sympathy. "The last thing your family needs is me adding to your troubles. I'll be out of here first light." His gaze swung to the window. "Which from the looks of things isn't far off."

"Don't get mad or take this the wrong way, and I know it doesn't help to say it, but—"

"But there are a lot of guys who no longer need matching shoes." He gave her a self-deprecating smile. "And when I'm not wallowing in a pity party—"

"I don't think you're wallowing. It takes time to recover emotionally and physically from the kind of life-altering blow you received."

"Those with brain injuries have it far worse." He swallowed. "Not sure I could handle that. Though I'm not doing too well coping with the injury I do have."

"Don't sell yourself short. You're still here, aren't you? Still standing on your feet." She elbowed him. "Proverbially speaking."

That earned her a real smile. "Proverbially speaking." There was a warmth in his eyes.

Blushing, she became glaringly aware she was sitting in her pajamas on a bed with a man. Not that her pajamas were skimpy. Her black shorts and pink nightshirt covered the essential places. But she probably looked a mess. Bed hair at its finest.

She tucked a strand of hair behind her ear. His eyes followed the movement of her hand. Stomach knotting, she stood so abruptly she saw stars. "There's a first-aid kit under the sink in your bathroom."

"You don't have to—"

"If you don't let me clean the wound, I'm not going to be able to sleep." She raised her chin.

His face didn't change from its usual maddening aloofness, but there was a softness in his eyes she'd not glimpsed before. "If it will make you happy . . ."

She threw him a smile over her shoulder as she glided into the bathroom. "It will."

Grabbing the kit, she returned and dropped to her knees on the floor in front of him. After pulling on the rubber gloves in the plastic kit, she opened a peroxide-soaked gauze pad. Gently, she touched the gauze to his raw flesh. He flinched.

Her eyes darted to his face. "I didn't mean to hurt you. I'm not good at medical stuff."

"You're doing fine. Go ahead."

She showed him the tube of antibacterial ointment. "Are you sure?"

He nodded, but his hands fisted the bedcovers on both sides of his body.

She worked quickly, then sat back on her heels. "Should you let the wound air overnight?"

"Maybe."

"You need to visit a wound specialist."

His mouth tightened. "I'm not going back to Reed."

She grabbed the cuffs of the gloves and pulled them inside out over her hands. "I meant the family medicine practice in Avon. Up the road."

He stared at the wall behind her. "I can't."

She closed the kit with a snap. "Consider it part of the job package. We'll need you on your feet to run the grill."

"At this rate I'll still be working off my debt to Skipjacks come spring."

"Consider yourself under contract."

"Thank you, McKenna."

She waved her hand. "I didn't do much. We better snatch what rest we can." She paused at the door. "Lovey runs a tight ship."

"Because if we're not there when the doors open, Lovey will skin us alive."

"Something like that." Her lips quirked. "I'll call first thing in the morning to see if the clinic can work us in after the lunch crowd dwindles. Earlene won't mind covering."

He rested his palm on Ginger's downy head. A new member in the Ginger Admiration Society? "Good night, McKenna."

"Good night to you too."

Stepping into the hall, she pulled the door shut behind her.

A man stepped out of the shadows and into her path. Hand to her throat, she nearly screamed.

"Dad," she hissed. "You almost gave me a heart attack."

Through the kitchen window, a moonbeam dappled her bare feet in shades of ivory. Her eyes darted to the guest room. How much had her father overheard? Enough to completely misread what just happened? Caden didn't need another reason for the police chief to hate him.

"Dad, I know this looks—"

"He can stay."

"W-what?"

Her father stepped into the swath of light. His rugged, beloved features were inscrutable, a block of marble. "There's been a suspicious fire on the waterfront. And another body found. I've gotta go." He adjusted the brim of his regulation hat.

"T-Thank you . . . Daddy." A catch in her voice.

"It's settled, then." Her father cast one brief look at the closed door before he moved away. "And that's my final word."

Chapter Eight

Skipjacks buzzed the next morning. The regulars were full of information. The fire had gutted an abandoned warehouse on the waterfront.

"The dead man was a drug dealer from Wanchese," Bob the Postman informed McKenna. "Dead before the building was torched."

Caribbean Jack—as she'd secretly dubbed the boating surfer dude with the stringy gray mullet—was chowing down on French toast in the corner booth. At this rate he might become a regular too. And like the regulars, he was doing his best to eavesdrop.

Weather-beaten Laddie pursed his lips. "Multiple stab wounds, but my source tells me the cause of death was the same as your first cook. Same MO."

Topping off Pastor's coffee, McKenna paused. What connection could there be between Alonso and a drug dealer? But Bob the Postman and Laddie's network of sources were widespread and always accurate.

"*Modus operandi.*" Earlene sauntered over with a pancake order. "Ooo, don't you sound professional, Laddie Ferguson."

The salty waterman blushed. Like most every man in Tuckahoe, eightyish Laddie was a little bit in love with Earlene Jones. Every man, except the one who mattered most.

Sometimes McKenna just wanted to knock some sense into her father. She was amazed that another man—a man of good sense—hadn't swept Earlene off her feet long ago.

Though she didn't know what she'd do if Earlene ever moved away.

The makeup, the teased hair—Earlene tried too hard. But she possessed the most generous heart of anyone McKenna had ever known.

Underscoring the fact that her father was a complete idiot.

From the tingling frisson across her shoulder blades, she became aware—without turning around—that Caden must be somewhere behind her. He'd taken offense when she asked him to stay off his leg today. As if she'd called him lazy.

Pivoting, she found him leaning against the counter, his unwavering gaze fixed on her. No one had looked at her that way in a long time. If ever.

Intense. Smoldering. Halflidded. Ridiculously stomach-quivering...

McKenna took a breath. Not happening. Not interested.

She nibbled at her bottom lip. So not true.

But Caden Wallis wasn't a safe man. He made her feel out of control. And after what had happened to Shawn, she couldn't risk another loss. She couldn't—wouldn't—betray Shawn.

Yet she'd brought Caden into their lives and insisted he stay. Not too smart for her heart.

Good thing she'd sworn off military men. Peeling her eyes off him, she readjusted her expression. This was about helping him. Friendship had been her idea.

Lovey shoved a plate of steaming scrambled eggs—the last order Caden had cooked—over to him. McKenna bit back a smile. Caden had proven as popular with her grandmother as Earlene with the village.

Breezing by with extra napkins for Caribbean Jack, Earlene hip-bumped McKenna. "Sweet tea and hush my mouth. That boy looks at you like you're a bowl of ice cream on a hot July day and he'd like to eat you with a spoon."

"Earlene!" She glanced to see if Caden had overheard. But he sat at a counter stool, hunched over his plate.

Once she got the heat in her cheeks under control—and when she couldn't think of another reason to linger with the customers—she finally ventured behind the counter. To be friendly. And neighborly. Because Tuckahoe was a friendly, neighborly place.

Caden shoveled food into his mouth like a starved man. Starved in more ways than one? She frowned. Bryce was right. It wasn't her job or within her ability to fix everyone. Especially when she was doing such a poor job with herself.

Seeing her in the mirror above the cutout window, he laid down the fork.

"Don't stop eating," she gestured. "Don't mind me."

Pressing his hands on either side of the plate, he stood up, speaking to the mirror. "I don't mind you." He scowled. "At all."

Try not to look so happy about it.

Obviously, she'd misread him. Who was the bigger idiot? Her or her dad? A toss-up.

She set the coffee pot on the warmer with more force than necessary.

His brow puckered. "I didn't mean—"

"It's all good." She gritted her teeth.

He propped his elbows on the counter. "Don't take it personal. I haven't been fit company for a long time."

But she took everything and everyone personally. Friend zone only. This was what she wanted. Right? He was her employee—actually Lovey's employee. Skipjacks, family-owned since the late 1940s.

"Shouldn't you be getting the kitchen ready for the lunch crowd?"

Pushing away from the counter, he glared. "You'll get your day's wage out of me." He turned his back and moved toward the swinging door.

She tapped her shoe against the linoleum. He was a hard worker. Why had she taken that tone with him? Some friend she was turning out to be.

But before she could apologize, Bryce stormed into the restaurant, his face a thundercloud of fury. Someone had told him about Caden working here.

Time for damage control. "Bryce—"

He strode past her and jacked Caden against the wall.

"Bryce!" She and Earlene cried out at the same time.

Caden winced but shoved back, nearly toppling Bryce, who clearly hadn't expected that kind of strength from the wounded veteran. McKenna hadn't expected that from Caden, either. Though after the way Bryce was behaving . . .

She glanced uncertainly at Caden's balled hands. A dangerous man, all the more frightening with his leashed anger. Like a volcano, white-hot fury lay just below the surface. And she'd hate to be on the receiving end when he exploded.

Bryce jabbed his finger at Caden. "Why aren't you on a ferry to nowhere? Or better yet, at the bottom of the trailer trash slime you crawled out of?"

Caden lunged, but McKenna inserted herself between them. Everyone had stopped talking, all eyes glued to the spectacle playing out before them. This was what passed for high drama in Tuckahoe.

She lifted her chin. "Skipjacks needed—"

"Murdered by the stranger you've hired." Bryce rammed her against Caden. "Don't imagine the chief doesn't figure you for the murder last night too."

Caden barreled forward. "You piece of—"

"Stop it, Caden," McKenna hissed. A hand on each of their chests, she forcibly thrust them apart.

Caden's gaze went from fire to ice so quickly, she felt the frost. He believed she'd taken Bryce's side, but that wasn't true. It would do his case no good in the court of public opinion for him to flatten her father's assistant chief. And recovering amputee or not, Caden Wallis could take Bryce, which would only land him right back where he'd started yesterday—in jail.

She had to diffuse this situation and fast. Even if it meant appeasing Bryce.

"Get back to the kitchen." She pushed at Caden's hard stomach muscles with the force of a sand flea. But catching him by surprise, he fell back. "Don't make me tell you again."

His seething but curiously raw look left her feeling off kilter. She'd hurt him, embarrassed him. A muscle ticked in his jaw, and she had the irrational urge to touch him, to feel the beat of his pulsing heart. Like an idiot, she actually stretched out her hand. But Bryce's low growl brought her to her senses. Just in time, too, before she made a fool out of herself. Again.

She redirected to Bryce. "We're still on for our lunch today, right?"

His face softened. "Wednesdays on my boat." He hitched his gun belt higher, widening his stance. "As usual?"

She gulped. "As usual."

With a self-satisfied smirk, Bryce leaned forward to plant a quick kiss on her lips. But at the last moment she turned her head, and his mouth brushed her cheek.

She felt the rush of air behind her as the kitchen door swung open and shut, leaving her with a chill of another kind.

❖ ❖ ❖

Caden banged around the kitchen. McKenna had disappeared about one o'clock. He was furious. And what was worse, he had no right to be furious.

She owed him nothing, and he owed her everything. Making him even more livid. At himself, most of all. For . . . For what?

He slammed the copper skillet on the stove. No need to kid himself. He hadn't felt such a stirring since . . .

Caden preferred not to think of "since." Because that would involve thinking of Nikki.

He threw a pot into the stainless steel sink. He'd do better to remember the cost of caring for someone. It wasn't like McKenna was the most physically alluring woman he'd ever met. Qualities Nikki possessed in spades.

Caden scrubbed his hand over his face. What McKenna possessed was far more beguiling than mere physical beauty. She possessed a kindness, a generosity of spirit. Offering him the most dangerous thing of all—hope. A rip current with the power to take him far beyond his depth to a point of no return. And after last night . . .

He was an idiot. They were nothing more than friends. Correction, he was her employee. He was glad she'd set him straight. He was glad she and that—

Caden white-knuckled the edge of the sink. He wasn't glad she and Hinson were an item. Hinson was a low life. She deserved better, but she'd made it clear that part of her life wasn't any of his business. Which was as it should be.

He tossed another pot into the sink.

"If you're done with your little temper tantrum . . ."

He whirled.

Lovey stood in the doorway, arms folded across her pale-blue cardigan. How long had she been standing there? Long enough. The door wasn't moving.

Heat crept up his neck.

"I'd like you to help me carry a box to the museum."

"The cleanup—"

"Earlene will finish. And since McKenna seems to be tied up . . ." Her denim-blue eyes flickered.

Lovey Dockery didn't appear any more pleased about her granddaughter's choice of boyfriend than he. Interesting.

She cleared her throat. "I'm taking you to the doctor."

"Don't bother," he grunted. "I'm fine."

She looked down her aquiline nose at him. A feat considering he topped the old lady by a half-dozen inches. "I surely hope you're not thinking you're the boss of me. Since I'm the one who signs your paychecks."

Paid his attorney too. And best he could determine, it was her house that had given him shelter. He hated—despised—owing anyone.

He was beginning to see more than a physical resemblance between McKenna and her grandmother. They were bossy. Steel hands in velvet gloves. And both, apparently, felt free to order him around.

But only until November, if he lived that long. And he wasn't thinking of the ocean.

"The doctor will be the judge of how fine you are, young man." She touched his cheek, her blue-veined hand gentle against his skin, softening the "Don't mess with a Banker" look in her eyes. "I won't sleep a wink tonight until I know you're not hurting."

Reminding him yet again of her granddaughter. And last night.

He shoved away from the sink. "If it makes you happy."

"It will make me happy, dear heart."

He'd never been anyone's "dear heart" before. It unsettled him. As if it somehow made him vaguely committed to someone other than himself.

Caden steeled himself against the good feeling. "It'll take more than a wound specialist to fix what's wrong with me."

She sniffed. "I expect you're correct."

Mouth tight, he wished to high heaven—if he believed such a thing existed for somebody like him—these Dockery women would leave him alone.

Not true. If not for the combined efforts of grandmother and granddaughter, he'd already be feeding the fishes.

"This isn't going to be one of those God talks, is it?" Following her outside, he scowled. "Because you ain't—pardon my English—been from where I've come. And you don't want to know what I think about your God."

"I think you'd be surprised where I come from." She motioned to her coupe. "I'll drive."

Of course she would.

She looked at him over the car, her auburn head just topping the roof. No way at her age the red didn't come from a bottle. "You can drive, can't you?"

He yanked open the door and wedged himself into the passenger seat.

She eased behind the wheel. "It's your left leg, isn't it?" She struggled to secure the seatbelt.

Reaching over, he clicked it for her.

"Then there's no reason in the world you can't drive." She patted his knee. "You can drive us to the clinic later. What happened to your car?"

He scratched his neck. "What makes you think I had a car?"

She cranked the engine. "I'm assuming you had an automobile before you deployed." She put the gear in Drive. "Most people do."

"It was a truck." He looked out the window. "And I sold it."

He'd sold it because once Nikki walked out, he didn't think he'd have a use for it. Though after deciding to return the quilt, he wished he'd waited to get rid of it.

"Might want to get another one."

He squinted at her. "Why?"

"Because going somewhere is going to be hard without transportation."

He snorted. "That's just it. I'm going nowhere. Fast."

"And with that attitude you'll get there for sure."

His lips flatlined. "Tell me what you really think."

She laughed, pressing the accelerator and crossing into the oncoming lane to pass a car. He grabbed the dashboard as a big rig barreled toward them. For the love of—

Lovey swerved back into their lane just in the nick of time. "I've reached the age where I ought to be able to say what I think."

He clutched the shoulder strap. "I get the feeling you said what you thought when you were sixteen."

She gave him a wicked grin. "True. But age has other advantages. I've lived long enough, seen enough, to know when someone deserves a second chance."

He didn't know how to respond to that.

"Someone a long time ago gave me a second chance. I like to think I've paid it forward over the years."

Lovey pulled alongside the curb outside a gingerbread-trimmed Victorian. A garish color, but probably historically authentic. Summers in high school, he'd helped one of his foster brothers flip houses. One of the houses had been in a historic district. He'd earned enough to get school clothes and go out after the Friday-night games.

Dating girls had never been a problem for him. He hadn't cared one way or the other until he met Nikki.

Unfolding from the car, he hurried around to lift the box out of the trunk for Lovey. Halfway up the wide-planked steps, he halted midstep. He'd transitioned without a second thought.

She gave him a faint smile. He swallowed. Her own brand of therapy?

A wiry, balding man with a high forehead and a bushy mustache came out onto the porch.

"Dr. Stanhope, meet my friend Caden Wallis."

Caden tightened his grip on the box. He wasn't overly fond of doctors. Mainly because a year ago they'd kept his heart beating.

Lovey inserted her arm through the crook of his elbow and tugged him forward. Grandma was stronger than she looked. "Paul is professor emeritus of the marine archaeology program at the university across the Sound."

Okay, not that kind of doctor.

"Dr. Stanhope was a soldier like you."

But Stanhope, in dockers and cargo shorts, looked like he still possessed both legs.

"Vietnam." The professor's shoulders rose and fell. "With deluxe accommodations at the Hanoi Hilton."

His gaze snapped to Stanhope's face. "That was a raw deal."

Stanhope's hazel eyes were shrewd but kind. "Better deal than some. I didn't come home in a body bag."

Whereas Caden had spent most of the last nine months wishing he had.

"GI bill took me through graduate school." He opened the door wider. "Lovey, I can't wait to see what you found in your attic."

Once inside, Caden set the box on a worktable with a thud. Glass encased exhibits filled the rooms on both sides of the hallway. Framed photographs, sepia toned with age, lined the walls.

"When Paul retired, he took on the task of putting together this collection of Tuckahoe history."

Stanhope rummaged through the box. It looked like junk to Caden. "To capture the memories of the final generation of Bankers who remember what it was like on the barrier islands before the highway and tourism came ashore."

Caden wandered over to the first exhibit. "Blackbeard?"

Lovey joined him. "Edward Teach met his demise off Ocracoke."

Stanhope removed a colorful stringed set of wooden buoys from the box. "Some folks believe he buried his ill-gotten gains somewhere on the Banks before he was caught."

Lovey nodded. "Banker kids have spent many a summer vacation treasure hunting in the sand."

Stanhope grinned. "It's the adults I see strolling the beach with metal detectors these days."

"And there are also sea glass hunters like my granddaughter."

Caden hadn't known that. "McKenna collects sea glass?"

"For Earlene. Her sea-glass jewelry is in several island galleries." Lovey moved to another exhibit depicting whaling ships. "McKenna loves any excuse to beach comb."

That didn't surprise him.

"Hello, hello." Talbot Rivenbark grinned from the door. "I told you I'd bring the box for you, Lovey."

"Caden was there." She flicked a look his way. "And we needed a break."

Stanhope rummaged deeper in the box. "I don't see the album you mentioned."

"For the love of sweet tea." She clamped a blue-veined hand on her throat. "I left it on the coffee table at home."

Rivenbark's face tightened a fraction. "What photo album?"

"Now that she's become interested in photography, McKenna wanted to see the old family pictures. My grandmother scrapbooked and journaled everything."

Rivenbark's eyes narrowed. "How far does the album go back, Lovey?"

She shrugged. "I'll bring it to you this week, Paul."

"Whenever you get around to it."

Caden studied the large relief map on the wall. "Hatteras Island. Ocracoke," he pointed, trying to identify the landmarks. "Portsmouth Island."

Stanhope didn't look up from Lovey's box. "In the old days, many Bankers made their living as wreckers."

Caden angled. "What's a wrecker?"

"Diamond Shoals is only thirty miles offshore. The Graveyard of the Atlantic." Rivenbark rolled his tongue in his cheek. "Any wreckers in your lineage, Lovey, my dear?"

She pursed her lips. "Luring a ship to its doom is evil. But what the tide brings to shore? That's finders keepers. A gift from the sea."

Rivenbark clapped a hand on Caden's back. "Spoken like a true Banker." He winked. "As I recall, a few years ago everyone became finders keepers. A lot of orange fingers in Tuckahoe."

Caden glanced at Lovey. "I don't understand."

Stanhope laughed. "A cargo container of Nacho Cheese Doritos went overboard off the coast and washed ashore."

"Doritos?" His mouth fell open. "Seriously?"

Stanhope pointed to a photo of chip bags floating on the surf. "Truth is often far stranger than fiction."

Rivenbark coughed. "And then again, sometimes not."

Caden returned to the map. "What's this little dot in the ocean off Tuckahoe?" He glanced over his shoulder. "Y-a-u-p-o-n—how do you say that?"

Lovey stepped back.

"*YO-pon.*" Stanhope nudged his chin. "There was a small village there until a hurricane drove away the last residents. Meteorologists estimate the storm was Category 5 when it hit the island."

Lovey twisted the cross around her neck.

"The hurricane made landfall about this time of year," Rivenbark added. "And the island's been uninhabited ever since."

Dropping her hold on the necklace, Lovey rubbed at her wrists.

"The weather bureau didn't name storms then. Locals refer to it as the Great Storm of 1944." Rivenbark tilted his head. "Is that the right year, Lovey?"

Caden's gaze cut from the attorney to Lovey.

Rivenbark took her hand. "Do you remember the storm, Lovey?"

She was visibly agitated. Ashen and a little scared. What was with Rivenbark?

Caden took her arm out of the attorney's grasp. "I'm ready to leave if you are, Lovey."

She threw him a grateful glance. Stanhope seemed as clueless as him. Rivenbark, on the other hand . . .

But nobody messed with Grandma on his watch. She leaned heavily on Caden as they went outside.

"After you look through the album, how about I drop it off for you, Lovey?"

She handed him the car keys. "I'd appreciate that, dear heart." She took a deep breath. "More than you know."

Chapter Nine

Perched on the dive board of Bryce's boat, the *Scheherazade*, McKenna dangled her feet in the cool water of the harbor. She lifted her face to the sky, relishing the feel of the sun's rays on her skin. So much had changed since she'd met Caden on the beach a few days ago. Or had it?

Time. Elusive and quick as water sifting through her fingers. The great healer . . . or the great enemy?

Bryce's boat was docked at a slip on the Tuckahoe waterfront. Off duty, Bryce was casual in cargo shorts and boat shoes. The remains of the picnic lunch from the deli at the Red & White lay on the deck.

"You know how I feel about you, McKenna." His voice became husky.

That got her attention.

Her mind elsewhere, she hadn't heard half of what he'd said. "You've worked on your boat since the last time I was here." She could smell the new paint and varnish on the deck.

"I wanted everything shipshape with my best girl coming aboard."

Was that what she was? His girl?

He toyed with a tendril of her hair. "You usually bring your camera."

When his parents were killed, as a boy Bryce had lived with his grandpa farther north on the Banks. Victims of a drunk driver, same as her mother. Something painful they shared in common.

After Bryce was hired on the police force, they'd become friends. Tuckahoe wasn't that big a place that you didn't run into every other year-rounder weekly. Especially in the off-season.

Her thoughts drifted to Shawn. She'd met him after a performance at the arts center in Virginia Beach. On leave from his ship, he'd won her heart in a whirlwind courtship. But after he died, her life had unraveled. Lovey required hip surgery. Skipjacks needed her. So she never returned to the contemporary dance company or the tour.

What was worse, she no longer possessed the burning passion to dance. It was like she'd lost something vital inside herself when she lost Shawn. And she didn't know how to get it back. How to find the way back to herself.

"Did you leave your camera at home?"

She jerked her focus to Bryce. "What?"

He brushed the ends of her hair against her cheek.

She pushed away his hand. "I think I left it on the boat the other day. Or at Skipjacks."

He blew out a breath. "I wish you wouldn't leave expensive stuff lying around. This isn't like the old days. There's a killer on the loose."

"You think the same person committed both murders?"

"Last night we found the dead dealer tied to a chair. Tortured before the building was set on fire."

She gasped. "That's awful. We don't usually see that kind of violence here. You really think Alonso was involved in drugs?"

He curled his lip. "I'd bet my badge it's no accident that Tuckahoe experienced its first crime wave the same time Wallis arrived."

She removed her hair and herself out of his reach. "You have absolutely no proof Caden was involved in either—"

"We're going to have to agree to disagree on that drifter." His pale blue eyes flamed. "I hate you having to work with him every day. The sooner he repays Lovey, the sooner he can leave. If we don't arrest him first."

"Bryce—"

"I'm surprised he didn't skip bail and leave Skipjacks high and dry."

No need to tell Bryce how Caden had almost done exactly that. It appeared Bryce still wasn't aware Caden was also staying at their house. She wasn't sure why her dad hadn't told him. Perhaps he'd figured Bryce would find out eventually on his own. Tuckahoe was a small place, after all.

"You know how much I care about your family." He leaned forward. "I want to be there for you."

Bryce had done his best to fill the hole Shawn's absence had left in her life. As if anyone could.

What about Caden?

She bit her lip at the thought. Bryce didn't deserve to be compared to anyone, much less to an angst-ridden, suicidal man she'd met only a few days ago.

Bryce had been nothing but kind and attentive. He'd covered for her dad with the town council. She owed him a lot.

". . . Which is why I need to say these things to you." He took her hand, bringing it to his lips. "Baby . . ."

She hadn't been listening. Again. She forced herself to look into his eyes. To answer his smile with one of her own.

McKenna couldn't deny that when he looked at her, she enjoyed his male admiration. But it wasn't the same knee-buckling, stomach-quivering, electrical zing she felt when—

Stop. Down that path lay only ruin. Those feelings belonged to Shawn.

McKenna swallowed.

With his piercing blue eyes, Bryce was a handsome, well-built man. A man who'd take care of her, if she'd let him. She'd spent the majority of her adult life taking care of others and Skipjacks.

Being taken care of for a change held more than a small appeal. And being with Bryce was easy. Safe. No fear of him eclipsing Shawn's memory.

With him, one day she might be able to move on from the emotional numbness in which she'd been entombed for the last three years. Being with Bryce gave her hope that she might be able to make a life for herself with someone other than Shawn. He didn't pressure her. He respected her need to grieve.

But after three years, even for a man as considerate as Bryce, his patience was wearing thin. His physical displays of affection had become more public over the last few days. The touching. The kiss at the diner earlier. Was he staking a claim?

Did she want Bryce to claim her?

He ran his hand up her arm, and she shivered. Taking her response as an invitation, he pulled her closer, the tip of his finger swirling a featherlight pattern on her skin.

"Bryce . . ." Her gaze darted to the boat in the next dock over, the *Margaritaville*.

The graying hippie Caribbean Jack stood on deck. But he didn't seem to be paying them any mind.

Bryce smoothed back a strand of hair dangling over her cheekbone. "I could make you happy again, if you'd let me."

Her relationship with Bryce felt different than with Shawn. And that bothered her. Which was ridiculous. Shawn's love had felt fresh and innocent, the feelings of a young man for his first love. Bryce's love was that of a mature man. He liked to be in control, and it was easier to allow him to steer the course of their relationship. To allow herself to float along on the tide of his passion for her.

A passion she was sure she'd find with him in time. Though deep inside, she feared she wasn't capable of feeling passion again.

Unbidden came the image of Caden's dark, probing eyes locked on hers that morning. Her stomach did that quivering, butterfly thing.

Bryce's lips touched her cheek, yanking her back to the present. Yet when his mouth inched closer to hers, she turned her head again. Why was she so confused? Why did she find it so hard with Bryce?

"Look at me, McKenna."

She jolted at the sharp note in his voice.

Bryce's lips had thinned, and though his hand cradled the curve of her jaw, he forced her to face him. She didn't deserve his devotion. But sometimes, the depth of his feelings scared her. How soon would he grow tired of waiting for her to make up her mind? Many women in Tuckahoe—not only the single ones—would trade places with her this instant if he put himself on the market again.

Perhaps the intensity of first love wasn't something that could ever be recaptured. Maybe her expectations were unrealistic. Perhaps she just needed to grow up.

"I wish I knew what went on in that beautiful head of yours."

She didn't want to lose Bryce or what they shared. A common heritage and background. Although the non-church thing was something he and Caden had in common.

But one day . . . when he fully came to terms with the devastating loss of his parents . . . with her help, maybe—

There she went again, trying to save people.

"Baby . . ." Bryce wrapped his hand around the nape of her neck, pulling her mouth close.

For the first time, she allowed him to kiss her. She squeezed her eyes shut, unable to relax. Despite the pressure of his hand, his lips were gentle but cold. Yet not as cold as she felt inside. What was wrong with her?

He released her with a sigh of satisfaction. His hands dropped to her shoulders, but he pressed his forehead to hers.

In time, she'd feel the same for him.

Time. Elusive and quick as water sifting through her fingers. The great healer or the great enemy?

In time . . . Surely, she would.

She closed her eyes. Wouldn't she?

❖ ❖ ❖

Going to the clinic wasn't the ordeal he'd feared, though its antiseptic aroma brought up unpleasant memories.

Dr. Austin handed him a supply of topical medications. "We caught it before the infection got too bad. I want you to soak your leg every night. It will help reduce the swelling."

Lovey carefully copied the instructions.

The doctor examined his prosthesis. "This is quite state-of-the-art. Waterproof?"

Caden nodded.

"Expensive, I'd guess."

Lovey paused, pen touching her chin.

"About the price of a car." The paper sheet crinkled beneath him as he eased off the examining table. "Courtesy of the DOD."

Dr. Austin whistled. "The price of a luxury car. The new technology automatically adapts to every terrain, right? Gait too. From walking to running, everything. Fascinating."

Head down, Caden slipped his stump into the liner sock and reattached the prosthesis.

Lovey capped the ballpoint pen. "How about you go get the car? I'll meet you at the entrance after I speak to the receptionist about the bill." She patted his arm, sending him on his way.

He'd spent his entire childhood on the receiving end of charity. He'd sworn he was done with that once he joined the army. And to find himself in such straits again . . .

Caden stalked outside. If it was the last thing he did in this life, he was going to repay the Dockerys for every dime they were wasting on him.

Lovey was smiling when she got in the car. "I think that was an afternoon well spent, don't you?"

He grunted.

Lovey faced forward. "Let's go home."

She had no idea what that word meant to somebody like him.

Driving through Tuckahoe, outside the station, he saw Bryce put his arms around McKenna. Breaking free from his hold, her lovely skin went lobster red. And spotting them passing by on the street, she dropped her gaze, tucking a strand of hair behind her ear.

Strangling the wheel, Caden pressed the accelerator and kept going.

"Giving up is not the answer, dear heart."

He didn't bother replying, but he did ease off the gas. Best to obey the speed limit. Bryce would like nothing more than to charge him with something, anything.

But when the silence lengthened to an uncomfortable level, Caden took the bait. "What is the answer, then?"

"Depends on the question, doesn't it?"

He glanced at Lovey.

"The real question . . ."

Here we go.

"The real question you have to answer first is whether you're going to sit around and slowly decompose. Or accept your new normal and move on."

"My new normal?" His voice darkened.

"You have to accept your leg is gone. You have to accept this is the way you are now. You can't change what happened."

He yanked the car to the shoulder of the road and screeched to a stop. "What would you know about what happened to me?"

"You have to grieve what you lost before you can embrace what you still have left. And what you have left is so much more than you imagine."

"Old woman, you have no idea what you're talking about." He jerked his thumb at the house visible through the branches. "You and your perfect family. Your perfect life. You're—"

"Bryce doesn't play well with others. Never has."

"What?"

She gave him a measured look.

"I thought we were talking about my leg."

"Were we?"

He glared at her. Then, without another word, he put the car in motion again. He wended the car through the dark tunnel of overhanging trees. Live oaks, dripping with Spanish moss. Dwarf red cedar. They emerged into the clearing where the house stood open to the wind and sky. He turned off the engine. When she told him to get out of her house—and it was only a matter of time before she would—he only needed to grab his ruck and go.

A life lesson learned early—always travel light.

He was surprised he'd lasted this long here. And more troubling, he was surprised by the sharp sting of loss he felt at the prospect of leaving.

"I shouldn't have said that." He forced himself to look at Lovey. "It wasn't respectful."

A soft look of compassion filled her wrinkled face. "I am old, Caden, but this old woman knew the minute you handed the quilt to McKenna you were just what our so-called perfect life needed. I'm mighty glad God brought you here when He did. You're an answer to prayer."

He'd never been an answer to anyone's prayer. More often than not, on the receiving end of a curse. Or a fist.

"Don't you want me to leave?" He'd been kicked out of foster homes for less.

She touched his arm. "Don't worry 'bout it, dear heart. We all say things we don't mean, but you're among friends. And because I am your friend, you can ask me anything." She eased her legs out of the car. "Or tell me anything." Something sad flitted across her lined features. "I'm real good at keeping secrets."

McKenna's truck barreled into the yard.

"I'll let you two talk." Lovey winked at him before heading into the house.

He got as far as the bottom step—

"What did the doctor say, Caden?"

Hand on the rail, he didn't turn around.

"Today would be a good day to do some therapy."

He rolled his eyes. Not that she could see.

"Unless he told you to stay off it."

Caden scowled at the closed front door. "He told me to soak it."

"That'll work with what I have in mind. But first, you'll need to undress."

His eyebrows rose. This ought to be interesting.

Turning, he cocked his head. "McKenna Dockery, the things you say."

Chapter Ten

HE HAD THE NERVE TO LAUGH. AND MCKENNA FELT A WAVE OF heat surge up her neck.

She gave him a quelling look. "Don't get any ideas, Wallis. We're going Soundside."

He narrowed his eyes. For the love of sweet tea, the eyelashes on that man! The envy of any girl. Not that there was anything remotely girly about Caden Wallis. She fanned herself with her hand.

"What makes you think I've got ideas?" He arched his brow into a question mark. "Maybe it's you that's got ideas."

She stopped fanning. Is that what he thought of her? He made her angry enough to spit. Sometimes she wanted to wipe that smirk right off his face. With her fist. And other times . . .

Against her will, her eyes drew to his mouth. Sometimes she didn't. At least, not with her fist.

She took a breath. "If you don't have swim trunks, my dad—"

"I can manage," he growled.

Fine. Be that way. She was just trying to . . . what? Oh, yeah. Help him get his life back.

The reason why was something she preferred not to examine too closely.

He folded his arms across his chest.

She forced her eyes away from the flexing muscles beneath his shirt. Her gaze shifted to his mouth again—Uh, no. Her heart thudded. Not a safe place to land either.

The eyes, she'd already established, were out. Just to be sure, she darted a swift glance at his smoldering look. And immediately dropped her gaze.

Eyes, definitely out. Perhaps she'd stay eye level with his . . . collarbone?

Or maybe it was better if she just stopped talking. And looking. And possibly breathing.

Turning on his heel, he went into the house. While he was gone, she loaded a paddleboard into the truck and covered it with a tarp.

He returned wearing navy-blue board shorts. A dark flush highlighted his cheekbones. He didn't like the prosthesis exposed. She was sorry as all get out about that, but he was going to have to get used to it. She peeled off her shirt and stepped out of her jeans.

"Do you always wear a swimsuit under your clothes, McKenna?"

She found that unwavering gaze of his focused on her again. Like she was a puzzle he couldn't solve.

Removing a band from her wrist, she skimmed the hair out of her face. "It's Hatteras."

"Or only when you plan to suck face with Hinson?"

She yanked open the truck door. "If you don't rethink that attitude, you and I are going to have a problem. Seeing as I have the ability to drown you."

His eyes flickered.

She bit her lip. "I wouldn't—you don't have to be afraid of the water. I'll make sure you're okay."

Jaw tight, he got into the truck. "What's under the tarp in the back?"

"You'll find out soon enough."

A handful of miles later, she turned into the parking lot at Canadian Hole between Avon and Buxton, where the calm, shallow waters of the Sound were better for a beginner. Water lapped gently against the stony beach. It was a perfect day. Autumn had not yet staked its claim on the Banks, and with the temperature still in the eighties, conditions were prime to enjoy the water. Especially since locals had the island virtually to themselves. Her favorite time of year.

She didn't like the flash of fear she'd seen in Caden's eyes. He wasn't a man who frightened easily. She understood that much about him.

And he hated being afraid. Of the water. Of being dependent. Of everything.

She released the bungee strap and threw off the tarp. "Could use a little help here." She wrestled the paddleboard off the truck bed.

"What's that for?" But he moved to help her.

"It's for parachuting out of an airplane." She batted her lashes. "What do you think it's for?"

"Parachuting I can probably still do. I'm airborne qualified." The corner of his mouth lifted in that one-sided smile of his. "But paddle boarding, McKenna . . . I . . ." He lowered his gaze.

"Standup paddle-boarding is the best kind of cross-training. A great way to improve your balance and increase your strength." Boost his confidence too. But she'd let him discover that for himself. And she counted on his pride forcing him to at least try.

His first attempt, however, proved anything but confidence building. Wading waist deep, she held the board steady for him. He knelt on both knees at first. And then, when he was ready, he brought one leg up. He kept his weight balanced and his other knee in contact with the board. Forehead scrunched in concentration, he made it to his feet, arms extended.

Then she let go, and three seconds later he fell into the water.

She sucked in a breath as he went under. Not terribly deep, but he completely submerged, then rocketed out of the water, sputtering, wiping his hand over his face. He scowled at her across the overturned board she'd righted, but he nodded and tried again.

And again. And again. Falling off sideways. Falling backward. She winced every single time. After the sixteenth try, she was sure he was going to stop. But without a word, he got on once more. Refusing to let it beat him.

That was when she knew for sure he was going to be okay. And she got a glimpse of the dogged determination that had enabled him to survive a rocky childhood. The same tenacious courage would enable him to overcome the loss of his leg.

On attempt number nineteen, he held his balance and managed to paddle for a full thirty seconds. He fell off, but this time when he came up, a grudging satisfaction filled his face. The next time, he stayed up over a minute. Once more and he'd gotten the hang of it.

He would've kept on, but she called it quits at sunset. He must've been a gifted athlete. It hadn't taken long for his muscle memory to return.

Coming out of the water with his shirt plastered against his body, he shook the hair out of his face, water droplets spraying. He laughed, the sound rumbling from somewhere deep in his chest. But it wasn't only his mouth smiling. His eyes were too.

A perfect day indeed.

It gave her an incredible sense of satisfaction to see him reclaim more of his life every day. To believe in himself again. To believe there was life for him beyond his injury. He'd lost that haunted look. Despair and resignation were slowly being replaced with dawning hope. And there were fleeting moments when she'd swear he was happy here in Tuckahoe. At Skipjacks. With her family.

With her?

She tried not to think about November and resolved to enjoy his presence in her life while she could. But it was becoming increasingly difficult to keep their friendship in perspective.

A week later found Caden still at the Dockerys, sitting in what had become his usual spot at the dinner table. Underneath the table, Ginger's warm, soft body leaned against the outside of his good leg. He snuck a piece of chicken from his plate, and when he was sure no one was watching, he reached down and offered it to Ginger. She gobbled it right out of his hand, even licked his fingers for extra measure. He couldn't help but smile.

McKenna tried to grill her father on the ongoing murder investigations.

Walt's eyes beetled under thick brows, but he kept silent.

"You've never shut us out before, Dad." McKenna lifted her chin. "So that means you've got nothing."

Lovey handed Walt the mashed potatoes.

"And having nothing means a killer is still out there, right, Dad?"

Walt put down the serving bowl. "Or maybe we've got the killer right here under our roof."

Caden looked up then.

Lovey laid aside her fork. "Walter."

"Dad," McKenna huffed.

Walt pointed the tines of his fork at Caden. "What I know is that six months ago, an alarming number of heroin overdoses started appearing on the I-95 corridor from Fayetteville to the Virginia border."

Caden stiffened. "I haven't been to Fayetteville since—"

"I'm aware." The chief squinted at him. "I checked."

Caden swallowed.

"An interagency Narcotics Task Force was formed when the bodies started piling up. When college kids in a beach rental died on my turf, my department was brought in."

McKenna's brow lowered. "That happened weeks ago. Caden wasn't—"

"There's nothing unusual about drugs on I-95," Walt continued as if she hadn't spoken. "It's a corridor for the entire eastern seaboard. Guns and human trafficking too."

She glowered. "So which one are you accusing Caden of trafficking, Dad?"

The chief leaned into his chair. "East of the Mississippi, drugs typically enter via Miami after running the Coast Guard gauntlet in the Caribbean. But no cases of this particular mix of heroin have been discovered outside North Carolina. Nor west of I-95 where you'd suppose—in the metropolitan areas of Raleigh or Charlotte."

Caden held the chief's probing gaze. "So they're coming in another way."

The chief dipped his chin in acknowledgment. "DEA and CGIS are monitoring our only deep-water ports—Wilmington and Morehead City. Norfolk, too, in case the drugs are coming ashore there and being transported over the North Carolina-Virginia line."

McKenna nodded. "A straight line from Tidewater Virginia to us."

"The feds are working point of entry. I've been tasked with identifying the local who's facilitating the traffic on the Banks."

Lovey gasped. "A local? Surely not, Walter."

"Or someone sent here." The chief's gaze never left Caden's face, as if they were having a private conversation. "Our latest vic was a well-known gangbanger and drug dealer whose distribution network included the Inner and Outer Banks."

McKenna rounded on her father. "You think Alonso was also a gang member and a drug dealer?"

The chief pursed his lips.

Caden cleared his throat. "I think what your father is saying is that there's a new local distributor facilitating the influx of the heroin. And he's eliminating the competition. A turf war."

The chief's eyes sharpened. "After what happened at the warehouse, we also know that this new player—and the South American cartel he represents—are extremely violent."

Caden straightened. "They won't hesitate to murder anyone who gets in their way."

"To make a point. Or for retribution." The chief's face clouded. "And in the most gruesome fashion imaginable."

Lovey frowned. "Must we have this conversation at the dinner table?"

"So you think I'm your—" Caden clenched his jaw. "Your facilitator?"

"As a *quiet professional*"—Walt raised an eyebrow—"I think you've been trained to act quickly and with extreme violence. I think you're more than capable of it."

Caden gulped. *A quiet professional . . .* So Walt knew.

McKenna scraped back her chair. "I cannot believe you think that—"

"Your father's right." Caden locked eyes with the chief. "As the situation demands, I am more than capable of it."

"I'll clean the kitchen." McKenna grabbed her plate. "I'm not as hungry as I thought I was."

An hour later, they'd moved to the family room when the doorbell rang. Caden rolled his eyes when Bryce Hinson let himself in the house. Did the man never work?

Hinson wasn't overjoyed to see him, either. "What's Wallis doing here?"

Walk away from every fight you can, his old football coach used to say. He was ready to do just that. But Lovey planted a firm hand on his arm, preventing him from rising off the couch.

"Evenin' Bryce." Lovey's smile belied the edge in her voice. "Didn't realize you were stopping by tonight."

Feet up in the recliner, Walt turned the page of the newspaper. "Did you want something, Bryce? Or have news to deliver?"

"Where's McKenna?"

Lovey gave Hinson a cool look. "Was she expecting you, Bryce?"

"Well, no, but—"

Screen door slamming, McKenna strolled from the kitchen into the living room, carrying a small glass bottle. Her eyes widened at their unexpected—and from Caden's perspective, unwelcome—guest.

But the fury of Frat Boy's glare landed on McKenna, giving Caden a stone-cold tightness in his chest like he used to get right before he pulled the trigger.

Caden stood without realizing it. Walt lowered his paper.

"He doesn't belong here." Hinson's nostrils flared. "Why is this one-legged waste of space in your house, baby?"

Caden balled his fists. "One leg or one arm, I can still—"

"Wallis, calm down. You, too, Bryce." Walt heaved to his feet, his eyes narrowing at Hinson. "Didn't realize I had to check with an employee before I took in guests."

"He's living here?" The area around Hinson's mouth whitened. "How can you let him near your family after what happened at the warehouse?"

Walt laid the paper on the coffee table. "It's because he's living here that I can positively alibi that Wallis was not involved in what happened to the dealer."

Hinson's eyes became glacial. "Doesn't mean he isn't working with the gang who killed him. Nor that he wasn't involved with Alonso's murder either."

Lovey laid aside her knitting. "What's in your hand, McKenna?"

"I found it in the surf." She frowned. "Same day as I found Alonso, I guess."

Hinson's nose wrinkled. "Same day you found this stray too."

Caden coiled to make a move, but one glance from Walt fixed him in place.

"It looks old." Knees creaking, Lovey got out of her chair. "Where did you say you found it?"

McKenna dropped her gaze to the four-inch clear-glass bottle. "Yaupon."

Her grandmother sucked in a breath.

Walt's mouth thinned. "I've told you not to go out there by yourself."

Hinson scowled. "Why would you want to go there? It's haunted."

McKenna shook her head. "I don't believe in stuff like that."

Eyes watering, Lovey sank onto her chair.

Walt rubbed his forehead. "You've upset your grandmother."

Caden was missing something here.

McKenna crouched beside the recliner. "I'm sorry, Lovey. I didn't think about that."

She patted McKenna's hand. "It was a long time ago. I'm being foolish." Lovey held the narrow-necked bottle to the lamp. "Let's take a look at what you found."

"It was covered in muck. On the bottom of the sea for a long time, I figure. I forgot about it until tonight. I'd left it in the bucket in the truck."

Her father leaned to get a better look. Hinson remain rooted in the middle of the rug. Caden wished he'd take the hint and leave.

"There's a word embossed in the glass." Lovey positioned her reading glasses onto her nose. "I can't quite . . . G-L-O."

"Glock . . . en . . . ." McKenna sounded out the syllables.

"Sounds like a gun," Walt quipped, shooting his officer a look. Hinson didn't respond.

"Glocken . . . Strasse." McKenna angled. "Anybody know what it means?"

Hinson jerked his head in the negative. The look in his pale, alien-blue eyes gave Caden pause. Probably searching for a way to get even. Caden would have to be careful to avoid dark alleys.

"Dr. Stanhope might know."

McKenna's face lit. "Great idea, Caden."

Caden gave Hinson a sidelong look. Hinson's creepy, bug-eyed gaze crawled from Walt to McKenna. "I should go." He wheeled.

McKenna's face puckered. "Bryce . . ." She went out on the porch.

Women. Good thing he was done with the lot of 'em.

Lovey excused herself for the night. Walt followed a few moments later, leaving Caden alone in the living room. Waiting for McKenna. He scuffed the rug with the heel of his boot. No, he wasn't waiting for her. That would be stupid. She was on the porch with Hinson.

He flopped onto the couch.

But not five minutes later she came inside, and her eyes flickered toward the stairs. "Everyone gone to bed?"

Calculating the distance? Had Hinson brainwashed her into believing he wasn't to be trusted? His mood went churlish.

"Don't worry. You'll be able to make it to your bedroom and lock the door long before I have time to ravish your virtue." His lips twisted. "I move slower than I used to."

"That's not what— You are the most . . . The most . . ."

He sat up. "Please, McKenna, enlighten me."

She flung out her hand. "Just when I think there's a decent human being buried—deeply though it be—beneath the bitterness and cynicism—"

"Do you know your eyes go all dark blue when you get mad?"

Eyes that now went large. "What?"

She positively vibrated with the desire to smack him. She wouldn't be the first.

"Then when I'm with you," she hissed, "all you must ever see is an ocean of indigo."

"Go upstairs," he grunted. "Since I scare you so much."

"I'm not scared of you, Caden Wallis."

"That's the thing, McKenna." Something ugly went awry inside him. "Maybe you should be."

She didn't move. And almost against his will, he found himself unable to look away. The oxygen trapped inside his lungs.

A man could drown in those blue, blue eyes of hers.

So why did he say the exact opposite of what he really wanted to say? What perverse instinct made him continually push her, challenge her, practically dare her to walk away?

McKenna made a point of taking a seat on the sofa. But at the far end, perched on the edge to flee if need be. Just the reaction he'd been hoping for. So why did his heart feel ripped to shreds?

He ran a hand down his neck. "What's with you and Officer Dud? I figured you for better taste in men."

"Present company included?"

He stuck his tongue inside his cheek. Beach Girl had claws. The weak didn't survive long in this world. And if she hitched herself to Hinson, she'd need all the survival skills she could muster.

"You're doing me a solid. The job. The *therapy*." Air quotes with his fingers. "Let me return the favor. As someone more acquainted with the ways of the world, let me help you wise up to a few realities about your boyfriend."

"Bryce is my *friend*."

"Ho! Kiss of death." He clutched his chest. "You know how to drive a dagger into the heart of a man. And by the way, friendship is not what Hinson's got on his mind."

"I don't know why you're picking a fight with me. Why are you in such a foul—" She slitted her eyes. "It's you who's scared. What are you running from?"

Heat flashed over his collar. She read him better than he thought. His mistake.

"No running for me, or did you forget, *baby*?" He gave Hinson's favorite endearment a nasty inflection.

"I'm not going to dignify that with a response, although as usual I think you sell yourself short." She crossed her arms. "I don't think there's much you can't do once you make up your mind."

How did she do that? Turn every mean-spirited thing he said into something affirming?

"Best piece of advice I can give?" Leaning back, he laced his hands on his head. "Rely only on yourself. Less hurtful when people fail you, as they inevitably do."

"He and I are friends. Nothing more."

Caden laughed, not amused. "Judging from that embrace last week,

I get the feeling Hinson thinks there's more—way more—between the two of you."

"That was a mistake." Blushing, she bit her lip, tucking her hair behind her ear. "But I do believe good relationships begin with friendship."

"Looks to me like he enjoys ordering you around. He tell you when it's okay to breathe too?"

She stood up. "You are—"

"Yeah, we've established that." He stood up too.

Her mouth quivered. "I'm sorry the two of you got off to such a bad start. You don't know him the way I do."

Caden arched his brow. "That is for sure."

"Bryce is a good man." She jabbed her finger into his chest and glared at him. "Are you?"

"No, McKenna." He scowled back. "I am not." The fight drained out of him. "But Hinson was right about one thing. I don't belong here."

And through eyes like a Carolina sky, another truth stared back at him. A truth that shouldn't hurt so much. But seeing himself reflected in the pure clarity of her gaze, it did.

He didn't belong anywhere.

Chapter Eleven

THE NEXT AFTERNOON CADEN ALMOST MADE IT OUT OF SKIPJACKS, but he wasn't fast enough.

"Where do you think you're going, soldier?"

So close. And yet so far.

"You need a haircut." Earlene propped her hands on her skinny hips. "Jolene is expecting us."

He'd made inquiries—Jolene of To Dye For Hair Salon. "No thanks, I'm good."

"We can't keep putting this off, Caden."

Yes, he could.

"I hate to think what the health inspector would say if he found you working in the kitchen." Earlene tapped her foot on the linoleum. "If you plan to continue working at Skipjacks, some of that hair needs to come off."

How did she waitress in those heels?

"I appreciate the thought but—"

"Do you want Skipjacks to fail the sanitation grade?"

"How *boot*—" He was starting to sound like these *hoi toiders*. "—how about I wear a head cover?"

Earlene got an evil gleam in her eye. "That might work." She arched her brow. "Hair nets are so manly."

He flushed.

"Besides." The look on her face boded ill. "Don't you want to see the empty storefront next to Jolene's where McKenna dreams of opening a dance studio?"

"McKenna wants to open a dance studio?"

Earlene propelled him out the door and down the sidewalk. She'd had him at "McKenna," and she knew it.

"McKenna graduated from the North Carolina School of the Arts. Danced professionally until Shawn died and Lovey got sick."

He got only a brief glimpse of the darkened storefront before Earlene dragged him into the salon next door. His first impression of the inner sanctum of womanhood? Pink. Everywhere. Pink walls. Pink-framed rail-thin models who needed to eat a hamburger. A strong chemical aroma stung his nostrils.

"Let's get you to the chair so we can get started."

Isn't that what they said to death-row inmates just before—

Jolene, a large, merry-faced woman, spun the chair around. Eyes widening, he dug in his heels. He hadn't realized electrocution chairs came in pink.

Still with the merry smile, Jolene took one of his arms and Earlene the other, stuffing him into it. Grabbing a cape—pink, what else?—Jolene whirled the fabric like a matador and snapped it closed behind his neck. Humiliation complete, he'd been reduced to this.

Jolene rummaged through a drawer in her cart, and the dread in his gut intensified. The instruments in this torture chamber were pink too. He recognized a flat iron plugged into the electric strip on the pink diamond linoleum. Sometimes Nikki had straightened her wavy dark curls. There was a hair dryer. Clips.

A strange blue liquid filled a cylindrical glass container. The shrunken heads of other men who'd ventured inside this female lair of estrogen? But there were combs inside, not heads.

Jolene brandished a gleaming pair of scissors. "Not often I get the chance to cut off so much hair."

What the— He half rose, the cape still attached. But Earlene pushed him into the chair. He scowled.

"Jolene's gonna make a new man out of you."

He gripped the armrests. "What I need is the old one back."

Then, as if the situation couldn't get more dire, McKenna strolled in. After their heated words last night, they'd steered clear of each other this morning at Skipjacks.

So he was surprised when she gave him a bright smile. "I was afraid I missed it."

He mumbled something under his breath.

She sauntered over. "I don't think I caught what you said."

His gaze darted from Earlene to Jolene Scissorhands to McKenna. "You are enjoying this way too much."

"Yes, we are. Don't look so miserable." She plopped into a nearby chair. "It won't be as bad as you think."

He gritted his teeth. "That's what nurses say right before they stab you with a needle."

Earlene patted his shoulder. "No worries, shoog. When Jolene gets through with you, you won't recognize yourself."

"That's what I'm afraid of."

Although maybe that wouldn't be a bad thing. The scissors glinted in the florescent lighting.

He gulped. "We're all friends here, right, Jolene?"

Jolene's eyes had taken on a fanatical gleam, her purple-tinted lips practically salivating. "What do you think, McKenna? A little here. A whole lot there?"

Stainless steel flashed before his eyes.

McKenna leaned forward, one elbow propped. "Not too much off the facial hair, Jo." She tilted her head, tapping her finger on the divot in her chin. "After all, he's got that whole pirate thing going for him."

His gaze shot to hers. "I thought you were into cowboys."

She looked at him through upswept lashes. "What girl doesn't love a little of both?"

Earlene and Jolene laughed.

McKenna's cell dinged. Reading the text, she hopped out of the chair. "I trust you ladies can take it from here. I forgot I promised I'd meet . . ." She dropped her gaze, moving away. "See you later."

His stomach roiled. Hinson. But it wasn't like Caden had any claim on her. Nor did he want one.

Keep telling yourself that, buddy.

He sat up, squaring his shoulders. "I'm ready whenever you are, Jolene." But his heart lay heavy in his chest.

❖ ❖ ❖

Still in his uniform, Bryce must've just gotten off shift. With the warm temperatures of an Indian summer, he had the top down on his personal vehicle. His car was a bold red, not unlike his personality.

The convertible wasn't easy to overlook. Nor was Bryce. He smiled as she approached.

"Everything okay with Dad?" Her father had been called out in the wee hours last night. There'd been another fire—this time at an empty beach rental property on the north end of town.

Bryce pursed his lips. "Let's grab coffee and we can talk."

Her gaze darted over her shoulder to the salon.

"I can come back after your hair appointment."

Bryce and Caden needed to stay far, far away from each other.

"It's nothing that can't wait." She smiled. "Coffee sounds great, but not at Skipjacks."

He grinned, dimples bracketing his cheeks. "You spend far too much of your life there as it is." Leaning across the seat, he thrust open the door for her.

She sank into the seat. "It's not like that."

Bryce cranked the motor, revving the engine. "It *is* like that." With a squeal of the tires, he peeled away from the curb. Down the block, Pastor Guthrie and Mrs. O'Neal stopped and stared. Caribbean Jack leaned against a black Dodge Ram truck.

She shrank deeper into the plush leather upholstery. Bryce gave Bob the Postman an airy wave. Bryce loved being noticed.

The scenery flashed by. Joe Bells bloomed along the road. Seaside, sandy, rounded dunes bordered the highway like the knuckles of a fist.

Bryce, in spite of being law enforcement, liked to drive fast. Or perhaps that was why he liked being law enforcement. No one, even in his personal vehicle, was likely to ticket him.

Gravel spinning, dust billowing, he pulled into the parking lot of The Dancing Turtle in nearby Hatteras Village. He switched off the ignition. "Sticky bun and a coffee?"

Being with Bryce always left her slightly out of breath. "Better not. Got to watch my girlish figure."

"Split one with me." He pushed open the driver-side door. "And I'll watch your figure for you." He slung his long legs out.

"Bryce—"

"Coffee to go." He shut the door with a decisive click, leaning over the frame. "I know how you like it."

She flushed at the innuendo.

Bryce laughed. "Blond as the sand."

His regulation boots crunched over the gravel as he headed toward the coffeehouse. People stepped aside to greet him. Bryce was well liked. Not born here, yet treated almost like a native. Or as close as an outsider could be.

Bryce returned bearing two steaming, lidded coffee cups in a cardboard carrier and a white paper bag tucked beneath his arm. He settled the carton on the seat between them.

When he reached over, she jerked. His eyebrows bunched. She reddened, steadying the already steady carton.

Opening the glove compartment, he withdrew a wad of napkins.

Napkins, what else? She focused her attention on removing the lid from her coffee. With the murders and arsons, everything had her jumpy these days.

Caden, most of all.

Taking a sip, she made a face. "Wrong one." She thrust the cup at him. "This one's yours."

He placed the sticky bun on a napkin between them. "Still warm." He rested his broad shoulders against the seat. "Dig in."

"You first." She gave him a teasing smile. "Cops and donuts aren't just a stereotype."

He laughed, but obliged.

"Anything new on the case?"

He stopped chewing. "Which one?"

She tore off a piece of pastry the size of her little finger. "Either." The scent of yeast and warm sugar wafted past her nose.

Bryce's jaw went tight. "This doesn't have anything to do with proving that army reject is innocent, does it?"

"He's not—" She bit her lip.

More flies with honey.

She started again. "Everyone in Tuckahoe is interested in what's happening, Bryce. There's a murderer out there. And someone's setting fires."

"Your father handed the arson investigation over to me. The accelerant used in the warehouse and rental house fires match. An accelerant easily acquired from most hardware stores."

She exhaled. "One arsonist then. Connected to Alonso's murder too?"

He ran his hand over his head, his blond locks feathering. "Who can say? The water washed away most trace evidence."

"Was Alonso killed in Tuckahoe?"

Bryce's eyes narrowed. "The coroner's finding came in right before I clocked out. The algae and sand in Alonso's remaining shoe doesn't match any ecosystem on Hatteras Island thus far."

She frowned. "So he was killed somewhere else and dumped on our beach?"

"Your dad's keeping both murder investigations pretty close to his Kevlar vest." Bryce didn't look happy about it.

And no crime scene to work made solving a case that much more difficult.

"There's some guy from the university whose specialty is diatom analysis."

"And in real speak, that would be . . . ?"

"It's stuff in the lungs of people who drown." He snorted. "Or the lack thereof. A no-brainer since it's pretty obvious the vic—Alonso—didn't drown."

She wrapped her arms around herself. The gaping holes in Alonso's skull had replayed themselves in her dreams this week.

"Professor Diatom says the algae is unfamiliar to him, but that will make it easy to match once he pinpoints an exact location."

"Which leaves you to focus on the arsons."

"The chief wants me to follow the chain of evidence. Establish where the arsonist may have acquired the accelerant." Bryce's eyes darkened. "It'll take several days to question every store owner from here to Manteo."

"Maybe the arsonist used a credit card."

Bryce's lip curled. "Only if he was an idiot. And unfortunately, most criminals aren't totally stupid."

"Nor are they as smart as you. You always get your man."

He gave her a significant look. "Even so, I'd prefer to get my woman."

She didn't rise to the bait. "Perhaps the store has a security camera. Maybe you'll catch the arsonist on film buying the materials."

"One way or the other, I'll get him." His expression cleared. "Good publicity for the department."

Not bad publicity for an up-and-coming assistant police chief either.

She punched him lightly in his bicep. "There's the old fighting Banker spirit."

A fond smile touched his lips. "There's my girl. Hadn't seen much of her lately. Now if only you'd listen to reason about your own career."

"I don't have a career, Bryce."

"Only because you stayed at home to take care of Lovey."

"Skipjacks needed me too."

"It's prime real estate." He started the engine again and backed out of the space. "And considering Lovey's medical bills?" He blew out a breath. "Trust me, I know about medical bills."

When no longer able to take care of his grandfather at home, Bryce had placed him in an assisted-living facility in Manteo. She'd been fond of the old guy. Grandpa Erich used to call her "little girl."

"A developer would pay millions for the waterfront location. You'd never have to worry about money again, McKenna."

She bristled. "Skipjacks is more than just a property. It's an institution. It's the heart of Tuckahoe."

"You've put your life on hold." He pulled onto the highway. "Lovey and Skipjacks are excuses, McKenna. For not moving forward with your life."

"Lovey needs me."

"If you're so determined to keep Skipjacks—one stiff breeze away from blowing into the Sound—hire a manager. You shouldn't have to be the hired help. You're better than that."

"We've been over this, Bryce."

He pressed harder on the accelerator. "Even the dance-studio fantasy of yours would be better than you wasting your life in that greasy spoon."

She stiffened. Whether on behalf of Skipjacks or her so-called "fantasy," she wasn't sure.

When Shawn died, so, too, had her desire for the bright lights. But Bryce was right about using her grandmother and Skipjacks as an excuse—an excuse to do the one thing she really wanted, which was to remain at home. Only when she'd had the sand between her toes again had she understood how much she'd missed Tuckahoe. Bryce couldn't seem to grasp that not only had Shawn's death changed her, it had changed her dreams too. Somehow the dancing seemed to belong to Shawn.

Now, working with children, mentoring others in the sheer joy of movement, was exactly what she wanted. A life in Tuckahoe. But even that felt so final, so impossible. Like she was denying all she and Shawn had meant to each other.

"You know what a great dancer I think you are." Bryce threw her a look. "And you still haven't told me whether or not you'll come with me to the club dance."

A sailing enthusiast, Grandpa Erich had been a member of the club. And Bryce wanted to show her off. Bryce liked to show off things that belonged to him. Did she belong to him?

"Baby . . ."

Recalling Caden's jibe, heat crept up her neck. Bryce had started calling her that a lot lately, and it made her uncomfortable. As if he assumed a future together was inevitable.

"You know how proud I am of you." He sighed. "But McKenna, your dad's never at the station. And when he is there, he seems unwell. Unfocused."

She straightened. "It's flu season, Bryce. Once he shakes—"

"I'm not the only one who's noticed. I'm not sure he'll be allowed to finish the murder investigation. The mayor . . ." Bryce frowned.

"Has the mayor said something to you?"

"It's becoming increasingly obvious to everyone that he's lost his edge. It's only a matter of time."

She was so sick of that phrase.

"My own job is in jeopardy. I've held the town council off as long as I can."

"I'm so grateful for everything you've done, Bryce."

He covered her hand, lying on the seat, with his own. And she let his hand remain without shying away this time.

"I don't want your gratitude, McKenna. It's what . . ." He swallowed. "It's what friends do for each other."

Friends wasn't what he'd wanted to say.

"The town is losing confidence in the chief's ability to keep Tuckahoe safe." Bryce bit his lip, staring fixedly out the windshield. "The town manager talked to me this morning."

She squeezed his hand. "As assistant chief, it's only right they offer you the job. And Dad would want you to take it. You've worked hard." Her vision blurred.

"I would do anything to keep your dad from being fired, baby."

Her throat clogged with tears. "I know, Bryce."

"But it's no good. Maybe it would be better if he stepped down. For the sake of the town. For the sake of his health."

To McKenna, her father had always seemed larger than life. But Bryce was right. Her dad wasn't himself. She'd seen the signs but hadn't wanted to acknowledge there might be something wrong with him. Really wrong with him.

He was tired a lot. Worse, he acted like his heart wasn't in it anymore. Maybe there was something wrong with his heart. And he was too stubborn and pigheaded—especially in the midst of a case—to take care of himself. No one, not even the best, strongest man she'd ever known, was immortal.

Sooner or later, if this recent decline in his stamina was any indication, she was going to lose him. A tear slid down her cheek. Like Shawn. Like her mother.

"He's going to have to resign soon, McKenna."

She breathed. "Or they'll fire him. That's what they said, right?"

"No matter what happens—" Bryce lifted her hand and brushed his lips against her fingers. "—I'll make sure you and Lovey are taken care of." He glanced at the road as a truck rumbled by. "Might be better to leave here. Leave the bad times behind."

She withdrew her hand. "Leave the Banks?"

"You are too talented to waste your life here, McKenna."

"This is what I want, Bryce. I don't care about those other things. Fame. Money."

His mouth tightened. "And I love that about you. That childlike . . ."

"Naiveté?"

"I was going to say *innocence*. But the world doesn't work like that. And that's why I'll always be here for you—to protect you, baby. From yourself, if I have to. It's what your dad would want."

Times like this were when she most missed having a mother. Times when she didn't know her own heart. Her treacherously unreliable heart.

"I should get back, Bryce. I'm on turtle duty at the rescue center tonight."

Bryce licked his lips. "No more going out to Yaupon, okay? I'll run by the beach there tomorrow morning before I go on shift."

After her last unsettling experience, she had no desire to return to the island.

He pulled the car into Skipjacks' parking lot. Her truck peeked from behind the restaurant.

She unfastened her seatbelt, sliding open the door. "I don't know what I'd do without you."

"Not something I ever want you to find out." Leaning over, Bryce planted a quick kiss on the tip of her nose. "The 'doing without me' part. See you Wednesday?"

On impulse, she kissed his cheek. He was such a good guy. Better than she deserved. Especially after the way she'd been treating him. All because of a transient Army vet. The person her father, the police chief, insinuated might be a part of a murderous drug-trafficking ring.

She backed away with a wave. Was she really that shallow? So easily disloyal to a friend that her head could be turned by a pair of broad shoulders and six-pack abs? To say nothing of those dark eyes . . . She blushed and shivered, toes curling, as she recalled the way his eyes had raked over her.

But she'd also never forget his courage in battling the kind of pain she never wanted to imagine. There was more to Caden Wallis than broad shoulders, six-pack abs, and yes, dark, melted-chocolate eyes.

And that was the part that kept her awake at night.

Chapter Twelve

AFTER THE SALON ORDEAL, CADEN WENT TO WORK REPLACING A sagging board on the back steps of the house.

Lovey handed him a glass of lemonade. "The outside of you cleaned up right nice. But then there's the inside to consider."

He drained the glass, not answering. He didn't intimidate easily, or he wouldn't have survived the places he'd been.

"It wouldn't do you any harm to come to church with us, young man. Or to look through the Bible I put on your nightstand."

He handed her the empty glass. "I'm not into religion."

Lovey smiled. "Me either. What I have is a relationship."

He fought the urge to roll his eyes. Joe used to say the same thing every time Caden used the religion excuse. Of all the islands in all the oceans, he had to land on the one with these God people.

But he'd been taught—no matter how haphazard his upbringing—not to disrespect his elders. Especially a woman for whom he possessed a true fondness. That, and he suspected if he riled her, she wasn't above taking a rolling pin to his backside.

"That's fine for you, Lovey. But what you're selling, I'm not buying."

"Good," she huffed, "'cause it's free."

That's where Joe and Lovey were wrong.

He folded his arms across his T-shirt. "Nothing's free."

She eyed him. "Can I give you some advice?"

"Why do I get the feeling you're going to give it anyway?"

"Best thing you could do is to accept your leg is gone."

He clenched his jaw.

"Same with any loss, you've got to grieve. But after you accept it, only then can you take inventory and cherish what you've got left." She touched his cheek with her work-worn palm. "Which is a lot."

How different would his life have been if he'd had someone like Lovey in his corner?

"You've got to learn to love your prosthesis. It's part of you now."

He grunted.

"But most of all, learn to see yourself as someone of great worth to God."

The compassion in her eyes, so like McKenna's, startled him. Swallowing, he turned his head. "I-I can't, Lovey. Wouldn't know where to start."

"I'll pray you will. Because life is precious. God gave you back yours, and I don't like to see His gifts wasted."

He bent to retrieve the hammer he'd propped against the railing. These God people had a way of slipping past his guard. He could get to like it here too much. Like them too much. Some more than others. As for a certain dancing waitress, maybe he already did—like her too much.

Time to get Lovey off his back. For now. Because when Lovey wanted something, like her granddaughter, she could be as persistent as a sandbur.

"I like that purple blouse on you, Miz Dockery. Looks good with your red hair."

She patted her hair. "If the butter doesn't just melt in your mouth. That charm of yours will either be your making or your undoing."

"Bet Talbot Rivenbark will like your outfit too."

Her lips twitched. "Don't think I don't know what you're doing. You and me are going to have this conversation again. You can mark my words, dear heart." The hinges on the screen door squeaked as she went inside.

Glancing at the slanting cast of the late-afternoon sun, he wiped his brow with his hand. Peeling off his sweat-stained shirt, he wadded it into a ball and dropped it behind the post. He wondered if McKenna's rendezvous with Hinson included dinner.

He hammered the nail with more force than required. He'd done some recon. Made discreet inquiries. No point letting his skills go rusty.

Caden grimaced. A poor excuse better than none. The board took another savage blow from the hammer.

He'd tapped two sources yesterday. Earlene, whose middle name didn't exactly scream discreet. And Bob the Postman, who as far as Caden could determine delivered the mail on a schedule of his own making.

According to Bob the Postman—never just Bob, but always Bob plus his professional capacity—Hinson had stepped up his game with McKenna over the last few weeks.

The thin man in blue—shorts, shirt, and a weird tan pith helmet—had raised his hand for a fist pump. "Give him heck, Wallis."

Good to know he had the mail carrier's vote. Not that he was—

He stilled at the sound of a truck. Three quarters of Hatteras drove trucks, but yes, he could tell the difference. McKenna's truck. Home for supper with the family.

Is that how she saw him? Like the brother she'd never had? He scowled.

Voices floated from inside the house. She must've joined Lovey in the kitchen. Gripping the hammer, he almost brained himself—like he needed to lose an eye too—when he started to run his hand over his newly shorn hair.

Suppose she didn't like it? His heart thudded painfully against his ribs. Not that it mattered whether she liked it or not.

Right . . .

Her feet slapped across the linoleum. That girl sure loved to go barefoot. Good thing she lived in a temperate climate.

The direction of the footfalls changed, heading toward the screened porch. Toward him. For the love of—

He dropped the hammer with a thud. Diving for his shirt, he turned away from the house, scrambling to insert his head and arms through the holes.

The door creaked. He closed his eyes. Project fourteen—still awaiting completion.

Fumbling to unroll the edges of the shirt to the copper button on his jeans, he turned.

"Hey, I—" McKenna's gaze went from his hair to his bare stomach. Her eyes widened.

Caden crammed the shirttail into his jeans. He ran his hand over his head. She hated it. His chest heaved. "That bad, huh?"

She lifted her chin toward the breeze blowing off the ocean. "Warm this afternoon, don't you think?" Fanning herself, she wouldn't look at him.

It must be that bad.

He'd never been vain, but his entire life, females—to his annoyance at fourteen, at eighteen not so much—had always liked his looks.

Of all the women in the world, McKenna Dockery would prove the exception.

Not that he cared. Right. Whatever helped him sleep at night. Not that he slept much with his thoughts full of the long-legged blonde in front of him.

"Yeah, well . . ." Retrieving the hammer, he came up the steps.

She smiled. "Look at you."

Ready to move on from her less than flattering appraisal, he realized she wasn't looking at his hair.

"You did that without thinking twice."

A few weeks ago, he would've had to grab the railing first. He saw himself reflected in her blue eyes. He'd do a lot to keep her approval.

"Let me get a good look at the rest of you." Before he could react, she took hold of his chin between her thumb and forefinger. "It's shorter, but not as short as I imagine you wore it at Bragg." She turned his face for him.

He was having a hard time catching his breath. "I-I only wore it like you mean the first few years. After that, my team, we . . . on our particular missions . . ." His Adam's apple bobbed. "We didn't . . ."

When her palm moved to cup his jaw, he thought his heart might stop.

"But you kept the beard." Her eyes fell to his mouth.

His mouth went dry.

She looked at him then. "Still rocking the cowboy pirate vibe."

Her fingers on his skin . . . He couldn't help it. He took hold of her hand. And they stood there—just stood there—looking at each other.

"McKenna."

Her mouth curved. "Caden."

This wasn't a good idea. But instead of beating a well-advised retreat, he leaned into her.

He really should stop this.

But he pulled her face, her mouth, closer to his. She didn't remove her hand from his cheek. And he didn't let go of her fingers.

What was he thinking? He flushed, well aware of what he was thinking. Intent on solving the mystery that had cost him hours of sleep. What *did* her lips taste like? Like the strawberry chapstick she wore? Or something as tropical as the light fragrance of her perfume?

McKenna's lips parted. No matter the flavor. He tilted his head. On her, he'd love them all. His heartbeat accelerated.

He—

"Dinner's on the table," Walt bellowed from the house.

They sprang apart like guilty teenagers.

He rubbed the back of his neck.

"Coming, Dad," she yelled.

Once inside the kitchen, the police chief glared at him. "Mighty hot out there."

Lovey stirred something on the stovetop. "And this time of year, only one thing breaks the heat."

He went to the sink to wash his hands. "What's that?"

Lovey smirked. "One good storm to clear the air."

Maybe not every mystery was meant to be solved. He stared at McKenna's lips. Smiling, she gave his hip a little bump as she brushed by.

Then again, maybe some were.

On Thursday night, Bryce's boat was vandalized, the cushions slashed and cabin items dumped overboard. Her little boat too. And another beach rental—the second property owned by the mayor—torched. But no more bodies.

Friday morning, McKenna left Skipjacks laden with enough sustenance for the entire station. Her dad was under tremendous pressure. The officers were working around the clock to catch the drug-dealing murderer before anyone else got hurt.

Gina, the lone female officer, buzzed her beyond the reception area door. "Bless you." The trim, petite young woman grabbed one of the Styrofoam cups in the tray. "The break room coffee is like sludge." Removing the lid, she closed her eyes, inhaling the pungent aroma of ground beans. "And we dare not touch the chief's coffee."

Leaving the acolyte at her altar of worship, McKenna worked her way past the cubicles, dropping off pancake orders until reaching her dad's office. Bryce didn't seem to be around.

She glanced at the burbling coffeemaker on a stand between the chief and assistant chief's offices. As far as she could tell, these days her father was living on coffee.

At her knock, he glanced up from his desk.

She held out a container. "Please try to eat this. Earlene thinks oatmeal might settle on your stomach better."

Her father grunted.

Taking that as a yes, she handed him a spoon and placed the bowl on his desk. "What's the news on the investigation?" Maybe if she kept him distracted, he'd get more than a few bites down.

He removed the plastic lid, and steam rose. "With brown sugar on top?"

McKenna smiled. "Earlene again. She remembered how you like it."

He stared at the bowl, an unreadable expression on his haggard face. He'd lost some weight.

"Dad? The case?"

He dipped the spoon into the oatmeal. "SBI believes someone is bringing the heroin across the Sound via boat to Tuckahoe." He took a bite.

"On the ferry?"

Her father swallowed. "Private boat. Someone we'd have no reason to suspect. Someone who makes regular trips across from Swan Quarter." He scooped oatmeal onto the spoon again.

"Like one of the watermen?" She shook her head. "Why?"

Her dad took another spoonful. "It's been hard to make a living from commercial fishing for a long time, McKenna. Many watermen whose families have fished these waters for generations have given up. Been forced to find other sources of income to keep their boats afloat. To keep a way of life viable."

"But drug smuggling? And with a cartel?"

Fourth bite. "A highly lucrative business opportunity. Playing with the bad guys is just an unfortunate necessity."

"Do you think it's someone we know?"

He laid down the spoon. "Probably. Maybe someone who found themselves in over their head. The task force is looking into financial records to see if any local watermen have come into a large windfall or paid off the mortgage on a boat. The Coasties are increasing interdiction patrols in hopes of catching our perpetrator in the act."

She motioned for him to keep eating.

"I'll be conducting interviews with the watermen in Tuckahoe." He sighed, stuffing another bite in his mouth. "Which will infuriate old-timers like Laddie."

"Not Laddie, Dad. He's already switched from fishing to charters."

"A switch he did reluctantly and recently." Her father's mouth flattened. "Bank records should tell us if he's making a go of it or not."

On the morning she'd found Alonso, she recalled running into Laddie at the marina. And how lately he was often at Skipjacks instead of out on the water. But he wasn't the only one behaving suspiciously. There was someone else always hanging around with no real purpose.

"What about that newcomer, Caribbean Jack—or whatever his real name is. Fancy boat. Brand-new black Ram."

Her father frowned. "Caribbean who?"

"Stringy gray mullet. Big guy. Hawaiian shirts. You know, the hippie."

Her dad eased his shoulder blades against his chair. "You're hoping it's an outsider. Not one of us."

She couldn't deny that.

Her father's eyes were shrewd. "But wasn't it you who told me it was too easy an explanation to pin the crime on an outsider? Or did that reasoning only apply to Caden?"

She crossed her arms. "You'll look into the guy I'm talking about?"

Her dad pushed away from his desk. "Stay out of it, McKenna. I'll get around to it sooner or later."

Only after he'd exhausted running Caden into the ground? It was like she didn't know her father anymore.

"The oatmeal was good." He'd actually eaten half of the container. "Thank you."

She flipped her hair over her shoulder. "Thank Earlene, not me."

"I . . ." He looked out the window. "Thank her for me."

Wheeling, she exited before she said something she'd regret.

❖ ❖ ❖

With this new turn in the investigation, paranoia dropped anchor in Tuckahoe.

Nerves on edge, friends and neighbors started to suspect each other of heinous crimes. People were afraid to go to sleep at night for fear they'd awake to their homes burning around them. And so far, Bryce hadn't been able to trace where the arsonist had bought his inflammatory materials.

Saturday afternoon, McKenna took Caden to the jetties off the old lighthouse site on the Cape to watch Ginger surf. Ginger bounded out of the truck and headed for the shoreline, eager to do her thing. They followed the half-mile path from the current lighthouse location to the beach.

Wearing cargo shorts and a gray T-shirt stamped *ARMY*, he'd insisted on carrying Ginger's child-sized board to the water. "When we were here before, I didn't realize the lighthouse had been moved."

"Coastal erosion and rising sea levels." She kept a watchful eye on Ginger as the dog frolicked in the waves. "Looks like we have the beach to ourselves today."

She shaded her hand over her eyes as Ginger dashed across the sand. The always encroaching sea was a constant reminder that nothing was forever. A reminder she should also heed when it came to the man standing beside her.

October already—a month from now he'd be gone as quickly from her life as he'd entered. She needed to be careful. It would be easy to get too attached. If only her heart would listen to her head. He'd been upfront about moving on. She needed to remember Caden was only passing through. But still . . .

The next day, Lovey was quick to notice her preoccupied thoughts. "Grab the clean towels for me, sweetie, and tell me what's wrong."

McKenna pulled the folded towels from the linen closet on the landing. "Nothing."

"I can hear the dissatisfaction in your voice. I can see how troubled you are, McKenna."

She looked away. "Bryce wants to be with me long term."

Lovey tilted her head. "And yet you continue to keep him at arm's length."

She hugged the towels to her chest. "I feel so disloyal. I loved Shawn, Lovey."

Her grandmother touched her cheek. "I know you did, sweetheart. But because I know Shawn truly loved you, he'd want you to be happy." Lovey moved toward the clothes hamper.

Would Bryce make her happy? After meeting Caden, for the first time she'd begun to wonder if there could be someone else for her. But it wouldn't be him. He was leaving. Unlike Bryce, commitment didn't seem to be on Caden's radar.

McKenna cleared her throat. "Why do you always do the wash on Monday?"

Sorting the clothes, Lovey paused. "Monday was the day my Grandmother Styron washed. I lived with my father's parents after . . ." Eyes dropping, she placed the whites into the plastic laundry basket.

McKenna replaced the bathroom towels with fresh ones. "You never talk much about your family."

"I've told you about working summers in high school at Skipjacks for the Dockerys."

She'd meant Lovey's other family—her mother and the maternal grandparents she'd lived with until the Great Storm.

Lovey grinned. "Skipjacks, where I caught the eye of the Dockery son, your grandfather." She did a little hip waggle. "When you've got it, girl, you've got it."

McKenna laughed. "Talbot Rivenbark still thinks you've got it."

"There's no expiration date on 'It.'" Lovey struck a pose. "You've either got 'It' or you don't."

"And I don't," McKenna sighed.

"I wouldn't be too sure about that." Lovey lifted the laundry basket. "Caden's eyes light up whenever you come into a room."

Her heart skipped a beat. "Really? You think—" She shook her head. "We're friends." To remind herself as much as her grandmother.

Basket tucked under her arm, Lovey's eyes sparkled. "I'm not too old to remember your grandfather giving me a look or two like that."

With another load of clean towels, she followed her grandmother downstairs. "Caden's better, don't you think?"

"Physically, yes."

Emotionally, something continued to eat away at him. Leaving him staring into the distance, a brooding look in his eyes. Anger too.

Bypassing Lovey in the laundry room off the kitchen, McKenna carried the fresh towels into Caden's bathroom—and came to an abrupt halt when she saw the photograph of a woman stuck in the corner of the mirror.

She swallowed. The woman was drop-dead gorgeous. A dark, exotic beauty perfectly matched to the soldier holding her in his arms. Caden, strong, healthy, fit. Before Afghanistan. Happy.

And everything became clear. Crystal clear. She sank onto the edge of the tub, the breath whooshing out of her.

She'd sensed it wasn't the amputation alone that had sent him spiraling into depression. He'd begun to make progress at Reed after the surgeries until something derailed him. The one thing he found himself unable to cope with—losing this woman.

A rush of anger like none she'd ever known filled McKenna. So this was the woman who'd broken his heart and his will to live. Who'd said those cruel things to him.

Was there anything lower on the planet—save a pedophile—than a person who Dear Johned a soldier, much less a critically injured one? What kind of inhuman, selfish monster walked away when someone you loved—

But she hadn't loved him, or she wouldn't have walked away. And if Caden Wallis had ever looked at McKenna like he was looking at the woman in the picture, she would've never walked away.

He was so much more than his injury. Losing a limb hadn't changed the man he was inside—strong, full of integrity. The only thing that had come close to destroying him was this woman. Leaving him to face the future alone.

At the moisture on her cheeks, she realized she was crying. Crying for the last, most devastating hurt in a lifetime of hurts that this woman had inflicted on him.

Yet he kept her picture where he could see it every day. Was she the real reason behind his desire to return to Bragg? Was he hoping to win her back?

McKenna's mouth trembled. Was he still so very much in love with this woman? A woman who didn't want him. Unlike—

Someone came into the connecting bedroom. Her cheeks heated, and she stood so fast her head spun. Her pulse raced. She mustn't let him see her like this.

Turning toward the towel rack, she hid her face.

Chapter Thirteen

"WHO'S—" CADEN POKED HIS HEAD AROUND THE DOOR JAMB. "OH, hey. It's you."

"Just changing the towels. Wash day."

Caden frowned. "Are you okay?"

Her voice didn't sound right. Too bright. Singsongy, like Mary Poppins. If Mary Poppins had worn flip-flops.

She fluttered her hand over her shoulder. "I'm fine."

He wished she'd turned around, but she seemed absorbed in folding the towel over the metal rod. He didn't like not being able to see her face. She wore every emotion on her face. Something had upset her.

"McKen—" Oh. She'd seen the picture. "I can explain."

"Not necessary." She did a sideways crab maneuver to get past him. "Lovey needs my—"

"Her name's Nicole Giordano." He didn't budge. "I called her Nikki."

"Not my business." Biting her lip, McKenna tried squeezing past him, but he propped his arms on both sides of the doorframe.

Blocked, she looked at him, a line between her brows. "Excuse me?"

He didn't move, their bodies incredibly close.

"Please, just—"

"What's wrong, McKenna?"

The wrong question. Her baby blues sparked, unleashing more than he bargained for.

"What's wrong is I don't understand why you have that . . . that . . ." She jabbed her index finger at the mirror before pressing her lips together. "Lovey would wash my mouth out if I said the words I'm thinking."

He dropped his arm. A mistake, because his fingers came into contact with her hand, shattering his attempted no-touch policy where McKenna was concerned.

She jerked away as if his touch scalded. "She's the one who derailed your recovery, wasn't she?"

He scrubbed his face.

"Paddleboarding showed you don't know the meaning of quit, much less quitting on life. It was her that dealt you the really crippling wound, wasn't it?"

McKenna looked absolutely livid. He'd never had anyone who had his back before, not on the homefront, leastways. He'd never had someone ready to do battle on his behalf. It gave him the strangest feeling. A feeling somehow he knew wouldn't be wise to examine too closely. No good could come from—

She poked him with her finger. "Why, Caden?"

"Ow." He rubbed his chest.

"What kind of masochistic moron keeps a photo of a woman who gutted him?"

"I—I—"

What could he say? Seeing himself—how he used to be—with Nikki goaded him to try harder. Looking at the picture every day gave him something to prove. He'd spent his life proving something. He didn't know how to live if he wasn't proving something.

And how could he explain that remembering the pain Nikki had dealt him fueled the rage he felt inside? The rage that—ironically—got him on his feet again so he could prove her wrong.

How could McKenna—of sunshine, sand, and sea—ever understand the dark motivations of a heart like his? Especially when he didn't understand the confusing tangle of emotions himself?

She tapped her bare foot on the bathroom tile. "I'm listening."

Caden scraped a hand over his face. "I have my reasons." He stepped aside to let her pass.

"It just goes to show you." McKenna raised her eyes to his. "She wasn't the one."

His brows drew together. "The one what?"

"The one who is supposed to love you the most and forever."

Was such a thing even possible for a throwaway like him?

He stared at her as she stalked out of the bedroom. What she said just might be true. If the someone who loved him was McKenna Dockery.

❖ ❖ ❖

McKenna found her grandmother in the living room. She shouldn't have let Caden upset her. His continued stupidity wasn't her problem.

On the sofa, Lovey glanced up from the old album in her lap.

McKenna threw herself onto the other end of the couch. "Men are idiots."

"Tell me something I don't know, sweetheart." Lovey returned to her perusal down memory lane. "Your father and Earlene, case in point."

Plucking the pillow between them, McKenna inched over. "What's that?"

"I guess I don't talk about my other family much." She shook her head. "I don't remember much."

"You were five when they died in the hurricane?"

Lovey lifted one of the photos. A little girl—Lovey. A woman, two older people, and a man in a World War II-era uniform. Despite the black-and-white picture, McKenna could tell the woman was fair haired with light eyes.

"My mother was an O'Neal. It was her people who lived on Yaupon. You look like her." Lovey traced the woman's face with her finger. "I have only a handful of pictures, taken by my paternal grandparents who lived in Tuckahoe. The only other photos were the ones my father had on him when he was killed at Bastogne."

She gave McKenna a sad smile. "I hope he died thinking we were safe at home. That he closed his eyes and opened them to find Mother. And that from then on, they were together."

"This house is where your father and later you grew up?"

She nodded. "It's the oddest things that stick in a child's mind. I remember Granny O'Neal made a rag doll for me." She sighed.

"Do you still have the doll?"

Lovey's forehead wrinkled. "Somewhere in a box. I should've loaned it to Paul Stanhope for the museum, but . . ." Her shoulders slumped. "Maybe after I pass, you could give it to him."

McKenna wrapped her arms around her grandmother. "You're going to live forever."

Her grandmother hugged her. "No one lives forever, darling."

Like Shawn. Like her mother.

Swallowing, McKenna removed a faded newspaper clipping sticking out from the peeling cover of the album. "What's this?"

"Grandmother Styron must've tucked it here for safekeeping."

McKenna bent over the newsprint. September 24, 1944. "Is that you, Lovey, holding your doll?"

Lovey adjusted the reading glasses on her nose. "It is."

"And who's the young man in the Coast Guard uniform?"

Lovey sat back. "There was a station on Yaupon during the war. He saved my life. We were the only ones to make it . . . after the storm surge."

"We don't have to talk about this, Lovey."

"Grandmother Styron discouraged me from talking about it. Or remembering." Lovey's eyes clouded. "But with age, I've come to realize it's in the telling that healing begins."

"What happened to the young Guardsman?"

"That was very sad." Lovey waved her hand. "He died not long after the newspaperman snapped this photo. Drowned, Grandmother said, rescuing someone else in the aftermath of the storm. His body lost forever to the sea."

"He was a brave man."

"If he hadn't saved me, neither Walt nor you would be alive." Lovey peered at the clipping. "I always thought it would be nice to write his family to express my thanks for saving my life. Though probably his family is long dead too."

"Maybe he left behind children and now grandchildren. Nieces or nephews who would love to hear about his courage. Dr. Stanhope could probably find them for you."

Lovey smiled. "I did promise I'd bring Paul the album—"

"I didn't know you lived on Yaupon, Lovey," Caden's voice rumbled. McKenna and her grandmother gasped.

Lovey put her hand over her heart. "You've taken a year off my life."

"Those ninja skills coming back, huh?" McKenna got off the couch. "Now that Nicole's given you so much to live for?"

Lovey's gaze shifted from McKenna to Caden. "Who's Nicole?"

"No one," he growled, his face like a thundercloud.

She removed the album from Lovey. "I'm headed into Tuckahoe. I'll drop it by the museum."

"Oh, that would be such a help." Lovey pushed against the cushions in order to rise, and Caden stepped forward, offering his hand.

"Such a gentleman," Lovey puffed, steadying herself. "Don't you think so, sweetie?"

McKenna curled her lip. "He's something, all right."

"Going so soon?" His lips tightened. "Is it Wednesday already?"

She crushed the seventy-year-old album to her chest. "Why wait for Wednesday?" And stalked out the door.

❖   ❖   ❖

"Oh, no!" McKenna flung out her hand, nearly knocking over her iced tea.

Bryce made a grab for the glass and steadied it in the nick of time. "What's wrong?"

"I forgot to take Lovey's book to Dr. Stanhope."

Leaving the house, she'd texted Bryce to see if he was available for an early dinner. They'd ended up here—an upscale eatery overlooking the Roanoke Sound on the outskirts of Manteo. And she'd completely forgotten her promise to Lovey.

Reaching across the table, Bryce took her hand. "I'll take you once we get back to Tuckahoe."

Infuriated at the unending thick-headedness of men—her father included—it felt nice to be with someone neither thickheaded nor insufferable. Someone who appreciated her. Whose eyes lit with admiration. Though Lovey had said Caden's eyes . . .

Biting her lip, she squeezed Bryce's hand. "Dinner was lovely."

He withdrew his wallet, extracting a bunch of bills. "Nothing but the best for my girl."

Was she Bryce's girl, though? Everyone in Tuckahoe, including Bryce, assumed she was. And it wasn't like she'd done anything to dissuade the town or Bryce of that opinion.

"You spoil me too much, Bryce."

He flashed her a smile, handing the cash to the waiter. "There is no 'too much' when it comes to you, baby."

She jiggled her knee underneath the table. "If I'd known we were coming here, I would've dressed more . . . appropriately."

"You make everything look good, baby." His pale-blue eyes caught hers and moved to her mouth, her neck, lingering on her fluttery plum-colored blouse.

She drew her blue tartan pashmina closer around her shoulders, covering the slight V in her neckline, though the shirt was anything but revealing. "Bryce . . ." She flushed.

But he only chuckled. "Can't help it. We were destined for each other."

Not if she'd married Shawn first.

Her breath hitched. Until today, how long had it been since she thought of him? A week? More?

The realization left her slightly sad and relieved at the same time. She'd been so busy with Skipjacks. She fingered the fringe on the shawl. And Caden . . .

McKenna darted a glance at Bryce's boat, docked at a slip in the bay. Fortunately, the damage from the vandalism had been easily fixed. In a completely romantic gesture, they'd motored up the Sound in the *Scheherazade*. She pinched her lips together. Some people should take notes on how to treat a lady.

Scraping back his chair, Bryce rose, extending his hand. "Come."

Her head jerked a fraction at his peremptory tone.

But he smiled at her. "We'd better get going so you can catch Stanhope."

On the boat, she kept her distance. Bryce stayed at the wheel, navigating past water hazards unique to this stretch of shore. It wasn't smart to be out on the water with darkness on the horizon. "We shouldn't have stayed so late, Bryce."

"No worries, baby." He grinned over his shoulder. "I know the shoals and sandbars as well as I know how many freckles you have across your nose."

She tapped the bridge of her nose. "I do not have freckles."

He cut the boat's engine and held out his hand. "Come over here, baby. Watch the sunset with me."

With reluctance, she let go of the railing. Bryce wrapped his arms around her and rested her back against his chest. They watched the sun descend. The afterglow bathed them in a wash of radiant pink.

This could be her life if she wanted it. So what if her toes didn't curl when he touched her? Like that moment on the porch when Caden had nearly kissed her. Her heart lurched.

Point was, Caden hadn't kissed her. Bryce's steady heartbeat thrummed against her back. Bryce was real. Caden was . . . a shadow.

It was dark when they reached the Tuckahoe marina. Light footed, Bryce jumped onto the dock. McKenna tossed him the mooring lines, one after the other, until the boat berthed secure. Down the block, a light shone from the repurposed Victorian-turned-museum.

He took her hand as she stepped over the gap. "The professor awaits us." He made a sweeping gesture.

"You don't have to come, Bryce. I know you have an early shift tomorrow."

He took her arm firmly in his. "No way am I letting you walk across a deserted wharf in the dark alone with a killer arsonist on the loose."

When he put it like that . . . "The book's in a bag in my truck."

"I'll get it. You wait here. I'll only be a minute, I promise."

She handed him her keys, and he left her under the streetlight. Rubbing her hand down her jeans, she spotted her father's Explorer in the station lot. Her father was probably consuming gallons of station coffee to stay alert.

Returning with the brown paper bag, Bryce escorted her to the door of the museum. "I'll wait here for you." He rapped loudly on the door with his knuckles.

After sounds of movement inside, Stanhope threw open the door and peered out at them under the porch light.

"I'm sorry to call on you so late. I meant to bring it earlier, but I forgot." McKenna held the bag out to him. "The album Lovey promised. And a hidden clipping."

"Come in, come in," Stanhope motioned. "Talbot and I were sorting through some files."

Bryce cut his eyes to the bag. "What's this about something hidden?" He followed her inside.

"A newspaper article from 1944. In fact . . ." Pulling out the clipping, she explained its significance.

Talbot and Stanhope pored over the newsprint, the ink and photo still amazingly clear.

Bryce frowned. "Why have you never mentioned this before?"

"Lovey found it this afternoon." She smiled at Dr. Stanhope. "Would you help us find the Guardsman's descendants?"

Talbot rubbed his aged hands together, the sound like rustling autumn leaves. "World War II. Paul's area of expertise."

"It would be my pleasure." The professor grinned at her, the florescent light above the display cases glinting off his bifocals. "I'll contact you as soon as I discover something."

Bryce was unusually quiet on the way back to her truck. Opening her door, he hung onto its frame while she stepped inside. "I would've helped you find info on the Guardsman, McKenna." His nose lifted. "I'm not without resources."

She'd offended him without meaning to. "Of course you have resources. It's just . . ." She verbally backpedaled. "I know how thin you've been stretched with the arson investigation."

"True." Coming around the door, he leaned inside the cab. "But there's nothing I want more than to be there for your family. You know that, right?"

Just when he kind of annoyed her, he could also be incredibly sweet.

"I know, Bryce. Thank you for a wonderful dinner." She tugged the door, forcing him to step out of the way.

He closed the door with a small click. "I'll sleep on the boat tonight. Do some undercover surveillance."

"Be careful, Bryce."

She was halfway home before she realized he hadn't asked for—nor taken—a kiss goodnight. The really disturbing thing, though?

How undisturbed she actually was.

Chapter Fourteen

CADEN PUNCHED THE PILLOW UNDER HIS HEAD. FLOPPING ON THE mattress, his gaze cut to the red glow of the digital clock on the nightstand. Ten thirty-five. He muffled the growl rising out of his throat with the pillow.

Almost eleven o'clock, and McKenna hadn't returned from her "date" with Hinson. Not that anyone else was losing sleep. Walt was at the station. Lovey slept upstairs.

He balled the pillow under his neck. Ten forty-two. Was no one worried about McKenna's reputation but him? Out carousing at this time of—

A gentle *snick* echoed in the silent house as the screen door settled into its frame. She'd returned. Safe and sound.

Or not so sound, if she was keeping company with Hinson.

Sidewalks rolled up in Tuckahoe about six o'clock. She'd come home late. Exactly—a quick look to confirm—ten forty-five. He stared at the darkened ceiling. Was she okay?

He was off the bed before he remembered his leg. Losing his balance, he fell, crashing onto the pine floor.

"Caden?" McKenna called from the other side of the door. "Are you okay?"

He thumped his forehead on the floor.

"Caden?"

Sounded like she was just fine. Him, on the other hand?

He lifted his head. "I'm good."

"Do you need me—"

"I told you I was good." That came out louder than he intended.

A pregnant pause.

"O-Okay . . . I'm sorry." Her soft whisper carried through the panel.

Now he felt like the jerk she believed him to be. Yelling at her when she was only concerned about him. But he didn't want her concern. He wanted—

He took a breath. A deep, long breath. "I didn't mean to shout. I'll see you in the morning."

The silence stretched. Had she walked away mad? Finally, about the time he didn't think he'd survive the increasing pressure in his chest—

"Good night, Caden."

"Good night, McKenna."

Hearing her move away, he let his head drop.

McKenna's determination to ruin her life wasn't his problem. He had his own issues to deal with. Welcoming his team home. Putting his life back together.

But he couldn't go on this way. The lack of sleep alone would kill him. He didn't know how Walt did it.

Then and there, he decided to just go with the flow and enjoy Tuckahoe, enjoy McKenna and her family, while it lasted. As long as he didn't fool himself into believing it could be forever. Nothing ever lasted. Nothing good anyway.

He pulled himself off the floor and returned to bed, pleased with his new resolution. Yep. That's what he'd do. Keep his head down and his shield high.

Caden sighed.

And try not to think about McKenna every waking moment of every single day.

❖ ❖ ❖

Later that night, someone broke into Skipjacks. Hinson proved himself almost useful for once. But giving chase, he lost the burglar in the crowd of the local watering hole.

Walt Dockery was burning the candle at both ends. Caden could see he wasn't looking so good. Everyone could see it except McKenna.

She had a blind spot when it came to the people she loved. Lucky for him.

Not that she loved him. It was obvious how hung up she still was on her dead fiancé. Caden had decided a long time ago not to love anyone again, but he'd broken his own rule with Nikki. And look how well that had turned out.

McKenna and Lovey insisted on inspecting the damage. He wasn't about to let two women—Banker-tough though they be—drive the desolate shoreline into town alone. So he got dressed and insisted on driving.

The forensic team had come and gone. But no joy—Bob the Postman informed them. The intruder wore gloves.

And the forensic team had left a mess for them to clean up before they could open in the morning. To Caden's surprise, a large contingent of regulars arrived to help the Dockerys put the place to rights. Including Caribbean Jack—McKenna's nickname for the man with the shaggy gray mullet.

One bright side—Hinson wasn't there. Too busy taking statements from neighbors on the off chance anyone had seen something.

Nothing was taken, but like the boats, the diner had been vandalized. At least, thanks to Hinson, the criminal didn't have time to set the restaurant on fire.

Grabbing a broom, Caden swept up broken glass. Walt barked orders into a handheld radio. Face bare of makeup and her hair hanging straight to her shoulders, Earlene rushed in and draped her arms around Lovey.

For a second Walt's eyelids flickered, and he stuttered to a brief stop before resuming his instructions.

McKenna righted the overturned chairs. "We've got to catch whoever is doing this."

Caden leaned against the broom handle. "Does your father think the vandalism is linked to the murders and arsons?"

"I don't know." She planted her hands on her hips. "But until now Tuckahoe hasn't exactly been a hotbed of crime. And I don't believe in coincidences."

He didn't either. "Leaving your father to wonder why this has all happened since I arrived."

She dropped her eyes. Did she believe him guilty? Her lack of faith in him pricked like a sharp needle.

"I didn't do this." He flung out his arm. "The murders or arsons either."

Her eyes snapped to his.

Caden clenched his jaw so tight his teeth ached. "What possible reason would I have for torching beach houses? Or vandalizing the place where I have a job?" His voice scraped low, like gravel. "Hurting people who've been nothing but good to me?"

"I believe you're innocent, Caden."

"Do you?"

McKenna lifted her chin. And not for the first time did he imagine what it would be like to touch the small cleft there. To brush his lips against her own. For a moment, his vision swam.

She bit her lip. "This isn't good for Lovey's heart."

This wasn't good for anyone, especially for a police chief under increasing pressure to bring the violence to an end.

"If your dad resigned, how soon before Hinson would find a reason to charge me?"

She pursed her lips. "All the more reason for us to be more proactive in uncovering the killer's identity."

"Us?"

"Laddie Ferguson's organizing a crime-watch night patrol in the village. I'm on call next week."

"I hardly think the police chief would sanction—" He frowned. "He doesn't know about this, does he?"

"How can he object to concerned citizens protecting their property?"

"Laddie Ferguson's going to get himself and possibly others killed. This kind of work is best left to professionals. Your father will never allow you to put yourself in harm's way, McKenna."

"He'll be glad enough if the crime watch stops this person from hurting someone else or destroying property. Catching this guy could save his job."

"McKenna," he growled, "promise me you won't do anything with-out talking to your father or me first. This isn't a game."

Spots of color peppered her cheeks. "I'm well aware this isn't a game. But my father doesn't get a vote in what I choose to do." She glared at him. "Neither do you."

"Hired hand, got it," he scowled.

"For someone as sweet as you, you can be such a . . ." She walked away.

Not something he'd ever been called. *Sweet* kind of fell into the same category as *friend*—the kiss of death. But coming from McKenna, sweet sounded good. More than good.

This crime-watch conversation wasn't over. She might think she was capable of handling herself, but he knew better. She was in over her head, and like it or not, he'd make it his personal mission to see that in trying to trap a killer she didn't get trapped in the process.

"It's only a matter of time until someone else gets hurt," Earlene whispered to him. "Exactly what Walt is afraid of."

Caden, too. Tuckahoe and its endearing, if quirky, inhabitants had a way of growing on a person.

❖   ❖   ❖

After Skipjacks closed the next afternoon, he found the house empty except for Lovey sitting on the couch, another album in her lap.

She waved him over. "Would you like to see McKenna's baby pictures?"

He melted inside at the photo of newborn McKenna in her mother's arms.

"Did McKenna tell you about her mother?"

"Only that she was killed in a car accident."

Lovey nodded. "Sara missed the mountains. I don't think she ever got used to the wide-open spaces."

"Sand, sea, and sky."

Lovey smiled. "I guess for those of us who are born here, the wind and waves become a part of us. Who we are in the deep places. We never like to drift too far. Not willingly, anyway."

The stark beauty of the barrier islands not only had a way of grow-ing on a person, but capturing the heart too.

Lovey's shoulders slumped. "Sara wanted Walt to transfer to a larger police department. Closer to civilization, she said. Walt didn't want to leave Tuckahoe any more than McKenna does now. But Sara wore him down."

"And what did you say?"

Lovey's eyebrows rose. "I stayed out of it. Sara made it plain the marriage was at stake if he didn't agree. So he stopped arguing and sent out résumés. He got a job in Asheville."

"I didn't realize McKenna and her dad lived somewhere else."

Lovey folded her hands. "They never made it to the mountains. Sara planned a house-hunting trip one weekend, but at the last minute McKenna got sick. The flu was bad that winter. I offered to let her stay with me. Sara said it would be like a second honeymoon for her and Walt."

"I'm sensing things didn't turn out that way, though."

"With most of the department down with the flu, Walt couldn't leave. Sara accused him of making excuses. Said that with or without him, she was finding a house that weekend."

"So she left alone."

"And never returned, thanks to a drunk driver west of Greensboro. Walt blamed himself. He believes if he'd been there . . ." Lovey pressed her lips together.

"If he'd been there, they'd both probably be dead."

Lovey knotted her hands. "Guilt, even if undeserved, may be the hardest thing to overcome."

"Is guilt the reason he won't give Earlene a chance?"

"My son doesn't believe he deserves a second chance."

Hitting a little too close for comfort, Caden shifted on the couch. He scrubbed the back of his neck. "Are we going to look at the pictures or not? Because if not, I should get started shoring up the front porch. Correcting the pitch."

"You need to learn to relax, Sergeant Wallis."

He crossed his arms and waited.

She shook her head, but a smile teased her lips. "Have it your way." She opened the album.

Photos of McKenna missing her two front teeth. McKenna holding a fish larger than she was. McKenna crouching on the sand in baby Wellingtons, solemnly contemplating a ghost crab.

Lovey's eyes were kind. "I don't suppose you have many childhood photos?"

His gaze dropped to the floor. "That kind of thing tended to go missing after your fourth foster home."

"Would you like to see a picture of Shawn?"

He'd been curious. Hoping that Bryce was not indicative of her taste in men. And every time McKenna said Shawn's name, she got this far away, dreamy look. Did he really want to see her with the love of her life?

Curiosity overcame his trepidation. "Okay." He took a breath.

Lovey flipped the page, and there he was. The man who'd loved McKenna. The man Caden believed McKenna probably still loved.

A Navy petty officer. Tall. Light brown hair. Blue eyes. Forever young.

Hinson, Caden grudgingly admitted, was far more handsome. And yet the younger man had something the policeman did not. A gentleness. A kindness. An honesty.

"One more," Lovey whispered, turning the page. "Their engagement photo."

They stood—where else?—on the beach. With waves foaming in the distance, the sailor had his arms around McKenna, tucking her against his uniform. She gazed at the camera lens with a lightness to her lovely face, a joy that grief had stolen from the woman he knew now.

And Shawn's face as he gazed at his bride-to-be?

Caden's gut clenched. Contemplating what she'd lost, unbidden moisture sprang into his eyes. For the way Shawn looked at McKenna . . . Caden had never seen such love, such devotion.

To his shame, something he'd never felt for any woman. Not even Nikki.

Shawn had been everything McKenna deserved and more.

"He looks like a good man," Caden rasped once he found his voice again.

"Yes, he was." Lovey squeezed his hand. "There's a lot of what made him so special in you."

He didn't see it. "I'll be working outside if you need anything."

But as he worked, he couldn't shake the image of what he'd glimpsed in that photograph. A picture of what true love looked like. It ignited within him a confusing yearning to not only be loved like that, but to love someone like that in return.

After Shawn, how could McKenna settle for someone like Hinson? Perhaps Caden wasn't the only one who'd given up. And that made him angry with her. Angry for selling herself short. For self-sabotaging a chance for real happiness.

Hinson was an arrogant, selfish, controlling bully. He'd never make Beach Girl happy. If only Caden could get her to see it, too. Before she made a mistake that ruined her life.

Chapter Fifteen

Despite the crime-watch patrol, there was another fire that night. Norman Gaskill's commercial fishing boat was torched in its mooring, a mere spitting distance from town. Like the others, the blaze erupted after midnight, and an entire family's livelihood went up in flames. Norman's grandfather and Laddie Ferguson had once worked that boat together.

It was a devastating blow for a Down Easter already struggling to make ends meet. The sheer viciousness of it in a community that relied on the sea to pay bills boggled the mind. In the old days, necks had been stretched for less.

The next day at Skipjacks, McKenna sensed the customers giving Caden increasingly hostile looks. So unfair. Caden hadn't left the house all night.

She knew that as fact because she'd lain awake for hours going over the events of the last month. Thinking on everything he'd said about himself, and more about what he hadn't. She'd never met anyone as closed off as Caden Wallis.

The downstairs lights were still on at midnight, and she'd gotten out of bed thinking he'd forgotten to turn them off. But she'd found him, head in his hands, exactly where she'd left him hours earlier when everyone went upstairs.

When he took his usual mid-morning break at the counter on the next stool over, boat captain Bill Scarborough made a point of leaving. Hunched over the plate, Caden's mouth thinned.

She pushed a mug of coffee toward him.

His lips twisted. "Do I have time to drink it before the lynch mob arrives?"

"Nobody is getting lynched, Caden."

He took a sip of coffee. "Southern justice, right?"

"My dad doesn't run that kind of town."

He set the mug down. "Hinson's pointing the finger at me, doing his best to lay blame on the outsider."

"Bryce wouldn't do that." Though she was less and less certain these days about what Bryce would or would not do.

"An outsider who temporarily lives downstairs from his woman."

"I'm not his woman," she growled. Although the "temporarily" part bothered her more.

"You tell him that yet? 'Cause if you have, I don't think he got the message."

She was about done with Caden's bad moods. Tempted to douse his eggs with Texas Pete, she was reaching for the spicy hot sauce when Paul Stanhope walked into the diner.

He joined them at the counter. "The newspaper clipping you and Bryce dropped by the other night. Out kind of late, weren't you?"

McKenna shot a look at Caden, who studiously ignored her, his shoulders hunkered, elbows planted on either side of the plate. But he was listening. Caden Wallis didn't miss much.

"Yeah, well . . ." McKenna waved her hand, hoping the professor would get on with it. "Have you found something?"

He took the stool next to Caden. "Once Talbot and I enlarged the photo, we got his name off the Coast Guard uniform."

McKenna hadn't expected anything so quickly. "That's wonderful."

"He's Seaman First Class Richard Freeman. Hometown, Newport News, Virginia."

"So close."

The professor nodded. "Unmarried, but a brother inherited the family home listed on his form. The brother's still living, although elderly, of course."

She flicked a look at Lovey, holding court at the register.

"The brother's wife kept photos Lovey might like to see. To get to know, even if posthumously, the man who saved her life."

McKenna smiled. "She'll be so pleased."

"Talbot insisted on driving there to make copies and show them the newspaper clipping. The brother wasn't aware a photo had been snapped of Richard just hours before his death."

"I have something else you might find interesting." She reached under the counter and opened the cabinet where they secured their purses. "Since you're here . . ." She pulled out the glass bottle.

Stanhope's eyes narrowed. "Where did you find this?"

"Buried in the sand on Yaupon Island."

"Don't locals steer clear of the place? Talbot advised me early on I ought to steer clear too."

Caden turned. "Why's that?"

"The official version I dug out of a 1945 report, declassified after the war, said there was a danger of unexploded ordnance."

Caden frowned. "From what?"

Unscrewing the top, McKenna refilled a saltshaker. "German submarines made this area Torpedo Junction in the early days of World War II."

Stanhope studied the menu on the wall. "The Allies lost more men, ships, and material during a seven-month stretch in 1942 than the rest of the war combined."

"Those constarned U-boats." Laddie Ferguson clapped Caden on the back. "The waffles were spot on this morning."

Caden scowled. But in his way, Laddie was trying to give Caden, the outsider, an insider seal of approval. She smiled at the old waterman. No way would she believe him guilty of drug smuggling.

She might just give Laddie free breakfasts for the rest of his life. Not as generous as it sounded. Laddie was eighty-two if he was a day.

"Rest your legs, Laddie." She pulled out a danish. "On the house. Can I get you a coffee?"

Laddie eased his arthritic bones on the other side of Caden. "Don't mind if I do."

Caden glared at them.

"Yep," Laddie warmed to the topic—one of his favorites—as she poured him a cup of joe. "Wolfpacks, they were called." Laddie frowned.

"Night after night, the house where I grew up shook from the force of the explosions."

Caden winced. She watched him out of the corner of her eye.

"Twenty or thirty miles out, the ships burned, lighting the sky." Laddie took a sip. "Leaking from the sunken boats, oil so thick my sister and I couldn't swim in the ocean that summer."

Caden got off the stool.

Stanhope sighed. "No one in America, except Bankers, ever knew until after the war how close we came to invasion." He fingered the raised lettering on the bottle. "This is German."

Caden crossed his arms, his hips wide. "How do you know so much about this stuff?"

She didn't like how Caden's breathing had become so rapid. They shouldn't have talked about this in front of him. She could only imagine—actually didn't want to imagine—the things he'd seen and experienced during his war.

"The professor's a maritime expert on the Battle of the Atlantic. He's mapped every sunken vessel along the entire Banks."

Stanhope turned the bottle over in his hand. "The tide of war turned not long after 1943. Using the convoy system, the Allies nullified the U-boat threat. Underwater sonar cables were strung along the barrier islands so the subs couldn't sneak spies onto land. Patrols swept the inlets for mines. And Ocracoke had a top-secret station with advanced detection devices."

"What does—" Laddie leaned over. "—*Glockenstrasse* mean? What is it?"

Stanhope pursed his mouth. "This is an empty perfume bottle used by German submariners to overcome the stench of the unwashed bodies of men cooped up for weeks in a tin can."

Laddie tilted his head. "Worth much?"

"Only to a historian." Stanhope shook his head. "I have no idea why you found this on Yaupon. No U-boat sank even close to there. Although . . ." His eyes took on a faraway glaze.

"Dr. Stanhope?"

He looked up with a faint smile. "Maybe just a belated gift from the sea."

"Yaupon?" Laddie grunted. "That's an evil place. Haunted ever since the Great Storm."

McKenna's eyes darted, making sure Lovey wasn't within earshot. "Laddie, that's a bunch of nonsense. Waterman superstition."

Laddie rose. "I know what I know. Every waterman will tell you about the mysterious lights over there at night where none should exist. You couldn't pay me enough to fish over there."

She rolled her eyes. "Seriously?"

Laddie straightened. "Say what you will, but I'm not the only one who's heard the bell over here in Tuckahoe."

"What bell?" Her eyes flicked to Caden.

"The bell in the church steeple on Yaupon." Laddie shivered. "They say it only tolls when someone is about to die."

She cocked her head. "That's some fish story you got there, Laddie. You ought to write fiction."

Laddie touched his finger to the side of his bulbous nose. "Mock me if you like. Your gran knows what I'm saying is true."

"Don't you upset my grandmother with your outlandish tales, Laddie Ferguson, or . . . or . . ." She snatched up a dishcloth. "I'll make sure you're permanently barred from Skipjacks."

Laddie rocked. "No need to get your flip-flops in a twist. I ain't saying nothing to 'er."

"Caden, are you—?" But he was gone, the kitchen door still swinging in his wake,

He was getting physically stronger every day. Learning to believe in himself again. Yet until he was willing to open up, she feared his invisible wounds of war would continue to fester.

But she could out-stubborn stubborn in her sleep. She'd had lots of practice.

❖ ❖ ❖

He wasn't surprised when McKenna followed him into the kitchen. She'd seen his reaction to the talk of war and its brutal realities, and she wasn't likely to let it go. Not until she dissected every nuance of every emotion he didn't even feel. She was such a girl.

"Long time since we talked."

Caden put his back into scouring the residue off the grill. "We talked last night, McKenna."

She did that jiggly thing with her foot and the flip-flop. "You never told me about your Army career."

"Nope. Never did." He carried a pan over to the sink. "Excuse me." He skirted around her.

"You know everything about me, and I know hardly anything about you."

Not true. He didn't know everything he wanted to know about her.

She played with the cobalt-blue sea-glass pendant dangling from her neck. He did know that blue—in every hue—was her favorite color.

"You never told me how you got hurt."

Caden looked her square in the face. "And I'm not going to."

Her eyes pulled at him. "It would help you to talk about it."

"It won't."

Sometimes, when she looked at him like that, he felt like he had both feet in the sand and an inexorable tide was pulling him out to sea.

McKenna's eyes welled. "You don't trust me."

How could he explain to her that to share even the smallest detail of his tours would taint her? She belonged to the sand, the sea, and the wind, not the blood-soaked horror from which he'd barely escaped with his life. From which Joe and Friday never would.

Instead of getting angry though, she did something worse. She walked out of the kitchen without another word, leaving him feeling like the lowest form of life.

That afternoon, Walt meandered into Skipjacks as Earlene flipped the sign to *Closed*.

Her face lit. "Walt, honey. Are you hungry? I can rustle you up some—"

Walt strode past her without so much as a word. It hurt something inside Caden's heart to see the light in Earlene's eyes die.

Caden stepped out from behind the counter. "Lovey's off with Stanhope."

Eyes downcast, Earlene grabbed her purse and left the diner.

The chief didn't speak until the bell stopped jingling. "It's you I want to see. Thought you and I ought to have a talk. Man to man." He slapped his palms on the counter. "Let's take a ride."

Seemed everybody wanted to have a chat with him today.

Gritting his teeth, he followed Walt to his Explorer. "Front or back, Chief?" His lip curled.

"Front seat." Walt leaned his elbows on the roof. "Unless you have a preference for the back of a police car."

Caden yanked open the door and got in. As the chief pulled out of Skipjacks, he wondered if this ride would end across the street in a jail cell. But Walt headed north on 12. Toward home?

It wasn't his home.

"We need to get a few things straight."

Caden clenched his jaw.

"Lay out a few ground rules for your continued association with my family." Walt tapped the side of his thumb on the wheel. "With my daughter."

He'd learned the hard way in Oklahoma, it was better when dealing with law enforcement to just keep your mouth shut.

"Until your recent misfortune—"

"You mean my unfortunate encounter with an IED?"

Walt appeared more amused than annoyed at the interruption.

Caden knew better. He'd certainly run enough interrogations of his own to know the drill. He'd been trained not to lose his cool. Anger was a weakness, an advantage you never bestowed on an enemy. Get angry, and you gave away your power.

"As I was saying, until your recent encounter with an IED, you had quite the distinguished service career. Bronze Star. The Bronze Star with Valor for heroism in combat. The Silver Star."

Yet the one time it really mattered . . . he would've died a thousand times over if he could have saved Joe and Friday.

"But your service record also indicates sometimes an almost reckless disregard for your own safety."

He clenched and unclenched his hands. "You're saying the IED was my own fault?"

"No, that would give you too much credit. Things happen." Walt took a quick glance at the passing scenery. "Chemical agents are unwittingly released while being destroyed. Pills supposed to keep you well make you sick. It's war, son. You don't mind if I call you son, do you?"

"You'd be the first who ever did."

A muscle ticked in Walt's cheek.

"I don't need your pity," he snarled.

Walt rolled his eyes. "Son, what amazes me is how you walked with *two* legs under the weight of that chip on your shoulder."

Caden's mouth fell open. He snapped it shut.

"You've done a good job at Skipjacks. The repairs on the house . . . I've never seen better."

"I haven't finished the window trim."

Walt pulled to a stop in front of the house and killed the engine but made no move to get out of the car. "I don't doubt you'll finish every project you've set your mind to. You're conscientious, I'll give you that."

"But?" There was always a but.

"No buts. My mother thinks you're the greatest thing since sliced bread. Earlene too. Although," he grimaced, "history has proven when it comes to her discernment of men—"

"Including you?" Caden wasn't about to let him tear down Earlene. She'd been kinder to him than his own mother. Though that in itself was hardly an endorsement.

Walt's chest heaved. "I'm not going to talk about Earlene with you or anyone else." He raked his hand over his face. "And there's McKenna to consider."

Caden's heart pounded. This man had the power to prevent him from ever seeing McKenna again. He'd do the same if he had a daughter and someone like him . . .

That's what this was about.

He was going to ask Caden—order Caden—off the island. He'd proven over and over, it didn't take long to wear out his welcome. "I'll be on the next ferry out—"

"Now that's exactly what I'm *not* asking you to do. Unless you want to."

He didn't want to. "What are you saying then?"

"I'm saying McKenna's got a lot invested in you. In your recovery." Walt pursed his lips. "I haven't seen her this . . . alive . . . in a long time.

So if you're looking for a place to put down roots, I'm telling you to think about staying."

Caden's eyes widened. Not what he'd expected.

"But if staying isn't your strong suit, then I think it would be kinder to leave before anyone gets more attached."

That he'd expected.

"You want a person of interest in a murder investigation to stick around?"

"Son, you are many things. Hardheaded, stubborn, prideful within an inch of your life—"

"I get the picture." Caden clamped his jaw tight.

Father and daughter were in perfect harmony on the finer points of his character.

"I'm not sure you do. You ever hear the old story about the hundreds of starfish stranded on a beach?"

"Uh . . . no."

"McKenna gathers strays. She can't help herself. It's her nature. She's like the girl in the story on the beach tossing one starfish after another back into the sea."

"So she should toss me back where I came from?"

"Can I tell this story, please?" Walt got an aggravated look. "Someone tells the girl to stop wasting her time. That she'll never be able to rescue all the starfish. Do you know what the girl said?"

His heart thudded in his chest.

"She said, 'But I can save *this* one. And I can save *this* one. And *this* one.'"

Which is exactly what McKenna had done on the beach that first day. Saved him from himself.

"But my daughter doesn't toss any of them out to sea. The turtles. The customers. Her family and friends."

Him.

"What she does is gather each one and hold them close to her heart. She has a hard time letting go."

Like Shawn. Giving oxygen to the insidious fear gnawing inside Caden that she would never love anyone else.

"I also think you have a lot of potential. McKenna saw it. Mother too. With your skills, the salt air and storms guarantee you'd be kept busy repairing beach properties. And I don't figure you for murdering Alonso." The chief gave Caden a steely-eyed look. "Not that I didn't thoroughly consider the idea. But the facts don't jive for you to have committed murder or set fire to those buildings."

"Chief, I appreciate your faith in me."

Walt slung open his door. "You think on what I said." He extricated his lanky form from the vehicle. "Let me know what you decide." He bent over, leaning into the cruiser. "Don't wait too long, or you and me are going to have a problem. Roger that, Sergeant Wallis?"

Caden climbed out of the cruiser. "Roger, Chief."

McKenna's father smiled at him over the roof. "I hear tell you used to play football."

"When I had two good legs."

The chief rolled his eyes. "Before you work yourself into a lather, a good friend of mine coaches the football team at the high school. They're headed for the playoffs if the kids don't derail themselves before then. Coach says the offensive line could use another trainer. A fresh approach."

Caden started to form an objection, but Walt beat him to the punch.

"Not talking about running plays." The chief leaned against the frame of the car. "Though I'm thinking you could, if you set your mind to wanting to. I'm talking about utilizing the benefit of your experience. The team-building skills you acquired, courtesy of Uncle Sam."

"What's the point? I won't be here come playoff season."

"That is entirely up to you. He'd need you on the field from three to five, two afternoons a week."

Returning to the gridiron held an irresistible appeal. A sure sign he should decline. "What about my projects?"

"What about showing a little community support? Besides, game time on Football Fridays are about the best thing going in Tuckahoe this time of year."

"Football Fridays, I'm guessing, are about the only thing going in Tuckahoe this time of year."

Walt's mouth quirked. "True." He rubbed his chin. "'Course, did I mention Football Fridays are one of McKenna's favorite fall activities?"

No, he hadn't. But Caden could imagine McKenna on the bleachers, him coaching from the sidelines, eating hot dogs . . . A perfect night.

He shut the car door. "Just remember, this was your idea."

"Now that we've got that settled." The police chief straightened, tapped the roof of the car with his palm, then started for the house. "The net is tightening around our local dealer."

Caden followed. "And desperate men do desperate things."

"Exactly. Fact is, with the hours I'm putting in, I'm glad you're here at night with Mother and McKenna." He undid the top button at the neck on his uniform. "The cartel not only has a local running the drugs, but another well-connected insider who enables them to stay two steps ahead of the task force. Alonso's body on my doorstep sent a message. A warning."

"Meaning if you don't back off, they could get to you."

The chief's gray-blue eyes went stormy. "Or worse, get to those I love. That's why it's also better if I don't—" His gaze bounced away.

Was he thinking of Earlene?

Caden frowned. "How do you figure the arsons fit with the drug trafficking?"

"That has perplexed me." Walt shrugged. "Maybe diversionary tactics. Muddying the waters. You've been trained for strategic problem-solving. What are your thoughts?"

"From what I know about drug trafficking," Caden rubbed his jaw, "cartel-connected individuals don't play around. They'll go to any lengths to achieve their objective, because if they fail, they pay with their lives."

"That's why I'd be grateful if . . ." Walt's mouth tightened and he scrubbed his neck. "We've heared chatter that a new shipment is about to make its way to the Banks soon."

"Why are you telling me this?"

The chief eyed him. "I'm trusting you with highly confidential task-force intel because the violence seems to be escalating. Whoever's behind this is painting a target on those of us trying to stop them."

Caden nodded. "McKenna's boat. Skipjacks. Hinson's boat."

"It's going to get worse before it gets better." The chief sighed. "I wanted to warn you. Stay on your guard, Wallis. And keep your eyes wide open."

Something inside Caden warmed at Walt's confidence in him. All his life, he'd felt like the guy on the outside looking in. But Walt was opening a door, giving him a chance to be on the inside for once. No matter what it took, he'd show McKenna's father that his trust wasn't misplaced.

Caden squared his shoulders. "I give you my word, sir. I won't leave until I know McKenna and your family are safe."

Chapter Sixteen

THE NEXT AFTERNOON FOUND MCKENNA STANDING IN FRONT OF the shuttered storefront next to Jolene's. At the sound of scuffled pebbles on the sidewalk, she whirled.

Talbot Rivenbark stood behind her, his Lincoln parked against the curb.

She placed her hand over her rapidly beating heart. He moved pretty stealthily for an old guy.

"You were doing some intense daydreaming."

She wrapped her arms around herself. "Wasting time."

"Nothing wrong with dreaming. Tuckahoe could use a dance studio."

"A pipe dream."

"I've been looking to invest in a local business." He studied the real-estate info taped to the window. "I know the listing agent." The glass mirrored their reflection. "The store has been vacant so long, I believe the agent would give us a good deal to get the place off his books."

Framed by the window, she saw herself reflected in the ripples of the glass. She pivoted, turning from the impossible. "Skipjacks needs me. Lovey and Dad need me."

The lawyer's grizzled brows wrinkled. "But that isn't the real issue, is it? That's the excuse."

She glanced away, his words uncomfortably close to what Bryce had said.

"Perhaps, deep down, you fear they might not need you after all. Or not as much as you need them to need you."

McKenna threw out her hands. "Suppose I try the dance studio and fail?"

"Suppose you try and succeed? Maybe that's the problem. If you succeed, it means you've moved into a new life, and that scares you to death."

"I like my life as it is, Talbot."

"What about your dreams? What about you and Wallis?"

"Caden's leaving soon, remember?" She hunched her shoulders. "And I stopped dreaming those kind of dreams when Shawn died."

"Shawn died, McKenna. Not you. Don't listen to the fear. Never lose your dreams. Once you do, you might as well be dead." He swung her around to the window. "What do you see when you look inside?"

Thanks to the ever-buffeting wind, her hair was a rumpled mess. She had no real skills other than dancing—something she could no longer do. Or was it something she no longer dared to do? Not so unlike Caden when he'd first arrived in Tuckahoe.

In saving Caden, was she also trying to save herself?

"Talbot . . ."

He wasn't letting her go. Not until she looked—really looked—at herself and what her future in Tuckahoe beyond Skipjacks could look like.

So she faced her reflection. And for the first time, the desire to dance again—but here in Tuckahoe—drowned out her fear. "I see Blue Marguerite."

"Pardon?"

She shrugged. "It's a paint color."

His mouth quirked. "What else?"

"Mirrors lining sound-proof walls."

He squinted through the smudged glass. "Good idea. And?"

"A ballet barre and a sound system. A free-floating hardwood dance floor in a natural maple finish with a cushioning suspension system, like on *Dancing with the Stars*."

"Excellent."

She frowned. "What I see is an enormous amount of work and expense."

"No harm in dreaming."

Actually, there was. And she wasn't thinking only of dance studios. "What happened with the Guardsman's family in Newport News?"

"Oddest thing . . ." He steepled his long-fingered hands on his chin.

Her eyes darted toward the waterfront. Commercial and recreational boats bobbed in the harbor. And as usual, Caribbean Jack loitered nearby. Maybe he lived on his boat. "What was odd?"

"The newspaper photo of Freeman. The family said it wasn't him."

Her attention returned to the attorney. "But his uniform . . ."

"Seaman Richard Freeman had dark hair." He removed an envelope from his shirt pocket. "Even in black and white, this man is as blond as you. As blond as little-girl Lovey in the photo with him."

"That doesn't make any sense. Who is the man? Why is he wearing Freeman's Coast Guard uniform?"

"I don't know." He dropped his eyes. "But I have friends with access to databases that go back decades."

"The Coast Guard must have records of the other guardsmen stationed on Yaupon in 1944." She nodded. "Perhaps he was sleeping when the storm hit. Maybe he grabbed the first thing he could get his hands on—a fellow Coastie's uniform."

"May not be easy to verify. The station personnel on Yaupon and Hatteras rotated every two weeks so no one was stuck too long on isolated Yaupon." He winked. "The dames and the dance clubs were farther north in Nags Head."

Her lips curved. "I bet you cut quite the rug in those days."

"I'm not that old." He tucked the folded clipping inside his pocket. "It was my father's war." His eyes became hooded. "And I've spent my life honoring his quest for justice."

"Did you hear Norm Gaskill's fishing boat was burned?"

Talbot's blue eyes sharpened. "If your father doesn't catch the arsonist soon, someone else is going to get hurt."

"Bryce is trying to find out where the arsonist acquired his materials."

"Is he now?" Talbot rubbed his hands together. "I've been invited to dinner at your house tonight. See you there?"

She shook her head. "I-I've got something else I promised to do at the turtle hospital."

Just as well she wasn't going home. She had the distinct impression Caden had been doing his best to avoid her. Maybe she should take a page from his playbook. He wasn't the only one who could do evasion.

❖ ❖ ❖

Caden had learned as a child that if you set your expectations low, you'd never be disappointed. His expectations had certainly been low when he pulled up to the small Dare County high school football field in Lovey's borrowed car.

But it turned out better than he expected. Coach Gray was great, talking plays and asking his opinion. It had been a long time since anyone had cared what he thought. Or believed that what he knew mattered. Despite himself, he enjoyed the afternoon. He even got to run the guys through a few drills.

And for the first time, he didn't get mired in the what-he-could-never-do-again but basked in the pleasure of the contribution he could still make.

The good feeling plummeted, however, once he returned to the Dockery house. Dinner was only him, Lovey, and Talbot. This was his life. Better get used to it. Third wheeling with the Bengay crowd.

Afterward, he cleared the table, but Lovey insisted on washing the dishes.

Talbot took up the drying cloth. "I'm surprised you're not with McKenna tonight. Lovey tells me you two have been near inseparable since you arrived on our fair shores."

Not only did he not like chitchat, Caden preferred not talking at all. In his experience, the less said the better. But the flip side meant he'd never been good at expressing his thoughts, much less his feelings, and that led to misunderstandings, like with McKenna over that stupid picture of Nikki.

If only conversations could be more like missions. Identify the target. Get in, do the job, and get out as quickly as possible.

Which, as soon as he put away the leftovers, was what he planned to do. Leave the geriatric lovebirds alone. Maybe he and Ginger could head to the beach and watch the moon rise over the ocean.

Lovey rinsed a plate. "McKenna said she wouldn't be sleeping here tonight."

He almost dropped the bowl.

What about her God talk? No surprise about Hinson, but he hadn't figured McKenna for that kind of woman, and he found himself stung by disappointment in her.

Not that he was any better than Hinson. The memory of how it had been with him and Nikki brought a burn of shame to his cheeks. Yet Nikki had been no innocent when he met her. As wise to the ways of the world as he was. Both out for a good time.

But McKenna . . .

Caden blew out a slow trickle of air. He'd believed she was different. He should've known better. Maybe Nikki and McKenna weren't as different as he'd hoped.

Lovey rested her hands on the sink. "I didn't want her going out alone, not with everything that's been happening, but she insisted she needed to keep watch over the turtles tonight. You know how head-strong she can be."

Turtles? "She's at the rescue center? I thought—" He clamped his lips shut.

From the smirk on Lovey's face, he had a feeling she already knew what he'd thought. "Crime-watch patrol."

He slammed the refrigerator door shut. He had a bad feeling about this. How could she be so foolish and stubborn? She was going to get herself—

"Lovey." His face felt tight enough to crack. "Would you mind if I borrowed your car again this evening?"

"A great idea." Her smile was broad. "A drive-by of the turtle hospital would be an even better idea."

"Suppose I hadn't asked to borrow the car, Lovey?" He crossed his arms. "What was your backup plan?"

From the pocket of her apron, she handed him her keys. "I had full confidence you wouldn't disappoint me."

Banker women—not Afghanistan or amputation—were going to be the death of him. Tucking his shirttail into his jeans, he headed out, letting the screen door slam behind him. Praying—yes, praying, another first—that he'd be in time to stop Beach Girl from making a potentially fatal mistake.

❖ ❖ ❖

McKenna had never fully appreciated how creepy the turtle rehab center could be at night. Situated at the far end of town on an isolated spit of land, the building was dark. The only sounds were the soft splashing inside the enormous tanks where Cecil and friends recuperated from their injuries.

"How ya doing big guy?" She shone the light from her cell phone into the water tank to locate Cecil. "Just you and me—"

She glanced over her shoulder. Was that the creak of a door? Or her imagination?

Laddie and his cohorts on the crime patrol weren't far. She had only to dial 9-1-1 and her dad would be here within minutes, lights blazing. Not that her father or Bryce had any idea where she was tonight.

Nor did Caden. She sniffed. He'd do better to concentrate on his own issues.

She leaned over the tank. "And let me tell you, Cecil, he's got plenty of those."

The loggerhead's remaining flippers propelled him to the other side of the tank and back. Cecil had come a long way. They'd release him by Christmas.

Soon Caden would return to his real world too. A sour taste filled her mouth. Back to that two-faced, not–to-be-trusted girlfriend of his.

Tomorrow he'd be angry when he learned she spent the night at the rehab center. Which served him right.

"Let that be a lesson to you, Cecil, my friend. Not to be a jerk or a moron or—"

Her pulse quickened. She hadn't imagined *that* noise in the adjacent waiting room. Like the scrape of a chair against the floor.

Ducking, she crouched at the base of the tank. Someone was in the reception area. Her heart pounded. Why had she thought this was a good idea?

Glass shattered on the other side of the wall, and a tremendous explosion shook the building. Screaming, she covered her head with her arms as fragments of something bombarded the walls and pulverized the observation window. A fire alarm shrieked.

She'd dropped her phone. Her hands scrabbled around the floor. But it must have skidded under the tanks.

Orange tongues of fire lapped at the walls. The front door was no longer an option. Smoke poured into the holding tank area. Why weren't the sprinklers going off?

Her sense of urgency mounted. The holding-tank room was on the exterior wall of the building. The smoke growing dense, McKenna couldn't stop coughing. Whirling, she raced toward the back, grateful for the glowing red *Exit* sign.

Stumbling into the door, she shoved the push-bar mechanism. But nothing happened. She slammed her body against the device, but it didn't budge. Why wouldn't it open? A half sob rose out of her chest. She pounded on the door.

"Help! Somebody help! Can you hear me? I'm trapped! Help me!"

She yelled until her throat burned. Her eyes watered at the haze of smoke rapidly filling the holding room. The turtles sensed something was amiss. Splashing increased as ash and soot rained upon the animals thrashing in the tanks.

Oh, God. Help me. Please . . .

She could no longer make out the outline of the tanks. There was only choking, black smoke and, beyond, an inferno. Disoriented, her breath came in short, rapid gasps as her lungs desperately craved fresh air.

Like shotgun blasts, everyday items began to explode in the intense, suffocating heat. Flames curled along the ceiling over her head. She dropped to her knees.

Was this how her life would end? So much she still wanted to do . . . to accomplish.

God, get me out of here.

She pressed her face against the smooth, still cool tile. Desperate for any last vestige of oxygen. And then there was time for only one final prayer.

Let the smoke take me, Father. Please don't let me burn.

People said in moments of extreme danger, their entire lives flashed before their eyes. Or the faces of the ones they'd leave behind. But not McKenna. Closing her eyes against the searing heat, she saw only the life she'd never get to live. A perfect day of blue sky, paddleboarding with Caden in the calm, shallow waters of the Pamlico Sound.

❖ ❖ ❖

Caden brought the car to a screeching halt beside McKenna's truck. The turtle hospital was engulfed in flames. Orange smoke billowed into the night sky.

In his worst nightmares, he'd never experienced the terror he felt now. McKenna was trapped somewhere inside the roaring flames. Crackling along the eaves, the roof buckled, groaning as if in a death throe.

He ran toward the entrance.

Stifling heat sucked the oxygen out of his lungs. He threw his arm over his face. Hinson raced around the corner of the building.

"Thank God, you're here." Hinson grabbed his arm. "We can't get her out through the front. There's a door at the back, but I need your help." His face reflected the same horror Caden felt inside.

Caden sprinted around the building, close on the man's heels. Near his parked cruiser, Hinson skidded to a stop in front of a large, metal door flush with the concrete wall. Caden grabbed the handle and pulled.

"The lock's been smashed," Hinson panted.

A dark abyss opened inside Caden, threatening to swallow him whole. "Deliberately?" He gritted his teeth.

Hinson looked away. "I'm guessing so."

Caden saw only black dots for a second as a killing rage engulfed him. If it was the last thing on earth he did, he was going to make this sicko arsonist pay.

He pounded his fist on the door. "McKenna! McKenna!"

Could she hear him through the steel door? Or was she past the point of hearing anyone? No. He couldn't think like that. He wouldn't stop until he had her out of there. Whatever it took.

Hinson pushed him aside and kicked the area below the handle with the force of his boot. The impact sent him staggering and clutching his knee.

What he wouldn't give for an explosive breaching charge. Caden wheeled toward Hinson. "Do you carry a ballistic shotgun in your vehicle?"

Hinson shook his head. "Not standard gear for a rural department like ours." Sweat poured down his face. He had a wild, crazed look in his eyes.

If Caden had ever had cause to doubt Hinson's feelings for McKenna, he doubted no more. No matter his opinion of the scumbag, Bryce Hinson cared about McKenna. Deeply.

"We've got to get her out, Wallis."

Think. He had to think. Fast. What about the hinges?

Caden scanned the wall. "The door swings outward. Have you got any tools in your car? We're going to have to break the hinges."

Hinson frowned. "I have a pry bar. A sledgehammer too."

"Get 'em."

Limping, Hinson rushed toward his cruiser and returned, a tool in each hand. "It's a two-man job. Hold the bar?" He hefted the hammer. "Or brute force? Which do you prefer?"

Hinson hated his guts. One slip-up—accidental or deliberate—and Hinson could smash his hands. But Hinson, with the balance of two good legs, had the strength to bring the greatest force to attack the hinges.

"I'll hold. You smash." Caden grabbed the bar.

Hinson's eyelids flickered. "You're sure? I'm right-handed, which means you'll have to—"

"Do whatever it takes." Caden placed the sharp point of the bar against the jam at a forty-five-degree angle. "Top hinge first."

Taking the corresponding position, Hinson gripped the wooden handle of the hammer. "Ready?"

"Ready." He tightened his grip on the bar and prepared for the jolt.

Hinson swung the hammer and struck. Caden's arms reverberated, but the force of the hammer drove the tip of the bar into the jam, gaining purchase. Caden shimmied the bar to force the blade face deeper into the gap.

"Again." He clenched his teeth. "Hit."

Hinson swung, burying the crowbar into the jam.

Thud.

Caden's arms throbbed, but he felt something solid beneath the bar. "Screws sheared." He yanked out the crowbar. "Middle hinge." He repositioned quickly. "Hit."

Thud. Strike. *Thud.* Strike.

Not only his arms ached, his jaw, too, from clenching his teeth. *Thud.* Strike. *Thud.*

"We're through. Bottom."

When the last hinge broke, Caden yanked out the pry bar and reinserted it at midpoint in the space they'd opened. It took the both of them lending their strength against the bar to pop the door from the frame. Caden dropped the bar with a clang to the concrete. With their bare hands, they wrenched open the door, pivoting it to the lock side. And they were through.

Both of them instinctively recoiled from the wave of heat. He could see nothing but thick smoke.

"McKenna!" yelled Hinson.

Caden stepped over the threshold. In the distance, sirens blared. Someone had called it in.

Hinson grabbed for his shoulder but missed. "Wait. The fire engines are here."

"McKenna!" Caden charged into the blackness. "Call out! McKenna! Where are you?" He couldn't find her. Had they been wrong? But her truck—

He ran smack into a holding tank. Water sloshed. With a splash, McKenna surfaced. Gasping, she clung to the rim of the tank, hair plastered to her head, water streaming off her face.

Caden touched her. "McKenna—"

Hinson shoved him aside. "I'm here, baby."

Sobbing, she raised her arms. He and Hinson dragged her out.

"Cecil," she choked. "The others."

A firefighter in turnout gear plunged into the room. "Go. We got this."

Caden and Hinson each took an arm. Between them, McKenna staggered into the night, falling against the cruiser. Other than smoke inhalation, she didn't appear to have sustained any burns or injuries.

Hinson crowded in. "Baby, baby, baby . . ."

Caden let go as Hinson enfolded her in an embrace. But over Hinson's shoulder, her eyes sought his.

An image floated through his mind of what could've happened to her. Her body, burned beyond recognition, in the smoking rubble of the clinic. He'd seen it countless times in—

Nausea roiled in his belly. Turning on his heel, he walked swiftly around the building. He passed several paramedics. A dozen firefighters battled the blaze, spray hissing from their hoses. He made it to the car before he succumbed. And there, ten-year combat veteran though he be, he was sick to his stomach.

He jerked upright at the screech of tires. Walt careened into the lot rapidly filling with other emergency vehicles. He flung himself out of the Explorer, his jaw working. "Where—"

Caden motioned. Walt didn't wait. Caden desperately needed to be anywhere but here. Yet he couldn't tear himself away. McKenna had Hinson and her dad, but he needed to be sure she was okay.

Escorted by the EMTs, McKenna emerged from the maze of firetrucks on a gurney, an oxygen mask over her face. Seeing him, she tried to sit up, pushing up on her elbows. But a paramedic forced her to lie back. The EMTs lifted her gurney into an ambulance, and accelerated away, lights flashing, sirens wailing. It turned north on 12 toward the hospital in Nags Head.

Walt stumbled to his cruiser, Hinson by his side. The younger man put a grimy hand on the chief's arm, but Walt shook him off.

"I can take care of things from here, Chief." Hinson appeared to have aged ten years. "You follow the ambulance. I'll make sure the scene is secure after the fire's extinguished and wait for the fire marshal."

Walt closed his eyes. "I didn't hear the call come in. I was—" He clutched his midsection. Pain distorted his features.

"I'll make sure Gina returns McKenna's car to the house." Hinson cut a glance at Caden. "But sir, if I hadn't been on patrol and seen the flames, McKenna could've lost her life because of this arsonist."

Truce over. Hinson had reverted to his true form. Not that Caden wanted praise. All that mattered was that McKenna was safe.

"No thanks to me," Walt rasped.

Caden winced at the raw torment in his voice. A man like Chief Dockery would take this as a personal failure. Especially when it came to his daughter.

"Maybe now you ought to consider, Chief, before something worse . . . It's gotten too personal for you to be—"

Walt pushed off from the Explorer. "Exactly why I can't quit now. Because it *is* personal."

Hinson's face darkened.

"I'd been thinking today about turning in my resignation. But now?" Walt ran his hand over on his jaw. "I can't quit. Not until I've put this maniac behind bars where he can't hurt anyone else."

Hinson's gaze went half mast, but not before Caden read seething fury in his eyes.

"Chief, I really don't think you're thinking—"

"That, Officer Hinson, is my final word."

Hinson's fists balled.

Walt faced Caden. "I'd prefer my mother not hear about this until McKenna gets home." He made a face. "Knowing my daughter, she won't allow them to keep her overnight. I'll need to stay here and find where this psycho has made a mistake."

Caden grunted. "Endangering McKenna, he's already made one mistake too many."

Walt's mouth thinned. "You and I think alike, son. Would you go to the hospital for me? McKenna will need a ride home."

Hinson jockeyed between Walt and Caden. "Let me go, Chief."

Walt folded his arms over his chest. "You've got an investigation to conduct. Or have you forgotten, Officer Hinson?"

Throwing Caden a murderous look, Hinson stalked toward the firefighters, barking demands.

"Keep me updated, Wallis."

Not a request. An order. But Caden did well with orders. He'd made a career of it. "Yes, sir."

Walt rapped the roof of the cruiser with the palm of his hand. "I knew I could count on you."

It scared Caden how much the older man's approval meant. But this stunt of McKenna's—not the IED—had easily taken five years off his life. Providing she wasn't on her deathbed, he planned to give her what-for and then some.

Chapter Seventeen

Hours later, McKenna stared at Caden's grim features, lit by the glow of the dashboard clock as he drove them home from the hospital.

A muscle tapped a steady drumbeat in his cheek. "I realize you're blonde, but this—"

"Wait right there, Caden Wallis." She twisted around. "There's no need to bring my hair into it."

One-handing the steering wheel, he plucked a piece of charred ash from her hair. "I like your hair."

She deflated against the upholstery. "Oh."

"You promised you wouldn't do anything without me."

"Did I?" She narrowed her gaze. "Did I really say that?"

His eyes darkened with a dangerous glint. She'd do well not to push this man. She might not be ready for the fallout.

"You're an intelligent woman, McKenna. Therefore, I know the only reason you went alone was that you were mad at me."

She fidgeted.

"It was stupid."

She reared. "Stupid?"

"And selfish." He strangled the wheel. "Do you know what your death would've done to your family? To the people who love you?"

Did he number himself among those who loved her?

"Your death would've wrecked their lives. Devastated them."

Them. Not him.

She flopped against the seat. "I didn't want anything to happen to Cecil."

Only the headlights pierced the darkness of the road. It was desolate in this stretch of the Pea Island National Wildlife Refuge. Dunes on both sides, the highway a thin ribbon superimposed by man. Vanity against what was elementally uncontrollable and unstoppable. The dark waters of the Sound and the rolling tide of the ocean were a palpable force.

She'd been so happy to see him outside the curtain in the ER, but the smile had died on her face once the tirade began.

"What were you thinking, McKenna?"

For a man whose few words were usually carefully parsed, why now did he become so vocal?

"That's the problem. You weren't thinking. Do you have some crazy death wish to—"

"You'd be the expert on death wishes."

His gaze snapped to hers. She beheld anger, bewilderment, and fear. Fear for her.

"Not anymore." He whipped face forward. "Thanks to you." He pinched his lips together so hard, they almost disappeared.

They went through the tri-villages of Rodanthe, Waves, and Salvo, one in quick succession after the other. At 10:00 p.m. most of the homes were dark, reminding her for a split second of the darkness of the tank. The blackness as the water closed over her head . . .

She must've made a sound.

"The nurse said your lungs didn't sustain permanent damage. But if we need to—"

"I'm fine. Banker strong."

"Almost Banker dead, McKenna." He shuddered. "If you hadn't gotten in the tank and under the water . . . No way we would've broken through the door in time."

"You didn't hurt yourself getting me out, did you?" She touched his hand on the wheel.

Jolting like he'd been tasered, he moved his hand. "I'm not some pathetic wimp. I'm tougher than that."

"Never doubted it."

His eyes narrowed as if he suspected he was being mocked.

McKenna bit the inside of her cheek. "Just glad you believe it now too."

Slowing the vehicle, he reached for her. His forefinger and thumb gently caressed the dimple in her chin.

McKenna leaned toward him, her heartbeat erratic.

His lips parted. "McKenna, I . . ." He swallowed. Returned his gaze to the windshield. Dropped his hand. "I called your dad from the waiting room."

Disappointment surged. What had she wanted him to say? What had she wanted him to do? She was the idiot. "Shall I anticipate another tongue-lashing from him?"

"You need one." He flicked her a look. "Since I suspect you're too old to be grounded."

She snorted.

"The firefighters extinguished the blaze before the turtles were harmed. Dr. Thompson arrived not long after. The building is pretty much a total loss, but with the help of the volunteers—"

"Minus me."

"Almost minus you permanently," he snarled. "The sprinkler system had been deliberately disabled. The smashed lock rendered inoperable."

She stopped talking. Silence fell between them.

Emerging into the welcome streetlights of the Avon shopping center, he cleared his throat. "The turtles have been transferred to the aquatic center in Manteo."

"I'm glad they're okay. I was starting to develop a real sympathy for boiled shrimp." She laughed.

He didn't. "Who knew you'd be at the center alone tonight?"

She stiffened. "Do you think someone targeted me? Why?"

"Who knew, McKenna, other than Lovey?"

"If you're implying that Bryce—"

"Hinson was out of his mind with terror when he discovered you were trapped inside."

Dread coiled in her gut. As soon as Bryce got off duty, she'd have a lot of explaining to do with him too.

"Alonso. Your boat. Skipjacks. Why is it you appear to be at the center of everything that's happened over the last month?"

She blinked. "Why would anyone want me dead, Caden?"

"You tell me." His mouth tightened. "Unless, of course, you're ready to believe this is my fault."

Bryce's theory. But what motive would anyone—much less Caden—have for targeting her family? Unless he was involved with drug traffickers and this was about retaliation against her father.

Had she been blinded by the feelings Caden Wallis brought to life within her?

"You *do* think I . . ." His jaw went hard as granite.

She'd waited too long to respond. "I don't think any such thing." But did she?

Her dad had taught her to trust her instincts. Bryce believed Caden was playing her. Taking advantage of her vulnerability. Was he right?

Even now, gazing at him across the car, the new haircut only accentuated the smoldering hot intensity of his dark eyes. As for his mouth—his lips were stern with disapproval. She looked away. His mouth made rational thought flee.

Good thing she was sitting down because Caden Wallis made her weak in the knees. Was that his intent? To keep her rattled? Yet, if he wanted her dead, why had he rescued her from the burning building?

Bryce would say to disguise his guilt. To make himself a hero. To ingratiate himself with her father and the police.

"I think—"

She jumped when he spoke.

"I think all of this—the murders, the fires, the vandalism—is a calculated distraction from something deeper that's going on."

"A smokescreen."

He glared at her. "This isn't a joke, McKenna."

"I realize that, Caden. I'm the one nearly lobster boiled tonight. You think the events are a ruse designed to keep my dad and Bryce running in circles? From finding out what is really going on?"

"Yes." He raked a hand over his head.

Her own hand twitched, a traitorous longing to run her fingers through his newly shorn locks. A yearning to satisfy her curiosity. Was his hair fine like hers, or coarser? She clenched her hand into a fist.

"Who knew you were at the center besides Lovey and Hinson?"

"Laddie, Norm, the others on the crime watch tonight. But Bryce didn't—" She gasped. "Talbot. I saw him this afternoon. I mentioned— But why would—"

"I don't know." He threw her a grim look. "People do crazy, contradictory things. It didn't take Afghanistan to show me people are capable of incredible evil. I learned to survive by never trusting anyone. Never putting my life in anyone else's hands. A lesson maybe it's time you learn."

The cynicism, the bitterness—no matter how much he believed them valid—that wasn't the kind of person she wanted to become. She cocked her head. "Does that include you, Caden?"

His eyes went hard. "I should be at the top of your list of most untrusted."

Arriving home, he parked in the driveway and cut the engine. The house lay dark. Her grandmother must be asleep. That meant . . .

"So Lovey doesn't know?"

"First thing in the morning, either you tell her or I will. Before she hears it from someone else."

McKenna sagged. "Because she *will* hear it from someone else."

His too handsome face smirked. "Gotta love the Tuckahoe grapevine."

She wasn't feeling the love. Thrusting open the door, she slung her legs out. "I get it, Caden. I screwed up. I'm sorry."

"McKenna . . ."

She closed her eyes. Good thing he didn't realize what her name rumbling between his lips did to her insides, or he'd think her a bigger fool than he already did.

"Please don't do anything like that ever again."

Just when she was almost ready to ignore her instincts and consider him the wretched human being he'd like her to believe him to be, he went and said things like that. Something that reeled her in again. Pulled her under. Like a riptide.

"I can't take another loss in my life, Beach Girl." He kept his face turned away, but there was an uncharacteristic hitch in his voice. "I'd be wrecked. Okay?"

A not so tiny thrill went through her.

"Okay," she whispered.

❖ ❖ ❖

Nothing happened over the next few days, except news of another tropical storm brewing off the Florida coast. The high school football team had done well at Friday's game. Caden was surprised at how much he looked forward to seeing the guys in the afternoons. They'd started calling him Coach Wallis.

He pushed the last order through the window to Earlene. Ambling out for his mid-morning break, the kitchen door swung behind him as he surveyed the crowded diner. Pastor Guthrie, Bob the Postman, and Laddie sat at a table for four. Earlene carried the breakfast order to the old hippie in a nearby booth. Wouldn't be long before Walt made his usual appearance.

Behind the counter, Caden grabbed a mug and poured himself some coffee. Bill Scarborough didn't look him in the eye, but he didn't get up and walk away, either. Empty stool or not, Caden would just as soon not sit next to anyone who didn't want his company.

Local hostility had thawed once it became common knowledge that he helped rescue McKenna from the burning building. Though, as Hinson told the story, he became the primary hero, not Caden. But Caden didn't care about getting the credit as long as she was safe.

Speaking of whom . . .

Leaving a customer, McKenna tucked a tendril of sunshine behind her ear and gave him a sweet smile. His gut squeezed, a sensation growing more familiar by the day. Like every time he got within ten feet of McKenna Dockery.

He didn't know what had possessed him to say what he did to her the other night. Except that sitting in the car, her face pale and her eyes luminous in the moonlight . . .

Caden hunched his shoulders. He had only to recall what could've happened and he got a sick—the Banker word was *quamish*—feeling in the pit of his stomach.

He hated being out of control. If this is what caring about someone involved, he wanted no part of it.

She was making her way over to him. He turned, absurdly panicked. He needed to stay far, far away from her. He'd been keeping his distance, taking evasive action all week.

Pastor Guthrie must've have noted his hesitation because he waved Caden over. Gripping his cup, Caden practically launched himself at their table. A pastor wasn't his first pick for companionship, but any port in a storm.

Eyes flashing, McKenna ground to a halt midway across the diner.

Dropping his gaze, Caden took a deep swig, forgetting it was coffee and not a shot of whiskey. The coffee scalded his mouth. He sputtered, eyes watering.

"They're calling it—" Without pausing, Laddie pounded him across his shoulder blades. "—Frieda."

McKenna pushed into the kitchen, a serves-you-right smirk on her pretty face. He scowled at his mug. Beach Girl had a mean streak.

Pastor Guthrie handed Caden a napkin. "I was hoping it would stay out to sea, but it's turned and intensified. They're predicting it'll be Cat 1 when it makes landfall somewhere along the Florida coast."

Bob the Postman settled in his chair, the pith helmet cocked precariously on his knobby knee. "It's always the *F*s that get us."

Pastor nodded. "Fran. Floyd."

"They all get us sooner or later 'cause we stick out. Like a broken fingernail snags everything," Laddie grunted.

Bell jangling, an agitated Stanhope rushed inside. He hadn't been to the diner for a while. Research, Lovey had mentioned.

"I've been looking everywhere for you." Stanhope's lip curled. "Should've known you'd be here." He snorted. "Where else?"

The pastor and Laddie appeared as mystified as Caden. Until he realized Stanhope was talking to Bob the Postman.

"Per union regulation, I'm allowed—"

"Where's my package?" Stanhope thrust out his hand.

The pastor and Laddie exchanged amused grins. Bob the Postman's face went florid.

Laddie clapped his palms on the tabletop and rose. "That's my cue."

Stanhope gritted his teeth. "Neither snow nor rain nor Skipjacks pancakes . . ."

But Laddie didn't venture far, his curiosity like Caden's, awakened. Bob the Postman rustled through the mailbag on the floor.

Stanhope grimaced. "Please don't overtax yourself."

Muttering, Bob the Postman extracted a large, padded envelope. "What's so all-fired impor—"

Stanhope snatched the envelope from his hands. "At last." He sank into Laddie's vacated chair and tore into it.

Pastor Guthrie peered across the table. "Those look official."

McKenna reappeared from the kitchen just then, chatting with Earlene and waving her hands like when something made her glad or mad. From the dire looks she shot his way, he figured mad. She slammed something on the counter.

Oh. He rolled his tongue over his teeth. She'd found the calendar he marked. Exactly as he'd meant her to. Part of a carefully planned, strategic retreat. Or was it self-sabotage?

Either way, if he'd minded his business instead of traveling to this sandbox at the end of nowhere, he wouldn't be in this—

"German?" Pastor Guthrie pursed his lips.

Stanhope did a quick scan of the papers. "A colleague made the copies for me. They'd been lost in the German archives since the Allies advanced on Berlin in 1945."

"Care to share?" Bob the Postman sneered. "Or if you do, will you have to kill us?"

Stanhope ignored him. "I think I've found it. The holy grail of missing U-boats."

Bob the Postman gave him a cock-eyed stare. "Haven't you found enough of those already?"

Pastor Guthrie raised his brow. "I didn't realize there were any left to be found."

"Around fifty were never accounted for." Stanhope poked his finger at the document. "*U-925* left the German submarine base in Kristiansand, Norway, in August 1944. Her first war patrol, she was to sail through the Icelandic passage to the North Atlantic for weather-reporting duty. But the U-boat and all fifty-one hands on board vanished without further transmission. There's been no plausible explanation for her loss."

Pastor Guthrie smiled. "I'm guessing you're going to say 'until now.'"

"Historians have always believed the boat lay somewhere at the bottom of the Norwegian Sea. Or the North Sea." Stanhope's eyes glinted. "But suppose it actually lies somewhere off Cape Hatteras?"

Bob the Postman whistled the opening bars from *The Twilight Zone.* "Nazi ghost ship."

Stanhope flicked him an annoyed look as Talbot Rivenbark strolled into the diner and joined them.

Laddie hovered over Caden's shoulder. "I ever tell you boys 'bout the time my dad set off to fish one morning, only to have one of them Nazi wolfpack subs rise right out of the water in front of him?"

Bob the Postman sighed. "Only 'bout five million times."

"Let me tell you, my dad got himself and the boat out of there quick as—"

"Why do you think the U-boat would be so far off course, Professor?" Caribbean Jack asked.

Caden blinked. A small crowd had encircled the table. Earlene. McKenna too.

"There were off-the-book missions." Stanhope paged through the document. "Not only crewman aboard, but also saboteurs. The glass bottle McKenna found got me thinking."

"But what leads you to believe something like that happened here?" Caribbean Jack probed.

Caden had a clear view of the man's eyes. Shrewd. Gray. Flat like a shark. A man who blended into the background yet was somehow always at the center of the action. Just nosy like the rest of Tuckahoe? Or did his presence indicate something sinister? Was he involved in transporting the heroin from the mainland?

"I remembered my oral-history interview with Wanda Ballance." Distracted, Stanhope had become engrossed in the paperwork. "Her cousin worked at the Loop Shack on Ocracoke. Night of September twenty-third, sonar pinged a vessel off the coast."

Pastor Guthrie's brow wrinkled. "September 1944, a hurricane was brewing off shore."

Stanhope flipped some pages, studying the contents. "The Coast Guard station on Hatteras received a transmission from the Yaupon station, but the signal dropped suddenly. Due to the approaching storm and high winds, no planes could take off to investigate."

"Yaupon?" Laddie hissed.

Caden cut his eyes to where, happily oblivious, Lovey made change for a customer.

"Secret-agent stuff. Cool." Caribbean Jack laughed but there was no merriment in his dead gray eyes. "Are you suggesting a Nazi U-boat attempted to land spies in North Carolina?"

Paul Stanhope's mouth tightened. "In 1942 other submarines landed German saboteurs in New Jersey and in Florida before the spies were apprehended. Operation Pastorius. Historical fact. Not so farfetched."

Bob the Postman's eyes bulged. "Any Nazi gold involved in this tall tale of yours?"

"Not gold." Stanhope drew himself up. "Diamonds. I mean—" He clamped his lips together.

A ripple of laughter echoed around the table. But Caden became aware of an undercurrent of tension.

Caribbean Jack folded his arms across his barrel-like chest. "I'm scuba certified." His mouth quirked. "Anyone else up for treasure hunting?"

"Lots of deep-sea diving talent around here." Bob the Postman plopped his helmet on his head. "Finders keepers. Banker motto."

"No treasure hunting." Stanhope gathered his papers in an untidy pile. "That U-boat, if it's where I suspect, contains the mortal remains of fifty-one souls. It's protected as a war grave."

Disapproving looks were cast at Stanhope, but the crowd drifted to their own tables. Laddie, Bob the Postman, and Pastor Guthrie took their leave as well. Stanhope clutched the file to his chest.

Caden scraped back his chair. "If you don't mind me saying so, that's some can of worms you've opened."

"This would be the discovery of a lifetime."

Caden scrubbed his hand over his beard. "Diamonds?"

Stanhope thumped the file. "Axel unearthed a postwar interview with the wife of a Nazi war criminal. Her husband was SS, part of the division that looted art treasures. She claimed a pouch of diamonds was given to a young German commando."

"Blood diamonds." Caden's lip curled. "No need to speculate the fate of the original owners."

"In the interview, you get the impression the bored, Aryan *hausfrau* had a relationship with the commando. He was shipping out on a secret mission to the United States. The diamonds were to be liquidated as the need arose to maintain the cover of the four-man team."

"A terrorist cell." Caden shook his head. "That sounds like something ripped from today's headlines."

Stanhope gave him a grim smile. "German commandos were highly trained. After the war, the Nazis who got away are known to have trained members of the Palestinian Liberation Organization."

But Nazi terrorists on Hatteras?

"Utilizing the rediscovered sonar reading and an unexplained explosion noted by the Hatteras station, I've been working on triangulating the precise area where the wreck could lie. Once I fix the location, I'll contact the National Institute of Oceanography to see if I can get them interested in launching a research vessel to explore the find."

"What do you think happened to the U-boat?"

"No Allied reports of a kill. Could've been the hurricane. An accident?" Stanhope shrugged. "Average life expectancy in the *Kriegsmarine* was measured in months, not years. The average age of the crew?" He tilted his head. "A lot younger than you."

The more things changed, the more they stayed the same. Young men died in the wars old men declared.

He didn't share Stanhope's fascination with a seventy-year-old mystery. "Perhaps what's buried should stay buried." Tuckahoe faced a more immediate, modern-day menace. Something Stanhope should consider before heading off by himself. "Professor, I know I don't have to tell you to be careful, but . . ."

Stanhope raised his chin. "It's probably no more than academic wishful thinking. Sheer speculation."

"Drug traffickers aren't particular." Caden grimaced. "Nazi diamonds would be right up their alley. Feed their greed."

"I hear you." Stanhope straightened. "I'll be careful."

Caden's internal McKenna radar went on alert. She sat at the counter in deep conversation with Hinson. When had he shown up?

It must be true that nature—and Hinson—abhorred a vacuum. At least when it came to McKenna. Since the fire, Hinson had become even more solicitous. Whereas Caden had made a tactical decision to withdraw.

Until he left, however, he'd promised Walt to see no harm came to her. Although, stubborn as she was, that was easier said than done.

But no matter his jumbled, conflicted feelings, he meant to protect her most of all from himself.

◈ ◈ ◈

When it came to Caden Wallis, sometimes McKenna didn't know if she was coming or going. He'd said that losing her would wreck him. But in the last few days, he'd done everything humanly possible to avoid her.

She plodded over the dune to her favorite spot near the house. There he sat in one of the Adirondack chairs. It had become his favorite spot too.

He was the most confusing human being she'd ever met. Or maybe it was just she who was confused. But he made her mad. So mad.

She rolled the wall-sized lighthouse calendar between her fists. He'd left it for her to find. She was sure of it. Making a point. He'd marked through every square since the first day they met with a big red X. And his departure date—two weeks and counting—goose-egged with an equally fat red circle.

Kicking sand, she plowed her way to him. He flicked a glance at her before returning his stony, dark-eyed stare to the churning waves. She chucked the calendar into his lap.

He didn't even flinch. "I'll finish my punch list for Skipjacks before I go."

She threw herself into the adjacent chair. "Sometimes I think the best thing I could do for you is to just take that leg of yours and beat some sense into you."

McKenna clapped her hand over her mouth. His eyes went large.

They stared at each other in shocked silence as the words hovered in the air between them.

For the love of— What kind of person said something like that to a man who'd lost a leg in the service of his country?

"Oh, Caden. I'm so—"

He laughed. Laughed so hard, he actually fell over in the sand. Tears leaked out of his eyes.

"I should've never—"

Still laughing.

"I don't know what gets into me sometimes. My brain disconnects from my mouth and . . ."

Gasping for breath, he crawled into the chair again.

McKenna pursed her lips. "It wasn't that funny."

Several beats passed before he got his unrestrained hilarity—at her expense—under control. "One of life's few certainties is that I can count on you to give it to me straight." He grinned. "Where have you been all my life?"

"Waiting right here in Tuckahoe." She looked at him. "What took you so long?"

Chapter Eighteen

THE GRIN SLID FROM CADEN'S FACE. WHAT DID SHE MEAN SHE'D been waiting? For what? For a broken-down soldier with a quilt in his arms?

Waiting, the gentler voice in Caden's heart whispered, *for me?*

Gathering his courage, he took a deep breath. "I went to the university for one year on a football scholarship, but I got hurt the first season. I didn't have the build to play anything more than college football anyway." He stole a look at McKenna's face. "And I thought, what's the point of taking the hits if you can't go pro?"

She'd gone motionless.

"The army seemed my best career option."

She fingered the hoop dangling from her earlobe. "You liked being in the army, didn't you?"

With a concentrated force of will, he peeled his gaze off her fingers . . . her earlobe . . . the slender curve of her neck . . . It was always easy to get distracted when he was with her. But he knew in his gut this was the moment he had to tell her. And when he set his mind to something, he didn't stop until it was done.

He gripped the armrests of the chair. "You can't possibly imagine how much I loved the army."

"What did you love about it?"

"Everything." His gaze flitted to the foaming tide. "The camaraderie. The friendships. Working together for a purpose larger than yourself."

"Belonging?"

His eyes cut to her.

"It became your family."

How did she know that when he'd only just begun to understand it himself? "The army was the only place I ever belonged."

"Until you didn't."

It had always been about more than losing the leg. More than losing Nikki. It had been about losing everything he was.

Drawing her knees to her chin, McKenna waited, letting him work through the turmoil. Letting him tell his story, his way. So he told her. He made himself speak in a matter-of-fact voice. He couldn't have said any of it otherwise. He wouldn't have been able to hold himself together.

He told her about Q course. How he'd loved being pushed to the breaking point and not breaking. The box. Rucking marches.

"Only thirty percent is physical. It's really a mental test."

Following his MOS training—military occupational specialty, in civilian speak—he'd flat out adored Robin Sage. Suggesting he might have more screws loose than the rest of them. He'd taken every hard thing they threw at him and asked for more. Begged for it, actually. Because, unlike the others, he knew he could handle what most could not. He believed he'd already faced the worst life had to offer and come out on top.

In hindsight, the sheer arrogance of such naiveté took his breath. Like he'd been daring disaster to strike.

Chin on her knees, McKenna listened, her eyes never leaving his face. The wind made a beautiful mess of her hair.

His voice quieted as he told her about his first tour. He didn't spare her any of the sordid details of who he was. Who he really was. The womanizing, the work-hard, play-hard mentality. The strange, white noise that filled his head during combat. The chaos of war.

She didn't flinch or blink.

"I was the MPC handler on the team." At the question in her gaze, he explained. "Multi-Purpose Canine." As a dog lover, she'd understand about his special relationship with Friday.

Her eyes were wide open. But when he got to the part about deploying for the last tour, he had to close his. He recounted for her the constant, sandblasting grit of the wind. The strange, stomach-churning smells. The noise. His team. Joe's favorite song.

Sanchez . . . and the last patrol. The sudden, roaring pain. The tide of blood dripping from his fingers. The sound of Velcro ripping on the second tourniquet. The blessed oblivion. The surgeries where they managed to save his right leg. Rehab.

Only then did he realize her fingers were twined in his. She gripped his hand.

Done with the telling, he fell against the chair. The words that had been locked inside him for so long were out. Floating free on a sea breeze high above their heads.

"Thank you," was all she said.

"You're welcome."

They sat there for the longest time. Thinking their own thoughts, staring out over the ocean waves. When the jerking in his chest from the leftover pain subsided, only then did he allow himself to wonder what she thought of him now.

He cleared his raspy throat. He didn't usually string that many words together. Okay, he never did. He wished he could see her eyes. He liked looking into her eyes.

She ducked her head, playing with his fingers. "You have great hands. Strong. Capable. Working hands." She hid her face in the blonde curtain of her hair. "Gentle hands."

Heart thudding, he wasn't sure how he should respond, if at all. So he went with, "Is that all you like about me?"

McKenna laughed. "Fishing for compliments?" She shoulder-butted him. "But okay, I'll play. You are very intelligent—although you like to keep it buried deep in that thick skull of yours."

"Not sure that qualifies as a compliment. What else?"

She made a show of rolling her eyes. "Shouldn't it be your turn?"

"That's easy." He shrugged. "I like everything about you."

Her eyebrow arched. "Everything?"

"I like how you make me laugh, usually at myself."

She raised one shoulder and let it drop. "It's a calling."

"I like how you make me want to believe things . . ." His throat closed.

Things he lacked the courage to say out loud.

"I like your heart." She placed her hand on his chest. "Though you don't like to admit you have one."

The warmth of her skin soaked through his shirt. "I-I forgot something else I like about you."

"And since we find ourselves in a mutual admiration society, what would that be?"

"I believe I'd like your mouth." She was so close he could feel her breath on his face. He swallowed. "But I'm not sure."

She tilted her head. "What should we do so you can be sure?" Her eyes had become a dark shade of blue. But this time he could almost guarantee she wasn't angry at him.

"A taste test." His Adam's apple bobbed. "For scientific purposes."

"For scientific purposes," she whispered. "Were you always this intense? Even before Afghanistan?"

His lips curved. "Yes."

She wound her hands into the short hair on the back of his neck. "I thought so." And she pulled him closer. Her lips parted.

Heart hammering, he unplugged his mind. Stopped listening to the voices inside his head telling him not to go there. To back off. That this wasn't a good idea.

Because it *was* a good idea. The best idea ever. An idea that had first taken root on a beach one morning in September. Moving inexorably toward this moment. As sure and inevitable as the tide.

Fingering the cleft in her chin, his mouth brushed her soft lips. His senses filled with the intoxicating scent and exquisite taste of her. He wanted to take his time. Go slow. Memorize the feel of her in his arms. Slipping his hand beneath her silken hair, his thumb caressed her cheek. Her breath hitched. Though she came willingly into his arms, she drew back an inch. But he gave chase to her lips. Capturing them.

The sweetness of her mouth blew him away, igniting an explosion within him. He'd never known such sweetness. The roar continued to build, more powerful than the breakers crashing on the shore. And he gave himself to the hunger.

A hunger for her. For her goodness.

McKenna Dockery was the most beautiful woman he'd ever known. Inside and out. And he might never get enough.

She cupped his face between her palms. Her skin scraped against the roughness of his beard as he buried his face into her neck. Held her. Breathed in the essence of who she was.

Caden had no words for her. There was only this moment. Who they were when they were with each other.

When she sighed—a sound of quiet contentment—a weight lifted off his chest. And something of what he believed he'd lost forever was restored.

Chapter Nineteen

SHE LOVED CADEN. MAYBE SINCE THE NIGHT SHE'D FOUND HIM grappling with pain. But love was a fragile thing.

That evening, Dr. Stanhope called. "I've been out on the *Cousteau*. Using sidescan sonar and a magnetometer, I think I've found the wreck of the *U-925*." He couldn't keep the excitement out of his voice. "I need to do a site survey to verify the location. Would you come and take underwater photos to document the find *in situ*?"

Phone pressed against her ear, she leaned against the headboard of her bed. "Me? Why me?" It had been a long time since she'd donned a wetsuit.

"You've done this before. With your fiancé, right?"

She had dived another U-boat, the *352*, in a popular dive spot off Beaufort with Shawn. The waters were warmer south of Hatteras. He'd loved exploring. She'd loved taking pictures of an undersea world filled with color beyond imagining.

They were supposed to go sport diving in the Caribbean on their honeymoon. She wasn't sure why she'd kept the suit, except that it had been expensive. But that wasn't the real reason. It had been something she'd shared with Shawn. And she hadn't been ready to give him up.

Until earlier on the beach.

"How about tomorrow, McKenna? With the storm raking the Georgia coastline and headed north, I think we're facing a short dive window."

"Does it have to be now?"

The professor's tone roughened. "I have a bad feeling I may not be the only one looking. That we're running out of time before it's plundered. So this needs to remain top secret between you and me, McKenna. Can I count on you for tomorrow?"

At dinner, Caden had been more quiet than usual. Brooding. Surely he felt the same as she for him or he couldn't have kissed her like that. Or was that only her inexperience talking? Either way, she wasn't sure she was up to facing him so soon tomorrow at Skipjacks. Not until she sorted her feelings.

She wrenched her attention to the phone. "I'll be there, Dr. Stanhope."

❖ ❖ ❖

At first light, she crept out of the house and headed to Tuckahoe. Laddie's boat was gone from its berth. Caribbean Jack's too.

Waving her over, Dr. Stanhope looked like a kid eager to embark on a great adventure. As soon as she was aboard, he guided the *Cousteau* out of the marina. "It'll take a few hours to get to the site. Until then, just relax."

On the gunwale, she wrapped her arms around herself. The waves brought to her mind the Ocean Waves quilt she'd made and the journey the quilt had taken. With a lot of help from Lovey, she'd poured her heart into every stitch. Her hopes and dreams for the future.

The boat motored past the channel markers where pelicans sat like enthroned aviary kings. They soon left behind the mudflats. But her thoughts stubbornly returned to Caden and the quilt.

Stanhope stood in the open wheelhouse behind the windscreen. "You didn't tell anybody what we were doing today, did you? Until my findings are verified and the proper authorities notified, I don't want to run the risk of the sub being looted for war trophies."

Dipping and lifting, the bow of the boat cut a *V* through the chop of the water. "Nope. Earlene is covering for me today."

She'd believed she was making the quilt for her new life with Shawn, and when he died, she'd sent it away. But God, in His sovereign providence, had brought it back to her . . . in the arms of another man.

From the beginning, had the quilt been meant for someone else? For a man she had yet to meet?

Dr. Stanhope threaded the twenty-foot Boston Whaler through the treacherous sandbars and shallows of the channel. Reaching open water, the land fell away, and he increased the speed to thirty knots.

After yesterday . . . One kiss. But what a kiss.

McKenna drew a lungful of salty air. An outstanding kiss. Caden Wallis might just be the world's best kisser.

She flushed. By his own admission, it was a skill he'd gained through experience. She felt so out of her depth with him. But when his mouth touched hers, all reason had fled.

Only later did she remember she needed to hold a little of herself apart. The way he did. Self-preservation of the heart. Yet yesterday . . .

McKenna ran the tip of her finger over her bottom lip. He'd tasted like cinnamon chewing gum. His sandalwood scent tantalized her nostrils. And he'd held nothing back. He'd been sweet, loving, gentle. The way she'd always imagined he could be if only he'd allow himself. As if in that moment he, too, had forgotten the need to guard himself, to hide. He'd given her a glimpse of his real self. Or was that just wishful thinking on her part?

She felt ready to open herself to new possibilities. There would always be a place in her heart that only belonged to Shawn, but she was ready to admit, the rest of it belonged to Caden Wallis. If he wanted it.

McKenna felt the Whaler lessen speed. Dr. Stanhope pulled back the throttle. "I think we're here." He dropped anchor.

She gazed at the open expanse of greenish-blue water. To the south, angry gray thunderheads billowed on the horizon. She strapped on her buoyancy compensator device.

In one smooth motion, Dr. Stanhope swung his twin steel eighties of compressed air over his head and onto the back of his BCD. "The photographs will help me secure funding for a thorough archaeological excavation."

She screwed the air regulator onto one of her tanks, bit into the mouthpiece, and took a deep, exploratory breath. He helped her mount her cylinders. She adjusted the straps on her shoulders.

Twenty-four miles off Cape Point, the water was much colder. Here, like mighty underwater rivers, the Labrador Current and the Gulf Stream met.

"I thought we'd be farther out." She fiddled with the weight belt around her midsection. She faced away from nearby Yaupon Island, too close for comfort in her opinion. Though from a distance, only scrub bush was visible on the low island.

Maybe Laddie was right. Maybe Yaupon *was* haunted.

Stanhope threw the dive flag buoy overboard. Not that there were any other boats around. "I believe the wreck is less than one hundred feet below. Relatively shallow."

A hundred feet didn't sound shallow to her.

"The sub must have been running along the surface when she failed. U-boats were capable of greater speed on the surface." He cinched the dive computer around his wrist. "Fitting my theory that the sub had just sent men in a raft to shore."

"But it doesn't explain why the sub ended up on the bottom of the ocean."

He shook his head. "Best-case scenario, there will be something obvious to indicate why the sub was lost. A hole in the hull from an unreported depth charge or an encounter with a mine."

She slipped fins over her booties.

"We will not attempt to enter the vessel. Stay close. It's easy to get disoriented. I'll go first to tie the anchor line off onto the wreck. When I return, we'll go along the line. In the meantime, stay alert." His eyes clouded as he did a three-sixty scan of the ocean. "There could be people who don't want this wreck discovered."

She jerked. The snorkel attached to her mask fluttered. "Would someone really kill to keep its location secret after seventy-plus years?"

"If there was a fortune in diamonds involved. Antiquities trafficking is a billion-dollar enterprise."

She peered over the railing. "Are the diamonds on the sub? Or did the commandos take them to the island?"

"Could be on the sub. Or with the storm surge, maybe the diamonds never made it off the island."

She shivered. "It kind of creeps me out. U-boats. Nazis."

"The Great Storm of '44 provided a perfect opportunity for an undetected landing."

"On Yaupon Island?"

"Makes sense, doesn't it?"

"You think the fake Freeman was one of the saboteurs?"

"Only your grandmother and he made it off the island alive after the storm."

McKenna's eyes widened. "You think he killed the people on Yaupon? Her family too?"

"I'm betting the real Freeman didn't give up his uniform willingly."

"But why didn't he kill Lovey?"

"We may never know. Perhaps he believed her too young to identify him. And time has proven him right. She hasn't remembered anything."

There'd always seemed to be a dense black fog in Lovey's mind when it came to recalling the events of that long ago time. Had her family died in the storm surge? Or at the hands of a ruthless killer? Had Lovey seen them murdered?

If so, maybe her "amnesia" was a self-protective mechanism. The mind's cushion against an unspeakable horror.

The wind kicked up. McKenna tucked her hair beneath the folds of the neoprene hoodie. "Lovey doesn't need to hear about this."

"Analysis of what's recovered from subsequent dives could take months, years before the press is informed. If we get lucky, I hope to recover the captain's notebook or personal items to prove the provenance of the *U-925*." He tilted his head. "Of course, I could've calculated wrong. There may be nothing below us."

"There'll probably be something. If not this wreck, then another."

In the Graveyard of the Atlantic, sometimes wrecks were stacked on top of each other. From the time of the Carolina colony, there'd been lost ships, their bones strewn over the sandy bottom like the dry bones of Ezekiel's vision.

McKenna curled her fingers around the strap of Stanhope's digital underwater camera hanging around her neck. "Why now? Why didn't someone come looking for the diamonds long ago?"

He clambered onto the boat rail. "You're assuming someone hasn't been looking. Until my friend Axel found the lost archives, no one but the missing German would've had any idea where to look. And it's only in the last few decades that we've possessed the technology to explore the deep."

It didn't make sense that the German could still be looking. Even if somehow he'd managed to evade the authorities, he was most likely dead by now.

McKenna shook her head. "I don't think—"

Stanhope secured his mask over his face, cutting off further conversation. At his thumbs-up, she nodded. Standing on the side with one end of the tied-off line, he gripped an LED dive light and stepped feet first into the water, shattering the surface into a thousand liquid shards. The sea soon settled itself over the spot where he'd disappeared. Only a momentary ripple marked his passing. The waves rocked against the hull. But for all intents and purposes, they were afloat over a graveyard.

Fathoms below, in the forever dark, icy waters of the Mid-Atlantic, fifty-one souls had met their doom. Forgotten until now. Or were they?

Surely there was nothing to be feared from long-dead Nazis. If Stanhope was correct, the U-boat posed a danger of a more recent kind. Treasure-hunters. Pirates. Antiquity traffickers. Men who wouldn't hesitate to kill.

Thinking of Alonso, maybe someone already had. Had they been too quick to assume Alonso was killed as a result of drug trafficking? It wouldn't be the first time thieves fell out with each other so as not to split the loot.

She swung her legs over the side. What was keeping Dr. Stanhope?

Just when she was ready to radio the Coast Guard, Stanhope's black-hooded head popped above the surface of the water. Although until he swam closer, it was hard to tell it was him through the mask.

He removed the regulator from his mouth and sculled in the water next to the boat. "It's there. We've found it." He pumped the air, his fist sending up a spray of water.

She hesitated. "I don't feel good about leaving the boat unprotected." Shawn had taught her to never dive alone and to always leave somebody on the boat.

"There was no one else I could trust."

She could think of many people in Tuckahoe more qualified than she. Her father, for instance. Bryce. Several deputies had diver certification.

Was she foolish to be on a boat in the middle of nowhere with

Stanhope? It was an easy place to make someone disappear. He'd lived in Tuckahoe for over a decade. Yet, like Alonso, how much did anyone really know about him?

His mouth had taken on a grim cast. "I've taken steps to ensure that if anything happens to me, the evidence I've uncovered will not be lost to history again." His eyes blazed. "Let's go. Time's wasting."

Time . . . Her great nemesis.

She adjusted the mask over her eyes and nose, tucked the regulator into her mouth, and bit into the rubber. Bending at the waist and hand to mask, she jackknifed forward. Slamming into the water.

Immediately, the water closed over her head. Engulfing her. Enfolding her in its cold embrace. With a slight hiss, she took her first breath from the regulator.

McKenna grabbed the anchor line, one hand coiled around it as she sank. At this depth, the water was pale green like an old soda glass. Farther down, it became a deeper blue.

She'd forgotten how peaceful it was here. The breathtaking colors. Where past, present, and future flowed together as one.

A school of silvery fish swam past her peripheral vision. She glanced upward as bubbles streamed toward the rapidly diminishing hull above her head. Gliding downward, she pinched her nose with her free hand to equalize the pressure on her eardrums as her depth increased.

Her ears popped. Good. But she couldn't see Dr. Stanhope.

She checked the gauge on her wrist. Fifty feet. Colder at this level. To sink at a more rapid pace, she vented air in her vest.

At seventy feet, a flash caught the corner of her eye. A shark. Her heart fluttered, increasing her breathing rate. Only a gray shark. Usually not aggressive.

She vented more air at eighty feet. Way colder now. The *Cousteau* was no longer visible. The watery sky over her head glowed a pea green. The current was strong here. Her body felt sluggish, like moving through thick, translucent mud. But below she spotted the glow of the dive light. Slowing her descent, she tightened her fist around the line to brake.

A black silhouette rose out of the murky gloom, lying starboard on its side. Her breath caught. All these years, waiting to be found. Were they the first to behold its final resting place?

Chill bumps rose on her arms beneath the neoprene skin. The U-boat's conning tower rose like a barnacle-encrusted monolith from the silt. Anything wooden on the deck had long since rotted away.

Dr. Stanhope signaled her over. His black-gloved finger pointed at the encrusted hatches. She brought the Nikon to her face. Peering through, she clicked the shutter.

A lump formed in her throat. Closed hatches. Had no one escaped the sinking sub? Did fifty-one men lay entombed within the steel tube of death? She cut her eyes at the sea floor. A lonely, wretched place to die.

The professor frog-kicked, surveying the naked underbelly of the hull. She followed, clicking shots as he directed. They found a hole. A gaping wound in the side of the beast. The probable death blow of the *U-925*. Its steel edges curled outward by the force of a blast.

She could tell from the narrowing of the professor's eyes that this surprised him.

The explosion had originated from within the vessel. Had there been no time to get out through the hatches? What could have caused such a terrible accident? After the sub shuddered to a stop on the sea-bed, had the crew died quickly or had pockets of air remained within the disabled vessel? A slow, agonizing death. The oxygen giving out long before the water seeped inside. Horrifying.

Dr. Stanhope held up his hand. Stopping, she hovered in the water above the wrecked submersible. He made hand motions, signaling his intent to explore the other side. For her to wait here until he determined it was safe.

He swam aft against the current, and she consulted her dive watch. Not much time had elapsed. It just felt longer in this eerie, forsaken place.

A large shadow emerged from the other side of the keeled over U-boat. Dr. Stanhope, finally. Surely they had enough photos to—

The masked second diver came out of nowhere. Gasping, McKenna started to call out before remembering she couldn't.

Sensing something, at the last moment Dr. Stanhope wheeled, but it was too late. The diver was on him, wrenching the regulator from the professor's mouth. The attacker wrapped his arms around Stanhope's neck in a crushing death grip. The dive light fell from his hand, settling to the bottom with a cloud of sand.

The diver hadn't spotted her yet. She had to do something.

Writhing, Dr. Stanhope propelled them away. The men rolled head over fins. Somersaulting. Stirring up the silt on the sea floor, further reducing visibility.

A jumble of black-coated limbs, the men were indistinguishable as they shot upward toward the surface at a dangerous speed. Too fast. Too swiftly for decompression. Without his regulator, Dr. Stanhope would get an air embolism and his lungs would explode.

Even as she thought it, it was already too late. They had disappeared above her, completely beyond her reach.

McKenna kicked hard toward the anchor line. But it wasn't where she'd expected it. She spun in a tight circle. It was so easy to get lost down here. She fought the panic burbling in her chest. Panic made breathing more rapid, decreasing her dwindling supply of air.

There. The anchor line. Had she been down longer than she'd realized? Her thinking was getting fuzzy.

Flutter-kicking her fins, she grabbed hold of the line and inflated her vest. As fast as she could, while still giving her body time to adjust to changing pressure, she began her ascent. Trying to calm her racing heart, she fixed her mind on Jesus. Her fortress. Her Defender. Her rock.

She shook her head. Not that. Not here. Rocks sank. She willed herself to remember her grandfather's favorite verse. The one about Jesus being her lifeline.

This hope we have as an anchor of the soul, sure and steadfast.

"Grab Him with both hands," her grandfather said. "And never let go."

As she rose, her heart skipped a beat. She tightened her grip on the line. *Grandad, are you here?*

Was she in narcosis? Her grandfather couldn't be here. His body had lain buried in the little church cemetery in Tuckahoe for twenty years.

But Jesus was here. Jesus was, as Granddad had told her, wherever she was. Even in the fathomless depths of the ocean blue.

It was growing brighter. The light above began to filter through the darkness around her. And finally, the dark outline of the *Cousteau's* hull. She almost wept with relief.

Breaking the surface of the water, a wave smacked her in the face. She bobbed like a cork as she watched the sleek outline of a boat speed away on the horizon.

McKenna wiped her arm across the mask, but never let go of the line. No longer buoyant, but weighted, she unbuckled the straps. Her BCD, loaded with what eerily resembled twin torpedoes, slid off and disappeared beneath the waves. Her legs weak as jelly, she hoisted herself up the ladder and collapsed on the deck, ripping off her mask and spitting out the regulator.

Where was the professor? How had the attacker found them?

She stumbled to the radio controls, certain they'd been disabled. But *Thank you, Jesus*, they were intact.

When the static cleared on Channel 16 and a strong, female watchstander answered her mayday, only then did she give in to the sobs building in her chest.

Chapter Twenty

AFTER DONNING JEANS AND A JACKET, MCKENNA HUDDLED ON THE gunwale of the *Cousteau*, her wetsuit discarded.

The Coast Guard rescue crew out of Station Hatteras Inlet had discovered Dr. Stanhope's body drifting about twenty minutes north in the current, lying face to the sun, his eyes forever sightless. Flecks of dried foam encircled his mouth. Blood had spewed internally once his lungs exploded. There were no other marks on him. CGIS would be brought in to investigate. Any crime on the water fell within their jurisdiction.

One of the crew steered the *Cousteau* into port. The station commander waited for them on the dock's silvery planks. As did her dad. And he looked furious.

Her stomach clenched. She'd never meant to cause him more stress.

It would be awhile before the CGIS agent arrived from the Sector North Carolina field office in Wilmington to interview her. The Nikon had been confiscated, although she'd been too stunned to take any pictures during the attack.

She followed her dad's long strides to the Explorer. She averted her face as the gurney with Stanhope's sheeted body was rolled into a waiting ambulance to be transported for autopsy.

They drove out of the Village in silence. She wished her father would say something. Anything.

She swallowed. "Are you okay?"

Eyes flashing, he turned so swiftly she shrank into the seat. "This isn't about me." His large hands gripped the wheel. "This is about what almost happened to you today."

"But nothing—"

"You're a witness to murder, McKenna. Once word of that gets out . . ." His face blanched.

"It happened so fast." She threw out her hands. "He was in a suit and masked. I couldn't pick him out of a lineup."

"Suppose the killer had disabled the radio?" Dad's mouth flatlined. "You'd have been out there alone on the open ocean, and no one would ever know what happened to you."

"I should've told you where I was going, but Dr. Stanhope asked me to keep the dive secret. I didn't want to bother—"

"This is the second time you've almost lost your life, McKenna."

"But he found it, Dad. It's really out there."

"I want you to tell me everything, McKenna. From beginning to end." He shot her a look. "And I mean everything."

So she began with the morning Alonso was murdered. The scare she'd passed off as nerves on Yaupon. The newspaper clipping Lovey found. Talbot uncovering the false Freeman. Stanhope's theories. The U-boat.

"Ancient history," her father barked, turning the wheel sharply into the Skipjacks parking lot.

"Something's going on out there on Yaupon, Dad. You should—"

"Not my jurisdiction. And you've been told to stay away from there."

"I haven't been out there again." She frowned. "But did you hear what I said? The professor believes—" Her mouth wobbled. "—*believed* there are antiquity traffickers involved."

"He had no proof of that," he snapped, whipping into a space. "I have real crimes to deal with. A drug trafficking ring to dismantle."

She gritted her teeth. He'd become obsessed with the task force. Why wouldn't he listen to her? "There could be a connection between what happened to Dr. Stanhope and what's happening in Tuckahoe, Dad."

He clicked off the ignition. "What I think is that once again you've found a convenient distraction instead of facing your loss and moving on with your life."

"You can't see the forest for the trees, Dad. From where I'm sitting, the forest isn't just on fire, it's blazing out of control."

He shoved open the door. "Almost ending up dead on the bottom of the ocean doesn't exactly give you a lot of credibility." A hand to his stomach, he grunted. Pain contorted his features.

"Dad, let me help—"

"Help yourself, McKenna. Stop using injured turtles and wounded men as an excuse."

She flinched.

"You aren't the only one who's ever lost someone."

"This is about Mom?" Her eyes watered. "Is that why— Talk to me, Dad. Don't shut me out."

He slammed his door so hard, the Explorer rocked. She scrambled out after him. The bell jangled as he strode inside Skipjacks. She followed her father as he waded through the usual lunch crowd.

Lips pursed, Lovey half rose from behind the register. McKenna's heart sank. The Tuckahoe grapevine.

The kitchen door swung wide, and Caden stood there, glaring at her. She wasn't looking forward to what he had to say to her.

Halfway to the coffee pot, her father staggered, his face a pasty white.

Immediately, Earlene was at his side. "Walt, hon. Let me help—"

"Why don't you fixate on someone who's interested?" He flung her off. "Preferably someone who doesn't beat you up this time."

McKenna gasped. The entire diner went silent. Lovey's face sagged.

"That's enough, Walter," Pastor commanded, rising. Chairs scraped as Laddie and Bob the Postman rose and moved as one toward her father. Ashen, Earlene held up her hand. They stopped, fists clenched.

"Chief Dockery's right." Earlene's voice was like steel. Thin, but rapier sharp. "Time I wised up."

Dad stood frozen, an inexplicable expression on his face. Brows furrowed, his eyes locked on Earlene. Only the sound of the coffee percolating on the burner broke the silence.

This was all McKenna's fault. It was her he was angry with, not Earlene. He wasn't well and not thinking straight.

Earlene pulled the loop at the front of her apron. "No sense in beating my head against a wall any longer." Her gaze never left McKenna's dad.

With painstaking deliberation, she untied her apron strings and unwound them from her waist. "It's time to take no for an answer."

The look in Earlene's eyes . . . Like a kicked puppy who'd finally accepted it didn't deserve anything better. The same expression she'd too often seen in Caden's eyes. Or at least the man she'd stumbled across that first morning.

McKenna wrenched her gaze to the swinging door, but Caden had already slipped back into the kitchen.

Peeling off the apron, Earlene wadded it into a ball and threw it at McKenna's father. "Two final words for you, Walter." She lifted her chin. "I quit."

And shoulders square, head high, Earlene walked out of Skipjacks.

Her father stared at the jangling bell, but he didn't go after her. Nobody moved. No one said a word.

"I'll get my coffee at the station," was all he said, his voice gravelly. Head bent, shoulders drooping, he left.

McKenna clapped her hand over her mouth to keep from crying out. Every hope, every dream she'd cherished over the years for her dad and Earlene had just crumbled.

Love was a fragile thing.

As fragile as a sandcastle at high tide.

❖ ❖ ❖

After the kiss yesterday—almost as soon as they'd returned to the house from the beach—Caden had begun the emotional backpedaling.

Him and McKenna? Big mistake. He was leaving in eight days, twelve hours, and . . .

Yes, he'd been counting.

How did he feel about leaving? Relief mixed with worsening dread. Come November 1, he wasn't sure which would have the upper hand. But with the panic he'd felt since yesterday's kiss, relief was winning.

Soon as he plated the last lunch order, he hightailed it out of Skipjacks like a house on fire. He frowned. Bad analogy after what had been happening in Tuckahoe.

Caden left to avoid facing McKenna. He didn't know what to say to her. And concerning what had almost happened to her this morning, he didn't trust himself to say anything at all.

He ought to work on his to-do list. He still hadn't gotten around to fixing her truck. But he needed a few minutes to decompress.

Caden grimaced, thinking of Paul Stanhope. Of what could've happened to McKenna. He'd been relieved she'd taken the morning off, never dreaming she was somewhere in the Atlantic in the crosshairs of a killer.

He plodded toward the chair on the beach. No one had known of the danger until, while drinking his morning brew, Walt got a call from the boat station commander. The police chief went flying out the door, leaving them to wonder and wait.

Caden had considered reaming McKenna out, but he figured her father had already covered that base. Thoroughly. And after what went down between Walt and Earlene?

He threw himself in the chair. Dockery was an idiot. The man didn't know a good thing when he saw it. What kind of man pushed away someone who loved him as much as Earlene? Women like her didn't exactly grow on trees.

Caden watched the waves roll in and out, crashing on the shore. What happened to Earlene could easily happen to him. Had happened to him, and he wasn't just thinking of Nikki. The look in Earlene's eyes had dredged up an uncomfortable memory of being yanked like a yo-yo from one foster home to another. The devastation of rejection was an experience he never wanted to revisit.

A flicker of movement down the beach caught his attention. Only then did he notice the discarded flip-flops between the chairs. And like the day they met, he noticed her legs first. In jeans this time. Legs that went on forever.

The unfurling of the sun highlighted the straight blonde hair framing her features. Her arms were outstretched, her face tilted upward. But her arched foot lifted out of the water. And eyes closed, she made a circling motion with her pointed big toe, balancing on her other leg.

She raised her arms above her head, her fingers artfully posed. Arching sideways, she kicked upward. Her feet scissored above the surface of the water. He held his breath, transfixed. She landed nimble, soft and sure footed. Her knees flexed and straightened.

Poetry in motion.

He shifted. The chair creaked beneath his weight, and she spun around, a frightened look in her eyes—blue like a Carolina morning—until her gaze fastened upon his.

Deja vú.

For a long moment, they stared at each other across the sand. An eternity, weighing the measure of the other. And once again, something in the fathomless depths of her eyes rocked him. Jarred him. Tugged at him. His heart skipped a beat. What kind of man . . .

A man like him, who'd rather walk away than get hurt again. He had to get away from here, from her. Before—

He pushed to his feet.

But in three long strides, she closed the distance between them, blocking his escape. "I didn't mean to worry anyone."

He willed his heart to settle. "I once believed I was bulletproof too." He kicked a mound of sand. "But I'm not, and neither are you. Why didn't you tell me what you were doing?"

She bit her lip, and his stomach did that crazy, somersaulting thing it did every time he thought about her mouth.

"It was supposed to be a quick scouting trip."

He jutted his jaw. "You didn't trust me."

She shook her head. "Dr. Stanhope insisted the expedition had to be top secret."

"No need for a deadweight cripple, huh?"

"That wasn't it. I do trust you." She stretched out her hand. "Dance with me, Caden."

His gaze went from the gentle curve of her palm to her face. "No."

Caden could barely shuffle through a dance with two good legs. With only one? Not happening. He'd had enough humiliation for one lifetime, thank you very much.

"There's no reason that you—"

"Except, I don't want to dance. With you." What she was asking of him went far beyond a dance, and they both knew it.

Dropping her hand, she lifted her chin. "I think it's you who doesn't trust me."

Not just her. Himself. Them, most of all.

"Please, Caden."

The missing portion of his left leg throbbed. He blanched at the racking torment of phantom pain. First time in weeks. And he recalled the night she found him, hurting and alone. The sweetness that took his breath. The comfort of her touch. The beguiling allure of something he could never hope to possess, much less deserve. Something he didn't have the will to resist. Something that scared him more than living handicapped. More than being alone.

"I'm not Shawn, McKenna." He gritted his teeth until the ache made him forget the agony in his leg. "I can't be him for you."

Her lips parted. "I wouldn't want you to—"

"Shawn was the lucky one."

Her brows furrowed. "Why was Shawn lucky?"

"Because . . ." Caden took care to infuse the right amount of bitterness into his laugh. "He died."

Her eyes widened. "How can you say that to me?"

Caden folded his arms as a sharp blast of cold wind buffeted his body. The forecasted change in the weather had arrived.

Her nostrils flared. "How dare you say that Shawn being dead is better than being alive with me?"

Good. He'd made her angry. Though he'd rather have taken a knife to the gut than see the hurt in her eyes. Hurt he'd inflicted.

"If you prefer being dead, Caden," her mouth flattened, "please don't let me stand in the way of your downward spiral to self-destruction."

She was beautiful, even when she was incensed at him.

"You don't want to dance with me?" She flipped her hair out of her face. "There are those who will." She stalked toward the house.

He almost called to her. But what was the point? He wasn't capable of saying what she wanted him to say. So he let her go.

❖ ❖ ❖

McKenna hadn't cleared the dune before she speed dialed Bryce. "Pick up. Pick up . . ."

Had she become such a selfish diva that she expected him to be at her beck and call? Reeling him in when it suited her, and casting him aside when it no longer did. She'd dodged him, never giving him an answer about the dance tonight—the upcoming event that had prompted her to ask Caden to dance when she should've been listening to her conscience about Bryce.

Approaching the house, she flushed, ashamed of how she'd treated him.

The call went to voice mail.

"Bryce? Would you give me a call? If you're not busy, I'd like to see you." She took a deep breath. "If it's not too late . . . please," she whispered.

Clicking off, she sank onto the bottom step. The step Caden had recently repaired. She was so, so tired of battling these feelings. Thinking of him constantly. The uncertainty. The self-doubt. The looming inevitability of what everyone but her had seen coming from the beginning.

Eyes closed, she lifted her face to the sky. The smells of home—her island home—wafted past her nostrils. The bayberry aroma of the yaupon holly. The wax myrtle. The wet sand coating her feet. The briny, saltwater punch to the air.

She was drained from the morning's events—physically, emotionally—and from the interview with CGIS. She was heartsick over what had happened between her dad and Earlene. It had resurrected feelings she believed she'd put behind her—the abandonment she'd felt in losing her mother. So she'd gone to the beach where no one could see her. Dancing was her way of processing life.

"What should I do, God?"

Prayer—the first thing she should've done weeks ago. Not when she'd hit rock bottom. She knew better.

She'd wanted to help Caden take back his life. Did his future include her? Or did her future —and Caden's—lay elsewhere?

McKenna about jumped out of her skin when the cell in her lap vibrated.

Her heart hammered. "Bryce?" Was this God's answer? "Could I meet you somewhere?" She frowned at the urgency in her voice. "I need to talk to you."

"What's wrong?" He inhaled sharply. "Are you all right?"

"I'm fine." She injected a breezy note into her tone. "No worries."

A brief silence. She feared he'd hung up. Something she richly deserved.

"I'm always happy to see you, McKenna," his voice gentled. "Whenever I can. Wherever you want." Plunging the knife of guilt deeper in her heart. "No matter what you have to say to me, McKenna."

Bryce must think she was severing their friendship. What else had her actions of late led him to believe?

Her heart constricted. "It's nothing bad, I promise. I-I just needed—"

"It makes me happy to hear you say you need me. You do need me, don't you, baby?"

Loneliness and confusion welled within her. "Yes, Bryce," she rasped. "I do need you."

They arranged to meet in his office. Fifteen minutes later, Gina buzzed her in beyond the reception desk. "Go on through. He's expecting you."

The door locked shut behind her. Venturing past the "bull pen," she hurried toward the two offices at the back of the station. One was empty. Her dad, though not feeling well, was on his way to a task force meeting in Nags Head.

Bryce emerged from the break room, a sugar bowl in his hand. His face lit. A balm over her scraped raw feelings. "Hey, baby." Placing the bowl on the coffeemaker stand, he opened his arms and she went to him.

He stroked her hair as she burrowed into his shoulder. "I nearly died when I spotted your flip-flops on the *Cousteau*, McKenna."

She raised her head. "I didn't see you at Hatteras Village."

"There was a crowd." His mouth pulled downward. "Your dad was there. I didn't want to get in the way."

One glimpse of her father's grim features and Bryce had probably headed straight back to the station. One look at her dad and she'd wanted to head straight to California.

"Maybe now the chief will listen to me. Arrest that mangled mental case and throw away the key."

She pushed back. "Caden was not responsible for what happened to Dr. Stanhope."

"And how do you know it wasn't him? You admitted you couldn't ID the killer."

Her lips tightened. "Caden never left Skipjacks this morning."

Bryce snorted. "If not him, maybe his accomplice."

"Seriously, Bryce?"

He pulled her into his office. "Did you know the museum was ransacked sometime after you two left on the Whaler? I took the call."

McKenna frowned. "Was anything taken?"

Her father used to tell her everything. But something had changed over the last few months. He'd clammed up, not only about the drug case, but about what was going on in his heart too.

Bryce rested his hip on the corner of the desk. "The papers Stanhope waved around the other day at Skipjacks were gone. And his laptop." He shook his head. "Saying that stuff with so many witnesses? He was begging to be taken out by someone with sufficient motivation."

"None of which automatically points to Caden."

"Why do you do that?" Bryce glared. "Always defend him?"

Yeah, why did she? Because she was a fool.

"I thought you were too smart to be taken in by the likes of him," he growled.

"Don't start on him again, Bryce."

"Sailors have a girl in every port."

McKenna stiffened. "Shawn never—"

"GIs too. Women throw themselves at Long Tabbers like Wallis."

Not sure what he meant by Long Tabbers, she crossed her arms over her sweater. "That's not how he is."

"That's always how it is with a man like him. Places he's been, things he's seen and done . . . Women are sport to him." Bryce's lip curled. "A contact sport."

She'd clued into the fact that Caden and Nicole had been living together until he deployed the final time. Her experience with men was far more limited. Shawn had been protective of her innocence. Perhaps

Bryce was trying to do the same. She believed the best about people. Long past the point when she shouldn't.

"McKenna, I've always looked out for you, haven't I? Your dad too." She allowed Bryce to wrap his arms around her again. "Wallis is bad news. A guy knows these things about other guys."

As she'd known, from the moment she laid eyes on the photo of the voluptuous Nicole, what kind of woman Caden was into.

"Wallis is only out for one thing, and it isn't love. He wouldn't know what to do with a real lady like you if his life depended on it."

She swallowed.

"Has he ever said anything about loving you?"

Caden Wallis wasn't a man who said much, period. Over and over again, he shut her out of his feelings. Was Bryce right?

"A long-term relationship like we have isn't on his radar. He's not capable of loving a woman like that, McKenna." Bryce's eyes flashed. "All a player like him wants is a little tail while temporarily sidelined. Until he can get back to his real life."

Had she read something into their relationship that wasn't there? Was she that lonely? Or just stupid? Was Caden using her? Was she merely the warm-up act until he returned to Nicole? If so, she didn't know him at all. Certainly not as well as Nicole knew him. In the biblical sense.

Her face flamed. "You're right," she whispered. "I've been foolish."

Bryce caught her face between his hands. "Of course I'm right, baby. I'm not afraid to say I love you. Because I do." His blue eyes welled. "Even if you never love me back."

She beheld herself in the reflection of his eyes. Whereas Caden was counting the days until his departure, Bryce would never leave her. Unlike her mother or Shawn.

He loved her. He wanted her. With Bryce, she'd never be alone again. A future with Bryce meant safety, security, steadiness.

She closed her eyes. "Forgive me?"

He pulled her to him, pressing her forehead against his. "One day I know that not only will you need me, but you'll want me too."

But would she? His words fueled her disquiet. This was so not fair to him. Was she setting him—them—up for failure? She had to stop pining for the impossible. Time to move forward. It wasn't only Shawn she needed to let go of.

Reaching a decision, she took a deep breath. "About the dance tonight? I'd like to go with you." She moistened her bottom lip. "If you still want me."

"I've wanted you since the first day I laid eyes on you, baby."

She forced down her doubts. Her fears.

His mouth moved to her cheek. "Tonight's going to be the first of something special. The beginning of the rest of our lives."

She was so lucky—blessed—to have a man like Bryce to care for her so deeply. Bryce might not be the one she yearned for, but he was the one—the only one—yearning for her. That would be enough. More than enough.

It had to be.

Chapter Twenty-One

IT WAS AWKWARD WHEN BRYCE PICKED UP MCKENNA AT THE house that evening—made worse by his insistence on speaking to her grandmother at length while Caden hunkered nearby, glowering.

Which served him right.

In Rodanthe, the setting sun cast a luminous glow over the Sound. Lanterns lined the pier behind the two-story yacht club, and a flotilla of recreational motorboats and sailboats festooned with twinkle lights anchored at their berths on the dock. Like something out of a fairy tale. But a beach girl at heart, McKenna had never wanted to be somebody's princess.

Once inside, they wended their way toward the glass-banked dining room overlooking the waterfront. Tables of eight were topped with ivory tablecloths and candlelight. Bryce kept his arm slung across her shoulders as he introduced her to Grandpa Erich's old buddies. The conversation and the liquor flowed, swirling around her. She was out of her depth with these people, whose table talk consisted of golf handicaps and exotic vacations.

A good dancer, Bryce swung her nimbly around the dance floor, his steps in perfect time with hers. They fit together in so many ways. She should be delirious with happiness to be on the arm of a man like him. A man who clearly adored her. She could be happy with Bryce. They could be happy together—she was almost certain of it.

But throughout dinner, his physical affection increased, and she grew increasingly leery of his familiarity. Looking at her, rubbing the top of his glass with his finger, he was drinking too much. And she was trapped between him and the real estate mogul he was chatting up.

"Bryce—"

He covered her mouth with his hand. "Let me do the talking, baby."

She stiffened, her gaze cutting to the Atlanta-based executive. The old guy patted her bare knee with his sweaty palm. She shrank into Bryce, but he interpreted her sudden closeness as something else.

He threw back his head and downed the remaining liquid in his glass in one smooth gulp. "When the lady says it's time to go, it's time to go."

Laughter broke out among the men.

He scraped his chair backward so fast, she had to catch hold of the table. His hand patted her rump.

She went hot, then cold. "No, Bryce," she hissed.

He grinned at their companions. "You heard the lady. Time for bed, ladies and gentlemen."

Before she could protest, he propelled her out of the crowded ballroom. Once outside, the sea breeze cooled some of the blaze from her cheeks, but not her temper.

"How could you insinuate we were sleeping together, Bryce?"

Bryce stumbled on the dock and lurched toward the marina. She caught hold of his tux to keep him from tumbling into the water. With effort, she held onto him. But he was bigger and heavier.

"Give me your keys. I'll drive us home."

He gestured wildly at the moored boats. "Home's here." The *Scheherazade* bobbed at the end of the row.

"No." Doubt gnawed at her insides, and a prickle of worry stabbed her chest. She let go of his jacket. "Dad's expecting me."

He gave her a supercilious smile. "The chief's at the station, pulling another all-nighter. Little good it'll do." He weaved toward his boat.

She followed, but only because she was worried about him slipping. "Lovey will expect me home."

Caden didn't care what she did. He was probably daydreaming about his reunion with Nicole.

"You need to sleep this off, Bryce."

He stepped onto the boat and pulled her with him. "Thought you'd never ask." He planted a wet, sloppy kiss on her mouth.

She wrenched back. "That's not what I meant."

He lolled at the top of the companionway above the cabin. "This night's going to be the first of something special, you said. The beginning of the rest of our lives."

"You said that. I never—"

"Why delay the inevitable, McKenna?" His eyes slitted. "We were meant to be together from the start."

"You're drunk, Bryce."

His boy-next-door features hardened. "It's past time to take our relationship to the next level."

"We're friends, Bryce." She folded her arms, chilled by the look in his eyes. "This has been a mistake. I should never have—"

"I've been patient. Watched you carry on with that waste of space." His fingers locked in a vise around her wrist. "But a man can only take so much for so long." His nostrils flared, a feral look in his eyes.

Her skin crawled. "Take your hand off—"

"Stop fighting me," he growled. "Stop fighting destiny."

McKenna gasped. "You're hurting me."

His breath hot against her throat, he held her chin and moved his lips closer.

"No," she cried out. "Stop." She beat at his shoulder, trying to push him off. But he was so strong. She fought against the wave of blackness threatening to drown her. "Please, no . . . Bryce . . ." she sobbed.

Jesus . . .

And then Bryce let go of her. "McKenna . . . I'm sorry . . ."

She clambered over the railing, bridging the gap to the dock.

"You know I never drink. I'm not used to . . . It went to my head."

She smoothed her dress but was unsteady in her heels.

"I'd never hurt you, McKenna. You have to know that." He extended his hand, but she skittered out of his reach. "Forgive me, please. Let me take you home, and we can talk."

No way was she getting into a confined space with him. The stretch on Highway 12 between Rodanthe and Tuckahoe was too deserted. Too isolated.

"The maitre'd will call me a cab." She stepped back a pace. And another. "I don't think we should see each other anymore, Bryce."

His face constricted. "McKenna . . ."

Wheeling, she ran toward the bright lights of the club.

During the cab ride home, she couldn't stop shaking. And once they reached her house, she fumbled in her purse. Her hand trembled as she passed her credit card to the cabbie.

He angled and gave her a sharp look. "Are you okay, lady?"

McKenna swallowed convulsively. "I-I am now."

She'd only been gone a few hours, but everything she'd believed about Bryce had changed.

Lights shone through the bay window. She heard the television. The hinges of the door squeaked as she slipped inside. A project Caden hadn't gotten to yet.

"Walt? Is that you?" Lovey called.

"J-just me." Closing the door, she set the deadbolt.

"McKenna?"

Schooling her features, she turned.

Lovey's eyes narrowed. "What's wrong?"

"Nothing."

"I didn't hear Bryce's car." Lovey frowned. "Did your father call him into the station?"

Shivering, she wrapped her arms around herself. "W-where's Caden?" Suddenly, nothing seemed more important than seeing him.

"Is that a bruise on your wrist?" Lovey laid aside her knitting. "McKenna?"

Uncrossing her arms, she tugged at her sleeves. "I-Is Caden in his room?"

No matter his lack of confidence in himself, he had a powerful physical presence. She felt safe with him. She was safe with him. She wanted to see—she gulped—she *needed* to see Caden. Now.

"Lovey," she barked.

Her grandmother got out of her chair. "He's not there."

For a second, she saw stars. "H-he's gone?" McKenna clutched the neckline of her dress as something tore inside her chest. The oxygen inside the house shrank. "Where is he?" She blinked stupid tears from her eyes.

"Same place since you left." Lovey motioned. "On the beach. Wouldn't come in for supper."

Relief washed through her.

Lovey's talcum-scented palm touched her cheek. "But I'm thinking it's not food he's needing."

"I didn't mean to get attached," she whispered.

"You never do." Lovey smiled. "But you brought home a really good one this time, sweetheart. One who thinks you hung the moon." She headed toward the stairs. "Best you go and put him out of his misery. See you in the morning, honey."

Caden was so closed off, so locked inside himself. Would he ever let her in? She was tired of second-guessing her feelings. Tired of wondering what or if he felt anything for her.

The moon was full, giving her enough light to pick her way across the path. Her heels sank into the soft, squishy ground. She stopped to take them off. The sand, as always, felt good between her toes. She climbed the access stairs. At the top, she spotted a flicker of light on the beach.

She wanted to be with him so badly she ached. She'd gone to the dance with Bryce because she'd been angry. To prove to herself someone wanted her, even if Caden didn't.

But if Caden didn't have feelings for her, why was he sitting alone in the dark? Before she lost her nerve, she crossed over to the beach.

❖ ❖ ❖

The flames from the bonfire curled upward, licking the star-studded sky. Blazing orange and hot, its sparks climbed higher and higher over the dark, roiling waves of the ocean.

Caden hunched in the low-slung chair. Tormented. Writhing as he recalled the look in Hinson's eyes earlier. Like a wolf licking his chops. A lascivious leer when no one but Caden was looking. And he'd made sure Caden was looking.

He'd wanted to wipe the triumph off Hinson's snarky face with his fist. But if McKenna was stupid enough to fall for a guy like Hinson, then she deserved him. Deserved exactly what she got. She was no better than Nikki.

Caden's hands clenched the wooden armrests. That wasn't true. No matter how angry and disappointed—hurt?—he was, McKenna was nothing like Nikki. It was his fault she was with Hinson tonight. He'd practically shoved her into Hinson's arms.

Fortunately this thing hadn't gotten beyond something chemical. He hadn't allowed anything between them to progress beyond physical attraction to something deeper.

So why was he sitting alone on a cold, late October night staring out at the rolling waves? Shoulders hunched, he watched the tide come in while his heart ached—the same heart he'd believed forever dead.

It made him sick to his stomach, imagining her in Hinson's arms. Images bombarded his mind of Hinson touching her. Kissing her.

Caden groaned. "Stop it," he growled. "Stop it."

The wind snatched his voice, carrying it over the dunes. A cold front was due to arrive after midnight ahead of a projected nor'easter.

He shouldn't have come to the Banks, much less gotten involved with the Dockerys and their problems. Once Rivenbark sprung him from jail, if he'd had a lick of sense he should've hightailed it out of Tuckahoe on the next ferry.

But he didn't. Have a lick of sense. Not when it came to the woman with sky-blue eyes and a cleft in her chin. Hair like corn silk brushing across her face.

The soft lips Hinson probably had pressed against his—

Stop. It.

At the sound of a footfall, he whipped around. Beyond the circle of light cast by the fire, a shadow hovered. He hadn't heard until it got close. Too close. He'd lost his edge. He balled his fists.

Then she stepped out of the darkness, and his mouth went dry. Barefoot as usual, high heels dangled from her hand.

He scowled. "What are you doing here?"

McKenna tilted her head. "You didn't come in for supper."

"Not hungry." He turned to the water. "And you're not my keeper, McKenna."

He chewed his lip. Yet another reason she'd turned to Hinson. Why did he say those things to her when what he really—

"Is your leg hurting? Are you having a bad night?"

He was having a bad night, all right, but not because of his leg. And he was hurting. Hurting with a jealous, lovesick—

Caden scrubbed a hand over his face. "My leg's fine. Go to the house. You must be tired. It's been a long . . ." He glanced at the luminescent dial on his watch. Actually, not that late.

Standing beside his chair, she contemplated the tide. Giving him the chance to take his first good look at her. He'd wanted to earlier, but not under Hinson's scrutiny.

Though not form fitting, the lacy black sheath dress with its scalloped neckline looked good on her. The hemline, ending just above her knee, showed off her long legs to perfection.

As for the lace? His pulse misfired. Sexy as all get out. At once forbidding and delectable.

She'd pinned her hair behind her head, but the wind loved McKenna. Tendrils had escaped to frolic around the faux diamond studs on her earlobes, teasing the slender curve of smooth skin on her neck.

It was then he realized how unnaturally quiet she was.

He'd known lots of men like Hinson. Men who didn't take no for an answer. Men who took what they wanted. The oddest sensation passed over him like a current of electricity.

Caden bolted to his feet. "Are you okay? Did Hinson—"

"I'm fine." Pulling at her sleeves, she averted her face.

She'd answered too quickly. Something had happened. Had she come out here to tell him she'd accepted a proposal from Hinson?

Caden took a ragged breath. "I-I've changed my mind."

She turned at the gruff note in his voice. "About what?"

He cleared his throat. "I'd like to dance with you. If the offer still stands."

A vein pulsed in the sweet hollow of her throat. "It does." She dropped her shoes on the sand and held out her hand.

"I'm not a good dancer." He wiped his palms down his jeans. "You may live to regret this."

"Either way—" The blue iris in her eyes darkened. "I'd still be living, wouldn't I?"

And after so much pain, so would he.

He twined his fingers in hers. "You're the expert here." His hands slid around her waist, drawing her close.

She smiled. "What shall we do for music?"

"How about we make our own?"

She laughed, the moonlight bouncing off the silkiness of her throat.

He bit the inside of his cheek. "That may be the cheesiest thing I've ever said."

"Or the sweetest that you've ever said to me." She blushed, looking at her toes. "There is a music here." Her eyes cut to the dark, pounding water. "Can you hear the rhythm of the waves and wind?"

"I hear it," he rasped. But it was a music he only heard when she was in his arms.

She rested her cheek against his shoulder and sighed. He buried his face in her hair as they swayed.

In that moment, he realized he loved her. It was hopelessly futile, but she felt so good, so right in his arms. Right for him. As if before the stars were hung in place, they'd been made for each other.

Yet he had nothing to offer her except a lifetime of caretaking. He needed to end this dance—the dance they'd been doing since the day they met on the beach.

Just one minute more . . .

He pressed his mouth to her neck. She quivered. How was he ever going to let go of her? How could he ever walk away? "McKenna, I—"

She cut him off with her lips, and an explosion went off inside him. Her mouth, like honey, offered him a sweetness he'd never believed possible. Not for someone like him. Thank God, she was like no one he'd ever known before. With a purity he found himself wanting to protect.

He longed to know the joy of ordinary days spent with her curled against him. He yearned for a thousand nights in which to fall asleep to the lull of the tide. He wanted her more than he'd ever wanted anything, more than life itself. Wanted her in a way that had nothing to do with sex—although the thought of his child within her belly almost buckled his knees. He wanted her in a way that had everything to do with someplace deep inside himself. A place he'd never known existed.

For the first time, hope was tangible. So real he was holding it in his arms. A future, possible only with her.

Mine . . . She's—

An engine revved somewhere on the highway. Headlights swept the beach, bringing Caden to his senses.

He jerked and dropped his hold on her. She staggered, her bottom lip swollen from his kisses. He clenched his fists to keep himself from reaching for her.

"I'm leaving next week, McKenna."

She flung out her hands. "What then was this about?"

"Getting it out of our system, I suppose."

A lie. But he was weak when it came to McKenna Dockery.

She shook her head.

"The road . . ." He was finding it hard to breathe. "Not taken."

Her chin wobbled. "That's what I am? The road not taken?"

She didn't understand. The longer he stuck around, the greater chance he'd ruin her. Ruin her chance for a future with a whole man. He was already ruined. Ruined long before an IED went off under his feet. As for his future and hope? He'd lost those a long time ago.

"Don't push me away," she whispered.

"Tuckahoe was never an option, and you knew it."

"I'd hoped . . ." Her throat convulsed.

So had he.

A log dislodged in the bonfire, sending a shower of sparks skyward. He jolted.

She walked away, but her shoes remained half buried in the sand, glinting silver in the glow of the dwindling flames. The embers of the fire were dying.

A metaphor for his life without her.

Chapter Twenty-Two

As the first beams of light filtered through the curtains, McKenna listened to the ever-present rumble of the waves on the beach. There was a heaviness in the air.

The events of last night replayed in her head. Bryce. The bonfire. Caden.

Flinging off the bedcovers, she winced as her bare feet touched the cold pine floor. The sky was a steely gray. In addition to jeans, she pulled on a sweater. And running shoes.

Downstairs, the radio blared. Lovey held her finger to her lips. "National Weather Service."

". . . noon today through eight p.m." The sonorous voice of the broadcaster filled the small kitchen. "The surface low will center off the North Carolina coast . . . deepening quickly as it moves northeast toward the Mid-Atlantic states."

Then Bart Bartleby from *In The Morning* returned to the airwaves. ". . . an old-fashioned nor'easter, folks, as this low pressure system collides with the remnants of Tropical Storm Frieda. Surf will be running seven to ten feet. Winds howling from the northeast at thirty-five to forty, with gusts to fifty-five. Soundside flooding expected and ocean overwash." Bart paused. "Good news, it's a fast-moving storm. So stay alert, hang tight, and be safe."

McKenna turned down the volume. They'd been through worse, and the Banks would surely go through worse in the future. It was the way of things. The price you paid for sandy beaches, blue sky, and living beside a capricious, elemental force of nature. Year-rounders never evacuated. It was an unspoken Banker code. A badge of honor.

"Where's Dad and Ginger?"

"At the station." Lovey switched on the dishwasher. "All officers are on duty."

Good—she'd be less likely to run into Bryce.

"I'm going to fill water jugs in case we lose utilities. Landfall coincides with high tide."

McKenna rolled her eyes. "Of course it does."

If the bridge was damaged, they'd be cut off from the mainland. And potentially without power for days.

Lovey returned from the pantry with several empty gallon jugs. "Since I know you're dying to ask, but won't, I'll go ahead and tell you where Caden is."

"I wasn't going to . . ." But she had been about to.

"Caden took my car. He's going to nail the plywood sheets over the windows at Skipjacks. I called Earlene, but she didn't answer."

McKenna felt the beginnings of an anxiety-laden headache.

"Remember to charge your cell." Lovey docked her own phone into the charger on the counter. "I'm worried about that girl."

That girl, Earlene Jones, all of fifty plus.

"Earlene's granddad helped the others rescue us that day."

McKenna blinked. "What?" Had the approaching storm jarred loose Lovey's memory. "What others, Lovey?"

"The men behind me and Coastie Freeman in the newspaper clipping." Lovey removed extra batteries from the refrigerator. "Their names were listed in the article."

She tried to recall the bearded men standing behind the five-year-old Lovey. "Who were they?"

"The mayor's pappy. Norm's grandpa. Laddie's pa. My Styron grandfather. Lloyd Dockery, my future father-in-law." Lovey planted her hands on her hips. "Where did I put the flashlights?"

McKenna followed Lovey onto the screened porch. "Norm, whose boat was torched?" Taking one end, she helped her grandmother lug the cooler into the kitchen.

Lovey dumped a bag of ice into the chest. "The wind and waves were terrible. Halfway across the channel, the motor conked out. And then I spotted Mr. Gaskill's boat. The men brought us into Tuckahoe."

"The same boat that burned a few weeks ago?"

Lovey pinched her lips together. "No, the Gaskills bought the boat that burned after the Great Storm." She glanced at the ceiling. "I should fill the tub with water too."

"But about Freeman?" She caught Lovey at the staircase. "What do you remember about him?"

Lovey rested her palm on the newel post. "Do we have to talk about this now, honey?"

"You never want to talk about it." McKenna swallowed. "I guess I do that too. Not want to face hard things."

An unidentifiable emotion flickered across Lovey's face. "Come. Let's sit down."

She settled herself beside Lovey on the sofa.

"What do I remember?" Lovey tilted her head. "The man played with me on the rug while Mother scrubbed the stain off his uniform. He had a big knapsack and the loveliest pale-blue eyes."

"Where were your grandparents?"

"Grandpop had gone to the Coastie station. The old church bell rang. That wasn't supposed to happen except in emergencies. Granny was worried." She frowned. "Then the man came. Mother mended the hole in his jacket too."

"Was he injured?"

Lovey shook her head. Her gaze narrowed. "Talbot left yesterday to consult a friend in DC, but he didn't tell me about his visit with Freeman's family. Was something wrong?"

The hole in the Coastie uniform. The stain. The real Richard Freeman's blood? "Did the man take you to the boat, Lovey?"

"No." Lovey plucked at the hem of her shirt. "Mother told me to hide in Grandpop's boat. That we were going to see Grandmother Styron in Tuckahoe, but Mother didn't come. Only the man."

"Why were you hiding?"

"I thought it was a game. But it wasn't." Lovey looked up. "Was it?"

McKenna broke the news about Talbot's discovery and what Dr. Stanhope had suspected about the U-boat's mission.

Lovey's soft eyes enlarged. "Paul Stanhope believed the Coastie was a German spy? But that would mean . . ." She shrank into the sofa. "Under the tarp, I heard loud bangs. But things were blowing around in the wind. My doll and I were scared."

She took her grandmother's hand.

"A four-man team? But there was only him. Unless the real Coasties fought back." Lovey went rigid. "Grandpop. The bell. He was trying to warn us. Get help."

"One of the Tuckahoe men must've heard the bell. That's why they came."

Lovey's chin wobbled. "The German killed my family, didn't he? My grandfather. My grandmother. My—" She squeezed her eyes shut.

Once the Guardsmen were eliminated, the old people would've been defenseless. And Lovey's mother, six months pregnant . . . Bile rose in McKenna's throat.

"The thrum of the engine vibrated through the deck boards."

She glanced at her grandmother, whose eyes had taken on a stricken glaze. "The boat rocked so hard I crashed against the crab pots. Lifting the tarp, he was surprised to see me. But he pulled me out."

Outside, the wind had picked up. McKenna quivered. It wouldn't be long before the outer bands of the nor'easter arrived.

Lovey's shoulders hunched. "He told the watermen everyone on Yaupon was dead. But the sea brings its own justice." Her mouth twisted. "He drowned."

They sat in silence for a second.

"I'm sorry, Lovey."

"It's better to know the truth."

Was it? Caden had told her the truth from the beginning about leaving. She had only herself to blame for daring to hope.

She kissed Lovey's papery-thin cheek. "I'll take care of everything outside."

In a storm, objects became airborne missiles if not properly secured. After donning her pullover fleece jacket, she removed the hanging pots and wind chimes from the porch, then toted lawn furniture across the back lawn to the shed.

From around the front of the house, car doors slammed.

Caden.

The first splatters of rain danced across her cheeks. Against a rising wind, she wrestled to close the shed. But after last night, she was in no hurry to see him.

Gravel crunched behind her.

She squared her shoulders. "Did you—"

A piercing sting. And she fell into blackness.

◈ ◈ ◈

The whirring, cordless drill bored the last screw in place. Plywood over the windows, Skipjacks appeared to have on blinders. Did he?

If Caden hadn't awakened to news of the nor'easter, he would've left today, a week early. Last night with McKenna had been a collision as tumultuous as the storm soon to make landfall on the Banks.

Across the street, the police chief exited the station with Ginger padding alongside. Walt clutched his mid-section and stumbled toward the Explorer in the empty lot, speaking into his shoulder mic. The rest of his officers must be on other calls. The day was going to get worse before it got better. And the Tuckahoe Police Department would be in the thick of it.

As the cruiser lurched onto the street, Ginger stuck her head out the open back window. The Explorer sped north on Main and disappeared from view.

Caden grabbed the toolbox and headed to Lovey's car. With Walt stretched thin, he couldn't abandon the Dockerys now. And he hadn't forgotten Walt's intel that a drug rendezvous was in the works. What better time than under the cover of a storm?

His gut said something big was about to go down. He'd learned to trust his gut long before Afghanistan. His instincts had made him a good soldier. Instinct had prompted his half turn when Friday cued down. A reaction that ultimately saved his life. McKenna would say a God-given instinct.

Maybe.

He never got why people had it in for Christians. The ones he'd met over the years—like Joe and Tavon Miller—were good guys. The Dockerys, including gruff Walt, were the best people he'd ever known.

Sometimes he wished he could be one of them. To believe in something so much. To belong to someone so completely.

But he couldn't. He didn't.

Instead, his job was to protect good people from bad guys. He'd been good at it. The only thing he'd ever been good at.

Over the last few weeks, he'd made a habit of quietly observing people in Tuckahoe. How they interacted. What they said versus what they actually did. People forgot he was there—a typical response, he was learning, to the disabled. Disregarded and underestimated, he blended into the surroundings. And his intelligence gathering had led to a few conclusions.

Talbot Rivenbark was a strange bird. Behind the good-old-boy charm, Caden sensed a calculating agenda. Rivenbark watched Lovey with an intensity beyond romantic interest.

And there was Caribbean Jack. Simply because he was an outsider, he was McKenna's number one suspect. An outsider himself, Caden didn't want to cast blame too quickly. But whenever something bad went down, the aging hippie seemed always on scene or conspicuously absent.

Caden wasn't sure if the murders of Alonso and Stanhope were connected. Perhaps there were two different criminal elements in play.

He threw the toolbox into the trunk. But at the sound of frenzied barking, his head snapped up. Ginger barreled toward him, tongue lolling, saliva drooling. He threw out his hands. "Ginger. Girl. Slow—"

She knocked him into the car, dropped on all fours, and caught his jeans in her teeth.

He tried yanking free. "What are you—?"

Ginger growled low in her throat.

Where was this coming from? Dogs had always liked him. "Ginger," he commanded. "Release. Now."

She went down on her haunches with a whimper—and his last image of Friday exploded across his brain.

The cue he'd missed.

He took a knee, rubbing his hand over Ginger's sodden coat. There were small lacerations along her nose and muzzle. "What are you trying to tell me, girl?" Dread crystallized in his belly. "Where's Walt, Ginger?"

He rose and scanned the deserted street. "Show me, girl." He opened the car door and she jumped in. "Take me to Walt."

On the edge of town, a pair of skid marks veered off the highway. Ginger's barking became frantic.

He spotted the crashed Explorer. Nose down in a neighborhood canal, the cruiser sat partially submerged and was filling rapidly with water.

Caden swerved into the cul-de-sac and slammed on the brakes. Ginger bounded out, barking non-stop. He raced toward the edge of the eight-foot canal and saw Walt trapped inside the Explorer, struggling with the seatbelt.

He fought the impulse to plunge into the water. He needed to be smart. Think before he acted.

Allowing the car to sink first, to equalize the pressure, was wrong. There was a golden minute—sometimes only thirty seconds—before the water would reach the windows. Walt was long past that marker. Ginger had been able to escape out the back, but Walt was unable to follow.

Caden ran for his tool box. He stashed a box cutter in his pocket, a hammer in his waistband, and raced back. He took a running leap, Parkour style, and flung himself on top of the Explorer. He landed with a jarring grunt.

No time for pain. He yanked the hammer, positioned himself over the rear windshield, and smacked the claw on the edges, where the glass was weaker. Cracks spread like the web of a spider. Another blow, and a large, relatively intact chunk of the tinted window fell inside the car. Ginger howled.

He dropped the hammer into the canal and folded through the opening. A shard pierced his sleeve. Drew blood. He ignored it. Water already covered Walt's legs.

Caden pulled out the box cutter and sawed at the seat harness. "I'm going to get you out, sir."

"If I don't get out of this, Caden, I—"

"You *are* getting out of this." Caden gritted his teeth, slashing at the fraying belt. Almost. A little more . . .

"Son, you need to get out of here." Water gushed to Walt's chest. "Don't worry about me."

"With all due respect, Chief—" He sliced at the fabric."—shut up." An unconscious echo of Sanchez.

The belt ripped in his hand, freeing Walt. "Hurry, sir."

Walt unstrapped his gun belt and clambered over the seat. The vehicle bucked. Water poured over the front seat.

"You go first," Walt gasped.

"No chance." Caden shoved him up and out through the shattered rear window. "I'll be right behind you."

McKenna's father slid out of the car into the water. Barking, Ginger paced at the top of the canal.

Caden scrambled out of the sinking car. Perching on the bumper, he dug his hands into the soil above the canal and hoisted himself street level. Ginger nosed him, but he pushed her aside. He grabbed the collar of Walt's police jacket and pulled.

Walt clambered over the edge, soaking wet but alive.

They both collapsed. Sucked in great draughts of air. Ginger pounced on Walt, showering him with doggy love.

"You saved my life, girl." Walt turned his head to look at Caden. "So did you."

Rolling onto his stomach, Caden pushed to his feet. "I reckon, in letting me stay this last month, you saved mine." He bent and kissed the top of Ginger's head, then rubbed behind her ears. "Good, good girl, Ginger."

Thank God the chief's cruiser didn't contain a prisoner cage like the other department vehicles, or Caden would never have gotten him out.

Wait. *Thank God?*

Caden ran his hand over his face. If he didn't get off Hatteras soon, he and God were going to be on a first-name basis.

He motioned to the totally engulfed vehicle. "What happened?"

The chief rose, but the effort cost him. "I gotta get home."

"What's wrong?"

"It's happening today." Walt grabbed Caden's arm to steady himself. "Tom's intel indicates that high-ranking cartel lieutenants have convened on the Banks to ensure the transfer goes smoothly."

"And Tom is who?"

"DEA agent on the task force. He's meeting me at the house. But in-bound, I got another call. I recognized the man's voice." Walt's profile hardened. "Said my family would pay for my interference."

Caden's breath hitched.

"I pray we're not too late. Maybe Tom got there first." Walt pulled at him. "You'll have to drive. I'm too . . ." He swayed.

Caden supported the chief's weight as they lumbered toward Lovey's coupe. Ginger darted inside as he tucked Walt into the passenger seat.

He shooed Caden away. "Let's get going."

Leaving the town limits, they raced into the no-man's-land of the national seashore. "So the call made you crash into—"

"It wasn't the call." Walt grimaced. "I'd already lost power steering. Then the brakes went too."

Caden negotiated a bend. "Total hydraulic failure? How often does that happen? This can't have been an accident."

"No accident." Walt pursed his lips. "Someone cut the hose."

"Who?"

"Someone who wanted to finish the job they'd already started." Walt threw back his shoulders. "Killing me."

Chapter Twenty-Three

McKenna awoke to the sound of water slapping against a hull. Disoriented, she sat up too fast. She clutched her head and flopped onto the mattress, letting the nausea pass.

Finally easing prone, she assessed her situation. She was on a boat. Below deck on a bed—

Oh, God, no.

She broke out in a cold sweat. But one quick glance reassured her that she was fully clothed. She peered out the porthole. The dark sky roiled with thunderclouds.

What had happened? Where was she?

She crawled off the bed, but standing produced a new round of queasiness. What was wrong with her? She staggered to the cabin door, surprised when the latch turned in her hand. She stumbled up the companionway.

Only yards from a beach, the boat lay anchored in the shallows of a vaguely familiar half-moon cove. A shiver oozed down her spine. Yaupon Island.

She'd been drugged and kidnapped. But by whom? Unbidden images rose in her mind of Alonso's bloated body. And Dr. Stanhope.

Antiquity trafficking or drugs? The police believed the arsons were an attempt to keep law enforcement distracted. Had she been kidnapped because her father was police chief?

No one appeared to be on board guarding her. The kidnapper's first mistake. She moved toward the wheelhouse, but the key was missing from the ignition.

Snatching the radio mic, she fiddled with the controls. She got nothing but static. No way to contact the outside world.

The storm hadn't arrived yet, so maybe she hadn't been unconscious long. She did a three-sixty, surveying her options. She had to get off the boat and hide. Once the storm blew over, her grandmother would alert—

Her vision blurred. She fell against the wheel. Lovey had been in the house. Had she been taken too? Or worse?

For Lovey's sake and her own, she couldn't panic. She needed to stay calm. Think like a police chief's daughter.

First order of business? Get off the boat. Second? Find Lovey.

She was going to assume Lovey was alive. And only after determining whether Lovey was on Yaupon or not would she hide to wait out the storm.

McKenna took off her shoes and rolled her jeans. Shoes tied together and strung around her neck, she climbed overboard into the calf-deep water. The bitter cold against her shins momentarily robbed her of breath.

Slogging onto the beach, she threw up her arm as a strong gust of wind blew sand into her face. She turned toward the boat and memorized the registration number on the bow. Home port: Swan Quarter, North Carolina.

According to the Tuckahoe grapevine, the task force believed the heroin originated on the mainland. Swan Quarter probably meant drug traffickers had taken her.

She plodded to the sandy ridge overlooking the ocean. At the top, she shuddered against the driving force of the wind and took a moment to get her bearings.

A month ago, she'd stood in this very spot. But something she'd done or seen had set off a murderous chain of events that had brought danger ashore to Tuckahoe. Arson. Vandalism. Murder.

She sucked in a quick breath. Was this where Alonso had been killed? Was it her fault—

No time for that. If Lovey was here, she needed to find her.

There weren't many places to stash someone on Yaupon. Destroyed over the course of a series of storms, no houses remained. Even before the Great Storm, everyone but Lovey's grandparents had abandoned the island.

Sitting on the dune, McKenna rolled down her jeans, dusted off the sand, and put on her shoes.

The dilapidated church lay over the rise, beyond the grove of stunted trees. A few other abandoned village buildings remained, too, but from this vantage point, only the church steeple was visible where it pierced the angry sky.

She shivered, thinking of the Yaupon bell—an Outer Banks boogey-man. Yet perhaps Laddie's stories weren't as farfetched as she once believed.

Crouching low, she kept to the waist-high grass and made her way to the other side of the cove. She was surprised to discover a warehouse—its aluminum siding not yet tarnished by the salt air—and a brand-new dock reaching into the channel.

Someone other than ghosts had been coming to Yaupon on a regular basis.

If Lovey was anywhere on Yaupon, odds were she was inside.

With one final look to make sure the coast was clear, McKenna dashed toward the warehouse. Flattening against the siding, she screwed up her courage, and poked her head around the corner.

Only to find herself face to face with a gun. She recoiled.

"Ah, señorita." Clad in jeans, boots, and a denim shirt, the man was swarthy, of an indeterminate age. "We meet at last. I trust you slept well. That you've suffered no lasting effects from the roofie."

The date-rape drug? Had she been—

"No worries, señorita. Our colleague was quite insistent. Mauricio did not exceed his instructions beyond bringing you here." He sneered. "You were not violated, I assure you."

She swallowed. "I don't know you."

"But I know you." His mouth twisted, slashing his features into something cruel. "You have cost my employer a great deal of time. And time is money in our business."

She frowned. "What are you talking about?"

"You had something we wanted, señorita."

She lifted her chin. "What have you done with my grandmother?"

His shoulders rose and fell. "Your *abuela* was simply the cost of doing business."

There was a flatness in his black eyes. An absence of light and soul. Like looking into an abyss.

He motioned the gun toward the steel door. "Come and see."

◆ ◆ ◆

Caden and Walt reached the house, but they were too late. Ginger bounded up the steps, barking once again. The doors on McKenna's truck were open and dinging. No sign of the DEA agent.

The house bore a slightly abandoned air. An emptiness that signaled no one was inside. No one alive, that is.

He tapped the unlatched door, and it swung wide. The wind flung granules of sand into his face. Shielding his eyes, he staggered inside, Ginger whining on the threshold.

Lamps were smashed. Furniture overturned. Every shelved book upended on its spine. The curtains and sofa had been slashed. The sheer vindictiveness of the violence set Caden's teeth on edge.

Someone had taken the house apart, searching for something. Had they found whatever it was? Had they taken McKenna and Lovey?

"Ginger, stay!" he ordered. "McKenna!" He clambered up the staircase. "Lovey!"

The upstairs had been tossed as well. He searched room to room, fearing what he'd find.

Walt called from below. "Are they up there, Ca—"

A crash. Barking.

Caden wheeled toward the stairs. Walt lay in a heap at the bottom. Whimpering, Ginger nudged the police chief with her nose. Caden rushed to him, but Walt pushed him away.

"My girls?"

"They're not here."

"Someone took them." Walt fell into the wall. "I have to get them back."

"You can't." Caden eased him down. "You're sick."

Walt shook his head. "No, I've been murdered."

Caden rocked back. "What?"

"I've been poisoned." Walt rested his head against the banister. "Over a period of weeks, I suspect. Just enough to incapacitate me. To keep me from uncovering the truth."

"Why would anyone—"

"He's been two steps ahead of me the whole time." Walt's gaze bored into Caden's. "You've got good instincts, son. McKenna too. Which explains why she could never—"

"Hinson?" His stomach turned. "Is he insane?"

"Not if you mean certifiable. Bryce does nothing without a reason. More often than not with him, it's about money." Walt's brow knit. "But he's played a long game. For the drug ring. For McKenna."

Caden gnashed his teeth. "So Hinson sabotaged your Explorer."

"Six weeks ago, our CI got a message to us just before we lost contact that a major smuggling operation was in the works." Frustration filled Walt's voice. "Something so unbelievable he wouldn't give us details until he could get proof. He was murdered before he could tell us what and where."

Caden's eyes widened. "Alonso was your confidential informant?"

"Lieutenant Commander Alonso Ortega, an intelligence officer in the Columbian Navy Special Forces. His body was dumped on my beach as a warning."

Caden fingered his chin. "You were his liaison at Skipjacks."

"The task force—sheriff's department, federals, and local police like myself—was formed a year ago by the Joint Interagency Task Force South."

Caden nodded. "I didn't realize they ran undercover missions."

"They work alongside counterintelligence agents from a dozen Latin American partner nations to detect, monitor, and interdict the flow of drugs from Latin America into the United States." Walt closed his eyes as pain rippled across his features.

Caden touched his arm. "Sir?"

Walt clutched his stomach, but with visible effort bit back the pain. "But for every fast boat they stop, three more get through."

Caden squeezed his shoulder.

Inhaling through his nostrils, Walt blew out a slow breath. "Tom got word this morning that another agent who'd infiltrated the cartel had located a submarine-building facility in the Venezuelan jungle. Something far more dangerous has altered the equation."

"Subs? So the drugs aren't arriving from the mainland?"

Walt squeezed the bridge of his nose. "We had the trafficking route in reverse order. The drugs are arriving on the Banks in the twenty-first century equivalent of a German U-boat and are then transported to the mainland."

"I thought drug subs only operated in the Pacific."

"The cartels have acquired the expertise of Russian scientists. The new subs targeting the Atlantic are bigger and better engineered. No longer the discardable, semisubmersibles the Coast Guard has interdicted off the Baja Peninsula. Task Force South now believes the cartels are running a triangular trade route from South America to Europe and Africa. Final destination—the U.S."

"Is it drugs for guns, cash, or humans?"

"Worse. The cartels have formed a coalition with terrorists. This unholy alliance has the potential to bring weapons of mass destruction to our shores. There's been chatter. An al-Qaeda operative may be en route."

Caden's gut clenched. "Enabling jihadists to carry out unimaginable attacks on American soil. But why the Banks?"

"This time of year, the islands are largely unpopulated. No true deterrent, except for the wind and waves. What better springboard to travel north to DC? Or to Norfolk, the largest naval station in the world? New York. Boston. Take your pick."

Caden slid his hands in his pockets. "But with the storm brewing . . ."

"Tom thinks the landing was meant to happen earlier. But something went wrong. Maybe when they caught Alonso."

"And the traffickers were forced to push back their timetable."

"I think Bryce is also our arsonist."

Caden fisted his hands. "McKenna almost burned to death at the turtle hospital."

"You saw his distress. I don't think Bryce ever meant to harm her."

"Other than putting her in the crosshairs of a murderous drug cartel. He's such a narcissistic, arrogant—"

"Bryce thought he could have his cake—drug money—and McKenna too."

The very idea of Hinson with his hands on McKenna made Caden want to retch. "We've got to stop him."

Walt's expression went bleak. "*You've* got to stop him. I'd be nothing more than a hindrance. You're going to have to go after them."

And put down Hinson like the dog he was.

"You trust your life to me, Chief?"

"Son, I'm trusting you with something that matters more than my life. I'm trusting you to save my family."

Caden glanced at the phone line ripped out of the wall. "I need to get you to the—"

"When the cartel gets what they want, my family's lives won't be worth a plugged nickel." Walt snorted. "And no surprise to anyone but him, neither will Bry—"

Overhead, a floorboard creaked. Ginger growled, baring her teeth.

"You checked the house?" Walt whispered in a hoarse voice.

Caden scowled. "Not well enough. But I'll rectify that. Ginger," he commanded. "Stay."

Hugging the wall, he took the stairs two at a time. He'd been about to check the bathroom, but he'd gotten distracted by Walt's collapse. An error he wouldn't make again.

He burst through the bathroom door and yanked aside the plastic shower curtain.

Nothing.

Something scuffled on the landing. He charged out. Snagged the intruder around the waist. The prowler gave a high-pitched scream as they fell to the floor.

Earlene?

The second before impact, Caden made a circular roll, landing on his back so his body would take the brunt of the collision. Earlene pummeled his rib cage with her fists, kicking his shins with her pointy shoes.

He raised his arms as the blows moved to his face. "Stop. It's me. Earl—"

"For the love of hush puppies, what are you doing here, Earlene?"

shouted Walt at the top of the staircase. Ginger scrabbled over to Earlene to love on one of her favorite people.

"They took Lovey and McKenna." Earlene staggered to her feet, chest heaving. "Tom and I got here too late to stop them."

Walt's gray eyes went stormy. "How do you know Tom?"

"I meet a lot of people at the diner. He's a nice guy. A good conversationalist." Her mouth pursed. "You should try it sometime."

Caden sat up, fingered his jaw. Apparently, everyone but him knew this Tom person. "How'd you two wind up here, Earlene?"

"Together?" spat Walt.

"He told me to wait for the chief. Said he was going after them. When I heard the car outside, I thought it might be the goons again, so I hid." She smoothed her crumpled jeans. "Tom thinks the sub is coming ashore on Yaupon."

"Tom told you about the— Just how well do you and Tom know each other, Earlene?" Walt snarled.

"What's it to you?" She brushed past them, clattering down the stairs. "Tom knew I could be trusted to keep my mouth shut."

Ginger loped after Earlene. Caden helped Walt downstairs to the sofa.

Earlene righted the overturned coffee table. "From Yaupon, the goods will be lightered onto a shallower boat and taken across the Sound, Tom says."

"Tom says." Walt made a face.

Ginger disappeared to sniff out the kitchen. Earlene gathered the remains of a cushion. "Tom says it's an easy drive through a largely unpopulated county to the interstate. And from there, access to the entire Eastern seaboard."

At the moment, the only thing Caden cared about was McKenna and Lovey. "So Hinson's taken McKenna to Yaupon. Why Lovey?"

"She probably got in the way when he came for my daughter. He won't bother with an elderly woman for long." Walt grunted. "He's cutting his losses. Relocating."

Anger churned Caden's belly. "Not with McKenna, he isn't."

Walt gave him a ghost of a smile. "Tom needs backup. I'll mobilize the task force, but that will take time my family doesn't have. You think you can find your way to Yaupon?"

Earlene dropped the cushion. "I'll go with him."

"No." Walt folded his arms. "Absolutely not."

She wagged her finger. "Walter Dockery, I will not sit idly by while some maniac and his drug buddies threaten my girl and the woman who's been a mother to me."

They glared at each other.

"Sir, you need to get to the hospital to counteract—"

The chief cut him off with a vicious glare.

"What's he talking about?" Earlene's eyes shot to Walt. "What aren't you telling me?"

"My cell phone's in the drink." Walt pushed up from the sofa. "I'll need your phone to call the task force, Earlene."

"And an ambulance." Caden's throat clogged with unaccustomed emotion. "Please."

Walt looked like death warmed over. "Nothing can be done, but if you insist . . ."

Hand on his chest, Earlene pushed him down again. "Think of me as a water taxi, because I'm taking your boat. Caden can figure out the exfil." She angled to Caden. "In your line of work, shoog, I reckon exit strategies are everything."

Caden's brow arched. "Exfil?"

"Exit strategies?" Walt sputtered.

She waved her hand. "I watched *SEAL Team Six*, the movie."

"I'm not a—"

"Adaptability. Mental fortitude." She ticked off on her fingers. "Intelligent. Resourceful. I know exactly who and what you are, Caden Wallis. Walt read in Tom, and Tom read me in."

"Tom Ferrell's got a lot of explaining to do," Walt bellowed.

Doubts squeezed Caden's chest. "That's who I used to be, Earlene."

"We do what we must." She shifted to Walt. "Right?"

He gave a reluctant nod. "I wish I could give you my S&W. That would give you stopping power. But you'll have to make do with the Glock 9mm you've got stashed under your bed. The seventeen rounds will at least give you capacity."

"You knew about my gun?"

"Son, there's not much I didn't make it my business to know about you, once you and my girl started cozying up to each other. Yeah, I searched your room." Walt rolled his eyes. "First day."

Caden rubbed the back of his neck. "I'd have done the same."

"Bryce has the same deadly-force duty weapon I have." The lines in Walt's brow deepened. "But the cartel foot soldiers will bring a different kind of firepower. And my AR-15 is lying at the bottom of the canal too."

"I'll manage."

Walt's mouth curved. "I like that. None of that 'I'll try' business. And think on this—the prosthesis wouldn't hinder you from making law enforcement a long-term career. I'd put in a good word for you at the academy." He blew a trickle of air between his lips. "Bring my girls home, son." His gaze darted to Earlene, but she didn't see. "All of them."

"I give you my word." Caden set his jaw. "They'll come home."

Chapter Twenty-Four

INSIDE THE WAREHOUSE, MCKENNA'S EYES ADJUSTED. UNDER THE glow of a dangling light bulb, Lovey sat unbound in a straight-back chair beside a wooden table.

Rushing forward, she draped her arms around her grandmother. "Did they hurt you?"

"I'm okay, honey." Quivering, Lovey clasped McKenna's hand.

McKenna faced the man. "What do you want from us?"

He smiled, his white teeth a stark contrast to his dark skin. "I already have what I came for." He gestured to the table.

McKenna's eyes widened. Her camera.

"Why did you want my camera?" She shook her head. "Never mind. I don't care. Now that you have what you want, let us go."

She was startled to find another man blocking the door.

McKenna gulped. "There's still time before the storm hits for you to disappear. No one has to know you were here."

"But señorita." Amusement danced in his flat, black eyes. "Why should we abandon our profitable operation? I think it is you who shall disappear."

"The police—my father—will be looking for us."

"I have a special relationship with your Tuckahoe police." He spoke toward the shadows, raising his voice. "Señor, our mutual employer has what he wanted. Therefore, I leave you to complete your business."

Bryce stepped out of the darkness.

Her eyes darted from the men to Bryce. "I-I don't understand."

Lovey tightened her grip on McKenna.

Still in uniform, Bryce raised his service weapon. "Destiny has brought our families together on the island one last time." He grimaced. "A reckoning seventy years in the making."

"Why are you working with these men? Your job—"

"Allowed me to provide insider information so the shipments weren't intercepted."

"But drugs, Bryce?" Her lip curled. "You've seen the awful ravages—"

"Do you know how much of a cut I get?" He shrugged. "More than I could make after years of working for the department."

She tried to make sense of it. "Is this because of Grandpa Erich's medical bills?"

Bryce flicked his gaze to Lovey. "It began with that, but I would've never had to get my hands dirty with scum like this in the first place if—" The man at the door shifted. "—if your family hadn't cheated mine of what rightfully belonged to us."

She looked at Lovey. "What's he talking about?"

"The resemblance is obvious once you know what to look for." Lovey's mouth thinned. "Though your eyes are not as lovely a shade. Too pale. Nothing but ice. I remember now . . ."

"I'm done waiting for my inheritance, old woman. Where have you hidden it?"

"Hiding in plain sight, Bryce." Lovey's eyes glinted. "All these years . . . Right under your nose."

Bryce took a step forward, and McKenna inserted herself between them.

"Grandpa Erich waited decades before he thought it safe to return to the Banks." Bryce beat the gun against his thigh. "We searched this stinking hellhole for years. If it was in plain sight, I would've found it. And in trying to locate the camera, I searched everywhere in Tuckahoe. On the boat. The restaurant."

How had she ever believed him handsome?

So much for the elusive intruder he'd supposedly chased. Vandalizing his own boat had thrown suspicion elsewhere. But what about . . . McKenna put her hand on her throat. "Alonso—"

"Alonso was their concern, not mine."

"Like a tangled quilt thread, everything's tied together, isn't it,

Bryce?" Lovey shunted McKenna aside. "Once you began to untie the knot, everything unraveled."

"The arsons kept Tuckahoe's finest too busy to notice our waterman colleague transporting the kilos to the mainland." He grinned. "And how perfect was it that the chief actually put me in charge of the arson investigation?"

She shook her head. "The tortured drug dealer . . ."

"That wasn't me either, McKenna. I'm not a monster." His gaze scudded toward the cartel men. "The dealer tried to muscle in on the distribution network. These men enjoy inflicting—" His mouth hardened. "Do you understand the lengths I've had to go to in order to protect you? If not for me, Lovey would already be dead. You too."

She gaped at him. "I almost burned to death because of you."

His Adam's apple bobbed. "If I'd known you were in there, I would've never—"

"So you're a hero?" She folded her arms. "For smuggling drugs? For lining your pockets? Burning the turtle center and Norm's boat? For terrorizing Tuckahoe?"

He broadened his chest. "Necessary evils, McKenna. To make a new life worthy of us."

"Nothing is necessary about evil, Bryce. And there is no us." She threw out her hands. "Why did they want my camera?"

"I'll show you." Bryce laid his weapon on the table. "Don't think about it." He locked eyes with her. "They have instructions not to harm you, but Lovey here . . . She'll be the one to eat the bullet, and you'll watch her die."

McKenna sucked in a breath.

"You have only yourself to blame, McKenna, that it's come to this."

She probed his clear, blue eyes. He honestly believed what he said.

"I told you to stay away from Yaupon. But you're so headstrong. You don't listen." He opened his hands. "That will, of course, have to change."

Her heart pounded. What was he talking about?

Bryce flipped through the digital display. "The camera captured something you didn't see." He turned the viewfinder toward her.

She'd been standing on the dunes snapping photos on Yaupon. But in the photo, just beyond the crest of the waves—something gleamed. Cylindrical, except for the metal pipe protruding from beneath the ocean deep.

A conning tower.

How much was a picture worth? More than a million dollars in illegal substances. To someone, this photo had been worth murder.

Silhouetted against the swirling pink clouds of dawn on the island's westerly point was the outline of a steel gray, tubelike container. A submarine, though not one of Dr. Stanhope's U-boats. She'd taken a picture of a drug sub.

"This is why you killed Alonso?" she rasped.

Bryce's eyes went glacial. "I didn't kill Alonso." He gestured. "Armando caught him outside the warehouse and dealt with him."

Armando—who'd also found her outside the warehouse—inclined his head.

The strange noise. The startled birds. That's what she'd heard. Gunshots. They'd been busy killing Alonso. Probably the only reason she made it off Yaupon alive that day.

"But why dump his body near my house?"

"You were seen. Mauricio—" The man at the door? "—got the registration number off your boat." Bryce sighed. "Imagine my surprise when I found out it was you. You can thank me it was only Alonso's body on the beach. I had to promise them I'd find the camera. You didn't make it easy."

At sudden static from the shadows, Armando stepped away. Opening a door, a burst of light revealed another room with a high-frequency radio. He pulled the door shut behind him.

"I left the camera underneath the truck seat and forgot about it. I meant to take it out, but I met Caden and—" She stopped.

Bryce's eyes hardened. He knew what had happened after she met Caden on the beach. "Always leaving valuable things lying around, but the one time you didn't . . ."

The exterior door opened, and a middle-aged Caucasian male entered. "The weather's worsening." He nudged his goatee chin at Bryce. "I brought your boat around to this side of the island. But if I'm taking cargo to the mainland, I need to go soon."

Judging from his accent, a North Carolinian. The boat from Swan Quarter must belong to him.

"Harvey's family has been lightering goods across the Sound for generations. Our enterprise has enabled him to keep his boat in the water and continue his heritage."

She was ashamed for suspecting Laddie of trafficking.

The office door opened again, and Armando rejoined them. "The captain has radioed his imminent arrival. The seas are getting rougher. He must offload our special package soon or risk running aground."

Palm over his heart, the Latino turned toward McKenna, bowing at the waist. "Señorita." The edges of his bushy mustache curved as he rotated to Bryce. "I wish you much happiness, *amigo. Hasta luego.*"

Lovey cleared her throat. "Do your associates know how much money is involved in your side venture, Bryce?"

At the door, the three men paused.

Bryce grabbed the gun off the table and yanked Lovey to her feet.

McKenna knocked his hand off her arm. "Leave her alone."

He waved the men away. "I'll deal with this situation."

"See that you do," Armando hissed.

"Let's go." Bryce jabbed the gun into the small of Lovey's back. "We'll continue this discussion on the *Scheherazade.*"

Following last, Bryce stepped over the gap onto his boat. "Tell me where you've hidden the diamonds, old woman."

McKenna stared at him. How had Bryce gotten involved with the blood diamonds from the U-boat? What did he mean about his inheritance being stolen?

Tied at the warehouse dock, the increasing ferocity of the swells made it difficult to stand on the *Scheherazade.* Lovey, coatless, shivered against the gusting north wind and stumbled. McKenna only just prevented her from face planting on the deck.

She eased her grandmother to the gunwale. "Sitting near the center will help, Lovey."

Bryce trained the gun on them. "When you showed me the perfume bottle, I knew what it was immediately. One of the four must've taken it off the sub. Dropped it on Yaupon."

Lovey knotted her hands. "The past wouldn't stay buried."

He waved the gun. "And then Stanhope had to go and—"

"You killed Dr. Stanhope?" McKenna felt sick. "Another necessary evil, Bryce?"

"The past needed to stay buried only until this final score, giving me the funds to start our new life out of the country." He flicked a contemptuous gaze toward the island. "Anywhere but this godforsaken strip of sand jutting into the Atlantic."

Our new life? "If you think for one minute I'm going anywhere with you, you're delusional, Bryce."

He leaned against the wheel, reholstered the pistol. "I only want what belongs to me, McKenna." He crossed his legs at the ankle. "And that includes you."

"I don't belong to you, Bryce. I never did."

"You did until that waste of oxygen came ashore. And you will again." Startlingly blue, his eyes burned. "And if you want Lovey to live, you'll come of your own free will. We will be happy."

His stance relaxed. And why not? He had McKenna's cooperation as long as Lovey was in danger.

Whatever he had planned, she needed to stall. They'd be missed in Tuckahoe. Her father would come after them. Yet how would he know where to look? She couldn't think about that now. She had to remain alert for an opportunity to escape.

"My own free will," she snorted. "Like last night, Bryce?"

His face constricted. "I never meant to hurt you, baby."

Scrambling to her feet, Lovey clutched the windshield screen for support. "Your bruises. Did he force himself—"

"I would never force myself on her." He angled to McKenna. "I wasn't myself. I was so afraid of losing you. You were slipping away. I love you, baby."

"You love me?" She gave a strangled laugh. "You can't be serious."

"When I saw your flip-flops on the *Cousteau* . . ." He placed his hand over his heart. "If I'd accidentally injured you, I couldn't have lived with myself. I didn't destroy the radio so you could call for help."

"But you could live with yourself after killing the professor?"

Lovey's gaze flickered, and she shifted away from the wheelhouse.

"I didn't want to kill him, my darling innocent." His tone was patiently condescending. "But he was meddling in things that weren't his concern."

Always someone else to blame for Bryce's "necessary" actions. He was a sociopath.

McKenna held on to her temper. "You were using me to get the diamonds, Bryce."

He came out of the wheelhouse, his back to the island. "I loved you long before I discovered the connection. It's destiny."

Lovey took another step backward to the stern. What was she doing?

"Why do you keep saying destiny, Bryce?"

He ran his finger along her cheekbone. She fought a shudder of revulsion. Yet if she angered him, Lovey would be the one to pay.

"You resemble her. Even in dementia, Grandpa Erich remembered."

"She looks like my mother." There was a strange, blank look on Lovey's countenance. "The man didn't drown?"

McKenna's eyes flitted from Lovey to Bryce. "Your grandfather always called me 'little girl.'"

"I was the little girl." Lovey's voice was like a hollow shell.

"Destiny brought us together. And when you took the clipping to the museum, I realized the diamonds had made it off the island during the hurricane." His eyes slitted. "With your grandmother."

Lovey gasped. "I remember. Grandmother Styron found the glittery stones. Mother must've sewn them into my rag doll when she mended his coat."

That charming old man—Bryce's grandfather—was the German commando.

Horror engulfed McKenna. "The jacket of the Coast Guardsman your grandfather killed."

Bryce dropped his hand. "Acts of war."

"Was killing Lovey's family an act of war?"

"It was . . . necessary."

She closed her eyes.

"After meeting you, Grandpa Erich told me he was sad about that."
Sad?

Lovey retreated even farther, placing McKenna at an awkward angle. She had to keep her attention on Bryce while making sure her grandmother didn't fall overboard.

"Grandpa Erich came from a prominent family. A brilliant man, he spoke flawless American English." Bryce's eyes shone with pride. "They spent his childhood summers sailing."

The Yacht Club membership. Miscellaneous pieces of a mass murderer's life fell into place.

"When he was ordered to lead a commando team to America, he saw his chance. He knew Germany couldn't win the war. He had no one left. No reason to stay. The diamonds were his ticket to a new life."

She visualized the U-boat hatches, forever sealed. "He sabotaged the U-boat. Leaving no one alive to know what he'd done."

"German High Command assumed, like many U-boats, the ship had simply been lost. His team didn't know his plan. He needed their help in dispatching the Guardsmen on Yaupon. They'd been told the island was otherwise abandoned." He grimaced. "Lovey's family being there was unfortunate."

Lovey sat as far from them as she could get. "Why didn't he kill me too?" She held out her hand to McKenna.

But McKenna didn't budge. She needed to stay close enough to disarm Bryce and take control of the boat. The *Scheherazade* was their only way off the island.

"Grandpa Erich wasn't a bad man. His entire family—parents, sister, niece—had perished a year earlier in the firestorm when the Allies carpet-bombed Hamburg." Bryce shook his head. "It changed him. He told me he saved the little girl because he couldn't save his niece."

"It twisted him," McKenna spat. "After your parents died, he twisted you, too, Bryce. Or was your entire family in on his lifetime deception?"

"He never told anyone else the truth—that he wasn't Erich Hinson—except me."

"A war criminal living out his life on American soil."

"He wasn't a war criminal," Bryce protested. "He was a soldier following orders. Same as that mangled mongrel you're so fond of, McKenna."

"It's not the same. Caden isn't—"

Bryce reddened.

She mustn't bring Caden into it. Bryce lost what little reason he possessed when it came to Caden.

"None of that matters now." Bryce took a breath. "You and I, McKenna, are destined. When Grandpa Erich explained, I knew. An atonement for what he'd had to do to the family. Full circle. Everything made right."

Bryce's alternate reality. She'd fallen through a black hole.

"I'm needed on the west coast of Africa to supervise future shipments. But I've installed a dance floor in the villa where we will live." His face was alight. "You can dance for me every day, baby," he breathed.

She recoiled.

"But first," he turned on Lovey. "Where are my diamonds?"

"One of your diamonds is where you eat breakfast most mornings. Another started the mayor's real estate company." Lovey laughed, high and shrill.

Bryce reared. Prickles rose on McKenna's arms. There was a glazed look in Lovey's eyes. Had she already lost her grandmother?

"Earlene's grandpappy drank up another diamond. Laddie Ferguson's pa went into the commercial fishing business with good buddy Gaskill." Lovey's mouth pursed. "The same boat you burned."

"What are you talking about?" A vein popped in Bryce's neck. "I'll kill you—"

A thud sounded at the bow. Bryce had no time to react before Caden tackled him to the deck.

With a crack of thunder, the sky opened and a cold deluge of rain fell upon them.

The storm had arrived.

❖ ❖ ❖

"Go!" Caden shouted to the women. "Get out of here!" He drove his fist into Hinson's shocked face.

Lovey moved quicker than he would've believed possible for a woman her age. She'd watched him creep along the shoreline and negotiate the dock. Kept Hinson too engaged to turn around and spot him. Every second, Caden had feared a creak of the boards would give him away and he'd lose his advantage.

McKenna stood frozen in place, water running in rivulets down her face.

Hinson fought back, and they rolled. A gun—Hinson's—skidded, clattering across the deck. Hinson scrabbled for it, but Caden kept him pinned. He bloodied Hinson. "You sick, son of a—" Punched him repeatedly. "You piece of—"

"This way!"

Caden jerked.

On the beach, clad in a yellow rain slicker, Earlene windmilled her arms. He'd told her to stay with the boat, hidden beyond the curve of the shore. But women never listened to him.

In that split-second of distraction, Hinson wrenched free and jumped to his feet. Caden lurched upright, came at him again, but he slipped on the wet deck. Hinson delivered a punishing blow to his gut.

Caden doubled over. Staggered. Reached for the gun at the back of his jeans. If Hinson retrieved his gun first . . .

"Stop right where you are, Bryce."

McKenna.

Caden swung around. Drew his gun.

McKenna, hair plastered to her head, had Hinson's gun pointed at the man's battered face. She stood in Caden's line of sight. He couldn't get off a shot without hitting her.

Swiping his hand over his face, Bryce smeared blood across his cheekbone. "Give me the gun, McKenna." He took a step.

McKenna stepped back. "I'll shoot you, Bryce."

Hinson cocked his head. "You're not going to shoot me, baby."

"I'm not your baby," she yelled and pumped the trigger.

Bryce yelped as the bullet landed next to his foot. Caden jolted too.

Arms extended, her hands around the gun remained rock steady. "Next bullet goes center mass, Bryce."

Who was this woman? And what had she done with Beach Girl?

Static broke out on the radio in the wheelhouse, but she didn't blink.

Hinson lifted his head, defiance etched in every boorish line of his body. "Without me, you don't stand a chance of getting off this island. Mauricio will hurt you, McKenna. In ways you cannot begin to imagine."

"Get out of the way, McKenna," Caden growled low in his throat. "I'll deal with this bast—"

"They've probably already found Lovey and Earlene." Hinson threw his arms wide. "Let's end this nonsense, McKenna. You're not a killer."

Her shoulders bunched, but she raised the gun.

Caden wouldn't allow Hinson to force her to make that choice.

"You're not going to hurt me, McKenna," Bryce sneered.

Caden sidestepped her. "No, but I will." He lunged and coldcocked Hinson.

Bryce dropped like a stone.

Swaying, McKenna lowered her arms. Caden caught her around the waist.

"Did you kill him?" she whispered.

If she hadn't been there, he probably would've. If anyone deserved to die, it was Hinson. A stinking cesspool of human filth instead of a soul. Caden would've done the world a favor by removing Hinson from it.

"He'll be out long enough for the cavalry to arrive."

She sagged against him. "My dad."

Now wasn't the time to tell her that her beloved father was probably dead.

"The cartel will have heard the shot. There's no time to tie up Hinson." He pulled her onto the pier. "I want you off the island."

On the beach, he tugged her toward the tidal creek where the Dockerys' boat waited. As they dashed toward safety, she told him about the camera, Harvey's boat, the two cartel men, and the arrival of the sub.

They rounded the pebbled shoreline, and Caden pushed in front of her. "In case Hinson was right, let me go first."

But beyond the stand of dwarf trees, the boat floated right where he'd left it, Lovey and Earlene on the deck. Sighting them, the two women visibly relaxed.

He stuck the gun behind his back again. "All clear."

McKenna splashed into the brackish water. But he stopped at the water's edge.

She whirled. "Why aren't you coming?"

"There's something different about this shipment, McKenna."

She nodded. "It's a special package."

"Not an it. A who." He grimaced. "The sub brought a terrorist. I have to stop him."

"Wait. No." She started to him, sluicing through the ankle-deep water. "The cavalry's coming."

Caden squared his shoulders. "Reinforcements may not arrive in time to stop them from getting away."

"But you can't do this alone." Her eyes flashed. "What about your leg?"

Caden smiled, recognizing her attempt to push a button. Not falling for it. "The same leg that got you out of Hinson's clutches will deal with them. I'm a warrior, Beach Girl. It's what I do."

"Then I'm coming with—"

"For once in your life, do what you're told. Earlene?" he bellowed to the boat. "Take them home, you hear me?"

Smirking, Earlene saluted him.

Turning on his heel, Caden strode toward the sandy ridge.

"Come home with us!" McKenna implored. "Please!"

He kept walking until she was beyond shouting distance.

That was the thing—

He *was* home. He'd come home the day he got off the ferry. He just hadn't known it.

Maybe the God stuff wasn't so outlandish. Perhaps God and the quilt had sent him here to protect home from evil men who wanted to send the entire world to hell.

It felt good to have a job to do. To be himself. If only one more time.

Chapter Twenty-Five

It had momentarily stopped raining.

Crouching under the cover of scrub brush, Caden watched the activities on the beach. Waiting for the right moment to make his move. Assessing. Thinking. Planning.

Two golf carts with hitched trailers emerged from a winding trail he guessed led to the other side of the island. At one wheel, a white male. At the other, two Latinos.

A fully surfaced submarine lay anchored next to a dock on a promontory point in the bay. The ocean-blue, camouflaged sub was almost twice as long as a city bus and about sixteen feet high. Four men crawled out of the hatch onto the deck of the sub.

The captain. Probably a navigator. Another with an AK-47 slung around his shoulder.

And the fourth—the special package wore the traditional Afghan shalwar kameez. In the driving wind, his long shirt and baggy trousers wrapped tightly against his tall, wiry frame.

Beside the five-foot conning tower, the four men handed off the plastic-bound drug bricks to the men waiting on the pier. Battling the spray of high waves and the wind, they transferred the cargo from the pier to the carts.

Seven tangos to neutralize.

Before leaving Tuckahoe, Caden had changed into a tactical shirt and pants that blended into the sand-covered terrain. Stealth was essential. His chances were better against one or two at a time. His odds against seven armed and ruthless men were slim to none.

When the trailers reached capacity, the white male and one cartel man drove away together. The other Latino and the special package rode away in the second cart. But they wouldn't get far. Before making his way over the dunes, he'd disabled the lightering vessel, still anchored where McKenna described.

Four tangos away. Neutralize the three left behind first.

Tango Number Five with the AK-47 headed toward the cluster of concrete bunkers farther down the headland. Maybe the remains of the former Coast Guard station. A bathroom break? Tango Number Six climbed inside the sub.

Leaving Tango Seven facing away from the beach. Engrossed in the mounting waves slamming into the coastline, the lone submariner hunched over and cupped his hands to light a cigarette.

Caden worked his way forward. The howling wind and blowing sand muffled his approach. He needed to swiftly and silently dispatch the three so as not to alert the others.

Taking a satisfying drag, the cartel lackey blew smoke. Caden sprung to his feet. Sprinting the remaining few yards, he grabbed the man from behind. Clamped a hand over his mouth and dragged him onto the beach. The tango thrashed, back kicked.

Caden lost his balance. They both went down, but Caden kept his hold. His Glock fell into the sand as they grappled with each other. Boots thudded on the pier.

"Behind you!" McKenna yelled.

What was she—

A spear gun lofted over her head, she ran across the beach toward him.

Bullets dinged the sand. He and the man flinched. So much for keeping it quiet. More bullets sprayed the sand beyond Caden. McKenna would be killed if he didn't—

With a violent wrench, he twisted the tango's head at an impossible angle and broke his neck. Caden wheeled. "Get down! Get down!"

But she kept coming.

Snatching his gun from the sand, he aimed. Squeezed the trigger. The gun jammed.

When he racked it, the Glock sounded like sandpaper rubbing. He pulled the trigger again. Nothing. The white noise roared in his head. The mag wasn't feeding.

Gunfire peppered the ground between them. Within seconds, the other tango would be too close to miss hitting her. But he'd have to go through Caden first.

"Use this!" She tossed the sixty-centimeter spear gun to him.

He dropped the useless Glock and caught the stock one handed. Loading the latex band with his free hand, he dove for the sand and rolled onto his belly. Aimed the steel shaft and waited for the shot. Pulled the trigger.

The barbed arrow penetrated the tango's chest cavity. Blood gushed from his mouth, and he fell sideways into the water.

Caden leapt to his feet and scrambled toward McKenna. She was bent over, hands on her knees, a curtain of hair obscuring her features.

"Are you hit?"

She straightened, taking in short bursts of air.

He threw down the spear gun. "I told you to get on the boat!"

She pushed the hair out of her face. "I wasn't hit."

Gripping her upper arms, he lifted her off her feet, raising her onto her toes. Her mouth opened into an *O*.

It took every ounce of self-control drummed into him, courtesy of Uncle Sam, not to shake her silly. "What were you thinking? You could've died."

Her eyes darkened. "I was thinking if I didn't do something, *you* were going to die."

"Better me than you." He gritted his teeth. "My life is not worth you losing yours."

"That's where you're wrong. You're worth dying for, Caden. And I'm not the only One who thinks so."

He let go of her so abruptly, she stutter-stepped.

"Table the God talk for another time." He scanned the bunkers in the distance. "Like when we're not running for our lives."

"I'm going to hold you to that, Caden Wallis."

Despite the danger from elements, both human and natural, he wanted nothing more than to hold her. But what she'd done could've very easily ended badly.

He got in her face. "I'm supposed to be rescuing *you*, McKenna."

McKenna got in his. "How about we rescue each other?"

Something she'd done since the first—she kept him from yielding to the dark lure of the water until he could see for himself the hope found in the dawn of each new day. Rebuilding his confidence. Rebuilding his shattered body. Giving him purpose.

And someone—her—to love.

Running his hand beneath her hair, he found her nape and pulled her tight against him. Bunching his shirt in her fists, she buried her head into the hollow of his shoulder. For a brief second, he held her. Even in the rain, she smelled like sunshine.

His gaze swept the beach. The other goon must've heard the gunfire. Why hadn't he shown himself? He released her and retrieved his Glock, tried to shake the sand out of it.

"Where are Lovey and Earlene?"

McKenna tucked her hair behind her ears. "On their way across the channel for help. I left Bryce's gun with Earlene in case the cartel boat followed them. She gave me the spear gun."

He shook his head. Banker women. He stowed the gun in his waistband.

And just when he believed things couldn't get any worse, the full fury of the storm fell upon them. They skittered back as the tide surged within inches of their feet.

"We've got to get out of the storm, McKenna," he shouted above the pounding breakers.

"There's the church." Wind whiplashed her hair across her face.

"Can you get us there?"

She nodded and tugged him along the beach.

Turbulent winds made it difficult to make headway. He towed her forward against the punishing wind. His strength alone kept her from being blown off her feet.

Once inside the maritime forest, the gnarled live oaks kept most of the wind off them, and their progress became faster. He never would've spotted the shortcut she took. The path between the dense holly was nothing more than a deer trail.

They emerged into the abandoned ruins of a ghost town. A general store sign swung wildly. The windows of every building were broken. They raced toward the paint-peeling, white-clapboard church at the end of the grassed-over street.

Battling the wind, he held the heavy oak door for her. As he slipped inside, the wind tore the door from him, banging it shut against the frame.

McKenna jumped.

They were out of the storm and, for now, safe. If they'd been forced to hunker, the cartel would have to also.

Rain drummed the tin roof. Behind the bare altar lay a set of rickety stairs leading to the bell tower. Due to a dripping leak in the ceiling, a puddle had formed in the aisle.

McKenna shivered and huddled on the edge of a scarred wooden pew. Removing the gun from his back, Caden sat beside her, and together they watched the street through the broken glass of a casement window.

"Where did you learn to . . . I mean . . . what you did to those men . . ." She frowned. "What exactly did you do in the army, Caden?"

He winced at the uncertainty in her voice. Like she was afraid of him. He stared, unseeing, at a jagged shard of glass.

"Or if you tell me, will you have to kill me?"

He looked at her then.

Smiling, she fluttered her lashes at him.

Caden gave her a lopsided smile. "No, I will not have to kill you. I was Special Forces."

Her brows arched. "Like the SEALS?"

"Why does everyone—" He rolled his eyes. "Green Berets."

She glared at him. "Why did no one think it worth mentioning you're Green Beret?"

"I'm not. Not anymore." He checked the Glock. "I told you about the Q course and Robin Sage. I thought you knew."

"How would I have known?"

"Everybody knew. Your dad knew." He turned the Glock over in his hand. Most reliable pistol in the world . . . Of all times to jam . . . "You were there when he said it."

She huffed. "When did I ever hear my father say you were a Green Beret?"

He stripped the magazine from the gun, examined it. "When he called me a quiet professional that night at dinner."

"So . . . ?"

He looked up. "A quiet professional, McKenna. Everybody knows that's what they call Green Berets."

"Everybody except me." She threw out her hands. "How was I supposed to know you were a prototype for Jason Bourne?"

He laughed and let the cartridge fall to the ground. He needed to set aside his plan to neutralize the tangos. The only thing that mattered now was getting McKenna off the island. If they could reach the *Scheherazade* . . . Nobody would expect them to return there.

He cocked his head and listened. The rain wasn't as loud. The wind had slackened too. They needed to move now.

She nudged his shoulder. "Able to kill in a dozen different—"

"More than that."

With his support hand, he grabbed a fresh magazine from the left pocket of his tactical pants.

"Lethal with nothing more than a shoelace, a paper clip, a croissant roll—"

"Don't forget duct tape." He smirked.

"—speaking a zillion foreign languages—"

"Only Urdu. Every operative is required to be fluent in one of a handful of significant languages."

"Stop showing off. I'm already impressed."

He snapped in the fresh cartridge. Palm over the gun, he racked it hard and fast.

She tilted her head, her eyes narrowing. "Lethal in more than a dozen ways? Seriously?"

He cut his eyes at her. "If nothing else, I can always take your very helpful suggestion and beat someone with my prosthesis."

"That's not funny."

"I thought you'd be pleased." He did a quick sweep of the street again. Far too exposed for his liking. "Shows how far I've come. Amputee humor."

She blew out a breath. "You are so full of it."

He stood up. "We do counterterrorism, but unlike the SEALS, we spend most of our time training and working with allied-nation partners." He pointed out the window. "We've gotta get to that building."

"But it's hunting season on Americans out there."

"Welcome to the last ten years of my life, Beach Girl. We have to assume the traffickers found Hinson. And that Mr. AK-47 has warned them about us. They could be preparing to storm our location."

There was a lot of ground between the church and cover.

Caden opened the door a crack. "When I tell you, I want you to flat-out run. I've seen what you can do in a strong headwind running full throttle on a beach. But this time your life is at stake if you don't make cover."

She tapped her foot on the planked floor. "What about you?"

He was thrilled that, for once, she wasn't wearing flip-flops. "After I know you're safe, I'll be right behind you."

"But—"

"McKenna. I'm the quiet professional here, remember?"

A vein pulsed in the sweet hollow of her throat.

He dragged his eyes away, scrutinizing the street. Her life depended on him staying at full operational readiness.

But she claimed his chin between her thumb and forefinger and forced him to look at her. "If you get yourself killed, I'm going to be really mad. You roger that, Sergeant?"

He brought her fingers to his mouth, his lips curving against the skin on her hand. "Loud and clear. No dying allowed today."

"You promise?" In her voice, a hint of tears.

There could be none of that. Emotion would get them killed. She was thinking of Shawn. Still so in love with Shawn.

Caden's gut clenched. But he vowed on his life that, for Shawn's sake if nothing else, he'd make sure McKenna survived to live the life she so richly deserved.

"This leg proves I'm mortal, McKenna. As was Shawn. Only your God holds the power of life and death."

Unable to stop himself, he leaned in and kissed her.

When he pulled back, she smiled at him. And he was happy that his touch pleased her.

"I'm going to do my best to see that both of us get off this island alive. But any prayers for divine assistance would be greatly appreciated."

"Will you pray too?"

He shrugged. "God's more likely to listen to you than me."

"God might surprise you, if you give Him the chance."

"Surprises kill." He firmed his grip on the Glock. "It's time to go."

The trickiest part? The first step out the door. He'd didn't think they'd been made, but he wouldn't know for sure until he stepped out and gained cover. Or felt a sharp flash of pain. Just as long as it wasn't McKenna who took the hit.

"When we get to the boat, I'm depending on your skills set to get us to safety. Deal?"

She pursed her lips. Lips he wished he had the time to kiss again. When they weren't dodging killers and al-Qaeda.

"Deal."

He patted her shoulder. "That's my girl."

McKenna's eyes flickered.

"The task force will be here soon." He hoped so anyway. And then despite what he told her—

God, if You can only manage to get one of us off this island alive, please make it her.

She glanced around him. "Maybe the worst of the storm has passed."

"On my mark."

Their eyes met.

"Now."

She darted down the sagging steps And raced hell-for-leather to the closest structure. When she reached it, Caden pitched himself across the street toward her. Reaching her, she squeezed his hand. He'd take a quick scan around the corner—

Footfalls crunched on the oyster-shelled path. He flung his arm across McKenna, plastering her against the weathered boards. Her eyes widened.

He tucked the Glock away. Slowed his breathing. Waited for the man coming upon them.

The barrel of the assault rifle came first. Stepping sideways, Caden grabbed the muzzle, jerked the AK-47 free, and rammed his fist into the tango's nose. The man reeled, writhing and screaming curses in Spanish. Using the stock, Caden hammered his broken nose into his skull. The tango collapsed, silent, unmoving.

Caden reached for McKenna, but her gaze was locked on the flecks of blood dotting his fist.

He swiped his knuckles against his pants. "I'm sor—"

"It's okay." She laced her fingers in his. "Let's go."

They tore down the street to the other end of the village. Where the trees gave way once more to sand, sky, and wind, two cartel foot soldiers bolted from the brush.

She screamed. "Cade—"

"Run!" He drew the Glock in one smooth motion. "Don't wait for me." He positioned himself in front of her and fired. The bullets chased the tangos back.

But then Bryce Hinson sprinted onto the beach, gun in hand. Caden had no sooner turned than Hinson grabbed hold of McKenna, snaked his arm around her neck, and pointed his gun at her head.

"Drop the weapon, Wallis," Bryce shouted. "If you don't want her hurt, drop it and interlock your hands on your head."

McKenna flailed, struggling to break his hold. "Don't listen to him, Caden."

As long as Hinson had McKenna, he had Caden dead to rights. Caden dropped the Glock into the sand.

"Your hands," the younger of the two Latinos demanded.

Swallowing hard, Caden locked his fingers behind his head.

"Now move away from the gun," the older man instructed.

Hinson pressed McKenna's spine against his jacket. "Check him for other weapons."

Caden gritted his teeth as the younger man relieved him of the Ka-Bar he'd strapped to his leg.

"Excellent." Hinson smiled. "One punch, left knee, should do it, Mauricio."

Gripping the Glock, the younger man delivered a crippling blow to where his stump fitted into the prosthesis. McKenna cried out as white-hot pain electrified his nerve endings. Blackness spiraled before his eyes. The ground rose to meet him.

"He'll give us no further trouble," Hinson gloated.

Stunned, Caden lay almost senseless at the edge of the water. Fighting to squeeze breath into his lungs. Anything to blunt the scorching agony. The tide rolled over him, the shock of the icy water nearly stopping his heart.

McKenna thrashed in Hinson's clasp, tried to reach for him. Hinson wrenched her back. "Enjoy yourselves, gentlemen. Take your time. Make him beg you to cut his throat."

◆　◆　◆

McKenna watched in agony as Armando and Mauricio seized Caden's arms and yanked him upright. He moaned, head lolling, feet dragging in the sand.

"No!" She wrested free and threw herself in front of Caden. "Don't let them hurt him, Bryce. I'll go with you—"

"McKenna!" Caden lunged, but the men jerked him to a standstill.

Bryce's mouth pursed. "What did you say, McKenna?"

"I'll go with you." She held her palms out to him. "Willingly, like you said."

Caden fought against their restraint. "No, McKenna!"

Bryce's eyes glinted. "How do I know you're telling me the truth, McKenna?"

"Don't—"

Armando cuffed Caden, busting his lip.

"I've never lied to you, have I, Bryce?" She faced Bryce. "We'll leave here. Start a new life together."

"No, McKenna. Don't—"

Mauricio knocked Caden to the ground.

Bryce lowered the weapon. "You'll come to me?" His gaze traveled over her body, undressing her with his eyes. "Give yourself fully to me?"

A silent scream built in her lungs.

Crumpled on the sand, blood oozed from a cut above Caden's eye. "Don't do this," he begged. "I don't want you to do this. Not for me."

But she'd do anything to save him.

Tremors racked her. "I-I'll come to you, Bryce."

Raising his arm, he pointed the gun in her direction and fired. She screamed, covering her head with her hands. But the bullet whizzed past. More bullets spurted, rapid fire, from Bryce's weapon. Her gut twisted in terror. *Has he killed Caden? Please, no.* She whirled.

Caden, curled into a ball, looked as stunned as she felt. But he was unhurt.

On either side of him lay the bodies of the other men. Mauricio sprawled, lifeless. Armando whimpered, clutching his chest.

Bryce stalked around her. Fear shown in Armando's eyes as he tried to crawl away. But Bryce planted his boot on Armando's chest and fired again. The bullet shattered Armando's skull, and he lay forever still.

When Bryce turned to Caden, McKenna's stomach convulsed. Was Caden next?

"If I let him go," Bryce said, kicking Caden hard, "you will dance for me every day?"

Groping on his hands and knees, Caden stretched out his hand. "McKenna . . ."

She couldn't stop shaking. And suddenly she got a glimmer of the unconscionable darkness that had once nearly broken Caden. Which was worse—a living hell that never ended, or death itself?

God, help me . . .

"I'll come, B-Bryce." She took a ragged breath. "Ev-every day." A cold dread that had nothing to do with the wind seeped into the marrow of her bones.

Bryce ran his tongue over his lips. "And every day, you will . . . ?"

Caden looked through her, his eyes fixed on something beyond her. She was glad. Glad she didn't have to look at him. Glad she wouldn't have to utter this unspeakable promise as he watched.

She stifled a sob. "I-I'll dance for you, Bryce."

Bryce smiled at her with unholy glee. "Let's get out of this hellhole then." He holstered his gun.

Now was not the time to fight. That would come later. She had to get Bryce away before he changed his mind about killing Caden. For now, she must play Bryce's game—

Caden exploded forward and crashed into her legs, knocking her off her feet. He wrapped around her body, pulled her down, rotated so his body hit the ground first. She landed with an *oomph* against his chest. They rolled.

Multiple shots rang out overhead, then silence. Deafening silence. McKenna lifted her head.

Her father stood behind them, hips wide, arms extended. Gun smoking.

A look of utter surprise rippled across Bryce's features, even as the color leached from his face. He glanced down. Three holes—center mass—burbled blood.

Bryce blinked twice before falling on his back.

"McKenna?" her father called. "Caden? You okay?"

Caden flinched but lumbered to his feet, pulling her with him. Dad strode to Bryce. McKenna started forward, but Caden stopped her.

"Don't look."

Yet if she was to truly believe he was dead, she had to. To make sure the nightmare was over.

"Atonement," Bryce rasped.

The bell in the steeple clanged.

Everyone jerked, including Bryce, their gazes cutting to the steeple. There was no one in the tower. No one ringing the bell. And yet, before their eyes, it rang twice more.

White faced, her father fell to his knees. Caden's arms tightened around her. She hid her face in the curve of his shoulder. Lovey's murdered family. Dr. Stanhope. Alonso.

Glancing up, she watched Bryce's face transform into a heart-wrenching, childlike disbelief. His body spasmed. And like a light winking out, suddenly there was nothing in his eyes anymore. He was gone.

The undulating tide, inexorable and unrelenting, foamed over his body.

Chapter Twenty-Six

THE CAVALRY ARRIVED, AND THE STORM BLEW OUT AS QUICKLY AS it blew in.

Hatteras Inlet Coasties took control of the supersub. Task-force members snared Harvey before he escaped. DEA agent Tom Ferrell—aka Caribbean Jack—had to be satisfied with seizing nine tons of heroin.

Within a handful of hours, men in black SUVs descended on Tuckahoe. FBI. Homeland. And an agency no one was supposed to know existed. McKenna was pleased that it was Officer Gina Montenegro who bagged the biggest prize of all—the special package. Custody of the special package went to the feds. Or whoever they were.

But whoever they were, Skipjacks became their gathering place. They crowded into booths, drinking endless mugs of coffee. Not saying much. Keeping an eye on her family. A lockdown of information.

Talbot Rivenbark had missed the excitement, but he and Lovey were making up for lost time.

"The world's turned upside down," her still weak but recovering father complained at the diner the next day, "when a son has to ask his elderly mother's suitor his intentions."

Lovey never looked up from tallying the receipts. "Get your own life, son."

Over the next few days, the year-rounders came to Skipjacks so often and stayed so long, McKenna considered charging rent. She couldn't blame them, though. Everyone wanted to know what was happening.

When Skipjacks closed that afternoon, the family and a few year-rounders assembled for an unofficial debrief.

After consulting with his "friend" in DC, only now did Talbot feel at liberty to share what he knew. "My father was the OSS agent sent to investigate after the storm in '44." He sipped his coffee. "Office of Strategic Services. The fact that a German agent of the Reich had landed on U.S. soil and gotten away was classified."

McKenna leaned against her father's chair. "Why still classified after all these years?"

"Same reason no one outside Tuckahoe will ever know a terrorist on the Most Wanted list managed to land on American soil and nearly got away." Talbot placed his mug on the table. "Also, after the war the OSS was in the middle of becoming the CIA. No one wanted to admit to such a failure then either. But my father never stopped investigating."

Bob the Postman shook his head. "How did your father learn about the diamonds, Talbot?"

"Working the Nuremberg trials several years later, he came across the rumor that a U-boat had disappeared with a fortune in diamonds. He made the connection to Yaupon."

Dad frowned. "But why did he conclude the diamonds were still on the Banks?"

"It came to his attention the Ferguson and Gaskill families bought a boat in '46." Talbot gestured at the counter. "The Dockerys built Skipjacks in '48. On and on it went. A great deal of money spent by the families who'd rescued Lovey Styron and the German."

Her father arched his brow. "So two and two together equal five?"

"My father believed there was a strong possibility that one day the German would return, looking for his diamonds." Talbot straightened his bow tie. "So he bought the summer house, watched, and waited."

Lovey touched his arm. "And when he died, you took up the mantle."

"Why didn't he turn in the Bankers who had the diamonds?" Norm Gaskill demanded.

"My father's team found the bodies of the Guardsmen, the dead commandos . . ." Talbot took Lovey's hand. "And your family. He never quite got over that. He believed they deserved justice."

"And possession of the diamonds insured our silence," Laddie sneered.

Talbot toasted Laddie with his mug. "Says the cynic."

"Says a realist," Laddie snorted.

"He felt in this particular situation, the government's interests—keeping quiet—aligned with the Bankers' best interests." Talbot shrugged. "Stanhope's colleague found Erich Hinson's real name in the German archives—Hans Ohlssen."

McKenna fretted the strings of her apron. "Information that cost Dr. Stanhope his life." He had mailed the missing file to the one place he knew it would be safest—*Tuckahoe Post Office, Attn: McKenna Dockery*—where it had languished in safety until Bob the Postman dug it out after the storm.

Talbot's shoulders slumped. "The sins of the father—or grandfather, in Bryce's case—are in the blood, perhaps."

McKenna's gaze cut to Caden, battered and bruised but quietly listening from a nearby stool. "I don't believe that. Everyone has a choice."

"Hans was clever. Living far enough north to stay off the radar of anyone old enough to remember him. When Bryce came to live with him as a teenager, he was at an impressionable age."

Lovey shivered. "So wicked."

"So evil." Talbot warmed his hands around the mug. "Imagine Ohlssen's horror when he realized the diamond pouch was empty."

"I'm not sure why my mother took the diamonds." Lovey swallowed. "Maybe to use as a bargaining chip to save our lives."

"Or finders keepers. The Banker way." Talbot glanced around the diner. "We'll never know for sure."

Laddie bristled. "After the war, the soldiers went home, and the economy tanked. Nobody knew to whom the diamonds belonged."

McKenna bit her lip. "But they didn't belong to us."

"Items weren't as easily traced like today." The craggy waterman lifted his hands. "What good would the stones have done anyone languishing in some government vault?"

For the first time, Mrs. O'Neal, retired librarian, spoke. "An entire way of life was dying."

Laddie nodded. "So old Miz Styron and the other men sold the diamonds one at a time over a space of years. The diamonds kept Tuck-ahoe alive until the highway finally came, bringing the tourism boom."

"Certainly a much better use than what Hans intended." Talbot nursed his coffee. "A gift from the sea."

The capture of a drug sub—in the Atlantic—was big news. And yet . . . it wasn't. Just a blip on the local news about a drug bust, and that was it. McKenna gradually realized that was all the United States government had to say on the matter of Yaupon Island. All it ever intended to say.

McKenna's family and Caden were interviewed by nearly every letter in the federal agency alphabet. In the week following the rescue, cuts and bruises healing, Caden finished the home repairs and spent a lot of time on the cell phone he'd bought. There were calls to Fort Bragg—lots of paperwork. Making his separation from the army official. A fact that stirred not a small amount of hope in her heart.

He took out a loan to buy a vehicle of his own. A sign he was looking forward, not back. Positive signs. But when he hired a short-order cook as his replacement, her confidence faltered.

The team was due to arrive in Fayetteville on Friday. She'd take him to the ferry first thing. Once across the Sound, he'd hitch a ride with a Marine to Jacksonville. There, he'd pick up the truck he'd bought online and drive himself to Bragg.

After which, he'd return to Tuckahoe. Where he belonged. With her.

Wouldn't he?

It would've been too simple for him to clarify his plans. He who spoke as if he had to pay for each word. And that was on a good day. Which drove her insane.

She could've asked him point blank. But something held her back. Fear of what he'd say?

He'd been aloof since getting off Yaupon. And when not working, he spent a great deal of time in the chair on the beach, staring into the fathomless depths of the ocean.

But the events of the past week had proven she was hardier than she'd ever dreamed. She wasn't giving up on him. She wasn't giving up on *them*. She had high hopes for a rosy future. For all of them—her dad and Earlene included. Though that wasn't going particularly well either.

Earlene hadn't returned to Skipjacks. And McKenna's sense of desperation mounted. Other than spotting her among the crowd when the Coasties brought them into the harbor, she hadn't seen or spoken to Earlene.

Nor, she was sure, had her dad.

Bryce had laced the sugar bowl next to her father's private coffeemaker at the station. But arsenic poisoning was an inexact science, subject to variables like an individual's genetic stamina. Sheer cussedness had kept her father alive. No surprise there.

The doctors were optimistic the damage caused by the arsenic was reversible. Time would tell. Something she was running out of on multiple fronts.

But Dad did look better. The lines around his eyes grew fainter by the day. But he wasn't happy. Happy, of course, they were alive. No more talk of resigning as police chief. Still . . . there was a forlornness in his eyes.

It broke her heart. Something was missing. *Someone* was missing.

Every morning he clomped into Skipjacks for his usual heart-attack breakfast on a plate. He'd scan the dining room—she doubted he even realized he was doing it—confusion written on his features. It was obvious to everyone but him that he missed Earlene. McKenna wished—oh, how she wished—he could see how much he needed Earlene in his life.

But he was stubborn. And she'd about had enough of stubborn. If her hardheaded father couldn't see what was right in front of him, it was time to take matters into her own hands.

"I hear tell Earlene sold her condo," Laddie volunteered Thursday morning during the breakfast rush.

Topping off a coffee at the next table, McKenna eavesdropped along with everyone else. Tuckahoe's favorite pastime.

Pastor nodded. "You heard right."

Sitting across from Pastor, her father heard too. But he said nothing. Just split open a biscuit with a butter knife and applied whipped butter with the methodical precision of a neurosurgeon.

Mrs. O'Neal veered to the booth. "She's moving to Raleigh."

Laying aside the biscuit, Dad picked up his mug and took a sip. Taking taciturn to a whole new level. For sheer recalcitrance, even Pay-For-Every-Word Caden Wallis could take notes.

Bob the Postman—on a break, of course—stopped to chat as well. "Going to live with her widowed sister." Shooting a look at the police chief, he adjusted the strap of the mailbag on his shoulder. "Tom Ferrell has family there."

Yet it appeared to have no effect on McKenna's dad. None. Zilch. *Nada.* His face was as stoic as the iconic drifter in a Clint Eastwood western.

A crowd—by Tuckahoe's standards—had formed. McKenna balanced a tray of pancakes on her shoulder And held her breath. Hoping. Praying.

Dad edged out of the booth. "Duty calls." He strode out the door, bells jingling in his wake.

She wanted to shake him. She wanted to lock her stiff-necked father and the uncharacteristically intractable Earlene in the meat locker and tell them to either get their act together or freeze.

Then she had an idea.

Later that afternoon, she called Earlene. "I hear you're headed out of town this week."

"No reason to drag it out," Earlene spoke in her ear. "I leave tomorrow."

Was everyone in her entire stinking life leaving Tuckahoe tomorrow? There was no time to lose. Not with her dad and Earlene's happiness at stake.

She took a breath. "I was hoping you'd stop by the house so we could talk." She left it at that, congratulating herself for not babbling. Didn't want to show her hand too soon.

A long silence. Then, "Did your father invite me or is this you?"

McKenna bit her lip. "Well, uh . . ."

"That's what I thought." Earlene sniffed. "No offense, hon, but I think I've said my last word on him."

Not going the way she'd hoped. "W-we owe you a paycheck, Earlene. Why don't you stop by Skipjacks in the morning on your way out of town?"

"It might be better if we said our goodbyes over the phone, shoog. Easier for both of us. Why don't you just mail the check to my sister's address?"

The thought of never seeing Earlene again was like a punch in the gut. Earlene was the heart of Skipjacks. She'd been a fixture in McKenna's life almost as long as she could remember.

"I-I'm not sure what I'm going to do without you, Earlene." Her voice wobbled. "You're the one who taught me how to use mascara." Her attempt at lightness came out shaky.

"Tampons too."

McKenna's mouth curved. "And much more than I could ever thank you for."

"Hush now," Earlene whispered. "You're going to make me ruin *my* mascara."

But this might be McKenna's last chance to let the hip-swinging, sassy-tongued, incredibly wonderful woman know how much she meant to her. "Thank you for being a mother to me after I lost mine, Earlene."

A quick, ragged breath on the other end of the line. "I . . . I guess I could stop by Skipjacks about nine o'clock." Earlene's voice softened. "Get one more hug from my best girl."

McKenna did a fist pump. "That would be great. See you then." She clicked off before Earlene changed her mind.

Now for the rest of her plan. She massaged the back of her neck, working out the kinks.

Getting Earlene to the diner had been the easy part.

Chapter Twenty-Seven

THURSDAY WAS CADEN'S LAST SHIFT AT SKIPJACKS.

No more steely-eyed men speaking into their sleeve cuffs. They'd all faded away as silently as they'd appeared. Conveniently, the National Parks Service had finally declared Yaupon off limits "due to unexploded ordnance" from World War II.

During the first few days after the rescue, slight tremors shook Tuckahoe, rattling the pans on the grill, and the dull, faint roar of repeated explosions sounded across the channel. Were the feds reinforcing the ordnance cover story? Getting rid of the U-boat? Obliterating any remaining traces of a seventy-year-old crime?

Walt made a deal with the feds in exchange for the family's continued silence—noninterference with his family. A deal which, to Caden's surprise, included him too. And whoever made those kinds of decisions realized the bargain was in the best interests of all concerned and agreed.

Or perhaps they reckoned dealing with the fiercely independent *hoi toiders* was more trouble than it was worth. Bankers were a prickly, self-sufficient lot. Distrustful of outsiders, they liked to be left to themselves. But past or present, they took care of their own. Kind of like Caden. Maybe that was why he liked it here so much.

At three o'clock on Thursday, he sent the new guy home. The sun-bleached California surfer might look spacey, but he could cook, and he was a good worker.

Caden took one last look around the empty diner. McKenna huddled in the corner booth, talking into her cell.

This week, in the crash of the cresting waves upon the shore, he'd come to the conclusion that he needed to leave. Too much remained unresolved from his life before Tuckahoe. With his team. With Nikki, too, although how she figured into it, he didn't know. The anger predated Nikki. He wasn't certain he could relinquish it. Not sure he wanted to.

Caden *was* sure, however, that he'd never love anyone in his whole life like he loved McKenna Dockery. It terrified him how much he loved her. In his experience, love only wrought disaster because everything came with a price. A price he'd been paying his entire life. Nothing was free. The good and the bad always cost somebody something. The piper had to be paid. And, in his experience, Caden usually did the paying.

He waited while she finished her call. She bent over the phone, locked in an intense conversation with someone. When her hair fell forward across her cheek, he sucked in a breath. A sudden tactile memory raced through his mind. Of her hair like corn silk through his fingers.

Could she hear the thudding of his heart?

Perhaps she could because she clicked off, caught him staring, and smiled.

In the space of a second, a thousand images exploded in his brain. Of sunlight dappling her hair the first time he saw her. Her graceful dance on the sand. The jolt of their gazes meeting. When she'd seen his leg. When she'd seen him. The pain. The fear. The despair. And in the blue—oh, the blue—of her eyes, a startling recognition. An unexplainable connection between strangers. A knowing and being known.

Enough . . .

Taking a cleansing breath, he scraped his hand down his jeans to erase the remembered sensation of her hair.

With a sweet smile—the smile he liked to think was his alone—she unfolded from the booth and glided toward him.

His chest rose and fell. He didn't know if he could do this. Surely not if he looked into her eyes.

Because today he intended to break her heart.

Which would break his own. But it had to be done. So that after he was gone, unlike after Shawn, she'd be free to move on. She deserved a life. Full of sea breezes and sand. Rich with the love of a good man.

Caden's legs almost buckled at the idea of her with someone else. But he loved her enough to want the best for her, and that wasn't him.

His expression must've given him away. The smile on her face died.

"McKenna . . ."

She held up her palm. "Don't say it."

He needed to say it. "I'm leaving tomorrow." She needed to hear it. "And I won't be coming back."

She flinched as if he'd struck her. "Why?"

He stuffed his hands in his pockets. "It doesn't matter."

"It matters to me," she rasped.

He clenched his jaw. "We agreed I'd only be here until the team returned."

"But I thought after—"

"You thought wrong."

Her lips trembled.

Not that. He couldn't stand to see her cry. Much less make her cry.

"Why are you doing this?" She stepped toward him.

Caden stepped back. Hurt flickered in her eyes. But if she touched him, he'd be lost. And if he stayed, he'd only hurt her more. Fail her. Because that's what he did—fail people. He'd rather leave now than watch the inevitable disappointment in him fill her eyes.

He steeled himself. "I don't belong here."

"That's not true."

"I don't belong anywhere. I'm probably not capable of belonging."

But despite his resolve, the throwaway kid still living inside him somewhere yearned to make Tuckahoe his forever home. To embrace the belonging it—she—offered.

"You belong with us." She opened her hands. "You don't have to work at Skipjacks. Coach is ready to offer you a job." A vein pulsed in the hollow of her throat.

He looked away.

"You belong, Caden. With me."

His eyes snapped to her face. A mistake. Maybe if he kept his gaze just above the cleft in her chin . . . But no, her mouth wasn't a safe place, either.

"You can do whatever you want, Caden." A pleading note entered her voice.

"What about what you want, McKenna?"

She blinked. "I am doing what I want."

"When are you going to stop hiding behind Skipjacks, behind Lovey, and open the dance studio? When are you going to stop using Shawn as an excuse?"

Her eyes narrowed. "You're afraid."

Caden's head jerked back a fraction. "I am not."

It was so easy to love her. He suspected, for whatever unfathomable reason, she loved him too. Or soon would if he didn't leave.

"You're afraid if you stay, you'll come to love it here too much."

Too late for that.

"You don't have to be afraid of losing us, Caden." She swallowed. "Of loving me."

Loving was the surest guarantee he'd lose. She didn't get it. And something inside him prayed—if he prayed—she never would. That somehow she'd remain cushioned from life's hardest lesson.

"This isn't about me, though, is it?" She folded her arms. "You're afraid if you love someone, you're going to get hurt. That's why you won't let anyone in."

Only because he understood what she didn't. Everything, *especially* love, came with a price. Inevitably, the piper would come calling. And today was that day. A cost exacted for the love he felt for her.

He shook his head. "I don't want to stay. I'm a loner. A rolling stone. Always have been. Always—"

"If that's true . . ." She cocked her head. "Tell me you're not afraid you're going to fall in love with me."

He jutted his jaw. "I'm not afraid I'm going to fall in love with you." Couldn't fear something that had already happened.

"All right, then."

He didn't like the look in her eyes.

"I'll be brave." Her mouth thinned. "I'll go first. I love you, Caden."

His heart hammered. No one had ever said that to him before. But despite its impossibility, something within him surged with bittersweet gladness.

"And you love me, Caden."

He had to clamp his lips together to keep from telling her that if he could live only in one moment for all eternity, it would be with her. That if he knew how to pray, he'd pray to always be with her. And when he died, it would be in her arms. But he couldn't.

She planted her hands on her hips. "Tell me you don't love me."

He flushed.

"You can't say it."

She didn't easily let go of those she loved.

He scrubbed his face. "Don't make me say things that will hurt you."

"But you do." She arched her eyebrow. "You. Love. Me."

He raked his hand over his head. "I don't love you, McKenna."

Caden took no pleasure when some of the blue fire dimmed from her eyes.

"I-I don't believe you."

He closed his eyes. For the love of hushpuppies . . .

"Prove it."

His eyes flew open. "The not staying kinda proves it, don't you think?"

"Show me you don't feel anything for me." She tucked her hair behind her ears. "Kiss me again. I dare you."

"That's—that's crazy, McKenna." He gaped. "In what world does kissing you prove I don't love you?"

"You kissed me before like you loved me."

"That was a mistake. We were both . . ." He gulped.

"Let's see just how platonically you can kiss me. I know how you love a good challenge."

This wasn't a good idea.

Caden crossed his arms over his chest. As much as anything to keep from taking hold of her. "No."

Her sweet, gentle face changed into the leave-no-man-behind McKenna he'd seen on the island. Unfolding, he widened his stance.

She came at him so quickly, he didn't have time to react. Face upturned, head tilted, she knotted her hands behind his neck and pulled his mouth down to hers. His breath hitched.

Her lips were pillowy. And she kissed him. Really kissed him. Within an inch of his life.

Not knowing what to do with his hands, he fisted them. He wouldn't touch her. He couldn't touch her.

Stretching on her toes, she tucked into him. "Caden . . ."

Eyes heavy lidded, her lips moved to the corner of his mouth. Her fingers plowed through the short hairs on the nape of his neck.

And then he was kissing her back. Desperately. Like a man drowning. Just this one last time. It was all he'd ever have of her. He needed to imprint the feel of her, the scent of her, the taste of her into his heart forever. Enough to last a lifetime.

Never moving his mouth from hers, he lifted her onto the stool. Level, he memorized the curve of her jaw with his lips. Claimed the fullness of her bottom lip. Relished the softness of her skin. Explored the divot in her chin. He drank her in like sand soaked in the rays of the sun.

But if he didn't stop now, he'd never be able to walk away.

Someone always had to pay. Pay for the pain. Pay for joy.

Chest heaving, he wrenched away. "No."

She held onto him. And if she hadn't, they would've both fallen to the floor. Her breath came in rapid spurts. He couldn't seem to find enough air to fill his lungs.

Undone, he'd more than proven he loved her. But he refused to be the one who ruined her life.

Her eyes blazed a smoky blue as she cradled his cheek with her hand. "You do love—"

"Don't mistake love for something else, McKenna."

She let go of him so fast, he stumbled, catching himself on the counter. He hated himself for flaying at her deepest insecurities, but what choice did he have?

"I don't believe you," she whispered, but doubt coated her voice.

He forced a laugh, layering it with just the right amount of self-mockery. "What Nikki and I had wasn't love, either."

McKenna slapped him.

Face stinging, he adjusted his jaw with his hand. No one had ever deserved slapping more than him. Better for her to hate him than for him to wreck her like Shawn nearly did.

She'd get over him. People always got over him. Just ask Nikki.

McKenna inserted distance between them. Her hair swung across her cheek. He didn't like not being able to see her face.

Genuine sorrow laced his voice. "I wanted us to end as friends."

Her silence unnerved him.

"You've been the best friend I ever had."

And this was how he repaid her kindness. But the way he figured it, he was doing her a favor.

"I'll say goodbye to your family tonight."

Hand on her throat, she looked at him then.

Caden jerked his gaze. "The new guy can take me to the ferry on his way to Skipjacks tomorrow morning."

"I'll take you myself."

Looking into her eyes, this time he was sorry he did.

Her mouth twisted. "Bring it full circle."

Despair seized his heart.

God help him—and only a fool didn't believe He was out there—Caden had indeed come full circle.

Chapter Twenty-Eight

THE NEXT MORNING, MCKENNA STARED THROUGH THE TRUCK windshield at the berthed ferry. "This is goodbye, then."

She was afraid to look at Caden. Afraid of herself. Afraid she'd act like a fool and beg him to stay. Recalling how she'd thrown herself at him yesterday, her face flamed.

Lovey had cried when he said goodbye last night. Her dad offered to help him pursue a career in law enforcement. Talbot wanted to help him finance a construction business. Caden had options—none of which mattered if he didn't want to stay. And he'd made it abundantly clear that staying was the last thing he wanted. Other than not wanting her.

There appeared to be no end to her naiveté when it came to men.

Caden had removed Nicole's photo from the mirror.

Humiliation sloshed through McKenna's veins. Yes, she'd checked while he said goodbye to Ginger.

Nicole—not McKenna—he was taking with him.

One small consolation—he'd also taken the Ocean Waves quilt from his bed. And the Bible Lovey gave him was no longer on the nightstand.

McKenna cleared her throat. "Passengers are boarding." How could she have so misjudged the thing between them? Romanticizing what for him had been nothing more than—a way to kill time? Convenience? Lust?

Heartache and mortification battled for supremacy.

"McKenna . . . would you look at me?"

No, thank you very much. She didn't believe she would.

She'd deluded herself. She hadn't known him at all. Only what he'd chosen to let her see. Her dad had tried to warn her.

Dear God, she closed her eyes. Even Bryce, although for his own self-serving purposes, had tried to protect her from this . . . this emotionally unavailable drifter.

McKenna should've taken better care of her heart. Protected herself from the emotional land mine named Caden Wallis.

She gripped the steering wheel. That would teach her. No more strays.

"You gave me back my life, McKenna."

Gratitude—the last thing she wanted.

She must be some kind of idiot. Helping him had guaranteed he wouldn't stay. And now he was leaving.

"McKenna, I wish . . ."

Heart pulsing with foolish hope, she looked at him then. What did he wish? But he bit his lip, saying nothing else.

She'd never seen him in his uniform before. He looked good in uniform. Then again, most men did. Shawn had too.

Nicole had been a complete fool to walk away from this incredibly smart, funny, handsome, sweet man. A courageous hero, not just on the battlefield but in life's adversities too.

A different man from the desperate stranger she'd met two months ago. New purpose and hope shone in his eyes.

Did he hope to renew his relationship with Nicole? Despite what he'd said yesterday, was he so stupidly in love with Nicole he couldn't see how wrong she was for him? Nicole didn't love him.

There was nothing right about Caden leaving a place where people cared about him. Leaving her, who did love him.

"McKenna, this is for the best."

She glared at him. "Best for whom?"

"You deserve so much more than a broken man like me."

She turned in the seat. "When I see you, I don't see brokenness. I see a man who has so much to offer."

"One day, you'll look back and realize I did you a favor."

"First my mother, then Shawn, now you. Why does everyone leave me?" Her chin quivered, and she was angry at herself. "What's wrong with me?"

"There's nothing wrong with you." He gritted his teeth. "The fault lies with me for not being enough."

"Not having a leg doesn't matter to me."

A muscle ticked in his cheek. "I'd stay if I could," his voice husky. "If I believed for a moment it was the right thing to do."

"Bryce believed he was acting in my best interests," she sniffed. "Maybe you two had more in common than I realized."

Caden took a quick, indrawn breath.

Okay, that had not been nice. Nor true. Part of her wanted to punish him. To hurt him the way his leaving was hurting her.

But she didn't really want to hurt him. She loved him. Whether he loved her or not.

"Many people are far more broken than you'll ever be, Caden. Yet until you see yourself as unbroken and whole, nothing else matters."

Silence fell between them.

"I'm sorry, McKenna."

She returned to her scrutiny of the harbor. "Just go, Caden."

If she didn't get away from him right this minute, she was going to lose it. And despite everything that had happened, she still had a few tattered remnants of pride.

He got out. She felt his gaze rake over her. But he closed the cab door. Duffel bag over his shoulder, he headed toward the gangplank. The early morning sunshine dappled his dark hair. His gait was even, his stride sure. His posture, soldier straight. Still had that pirate thing going. She choked back a sob as he vanished out of sight on board the ferry.

She sat there, like the idiot she was, until the last car rolled aboard. The gate closed. Anchor raised, the ferry moved into the harbor. Choppy waves splashed against the boat, spraying the passengers who braved the cold on deck.

But Caden wasn't one of them. No looking back for him. No fond farewell to the island that had helped make him whole, at least on the outside. The inside? Only God could do that.

The ferry chugged out of the marina, leaving foam in its wake. She watched until it became no more than a distant white dot, then at last disappeared over the horizon. Only then did she allow herself to cry. A storm surge of tears flowed down her cheeks. She was so angry with him. She throttled the wheel. It didn't have to be this way.

The anger was easier than facing the pain of love spurned. But the ache—which she'd almost succeeded in forgetting over the last few months—resurfaced like flotsam after a shipwreck.

Everything was a mess. Earlene was leaving town. And McKenna couldn't blame her. Her dad was being impossible and pigheaded. About as impossible and pigheaded as a certain Army sergeant.

"Men are such jerks," she shouted to a startled sandpiper, scurrying away.

Blowing out a breath, she scrubbed her forehead. She could only leave Caden to God's care. But there was still a chance for her dad and Earlene. Somehow she had to figure out a way to get them together before they threw away their chance for happiness.

Like Caden had thrown away his chance with her.

Her anger subsided as quickly as it flared, leaving devastation in its wake.

"When You told me to wait, I thought he was Your answer," she whispered.

How had she misunderstood God so completely? Had she been so consumed by her own wants that she'd closed her mind to God's plan? A plan that didn't include a future for her and Caden?

For the first time in her life, she had no desire to go to the beach. The ocean had lost its ability to comfort her. She didn't want to dance.

Her eyes flicked at the raucous call of the gulls wheeling in acrobatic figure eights above the marina. She'd been patient. She'd held on to her hope. And where had that gotten her?

Right back where she'd begun. Alone. And in far worse condition.

Caden had taken with him her dreams, her heart. How was she going to make a life after him, when everything and everyone on Hatteras reminded her of him?

In some ways, losing Caden was worse than losing Shawn. Shawn hadn't left by choice. Caden had. And losing Caden would hurt for a long time.

Because grief takes as long as it takes.

Loneliness swept over her. She laid her forehead against the steering wheel and wept, for herself and for him.

For what they could've been together.

❖   ❖   ❖

With her own life in shambles, if things didn't work out for her dad and Earlene, McKenna didn't know what she was going to do.

She'd come to Skipjacks after dropping Caden off at the ferry. One of these days, she'd like to be the one who left. To walk away and never look back. But she knew she wouldn't. That was just the anger talking.

McKenna moved between the tables of the breakfast crowd, delivering one man's order, inquiring about a woman's grandchild. Truth was she needed these people with their endearing speech. She loved Tuckahoe. She belonged here. She never wanted to live too far from the sound of the sea. She needed to feel the sand between her toes. Breathe the salt-laden air fanning across her skin. This was home. This was who she was.

The waves would call her again. The tide would once more soothe her soul. And where the land met the sea—a thin place—she'd wrap herself in the warmth of God's unchanging love.

But today? She wasn't in the mood for obstacles today. If people knew what was good for them, they'd stay out of her way.

She glanced at the clock. Eight fifty-eight. Earlene would be here any minute, but where was her father? Of all days . . .

Ringing up a customer, Lovey cut her eyes at McKenna, giving her a nervous look. This had to work. McKenna wasn't sure she could take much more loss. Especially today.

God, please . . .

This was her father's last chance. McKenna had a bad feeling that if he let Earlene leave Tuckahoe, she wasn't ever coming back.

Eight fifty-nine.

The diner was packed. Pastor, Laddie, Mrs. O'Neal, Bob the Postman—you name 'em, they were here. As if everyone sensed there might be more than coffee brewing at Skipjacks today. Or maybe they were here to say goodbye.

The bell jingled. Earlene, thank goodness. But still no Dad.

McKenna got her first glimpse of Earlene in a week. And whoa . . . what had Earlene done to herself?

Instead of black jeans, Earlene wore a gray wool skirt with ankle boots. A pink tartan scarf draped artfully over her gray silk blouse. And it wasn't only her clothes. No longer teased and sprayed, Earlene's hair hung straight to her shoulders. The florescent lights brought out the corn-yellow highlights. Her natural color, Earlene was quick to tell people. She'd never dyed her hair. With that gorgeous color, she didn't need to.

Bob the Postman hugged Earlene at the door. Other diners called greetings, and Earlene stopped to speak with each one.

Nine o-five.

Earlene's makeup was very subdued. A touch of rose on her cheekbones. Pale pink gloss on her lips. Her bangs lay strangely young and vulnerable on her forehead.

McKenna turned to her grandmother. "Earlene never needed that goop on her face."

Lovey's eyes softened, watching Earlene wend her way through the throng of well-wishers. "Reminds me of the sweet girl from the wrong side of the proverbial creek that your father took to prom forty years ago. He called her Lenie then."

Mrs. O'Neal took Earlene's hands in hers, murmuring something in a low voice. Earlene nodded, pressing her lips together.

Lovey wrapped her arm around McKenna. "She never believed she was good enough. Not as smart or pretty as your mother."

"All she ever had to be," McKenna whispered, "was the generous, loving person she already is."

When it came Laddie's turn, he couldn't speak. The rough-mannered, no-nonsense waterman's face was a mask of grief. It was Earlene who'd taken his wife across the bridge to chemo in her final days. Earlene took her time with him. And McKenna was grateful for every delay. Anything to stall Earlene until her father arrived.

McKenna swiveled to the clock. Nine sixteen. Where was he?

Lovey frowned. "That son of mine is about to miss out on one of the best things that ever happened to him."

Then it was their turn with Earlene, whose lashes were spiky with tears. "I guess it's time to say goodbye." Resignation clouded her blue eyes.

McKenna thought her heart might burst. The three of them—three who had shared so much—took each other's hands.

"Survivors." Lovey swallowed. "That's what we are. Don't forget that, Earlene."

With a breathy sigh, Earlene let go. "It's a long way to Raleigh. I best collect my paycheck and be on my way."

McKenna shot her grandmother a desperate look. *Do something . . . anything . . .*

Nine twenty.

"I'll get your check." Usually spry, Lovey limped in slow motion toward the register.

Good thinking, Lovey.

Lovey pretended at first she couldn't locate the key to punch open the drawer. She removed the till in a leisurely fashion. Languidly, she sorted through sundry items until at last, with minute deliberation, she withdrew the white envelope.

But when Lovey took halting steps to return, Earlene's eyes narrowed. "Lovey, are you feeling all right?"

Nine twenty-five.

Lovey fanned herself with the envelope. "At my age, I have good days and bad days."

"If I could . . ." Earlene attempted to capture the flapping envelope in Lovey's blue-veined hand. "If you'd just—"

The bell jangled. Lovey and McKenna's gazes cut to the door. Earlene snatched the envelope and stuffed it in her skirt pocket.

"Dad!" McKenna almost shouted in relief. "Earlene's here to get her last paycheck before she leaves for Raleigh."

Hatless, Walt Dockery stalked into the diner. Lovey's face lifted. McKenna rose on her tiptoes in anticipation. Everything was going to work out. Her father and Earlene would get the happily-ever-after they deserved. Joy bubbled inside McKenna until—

Her father strode past them, heading toward the coffee station. Lovey's face fell. McKenna came down hard on her heels.

Earlene didn't even blink.

Uniform stretched taut across his broad shoulders, he helped himself to a cup of joe.

"Dad!" McKenna barked. "Did you hear me?"

He could see them in the mirror, but still giving them a nice view of his back, he propped his elbows on the counter.

Earlene raised her chin, dry eyed.

Lovey shook her head. "You don't know how sorry I am, sweetheart, that my son is such an idiot."

This couldn't be happening. No one appeared to be getting a happy ending today.

A choking feeling squeezed McKenna's chest. "What am I going to do without you?" Her voice, a half sob, came out louder than she intended.

No one in the diner even pretended to mind their own business.

"Lovey is right." Earlene draped her arm around McKenna. "You're a survivor." Her words fell gentle. "And you're strong enough for me to leave you now."

"I'm not strong. Caden—" She gulped past the knot in her throat.

Earlene cupped McKenna's cheek. "I wouldn't write him off yet. That man loves you. You can see it in his eyes when he looks at you. But with or without him, you're going to be fine."

McKenna threw out her hands, fluttering like a frightened bird. "Lovey, do something."

But her grandmother just pleated the folds of her apron and quietly cried.

"Your father has been the great love of my life." Earlene tilted her head. "But you either love someone or you don't, shoog."

Love, such a fragile thing.

"Please, please, don't go," she whispered.

"Walt's never going to love me the way I love him." A fleeting, sad smile. "It's time for me to go." She took a tentative step toward the counter. "Goodbye, Walter."

Her father stiffened.

Like spectators at Wimbledon, fifteen faces swung from Earlene to the chief.

In the reflection, McKenna watched his face contort. Earlene didn't see because she was halfway to the door when he whipped off the stool.

"Earlene, wait."

In two strides he reached Earlene and swung her around. There was a collective gasp. Earlene's eyes widened.

Dad swept her into his arms, bent her over backward, and gave her a lip-smacking, V-J Day-worthy kiss before God, his mother and daughter, and the year-rounders in Tuckahoe.

Earlene's arms slipped around his neck—where they'd always belonged.

Crying, Lovey grabbed McKenna into a hug.

When her father finally came up for air, he set Earlene on her feet but didn't let her go, not for a minute. "Can you forgive me for what I . . . After McKenna's mother died, I felt so guilty. Then I was afraid the cartel might . . ." He dropped his gaze. "Please stay, Lenie." He swallowed. "I love you."

Earlene nodded, bemused but oh so happy. When he kissed her again, everyone broke out into spontaneous applause.

Though there'd be no happy ending for McKenna, she smiled through her tears.

Some dreams did come true.

Chapter Twenty-Nine

CADEN WOULDN'T HAVE BELIEVED IT POSSIBLE TO HURT MORE than he had on that final mission in Afghanistan. But this time, the pain only increased as the shoreline of Hatteras grew more distant. He ached with the loss of what would never be.

On the ferry, he and the Marine soon found each other. The man reminded him of Scruggs, the youngest member of Caden's team. All testosterone, all mouth. Caden climbed into the Chevy to wait out the crossing.

Driving off the ferry at the Cedar Island terminal, the young Marine turned the radio to heavy metal. Caden let the music fill the space between them. It wasn't hard to blank out the aggressively distorted chords. He had a lot of practice in finding white noise—the surreal silence that played in his head when bullets began to fly. And later, when the physical and emotional pain had become too much, he'd sunk into white oblivion. Wrapped himself in numb nothingness.

Today, though, comfort eluded him. But he consoled himself. He'd been thinking of McKenna's welfare, not his own.

In Jacksonville, the Marine dropped him off at the car dealership to pick up the new set of wheels. For his new life. The life he'd spend alone.

Once he was on the highway, the flat marshland of the coastal plains gave way to isolated farms, pastures, and small towns. Loblolly pines arched over the highway. The road closed in on him. He felt a peculiar weight on his chest, a claustrophobia. In Oklahoma, the land was flat and treeless. A body could see for miles. The same, he now realized, as the Banks. Clear, open sky and blue ocean in every direction.

Reaching Fayetteville, he drove to the old apartment where he and Nikki used to live. Pulling into the lot, he parked under the barren branches of a river birch. Apartment 3C. Third floor. First window on the right.

An all-too-familiar woman skipped down the open staircase. His breath hitched, not quite believing his eyes. And despite the cold November day, the low—very low—neckline displayed Nikki's "assets" to maximum advantage.

Shame crept up his neck. He'd been proud of how she looked on his arm. The envy of the other guys. Proving that, of all men, Caden Wallis had captured her heart.

But he hadn't. Far from it. What you saw with Nikki was what you got. *All* that you got. It was because of *his* inexperience with love that he hadn't understood there should be more. So much more.

A white-hot desire for revenge burned like acid in his belly. He'd come to release the torrent of bottled words inside him. To tell her exactly what he thought of her.

She opened the door of a Lamborghini.

He had to hand it to her. She'd certainly worked her way more than a few notches up the food chain since deserting him.

Placing her designer purse inside the car, she tossed her long, black curls over her shoulder. The hair that used to so allure him now left him feeling empty. Turning, she called to the stairwell, and her newest lover—his replacement with two legs—emerged.

Gut clenching, pent-up rage churned in Caden's chest.

Women probably found the man handsome with his arrogant swagger and expensive watch. The big spender who turned Nikki's head. Although to be fair, Nikki had been more than willing to turn her own head.

How many nights had Caden lain awake thinking of what he'd like to do to the scum who stole his girl? His temples pounded. His ears filled with a roaring sound.

As Caden moved to open the door of his new truck, the man planted a kiss on Nikki's lush lips. The cherry-red mouth Caden used to know so well. If the man had been a tree, Nikki would've climbed him there in the parking lot.

Caden braced for roiling jealousy, but to his surprise he felt nothing. Nothing at all.

Blinking rapidly, he took a deep breath just to be sure. Nope. She left him neither jealous or hurting. He let go of the door handle.

Nikki's version of the good life wasn't his idea of the good life at all. Maybe never had been.

Caden leaned against the seat. The blame went both ways. He'd used her as much as she'd used him. A mutual exploitation. Together for all the wrong reasons.

Her betrayal had come last in a long line of other betrayals, but he hadn't missed Nikki while in Tuckahoe. Her memory had only served as a goad to push himself to get better. To prove her wrong.

McKenna had shown him what really mattered in life. And what really mattered wasn't Nikki, nor what she had to offer. He might've tangled with an IED, but he'd dodged a bullet with her.

The man swatted her rump. And Caden couldn't have cared less. He didn't want her back. Not after a glimpse of what real love was like.

Yet the anger kept him as tied to Nikki and the past as McKenna's grief kept her tied to a dead man. He needed to let both Nikki and the anger go. As Nikki and her latest sugar daddy drove away, he found himself bestowing forgiveness. He wished her well.

Blowing a breath between his lips, he felt lighter. A burden lifted as he let the flame of his anger go.

He didn't know what his future held, but it wouldn't include Nikki. And he was okay with that. More than okay. He headed toward Bragg.

It felt a little weird being in uniform again. He'd gotten used to beach casual. He'd stopped thinking of himself as a soldier. He'd moved on.

Nothing much had changed at the base. Everything looked familiar, yet inexplicably different. Or maybe he was the one who was different.

He parked and made his way to Memorial Plaza outside the Army Special Operations Command headquarters. There, the thirty-foot long and six-foot high black granite wall commemorated the over twelve hundred special operators killed since the Korean War. He'd still been at Reed when this year's names had been added in the Memorial Day ceremony held for their Gold Star families.

Finding Joe's name, he traced the letters with his finger. "I miss you every day, bud." He probably always would.

Over the last year, Tavon had determinedly kept in touch with him. The team had wanted to wait until Caden could be with them to honor their fallen comrade.

Not wanting to intrude on reunions with loved ones, he texted Tavon that he'd meet the guys at the Airborne and Special Operations museum just off base. He made the short drive there.

In front of the museum entrance, a bronze, life-size Belgian Malinois stood sentry. And Caden struggled to come to grips with what else Afghanistan had cost him.

As in life, the dog in full deployment gear sat alert, ears perked. Around the granite base, pavers were inscribed with the name of each Special Forces MPC K-9, the year, and theater of operations in which the dog was KIA. Someone—maybe Tavon's wife—had placed small American flags next to each stone.

The plaque read:

CONSTANT VIGILANCE

The Bond Between a SOF Handler
& His K-9 Is Eternal Trusting Each Other
in a Nameless Language.

Here We Honor Our SOF K-9'S
that Have Paid the Ultimate Price.

He crouched beside the inscribed name of one other fallen hero from that fatal last mission. Friday.

Car doors banged in the parking lot. Caden rose as his former Alpha team clambered out of SUVs with family members. It hit him then just how much he'd missed them. Even Scruggs, the foul-mouthed kid from Mississippi whose arm was draped around a young woman with the perfect skin of a magnolia blossom. Caden smiled, looking forward to ribbing him. Scruggs had obviously somehow managed to acquire a girlfriend way above his pay grade.

Serving the nation that had once enslaved his ancestors, today Tavon clutched his wife like he meant to never let her go. Two little girls with brightly colored barrettes in their hair raced ahead of them.

Pulaski. Yazzie. The others.

Suddenly Sanchez, the man who'd saved his life, stood in front of him. "Sergeant."

A lump formed in Caden's throat. "Sanchez," he grunted.

"Last we heard—" Sanchez looked away. "I didn't know if we'd ever see you again."

"You and me both," Caden whispered. "I wanted to thank you for saving my life."

Sanchez's dark eyes gleamed with something suspiciously like tears. "I wasn't sure . . ." His Adam's apple bobbed. "That I'd done you any favors."

"A year ago, I would've agreed. Cursed you even. But now . . ." So much had changed over the last few months. "You gave me the opportunity for another chance." Caden took a deep breath. "And for that, I'll always owe you, Rick." He stuck out his hand.

Sanchez stared at him before grasping hold, his grip firm. "You've been missed."

The remaining members of the team swarmed him. Thumped him on the back, thrilled to see him on his feet. Caden had been wrong about people. Lots of people cared about him.

If they only knew what it had taken to get him here today. A nor'easter, a drug cartel, and a woman who refused to let him drown in his own misery.

Despite how things had ended, he was so thankful for the chance to know McKenna Dockery. To love her. To find out what it meant to be part of a family. To glimpse what home was meant to be.

What was the loss of a limb in comparison to what he'd gained?

Tavon's wife placed a miniature wreath of autumn flowers with Friday's name on the ribbon next to her paver. Tavon called for prayer.

At the "Amen," Yazz's teenaged son got out his iPhone, and the national anthem broke the quiet.

The land of the free . . . and the home of the brave.

Home of the brave. Like Joe, Friday, and others lost to war.

The last notes of the noble ballad rose, drifting high in the cloudless blue sky. For a second they floated, lingering.

Tavon squared his shoulders. "Who would like to say a few words of remembrance for Sergeant First Class Friday?"

Pulaski stepped forward. "I wanted to express my thanks—and our nation's gratitude—for Friday's service."

Sanchez went next. "Friday represented the Third Special Forces Group—this battalion, this team, most important, her country—with great courage and distinction."

The remaining members of their original twelve-man team offered their condolences.

"Wallis?" Tavon turned. "Would you like to say anything?"

"You're my hero, girl." Caden's voice choked. "Strong, fiercely loyal, beautiful. You gave me my life by sacrificing your own, and I will be forever grateful."

The men joined him in a salute. A silence fell.

"Is it time, Daddy?" whispered one of Tavon's girls.

Tavon nodded. The oldest reached into her mother's voluminous purse and withdrew a wooden box. Both girls took great care to hand the framed box to Caden. Inside the memorial box lay a folded flag, an enlarged picture of Friday with Caden, and Friday's medals pinned against the black velvet.

"Welcome home, soldier," the littlest one said.

Caden gulped, glad he wasn't the only tough guy who needed to wipe his eyes.

"Sergeant Nelson's wife couldn't be here today." Pulaski's brow furrowed. "We weren't allowed to bury Friday in a national cemetery, so she asked that Friday's body be buried next to Joe's on the family farm. She said to tell you to visit them in Roanoke whenever you're ready."

Yazz shuffled his feet. "And since you weren't able to be at Sergeant Nelson's funeral . . ." His eyes darted to Sanchez.

Sanchez pursed his lips. "The team thought we should sing the song he liked so much. To honor him."

Caden's heart began to pound as the team gathered, arms around each other's shoulders.

"Let Pulaski start it." Yazz grinned. "He's the only one who can sing worth a flip."

> *Here is love, vast as the ocean,*
> *Lovingkindness as the flood*
> *When the Prince of Life our Ransom,*
> *Shed for us His precious blood,*
> *Who His love will not remember?*
> *Who can cease to sing His praise?*
> *He can never be forgotten,*
> *Throughout Heaven's eternal days.*

It hit Caden then. It wasn't a love song to God. It was God's love song to man. The words reverberated in the deep places of Caden's soul, and everything came together. Crystal clear. Like a brisk sea wind.

He'd actually had it right. Or at least, right in part. Everything did come at a price. Caden wasn't good enough. No one was good enough. Someone always had to pay.

But what he hadn't seen until now? Someone already had.

Love made the sacrifice.

The rest of the men continued singing, but the realization robbed Caden of breath. Jesus had born his sin and shame. He'd already paid the price Caden owed.

You've always been there for me. He squeezed his eyes shut. *Lord, forgive me. I want to be Yours always. So take my life, Lord, and do with it as You will.*

Had he been wrong to walk away from McKenna?

It was fear that made him leave. He'd acted in his own best interests, not hers. Protecting himself from loss. Was he brave enough to grasp hold of the life God offered?

He felt ready to embrace what he had left. And what he had left—what could be his—was so much more than he could've ever envisioned.

Caden opened his eyes.

After the last line, they gazed at each other, arms still clasped. Men dearer than brothers. A bond he knew would never be broken.

Then boot scuffing. Sheepish grins. A little, gentle head slapping.

Caden prayed none of them would ever experience the anguish of body and soul he'd endured over the last year. A prayer from the depths of his reclaimed soul.

Tavon squeezed his arm. Something in his ebony black eyes made Caden think he suspected what had just happened to him. "Call me," he spoke in Caden's ear. "Day or night. Anytime."

Could his face possibly reflect the extraordinary change he felt inside? Finally—as McKenna urged him from the first—he'd chosen abundant life, not death. Because of what he was worth to God, McKenna had shown him it was okay to invest himself in other people. Though Ginger would never replace Friday, it was Ginger who'd shown him it was possible to love other dogs too.

And something akin to purpose shimmered before his eyes. Almost within reach . . . like if he just stretched out his hand . . .

Sanchez touched his shoulder. "Where are you headed now?"

"I was thinking about staying somewhere around here." Caden gauged their reaction. "Not too far. What do you think?"

Sanchez smiled, his teeth white against his skin. "I think that would be a fine idea."

Caden understood something else then. God had given him another gracious gift—time.

Thank You.

Time to become a part of their lives—if they'd allow him. To pay it forward, as Lovey put it. Share his journey from despair to healing. Show them that it was okay for tough guys to ask for help.

He'd be forever grateful to the army for the investment they'd made in a throwaway foster kid going nowhere. But it was time to close the door on being a soldier.

Instead of sorrow, he felt only a strange sense of hope.

Somewhere along the way, he'd accepted the prosthesis as an essential part of himself. This was the way he was now. And the way he was . . . was all right.

He also owed this to McKenna. Able to see himself through her eyes.

Promising to get together again soon, Caden headed out as the men drifted back to their families. For a long while, he hadn't believed there was anything for him beyond this moment. Now he had time to discover his future.

Could his future include McKenna?

He scrubbed his face with his hand. This morning when he'd gotten out of her truck, she'd looked at him as if she hated him.

Oh, God. What have I done?

Caden's heart thumped in his chest. Why had he walked away from God's most precious earthly gift—love?

And love—Love—changed everything. Every. Single. Thing.

Was it too late?

Glancing at his watch, his pulse raced. If he left right now . . . pushed the speed limit . . . But was there anything left to return to?

Resilience. Mental fortitude. Adaptability.

He got into his new truck. No more second-guessing. The decision would be hers.

On the ferry, he'd text her his ETA. Tell her that if she still wanted to see him—his throat clogged—then she should meet him on the lighthouse beach. Because he was coming.

Coming home.

Chapter Thirty

FOR MCKENNA, THE REST OF THAT DAY FELT INTERMINABLE.

The surfer Caden hired—Valdimar, seriously?—was great handling the grill.

In Icelandic, Valdimar meant "Ruler of the Ocean," the latte-guzzling millennial originally from North Dakota informed her.

And since his sole aim in life was to catch waves, the schedule at Skipjacks worked well for him. Actually, he used words like *stoked* and *rad*.

Lovey got a pained look whenever Valdimar spoke. McKenna might have to invest in a book so her grandmother could communicate with the young surfer. Or hire a translator.

McKenna could foresee the day Earlene would take Lovey's place at the register. Lovey had her own fish to fry these days with Talbot. Maybe it was time to hire another part-time waitress too.

Random thoughts filled McKenna's mind as she worked through the enormous lunch crowd—the year-rounders who hadn't made it to the diner this morning to congratulate Tuckahoe's sweetheart couple, Walt and Earlene. Yet her family understood how much she was hurting. In-between customers and wedding plans, there were lots of hugs for her.

She also had time to admit Caden had been right about one thing. She'd been hiding behind Skipjacks and her aging grandmother. Using Shawn's death as an excuse to not do life. Caden wasn't the only one who needed to choose life.

It was time—past time—to move out of her childhood home. Perhaps she'd rent one of the oceanside bungalows. She and Earlene could shop at the Nags Head outlet for home furnishings. A tingle of excitement began to build in her chest.

Stacking the dirty plates in the bin, she bused the last table. Ginger was Dad's dog, but she had a feeling he'd say McKenna needed Ginger now more than he did. So she added a new coordinating doggy bed to her mental shopping list.

Three middle fingers curled *shaka* style, Valdimar—who on God's earth named a child Valdimar?—waggled his hand on his way out. "Till tomorrow, Boss Lady."

"Right back at you, dude," she called.

Valdimar. She shook her head. That could *not* be his real name.

The dishes and silverware rattled as she lurched into the kitchen. It was time to do what she wanted for a change. Like . . . more time for turtle patrol?

McKenna plunked the bin on the counter.

Turtle patrol was what had gotten her into trouble in the first place. Turtle patrol had also brought her Caden—trouble of a different kind.

She scraped the plates and loaded the dishwasher. With the diner in the hands of the soon-to-be Mrs. Walter Dockery, McKenna could set her own hours. Or not.

Was she brave enough? The storefront next to Jolene's had been empty a long time. Maybe it was time to open the dance studio. To pursue her dreams.

She pressed the button to start the dishwasher. She'd contact Terry at the realty office tomorrow. But enough important life decisions for one day.

When she returned to the dining room, her dad and Earlene were gone. Something about a jeweler. She smiled. At least one thing had gone right today.

Flipping the sign to *Closed*, she remembered her phone. She'd turned it off after Caden left this morning. When she wasn't fit to talk to another living soul, but she usually didn't leave it off this long. She hoped she hadn't missed anything important.

Perhaps she should hire two waitresses. Planning the wording of the ad in her head, she took her cell out of her pocket and powered it on.

◆ ◆ ◆

Was it Caden's imagination, or was the returning ferry from Ocracoke back to Hatteras slower than the outgoing one this morning? Had it only been this morning?

So much had changed. Anger relinquished. Heart regenerated. He felt as if he'd fought a dozen dragons to stand where he was right now.

At the railing, the wind whipped his coat and pants. The spray stung his eyes. He strained forward as if by sheer willpower he could force the boat to go faster.

But in the back of his mind, an insidious voice whispered, *She hates you, loser. You blew your chance with her.*

The pit in his stomach tightened. McKenna wouldn't be there. She'd never forgive him. He'd hurt her too badly. He didn't deserve—

Old thinking. He'd need to study the Bible Lovey had given him. It would take time to reprogram the thought patterns of a lifetime.

The boat sliced through the waves. He kept his knees flexed, adjusting to the dip and play of the swells.

He'd messed up so bad with her, and where he came from, life didn't come with do-overs, much less second chances at love. She'd been so hurt and angry with him. Suppose she didn't want him now? His heart clamored against his ribs. After what he'd said, she couldn't possibly love him anymore.

Then why was he hurrying back?

Because he was hoping this time would be different. Praying that this time, unlike the meager love he'd received his entire life—withdrawn once he didn't meet expectations—McKenna's love would prove real. He was beginning to understand that God's love was unchanging, everlasting. But could such a love exist between a man like him and a woman like her?

Caden sucked in a breath. What was he doing? Even if by some miracle, she forgave him—again, forgiveness not his norm—he would ruin her life.

He was babbling. Not out loud. Just internally losing it.

Caden glanced around the nearly deserted deck. Everyone else had sense enough to stay in their vehicles on this chilly November afternoon. Behind him, the sun already hung low on the western horizon.

This. Was. A. Mistake. Of epic—

He'd sleep in his truck tonight, and with no one the wiser, he'd be on the first ferry back to the mainland come morning.

When the captain blew the horn, he nearly jumped out of his skin. Ahead, Hatteras Island shimmered golden in the late afternoon glow. Chest tight, he crawled into his truck. The ferry chugged into harbor. Somebody at the Coast Guard station waved. He felt sick with fear and dread.

Nevertheless, when the cars around him sprang to life, he, too, started his engine. With the usual dire clanking, he exited the gangplank for solid ground. He pulled out of the terminal and circled past the Graveyard of the Atlantic Museum and shops.

It had been a clear day. There'd be a clean sunset tonight. No dust or haze. Only vibrant reds and oranges.

He headed north on 12. Tuckahoe was a blur. He passed the art gallery in Frisco. The Buxton Bookstore. He turned off at the lighthouse and parked in the lot. Let the engine cool. Tried to get his pulse to settle.

The dashboard read four twenty. Time to head over the dunes. Wait at the water's edge . . .

Would she be there? Would she come?

His forehead broke into a sweat.

Caden needed to get ahold of his nerves. He flung open the door, grabbed his ruck from behind the seat, and headed toward the access path.

She'd either be there or she wouldn't. By his watch, four twenty-five . . .

Caden slogged through the sand. She'd either forgive him or she wouldn't.

The wind whistled. She'd either want him or she wouldn't. Four thirty . . .

He began the slow descent on the backside of the dune. She'd either still love him or she wouldn't. Four thirty-five . . .

Caden refused to look. Not . . . until . . . he . . . stood on the sand. There. Finally. Still, he kept his head down. The sound of the waves thundered, crashing onto the shore. If she were here, wouldn't she have called out? Perhaps she was waiting for him to say the first word.

Eyes on the driftwood in front of him, he moved toward the edge of the water. A sand crab skittered into a hole. His breathing seemed extraordinarily loud. Louder than the surf itself.

Past tidal pools. Bits of battered shell. Precarious sand castles. The tide would soon reclaim the strip of sand.

Four forty . . .

His heart clamored inside his chest. His pulse pounded. The tide foamed over his boot.

Four forty-five . . .

He balled his fists. Said a prayer. Closed his eyes. Opened them.

To an empty expanse of beach.

Caden staggered. The blow felt like a mortal wound. In the distance, the lighthouse stood sentinel, its black-and-white spirals stark against the lavender sky. But there was nothing—and no one—else.

Maybe—

He whipped around. Only his footprints told a story in sand.

So that was that. McKenna wasn't coming. She didn't forgive him. She didn't want him. She . . . He choked off the moan ripping through his chest.

McKenna didn't love him.

He didn't know how long he stood there, staring out over the blue-gray water and fiery blaze of sunset. Clutching the ruck. Trying to numb his heart. Trying to breathe. Trying to find oblivion. Failing.

Instead, he found a peace he didn't understand. A voice, not the insidious one, telling him to hang on. To trust.

Caden was going to hurt over this a long, long time, but God would make it okay. How, he didn't know. He just knew that God would.

He took one last look at the ocean waves that had brought him here. Where for a time he'd almost had a place to belong, a home, a family. McKenna. Then he turned and plodded back the long way he'd come. Past the tidal pools. The precarious sand castles. Driftwood. Bits of shell.

Muffled against the crashing waves, a faint sound reached his ears. There it was again. Getting louder. Moving closer.

He glanced over his shoulder and froze.

She was running. Those long legs of hers eating up the sand. Running. Crying. Screaming his name. "Wait! Caden!"

The wind loved McKenna. Her hair blew across her face. Her lovely face.

"Caden, wait. Wait for me!" She raced across the beach. Kicking up sand. Dashing through the foaming surf. "Don't leave," she called. "Please. Wait for me."

"I'm waiting," he whispered to the tide. "Waiting my whole life."

She skidded, and he had to grab her arms to keep her from plowing into him.

"My phone . . ." she gasped. "Off all day." She took a great gulp of air. "Didn't see your message until after four." Tears ran across her cheeks, glistening in the final sunburst of light. "The truck—that stupid, stupid truck—wouldn't start," she panted.

The only item on his to-do list he hadn't checked off.

Her chest heaved. "I couldn't reach anyone, except Bob."

"Bob the Postman?" Caden shook his head. "Never mind. Slow down."

She fluttered her hands. "He could only take me as far as the bookstore. Union rules. He has to clock out at exactly—"

"You ran all the way from the bookstore?" That had to be over two miles.

"I was so afraid—"

"McKenna." He gripped her upper arms. "Breathe."

She took a shuddering breath. Then, as if gathering her dignity, she removed herself from his hold. Suspicion shadowed her eyes. "Why did you come back?"

It was going to take a long time to repair the trust he'd shattered. But she was here. Giving him a chance. "I wanted to tell you what happened at Bragg."

Her brows drew together. "Your team—they were glad to see you, weren't they?"

She must care a little if she was worried the team's unofficial coming home ceremony had hurt him. But the only coming-home cere-mony he wanted was with the woman standing in front of him. *Please, God.*

Caden beat back the fear threatening to resurface. "You were right. I was terrified. Terrified to let anyone in. You most of all."

Her chin quivered, but she said nothing.

"Loving someone has always meant losing another piece of myself." His eyes darted toward the dunes. "I didn't expect . . . I didn't want to love this place. But for so long I believed a lie about myself." He swal-lowed. "Everything I said to you yesterday was a lie. A lie to push you away before you got too close."

She folded her blue tartan pashmina around her body. "Congratu-lations. You succeeded."

How could he make her understand what was really in his heart? "I'm sorry about what I said, McKenna."

"So you've apologized. Now you can leave." Her mouth flattened. "Since leaving is what you do so well."

"This isn't coming out right." He raked his hand over his head. "I'm not good with words."

She pursed her lips. "Oh, I think you've made yourself perfectly clear."

Caden shook his head. "It wasn't until I was with the team. We sang Joe's favorite song—I told you about it." He reached for her, but she took a step back. Pain knifed his chest.

"What do you want from me, Caden?"

Everything. Absolutely everything. But he couldn't say that, not until he tried to explain.

"As we were singing, the strangest sensation came over me." His heart started beating fast again. "And I got it."

McKenna wasn't looking at him.

"Suddenly, I understood what made your family different. I under-stood about the faith that made you different."

Her eyes flicked to his.

"I didn't have to be broken anymore. He was broken so I wouldn't have to be. Ever again." He sighed. "So that's what I did. I asked Him to . . . to mend me."

Her lips trembled.

"I can't explain it, but I think He did," he whispered. "And God used a quilt to bring me to the Home I was truly made for."

Swaying like sea oats in the wind, she put her hand over her mouth. He closed the gap between them, lifted his hand to touch her face. Let it drop.

"I didn't mean to make you cry. I always seem to make you cry."

"This is what I've hoped since . . ." She looked away. "Thank you for coming back to tell me."

Now for the hard part. He wasn't sure how she'd respond. "Something else happened this afternoon."

She turned toward the water. "You and Nicole are getting back together."

"What? No." He stiffened. "Why do you always call her—" He shook himself. "What I felt for her was never love. But what I feel for you . . ." He removed the strap from his shoulder and dropped the ruck on the sand.

She looked at him then.

Bending, he unzipped the bag at his feet. "I made another earth-shattering realization today."

She raised her chin. "And what realization is that?"

Caden withdrew the quilt from the ruck and straightened. "I realized that you, McKenna Dockery—" He held the quilt close to his heart, his gaze boring into hers. "—you are the one."

Her eyes flooded, twin pools of blue water.

Caden took a step toward her. "You are the one I will love the most and forever. I love you, McKenna. I think I have from the moment we met."

Only the quilt stood between them. She pressed her lips together. Why didn't she say something?

His heart quavered. "You hate me, and I don't blame you."

McKenna's gaze dropped to the quilt in his arms. "I don't hate you."

"I know you could never love me the way you loved Shawn."

Her eyes jerked to his. "That's not—"

"But if you'd give me a chance . . ." Caden unfolded part of the quilt. "I promise you, McKenna, I'll never leave you again."

She shook her head. "Don't compare yourself to Shawn. Not ever again."

His heart sank.

She took one end of the quilt and ran her hand over the ocean waves of blue fabric. "God never meant this quilt to be for Shawn. I know that now. And I know that God brought the quilt and you—" Her voice hitched. "He brought you—like a love letter—to me. I will always love Shawn, but . . ."

Caden braced himself for the killing blow.

"But my love for you, Caden Wallis . . ." Her eyes held a bemused wonderment. "It's as vast as the sea. As fathomless . . ." She bit her lip.

"You love me? Still?" His heart jackhammered.

There was a sweet longing in her gaze. "You're the one I'm going to love the most and forever."

Caden opened the quilt full length and draped it around her shoulders. "*Always come home*, it said." He loved her so much. "That's why I came back. Home to you, Beach Girl."

McKenna drew the other side of the quilt around him, too, so that it held them both in its warm embrace.

She cradled his cheek. "Welcome home, Caden."

Under an indigo Carolina sky, the sea crashed onto the sand. He turned his mouth into her palm. Sunshine.

"Suddenly so much talk." Smiling, she leaned in, her lips a whisper away. "When are you going to kiss me?"

He cocked his head. "Kiss you?"

"What are you waiting for?" Her mouth curved. "I dare you."

And on the wave of a gracious tide, he did.

Vast and unchanging,
God's love is like the ocean.
We can find love's beginning,
But never, ever, its end.

Author's Note

I have changed various aspects of the geography of the Outer Banks to better suit the story. Tuckahoe and Yaupon Island are imaginary, but most of the places mentioned are not—like Manteo, Nags Head, the tri-villages, and Avon.

Cape Hatteras—the tallest lighthouse in America—is well worth a visit. The Buxton Bookstore and its fabulous proprietor are also delightfully real. Portsmouth Island formed the basis for the ghost village on Yaupon. It, too, was long ago abandoned, and now only wildlife inhabit its windswept terrain. The Graveyard of the Atlantic Museum in Hatteras Village is great fun, as is taking the free ferry over to Ocracoke to spend the day wandering.

A top-secret sonar station on Ocracoke once listened for the pings of German U-boats. During the first two years of the war, no one in America outside the Banks understood how close the Germans came to winning the war in the Atlantic. Aptly named Torpedo Junction, older folks on the Banks still remember as children watching the ships burning offshore. And yes, one Banker waterman did accidentally come upon a surfacing U-boat. He beat a hasty retreat.

Operation Pastorius actually happened. In 1985, Georg Gärtner, a German soldier who escaped from a POW camp, turned himself in to American authorities after nearly forty years of hiding in plain sight. On her first war patrol, the *U-925* was never heard from again after September 18, 1944—five days before the Great Storm—with all fifty-one souls presumed lost. Who knows? Maybe she does lie somewhere in the Graveyard of the Atlantic. Stranger things have happened.

Because sometimes the past refuses to stay buried. In September 2017, two unexploded ordnance mines from World War II washed up on an Outer Banks beach.

The work of the Joint Interagency Task Force South is real, as is the threat of a drug-terrorist coalition. There are many unsung heroes from this agency in the war on terror and drugs. Submarine facilities have been found in the jungles of Venezuela. The first Atlantic drug sub was discovered beached in Spain.

It is no coincidence that captured submarines display Russian engineering and contain Chinese-made parts. Military experts say that if al-Qaeda or Iran wanted to attack our homeland, this would be the way they'd get in. As in the past, one of America's first lines of defense is the Outer Banks. Military authorities fear it is only a matter of when—not if—there will be an incursion along the Eastern seaboard.

Acknowledgments

I owe a debt of gratitude to so many for helping this book see the light of day.

A big thank you to my agent, Tamela Hancock Murray, for your encouragement and support throughout this endeavor. To the team at Gilead—Becky Philpott, Sue Brower, Jane Strong, Jordan Smith, Katelyn Summer Bolds, and others—for allowing me to tell the story of one man's long journey home. Also, thanks to dear friends (you know who you are) whose prayers brought this book to completion.

Many thanks to retired Thibodaux police chief and author Scott Silverii for his invaluable guidance in creating a combat veteran amputee character and for guidance on plot possibilities.

Thanks to fellow suspense author Jodie Bailey for her boots-on-the-ground perspective as a former army wife. And for including me in a girl-writer week at Hatteras, where I was able to research this story.

I am very grateful for the scuba expertise of Bob and Sue Kennedy, who painted word pictures for me of the beautiful undersea world and who helped me plot murder there—while eating pizza at a crowded restaurant. Sometimes I wonder why no one has called the cops on me yet.

Thanks to D. P. Lyle, author and doctor, for his medical expertise in answering questions and brainstorming forensic scenarios.

Thanks to Louis Brown of EastPoint Prosthetics & Orthotics for walking me through the prosthesis devices available for amputees today. He also provided compassionate insight into the mental, spiritual, and emotional challenges these wounded warriors face.

I have taken their advice as it suited the plot. Any errors are my fault, not theirs.

And last but not least, thanks to my husband and fellow life adventurer, who ate a lot of takeout in the final weeks of writing this story.

Lisa Carter is the bestselling author of seven romantic suspense novels, four historical novellas, and a contemporary Coast Guard series. Blending Southern and Native American fiction, she likes to describe her suspense novels as "Sweet Tea with a Slice of Murder." *The Stronghold* was a 2017 Daphne du Maurier finalist. *Under a Turquoise Sky* won the 2015 Carol Award for Romantic Suspense. *Beyond the Cherokee* Trail was a 4-1/2 star *Romantic Times* Top Pick. Lisa enjoys traveling to romantic locales and researching her next exotic adventure. When not writing, she loves spending time with her family and teaching writing workshops. A native North Carolinian, she has strong opinions on barbecue and ACC basketball.

Connect with Lisa!

Website: *www.lisacarterauthor.com*
Facebook: *www.facebook.com/lisa.carter.1272*
Twitter: *www.twitter.com/lisacarter27*
Instagram: *@lisacarterauthor*